Wild and Wanton Edition

Persuasion

Micah Persell
and Jane Austen

Crimson Romance
New York London Toronto Sydney New Delhi

CRIMSON
ROMANCE

Crimson Romance
An Imprint of Simon & Schuster, Inc.
1230 Avenue of the Americas
New York, NY 10020

ISBN 978-1-4405-6707-0
ISBN 978-1-4405-6708-7 (ebook)

For Laci, on the occasion of marriage to her very own Fred—
You two are further proof that
every great love deserves a second chance

Prologue

Frederick looked at his pocket watch for the fifth time in as many minutes. *She is late*, he thought while slipping the warm metal back into the front pocket of his waistcoat. She was never late.

His foot jiggled a little against the leg of the bench, and he tried to focus on anything other than how slowly Father Time was passing. The bench was hidden behind a hedge of shrubberies that were dotted with delicate pink flowers; the same distracting shade as Anne's perfect, mouthwatering nipples.

With a jerk of his head, he forced himself to look elsewhere. The traitorous shrubberies were offering no distraction except the one he needed to avoid. If he continued to remember what her body looked like bare, he would not be able to sit still any longer. Already, his breeches were painfully tight and cutting off the circulation he would need very soon.

If only she would arrive.

His fingers traveled with a mind of their own to his watch yet again, but he was saved from the mortifying action of checking the hour for the *sixth* time by the snap of a twig nearby.

His hair fell into his eyes as he unerringly swiveled to face the sound and was greeted by his favourite sight in the world.

"*Anne.*"

The word was a breathless plea, and the next moment, he was launching forward, nearly sprinting toward her.

She had yet to look at him; her face was downturned to check the path as she placed her feet carefully over the terrain. He caught the sight of one shapely ankle and picked up his speed. He did not slow once he reached her, but used his momentum to swing her up into his arms and around in a circle while he pressed his lips against hers.

As soon as their skin touched, something unwound within his chest, and he could breathe once again. He was never easy apart from her.

Her lips trembled beneath his, and his knees grew weak. She was always so responsive, his Anne. He deepened the kiss, thrusting his tongue within her mouth, as he made his way back to the bench he had just vacated.

He fell to the seat with no amount of grace, eager only to cradle her even closer. He settled her within his lap and could not prevent a husky groan when the warm curve of her bottom ground against his hard shaft.

He threaded his fingers into her hair, knowing he was ruining her meticulous style of the day, but caring little. He would help her return it to some semblance of normal after. He rotated them slightly, tucking her head against his shoulder while continuing to explore her mouth with his tongue.

When her arm tightened around his neck and her tongue slid against his, he was nearly undone. His hand fell from her hair to blindly grope for the hem of her gown. Incoherent words fell from his lips in between desperate kisses as he slipped his hand between cloth and warm woman. His fingers trailed past her knee, and he clutched her even closer so that her breasts were flattened against his chest. He groaned anew, the choice between the treasure at the apex of her thighs and the treasure concealed within her bodice pulling him in opposite directions. He cursed the fact that he had only two hands, one of which was supporting her back. He pressed on toward his ultimate prize with the hand that now caressed the soft skin of her inner thigh.

"Oh, how I love you," he murmured against her lips.

That was when he tasted salt. It was so at odds with her usual sweet taste that he pulled back in alarm.

Tears tracked down her cheeks, the sight of which landed like a blow to his heart. He cupped her face with the hand that had been beneath her skirt and brushed a tear aside with his thumb. "Anne?" he whispered hoarsely. "Darling, what is wrong?"

She pushed against his chest with more strength than he had imagined she possessed and scrambled away from him and to the other side of the bench.

A cool breeze blew by and chilled the parts of him that had been warmed by her flesh, but it was not even close to the dreadful chill that edged into his gut. "Anne?" He had to fist his hands in his lap to keep from reaching for her.

She huddled into herself and covered her mouth with a shaky hand. Her words carried through the barrier as clear as a death knell: "I am here to end our engagement."

Surely he had misheard. "What?"

A ragged sob sounded from behind her hand. "Please do not make me repeat it!"

That was the moment he knew for certain his life would never be the same. "End our engagement?" He launched himself to his feet and towered over her. "Surely you cannot be serious!" *Please do not be serious*, a part of him pleaded desperately.

"I am so sorry."

"No."

Now her eyes met his. He realized it was the first time they had done so since he'd first spotted her walking toward him. They were flooded with tears and darker than they had ever been. He noticed half-moons of shadow beneath each eye. "No," he said again, more firmly this time.

She shook her head, and he poured through his mind to try to find something he could say that would prove this enterprise of hers would never work. He sat beside her quickly and grabbed one of her hands. Her fingers were ice-cold within his palm. "Anne, no," he said. "Even now you could be carrying my child."

Memories of their first time together, of the greatest moment of his life, filtered through his mind. The scent of her skin; the feel of her tight, warm centre; the breathless cries he had captured and savored with his kisses. That had been only last week. She would *have* to stay betrothed to him for a while until she knew for certain that she was not with child. And he would do everything within his power in the meantime to ensure that she *did* conceive.

She pulled her hand from his grasp, and with it, his mind from his thoughts. "My courses started this morning," she said in a dead voice.

Utter defeat rose up within his throat, and choked him. He worried for several moments that he would disgrace himself with tears. "Anne," he began, his voice cracking on her name. "Do not do this."

"Lady Russell says—"

"*Lady Russell.*" The name was a growl erupting from his chest.

Another sob shook her small frame, and he immediately felt like a complete heel. "Forgive me, love," he whispered quickly, reaching for her once again.

She jumped to her feet and dashed a tear from her cheek violently. "I cannot abide any more of this. It is over. I am sorry." She broke into a run, the wind thrusting her skirt behind her in billows of white.

He rose to his own feet unsteadily and reached out to brace himself on a nearby tree. "Anne!" he called after her. "We can find a way!"

She never slowed.

He stood staring off into the direction she had fled long after any glimpse of her had faded into air, hoping every moment that she would return—that they could work this out. That she would still be his.

When the sun dipped below the horizon, and he shook from more than just the chill of his shattered heart, he once again reached into his waistcoat pocket and withdrew his pocket watch. His initial wish had been granted; hours had flown by as mere minutes. He knew the rest of his life would not pass so quickly without the one thing that had made it sail.

Chapter 1

Eight Years Later

Sir Walter Elliot, of Kellynch Hall, in Somersetshire, was a man who, for his own amusement, never took up any book but the Baronetage; there he found occupation for an idle hour, and consolation in a distressed one; there his faculties were roused into admiration and respect, by contemplating the limited remnant of the earliest patents; there any unwelcome sensations, arising from domestic affairs changed naturally into pity and contempt as he turned over the almost endless creations of the last century; and there, if every other leaf were powerless, he could read his own history with an interest which never failed. This was the page at which the favourite volume always opened:

"ELLIOT OF KELLYNCH HALL.

"Walter Elliot, born March 1, 1760, married, July 15, 1784, Elizabeth, daughter of James Stevenson, Esq. of South Park, in the county of Gloucester, by which lady (who died 1800) he has issue Elizabeth, born June 1, 1785; Anne, born August 9, 1787; a still-born son, November 5, 1789; Mary, born November 20, 1791."

Precisely such had the paragraph originally stood from the printer's hands; but Sir Walter had improved it by adding, for the information of himself and his family, these words, after the date of Mary's birth—"Married, December 16, 1810, Charles, son and heir of Charles Musgrove, Esq. of Uppercross, in the county of Somerset," and by inserting most accurately the day of the month on which he had lost his wife. Sir Walter did not care for many people, but he had cared for Lady Elliot. The day she was lost was one of the few days of his past that remained fixed in his mind as a devastating one.

Then followed the history and rise of the ancient and respectable family, in the usual terms; how it had been first settled in Cheshire; how mentioned in Dugdale, serving the office of high sheriff, representing a borough in three successive parliaments, exertions of loyalty, and dignity of baronet, in the first year of Charles II, with all the Marys and Elizabeths they had married; forming altogether two handsome duodecimo pages, and concluding with the arms and motto: "Principal seat, Kellynch Hall, in the county of Somerset," and Sir Walter's handwriting again in this finale:

"Heir presumptive, William Walter Elliot, Esq., great grandson of the second Sir Walter."

Vanity was the beginning and the end of Sir Walter Elliot's character; vanity of person and of situation. He had been remarkably handsome in his youth; nature had gifted him with a marvelous build, full, black hair, and eyes the colour of a cresting wave. Women had naturally noticed him when he was young, and, at fifty-four, he was still a very fine man who turned many a lady's head. He was never in want for company, and gifted his body to most who expressed a desire for it. It was, after all, his duty to allow as many as possible to partake of the perfection of form so many other men lacked. Few women could think more of their personal appearance than he did, nor could the valet of any new made lord be more delighted with the place he held in society. He considered the blessing of beauty as inferior only to the blessing of a baronetcy; and the Sir Walter Elliot, who united these gifts, was the constant object of his warmest respect and devotion.

His good looks and his rank had one fair claim on his attachment; since to them he must have owed a wife of very superior character to any thing deserved by his own. Lady Elliot, a beautiful woman with wheat-blonde hair and eyes the colour of chestnuts, had been an excellent woman, sensible and amiable; whose judgement and conduct, if they might be pardoned the youthful infatuation which made her Lady Elliot, had never required indulgence afterwards. She had not cared that Sir Walter was vain; anyone could look upon him and appreciate his beauty, so why should he be faulted for doing the same? It was this physical beauty that had drawn her to him, and against all reason, had caused her to fall desperately in love with him.

Shortly after the wedding, her eyes had been opened to all of Sir Walter's shortcomings; however, he more than made up for them in the efforts he took in the bedroom. Lady Elliot had never known such pleasure between a man and woman was possible. The soft way he touched her, the gasps he wrung from her, the ways he caused her to forget his foolishness in other areas—all combined to make her moderately happy as Sir Walter's wife. She had humoured, or softened, or concealed his failings, and promoted his real respectability for seventeen years; and though not the very happiest being in the world herself, had found enough in her duties, her friends, and her children, to attach her to life, and make it no matter of indifference to her when she was called on to quit them. Three girls, the two eldest sixteen and fourteen, was an awful legacy for a mother to bequeath, an awful charge rather, to confide to the authority and guidance of a conceited, silly father. She had, however, one very intimate friend, a sensible, deserving woman, who had been brought, by strong attachment to herself, to settle close by her, in the village of Kellynch; and on her kindness and advice, Lady Elliot mainly relied for the best help and maintenance of the good principles and instruction which she had been anxiously giving her daughters.

This friend, and Sir Walter, did *not* marry, whatever might have been anticipated on that head by their acquaintance. Thirteen years had passed away since Lady Elliot's death, and they were still near neighbours and intimate friends, and one remained a widower, the other a widow.

That Lady Russell, of steady age and character, and extremely well provided for, should have no thought of a second marriage, needs no apology to the public, which is rather apt to be unreasonably discontented when a woman *does* marry again, than when she does *not*; but Sir Walter's continuing in singleness requires explanation. Be it known then, that Sir Walter, like a good father, (having met with one or two private disappointments in very unreasonable applications), prided himself on remaining single for his dear daughters' sake. At least that was what he told his dear friends and acquaintances. The truth, that Sir Walter very much enjoyed dallying with a wide array of women, and matrimony would impede if not completely cut off his amorous activities, was a fact best kept to himself. His children were a well-accepted, polite excuse. For one daughter, his eldest, he would really have given up any thing, which he had not been very much tempted to do. Elizabeth had succeeded, at sixteen, to all that was possible, of her mother's rights and consequence; and being very handsome, and very like himself, her influence had always been great, and they had gone on together most happily. His two other children were of very inferior value. Mary had acquired a little artificial importance, by becoming Mrs. Charles Musgrove; but Anne, with an elegance of mind and sweetness of character, which must have placed her high with any people of real understanding, was nobody with either father or sister; her word had no weight, her convenience was always to give way—she was only Anne.

To Lady Russell, indeed, she was a most dear and highly valued god-daughter, favourite, and friend. Lady Russell loved them all; but it was only in Anne that she could fancy the mother to revive again.

A few years before, Anne Elliot had been a very pretty girl. She was small in stature, but so rounded in the correct places as to draw a man's notice. Her light brown hair and the beautiful eyes she had inherited from her mother had been the crowning glory of the Elliot family, but her bloom had vanished early; and as even in its height, her father had found little to admire in her, (so totally different were her delicate features and mild dark eyes from his own), there could be nothing in them, now that she was faded and thin, to excite his esteem. He had never indulged much hope, he had now none, of ever reading her name in any other page of his favourite work. All equality of alliance must rest with Elizabeth, for Mary had merely connected herself with an old country family of respectability and large fortune, and had therefore *given* all the honour and received none: Elizabeth would, one day or other, marry suitably.

It sometimes happens that a woman is handsomer at twenty-nine than she was ten years before; and, generally speaking, if there has been neither ill health nor anxiety, it is a time of life at which scarcely any charm is lost. It was so with Elizabeth, still the same handsome Miss Elliot that she had begun to be thirteen years ago. Where Anne was small, Elizabeth was statuesque. Where Anne had her mother's eyes, Elizabeth had Sir Walter's. Lady Elliot's blonde hair was most becoming and youthful on Elizabeth, and Sir Walter might be excused, therefore, in forgetting her age, or, at least, be deemed only half a fool, for thinking himself and Elizabeth as blooming as ever, amidst the wreck of the good looks of everybody else; for he could plainly see how old all the rest of his family and acquaintance were growing. Anne haggard, Mary coarse, every face in the neighbourhood worsting, and the rapid increase of the crow's foot about Lady Russell's temples had long been a distress to him.

Elizabeth did not quite equal her father in personal contentment. Thirteen years had seen her mistress of Kellynch Hall, presiding and directing with a self-possession and decision which could never have given the idea of her being younger than she was. For thirteen years had she been doing the honours, and laying down the domestic law at home, and leading the way to the chaise and four, and walking immediately after Lady Russell out of all the drawing-rooms and dining-rooms in the country. Thirteen winters' revolving frosts had seen her opening every ball of credit which a scanty neighbourhood afforded, and thirteen springs shewn their blossoms, as she travelled up to London with her father, for a few weeks' annual enjoyment of the great world. Thirteen summers had seen her beneath the arbor in the garden with men in their prime teaching her through touch with their hands only—she would not abide too much liberty with her person—the ways her body could bring her pleasure. Their trembling hands as they tentatively raised her skirts; their impassioned groans as she stroked them through their breeches; their desperate pleas that she give herself to them—pleas that were always answered with an emphatic *no* out of necessity— these were the powerful moments of her life that she treasured most. She had the fond remembrance of all this, but now felt she approached the autumn of her life. She had not much cared for the thirteen autumns. She had the consciousness of being nine-and-twenty to give her some regrets and some apprehensions; she was fully satisfied of being still quite as handsome as ever, but she felt her approach to the years of danger, and would have rejoiced to be certain of being properly solicited by baronet-blood within the next twelvemonth or two. She craved, with a violence that startled her, to know what it felt like to fully join with a man. Thirteen years of slight dalliances had only whetted her appetite, not quenched it. Her future baronet would be able to show her at last what she had denied others for so long. Then might she again take up the book of books with as much enjoyment as in her early youth, but now she liked it not. Always to be presented with the date of her own birth and see no marriage follow but that of a youngest sister, made the book an evil; and more than once, when her father had left it open on the table near her, had she closed it, with averted eyes, and pushed it away.

She had had a disappointment, moreover, which that book, and especially the history of her own family, must ever present the remembrance of. The heir presumptive, the very William Walter Elliot, Esq., whose rights had been so generously supported by her father, had disappointed her.

She had, while a very young girl, as soon as she had known him to be, in the event of her having no brother, the future baronet, meant to marry him, and her father had always meant that she should. He had not been known to them as a boy; but soon after Lady Elliot's death, Sir Walter had sought the acquaintance, and though his overtures had not been met with any warmth, he had persevered in seeking it, making allowance for the modest drawing-back of youth; and, in one of their spring excursions to London, when Elizabeth was in her first bloom, Mr. Elliot had been forced into the introduction.

He was at that time a very young man, just engaged in the study of the law; and Elizabeth found him extremely agreeable. He was tall and brooding. To Elizabeth's young eyes, he was the most handsome man she had ever encountered. Broad shoulders stretched almost farther than she could reach. His thick, black hair fell in waves to his collar, and his eyes were so dark as to be almost black themselves. They were eyes that she could see herself falling into forever, and every plan in his favour was confirmed. He was invited to Kellynch Hall; he was talked of and expected all the rest of the year; but he never came, to Elizabeth's eternal disappointment. The following spring he was seen again in town, found equally agreeable, again encouraged, invited, and expected, and again he did not come; and the next tidings were that he was married. Instead of pushing his fortune in the line marked out for the heir of the house of Elliot, he had purchased independence by uniting himself to a rich woman of inferior birth.

Sir Walter has resented it. As the head of the house, he felt that he ought to have been consulted, especially after taking the young man so publicly by the hand; "For they must have been seen together," he observed, "once at Tattersall's, and twice in the lobby of the House of Commons." His disapprobation was expressed, but apparently very little regarded. Mr. Elliot had attempted no apology, and shewn himself as unsolicitous of being longer noticed by the family, as Sir Walter considered him unworthy of it: all acquaintance between them had ceased.

This very awkward history of Mr. Elliot was still, after an interval of several years, felt with anger by Elizabeth, who had liked the man for himself, and still more for being her father's heir, and whose strong family pride could see only in *him* a proper match for Sir Walter Elliot's eldest daughter. There was not a baronet from A to Z whom her feelings could have so willingly acknowledged as an equal. She had taken her revenge on members of Mr. Elliot's sex every summer since by taking her own pleasure and denying them theirs. It was of great comfort, yet it did not satisfy her completely. So miserably had he conducted himself, that though she was at this present time (the summer of 1814) wearing black ribbons for his wife, she could not admit him to be worth thinking of again. The disgrace of his first marriage might, perhaps, as there was no reason to suppose it perpetuated by offspring, have been got over, had he not done worse; but he had, as by the accustomary intervention of kind friends, they had been informed, spoken most disrespectfully of them all, most slightingly and contemptuously of the very blood he belonged to, and the honours which were hereafter to be his own. This could not be pardoned.

Such were Elizabeth Elliot's sentiments and sensations; such the cares to alloy, the agitations to vary, the sameness and the elegance, the prosperity and the nothingness of her scene of life; such the feelings to give interest to a long, uneventful residence in one country circle, to fill the vacancies which there were no habits of utility abroad, no talents or accomplishments for home, to occupy.

But now, another occupation and solicitude of mind was beginning to be added to these. Her father was growing distressed for money. She knew, that when he now took up the Baronetage, it was to drive the heavy bills of his tradespeople, and the unwelcome hints of Mr. Shepherd, his agent, from his thoughts. The Kellynch property was good, but not equal to Sir Walter's apprehension of the state required in its possessor. While Lady Elliot lived, there had been method, moderation, and economy, which had just kept him within his income; but with her had died all such right-mindedness, and from that period he had been constantly exceeding it. He found himself requiring more and more earthly possessions to acquire and keep the happiness that had been elusive at best since the passing of Lady Elliot. It had not been possible for him to spend less; he had done nothing but what Sir Walter Elliot was imperiously called on to do; but blameless as he was, he was not only growing dreadfully in debt, but was hearing of it so often, that it became vain to attempt concealing it longer, even partially, from his daughter.

He had given her some hints of it the last spring in town; he had gone so far even as to say, "Can we retrench? Does it occur to you that there is any one article in which we can retrench?" and Elizabeth, to do her justice, had, in the first ardour of female alarm, set seriously to think what could be done, and had finally proposed these two branches of economy, to cut off some unnecessary charities, and to refrain from new furnishing the drawing-room; to which expedients she afterwards added the happy thought of their taking no present down to Anne, as had been the usual yearly custom. But these measures, however good in themselves, were insufficient for the real extent of the evil, the whole of which Sir Walter found himself obliged to confess to her soon afterwards. Elizabeth had nothing to propose of deeper efficacy. She felt herself ill-used and unfortunate, as did her father; and they were neither of them able to devise any means of lessening their expenses without compromising their dignity, or relinquishing their comforts in a way not to be borne.

There was only a small part of his estate that Sir Walter could dispose of; but had every acre been alienable, it would have made no difference. He had condescended to mortgage as far as he had the power, but he would never condescend to sell. No; he would never disgrace his name so far. The Kellynch estate should be transmitted whole and entire, as he had received it.

Their two confidential friends, Mr. Shepherd, who lived in the neighbouring market town, and Lady Russell, were called to advise them; and both father and daughter seemed to expect that something should be struck out by one or the other to remove their embarrassments and reduce their expenditure, without involving the loss of any indulgence of taste or pride.

Chapter 2

Mr. Shepherd, a civil, cautious lawyer, who, whatever might be his hold or his views on Sir Walter, would rather have the *disagreeable* prompted by anybody else, excused himself from offering the slightest hint, and only begged leave to recommend an implicit reference to the excellent judgement of Lady Russell, from whose known good sense he fully expected to have just such resolute measures advised as he meant to see finally adopted.

Lady Russell was most anxiously zealous on the subject, and gave it much serious consideration. She was a woman rather of sound than of quick abilities, whose difficulties in coming to any decision in this instance were great, from the opposition of two leading principles. She was of strict integrity herself, with a delicate sense of honour; but she was as desirous of saving Sir Walter's feelings, as solicitous for the credit of the family, as aristocratic in her ideas of what was due to them, as anybody of sense and honesty could well be.

Though she had no desire whatsoever to enter into a second marriage, the close daily interaction she had with the Elliot family had, in fact, endeared Sir Walter to her in a fashion that could not be contained by the mere title of *friend*. She was a benevolent, charitable, good woman, and capable of strong attachments, most correct in her conduct, strict in her notions of decorum, and with manners that were held a standard of good-breeding, but even she could not ignore Sir Walter's physical beauty. She had a cultivated mind, and was, generally speaking, rational and consistent; but she had prejudices on the side of ancestry; she had a value for rank and consequence, which blinded her a little to the faults of those who possessed them, and this had her in the very unfortunate position of loving Sir Walter, a feeling that was much unrequited, while overlooking many of his shortcomings. Herself the widow of only a knight, she gave the dignity of a baronet all its due; and Sir Walter, independent of his claims as an old acquaintance, an attentive neighbour, an obliging landlord, the husband of her very dear friend, the father of Anne and her sisters, was, as being Sir Walter, in her apprehension, entitled to a great deal of compassion and consideration under his present difficulties.

She had not personally witnessed Sir Walter's prowess in the bedroom, but her dear friend Lady Elliot had often divulged what went on behind their closed doors. Lady Russell's own knight had been much worse than simply a distasteful husband in the conventional sense; he had been an absolute trial in the fulfillment of marital duty. Her first experience with intimacy, her wedding night, had been most disappointing. Sir Russell had rolled atop her, thrust himself inside, ignored her cry of pain, and finished his job in the next handful of moments. It was a performance that he'd repeated frequently, and the quality never improved. If Lady Elliot were to be believed, Sir Walter was able to produce a different experience, and Lady Russell had often wished she were the one he took to his bedroom to ease his needs rather than the parade of women he seemed to enjoy bedding. But he looked to Lady Russell solely as a friend. He sought her never for physical comfort, but often for advice. Now, in this most dire of fiscal situations, he again required her aid.

They must retrench; that did not admit of a doubt. But she was very anxious to have it done with the least possible pain to him and Elizabeth. She drew up plans of economy, she made exact calculations, and she did what nobody else thought of doing: she consulted Anne, who never seemed considered by the others as having any interest in the question. She consulted, and in a degree was influenced by her in marking out the scheme of retrenchment which was at last submitted to Sir Walter. Every emendation of Anne's had been on the side of honesty against importance. She wanted more vigorous measures, a more complete reformation, a quicker release from debt, a much higher tone of indifference for everything but justice and equity.

"If we can persuade your father to all this," said Lady Russell, looking over her paper, "much may be done. If he will adopt these regulations, in seven years he will be clear; and I hope we may be able to convince him and Elizabeth, that Kellynch Hall has a respectability in itself which cannot be affected by these reductions; and that the true dignity of Sir Walter Elliot will be very far from lessened in the eyes of sensible people, by acting like a man of principle. What will he be doing, in fact, but what very many of our first families have done, or ought to do? There will be nothing singular in his case; and it is singularity which often makes the worst part of our suffering, as it always does of our conduct. I have great hope of prevailing. We must be serious and decided; for after all, the person who has contracted debts must pay them; and though a great deal is due to the feelings of the gentleman, and the head of a house, like your father, there is still more due to the character of an honest man."

This was the principle on which Anne wanted her father to be proceeding, his friends to be urging him. She considered it as an act of indispensable duty to clear away the claims of creditors with all the expedition which the most comprehensive retrenchments could secure, and saw no dignity in anything short of it. She wanted it to be prescribed, and felt as a duty. She rated Lady Russell's influence highly; and as to the severe degree of self-denial which her own conscience prompted, she believed there might be little more difficulty in persuading them to a complete, than to half a reformation. Her knowledge of her father and Elizabeth inclined her to think that the sacrifice of one pair of horses would be hardly less painful than of both, and so on, through the whole list of Lady Russell's too gentle reductions.

How Anne's more rigid requisitions might have been taken is of little consequence. Lady Russell's had no success at all: could not be put up with, were not to be borne. "What! every comfort of life knocked off! Journeys, London, servants, horses, table—contractions and restrictions every where! To live no longer with the decencies even of a private gentleman! No, he would sooner quit Kellynch Hall at once, than remain in it on such disgraceful terms."

"Quit Kellynch Hall." The hint was immediately taken up by Mr. Shepherd, whose interest was involved in the reality of Sir Walter's retrenching, and who was perfectly persuaded that nothing would be done without a change of abode. "Since the idea had been started in the very quarter which ought to dictate, he had no scruple," he said, "in confessing his judgement to be entirely on that side. It did not appear to him that Sir Walter could materially alter his style of living in a house which had such a character of hospitality and ancient dignity to support. In any other place Sir Walter might judge for himself; and would be looked up to, as regulating the modes of life in whatever way he might choose to model his household."

Sir Walter would quit Kellynch Hall; and after a very few days more of doubt and indecision, the great question of whither he should go was settled, and the first outline of this important change made out.

There had been three alternatives, London, Bath, or another house in the country. All Anne's wishes had been for the latter. A small house in their own neighbourhood, where they might still have Lady Russell's society, still be near Mary, and still have the pleasure of sometimes seeing the lawns and groves of Kellynch, was the object of her ambition. But the usual fate of Anne attended her, in having something very opposite from her inclination fixed on. She disliked Bath, and did not think it agreed with her; and Bath was to be her home.

Sir Walter had at first thought more of London; but Mr. Shepherd felt that he could not be trusted in London, and had been skilful enough to dissuade him from it, and make Bath preferred. It was a much safer place for a gentleman in his predicament: he might there be important at comparatively little expense. Two material advantages of Bath over London had of course been given all their weight: its more convenient distance from Kellynch, only fifty miles, and Lady Russell's spending some part of every winter there; and to the very great satisfaction of Lady Russell, whose first views on the projected change had been for Bath, Sir Walter and Elizabeth were induced to believe that they should lose neither consequence nor enjoyment by settling there.

Lady Russell felt obliged to oppose her dear Anne's known wishes. It would be too much to expect Sir Walter to descend into a small house in his own neighbourhood. Anne herself would have found the mortifications of it more than she foresaw, and to Sir Walter's feelings they must have been dreadful. And with regard to Anne's dislike of Bath, she considered it as a prejudice and mistake arising, first, from the circumstance of her having been three years at school there, after her mother's death; and secondly, from her happening to be not in perfectly good spirits the only winter which she had afterwards spent there with herself.

Lady Russell was fond of Bath, in short, and disposed to think it must suit them all; and as to her young friend's health, by passing all the warm months with her at Kellynch Lodge, every danger would be avoided; and it was in fact, a change which must do both health and spirits good. Anne had been too little from home, too little seen. Her spirits were not high. A larger society would improve them. She wanted her to be more known.

The undesirableness of any other house in the same neighbourhood for Sir Walter was certainly much strengthened by one part, and a very material part of the scheme, which had been happily engrafted on the beginning. He was not only to quit his home, but to see it in the hands of others; a trial of fortitude, which stronger heads than Sir Walter's have found too much. Kellynch Hall was to be let. This, however, was a profound secret, not to be breathed beyond their own circle.

Sir Walter could not have borne the degradation of being known to design letting his house. Mr. Shepherd had once mentioned the word "advertise," but never dared approach it again. Sir Walter spurned the idea of its being offered in any manner; forbad the slightest hint being dropped of his having such an intention; and it was only on the supposition of his being spontaneously solicited by some most unexceptionable applicant, on his own terms, and as a great favour, that he would let it at all.

How quick come the reasons for approving what we like! Lady Russell had another excellent one at hand, for being extremely glad that Sir Walter and his family were to remove from the country. Elizabeth had been lately forming an intimacy, which she wished to see interrupted. It was with the daughter of Mr. Shepherd, who had returned, after an unprosperous marriage, to her father's house, with the additional burden of two children. She was a clever young woman, who understood the art of pleasing—the art of pleasing, at least, at Kellynch Hall; and who had made herself so acceptable to Miss Elliot, as to have been already staying there more than once, in spite of all that Lady Russell, who thought it a friendship quite out of place, could hint of caution and reserve.

Lady Russell, indeed, had scarcely any influence with Elizabeth, and seemed to love her, rather because she would love her, than because Elizabeth deserved it. She had never received from her more than outward attention, nothing beyond the observances of complaisance; had never succeeded in any point which she wanted to carry, against previous inclination. She had been repeatedly very earnest in trying to get Anne included in the visit to London, sensibly open to all the injustice and all the discredit of the selfish arrangements which shut her out, and on many lesser occasions had endeavoured to give Elizabeth the advantage of her own better judgement and experience; but always in vain: Elizabeth would go her own way; and never had she pursued it in more decided opposition to Lady Russell than in this selection of Mrs. Clay; turning from the society of so deserving a sister, to bestow her affection and confidence on one who ought to have been nothing to her but the object of distant civility.

From situation, Mrs. Clay was, in Lady Russell's estimate, a very unequal, and in her character she believed a very dangerous companion; and a removal that would leave Mrs. Clay behind, and bring a choice of more suitable intimates within Miss Elliot's reach, was therefore an object of first-rate importance.

This desire was firmed even more by what Lady Russell discovered one afternoon when she believed Sir Walter to be alone in the house. She had known that Elizabeth was to walk in town that day, and naturally assumed that Mrs. Clay, odious creature that she was, would join her. It would have afforded Lady Russell some much-coveted time with Sir Walter. Lady Russell was already planning the various things they could discuss to excuse her unannounced visit when she was distracted from her musings in the Elliot foyer by some very peculiar noises indeed. Being such a good friend of the family, the Elliot staff had admitted her to the house and promptly left her, knowing Lady Russell could find her own way. But the very feminine moan that echoed throughout Kellynch Hall stopped Lady Russell in her path and had her immediately wishing the Elliot staff had shown perhaps a modicum more of the proper social niceties.

"Oh, dear," Lady Russell said, wringing her silk purse within her hands in the midst of the foyer. This was quite the conundrum. A feminine moan on its own could be nothing. Perhaps Anne had fallen and injured herself? The moan had sounded quite distressed.

Knowing she was fooling herself, but unable to ignore the very real pang of concern that the thought of Anne in distress caused, Lady Russell began the misbegotten journey toward the parlour.

Just as Lady Russell reached the partially ajar door, the feminine moan sounded again, escalated, and ended with a very enthusiastic shout of "*Walter!*"

Dread settled like a stone in her belly, but Lady Russell could not prevent her hand from reaching out and pushing the door open a tad more. Her horrified gasp was overshadowed by yet another moan.

Across the parlour, against the bookshelves of all things, Sir Walter and Mrs. Clay were engaged in an act of most impressive fornication. He had her pressed up against the rows of books, her bottom firmly seated on one of the shelves. Her legs were wrapt around his waist, and her skirts were bunched between them. Mrs. Clay's stocking-clad calves hugged Sir Walter's naked arse, and said arse was bunching and releasing in the most tantalizing fashion as Lady Russell's oldest, dearest friend pumped in and out of the world's vilest tart.

The woman's head was thrown back, and she emitted another of those throaty moans. Sir Walter picked up his pace and added his own guttural groan.

"Oh, *Pen*," Sir Walter muttered desperately. His body stiffened before Lady Russell's eyes, and, as a shudder ran through him, he made a noise that sounded close to the noise one would make while in midst of most desperate peril.

Lady Russell gasped again, and her hand flew to her lips.

Mrs. Clay's head snapped up, and those green eyes of hers connected with Lady Russell's.

There was a moment of horrified silence as Lady Russell wondered if the dreadful woman would out her, but then Mrs. Clay's lips twisted up into a cruel smile. She wound her arms tighter about Sir Walter and stroked his back while murmuring quiet, soothing words that Lady Russell could not hear.

Lady Russell stumbled back, more wounded by that cat-with-the-cream grin than she cared to admit. She staggered through the manor blindly, and when she once again found herself outside, it took several minutes before her harried thoughts calmed and narrowed down to one:

Mrs. Clay must go.

Chapter 3

"I must take leave to observe, Sir Walter," said Mr. Shepherd one morning at Kellynch Hall, as he laid down the newspaper, "that the present juncture is much in our favour. This peace will be turning all our rich naval officers ashore. They will be all wanting a home. Could not be a better time, Sir Walter, for having a choice of tenants, very responsible tenants. Many a noble fortune has been made during the war. If a rich admiral were to come in our way, Sir Walter—"

"He would be a very lucky man, Shepherd," replied Sir Walter; "that's all I have to remark. A prize indeed would Kellynch Hall be to him; rather the greatest prize of all, let him have taken ever so many before; hey, Shepherd?"

Mr. Shepherd laughed, as he knew he must, at this wit, and then added—

"I presume to observe, Sir Walter, that, in the way of business, gentlemen of the navy are well to deal with. I have had a little knowledge of their methods of doing business; and I am free to confess that they have very liberal notions, and are as likely to make desirable tenants as any set of people one should meet with. Therefore, Sir Walter, what I would take leave to suggest is, that if in consequence of any rumours getting abroad of your intention; which must be contemplated as a possible thing, because we know how difficult it is to keep the actions and designs of one part of the world from the notice and curiosity of the other; consequence has its tax; I, John Shepherd, might conceal any family-matters that I chose, for nobody would think it worth their while to observe me; but Sir Walter Elliot has eyes upon him which it may be very difficult to elude; and therefore, thus much I venture upon, that it will not greatly surprise me if, with all our caution, some rumour of the truth should get abroad; in the supposition of which, as I was going to observe, since applications will unquestionably follow, I should think any from our wealthy naval commanders particularly worth attending to; and beg leave to add, that two hours will bring me over at any time, to save you the trouble of replying."

Sir Walter only nodded. But soon afterwards, rising and pacing the room, he observed sarcastically—

"There are few among the gentlemen of the navy, I imagine, who would not be surprised to find themselves in a house of this description."

"They would look around them, no doubt, and bless their good fortune," said Mrs. Clay, for Mrs. Clay was present: her father had driven her over, nothing being of so much use to Mrs. Clay's health as a drive to Kellynch: "but I quite agree with my father in thinking a sailor might be a very desirable tenant. I have known a good deal of the profession; and besides their liberality, they are so neat and careful in all their ways!" Mrs. Clay paused a moment in her speech to remember another trait of sailors: their ways in bed. They were so very robust and enthusiastic. Mrs. Clay had never encountered a sailor who did not make her time with them in private well worth her while. With a secret smile upon her lips, she continued, "These valuable pictures of yours, Sir Walter, if you chose to leave them, would be perfectly safe. Everything in and about the house would be taken such excellent care of! The gardens and shrubberies would be kept in almost as high order as they are now. You need not be afraid, Miss Elliot, of your own sweet flower gardens being neglected."

"As to all that," rejoined Sir Walter coolly, "supposing I were induced to let my house, I have by no means made up my mind as to the privileges to be annexed to it. I am not particularly disposed to favour a tenant. The park would be open to him of course, and few navy officers, or men of any other description, can have had such a range; but what restrictions I might impose on the use of the pleasure-grounds, is another thing. I am not fond of the idea of my shrubberies being always approachable; and I should recommend Miss Elliot to be on her guard with respect to her flower garden. I am very little disposed to grant a tenant of Kellynch Hall any extraordinary favour, I assure you, be he sailor or soldier."

After a short pause, Mr. Shepherd presumed to say—

"In all these cases, there are established usages which make everything plain and easy between landlord and tenant. Your interest, Sir Walter, is in pretty safe hands. Depend upon me for taking care that no tenant has more than his just rights. I venture to hint, that Sir Walter Elliot cannot be half so jealous for his own, as John Shepherd will be for him."

Here Anne spoke—

"The navy, I think, who have done so much for us, have at least an equal claim with any other set of men, for all the comforts and all the privileges which any home can give. Sailors work hard enough for their comforts, we must all allow."

Everyone in the room paused in what they were doing and turned toward Anne, for all of them had forgotten she was in their presence. Anne, however, noticed none of them. Her mind was otherwise occupied with a disturbing flash of eyes the exact shade of sea foam, and a smile that turned up more on one side than the other. Anne was brushing her fingertips across her bottom lip when an abrupt male voice pulled her from her reverie.

"Very true, very true. What Miss Anne says, is very true," was Mr. Shepherd's rejoinder, and "Oh! Certainly," was his daughter's; but Sir Walter's remark was, soon afterwards—

"The profession has its utility, but I should be sorry to see any friend of mine belonging to it."

"Indeed!" was the reply, and with a look of surprise.

"Yes; it is in two points offensive to me; I have two strong grounds of objection to it. First, as being the means of bringing persons of obscure birth into undue distinction, and raising men to honours which their fathers and grandfathers never dreamt of; and secondly, as it cuts up a man's youth and vigour most horribly; a sailor grows old sooner than any other man. I have observed it all my life. A man is in greater danger in the navy of being insulted by the rise of one whose father, his father might have disdained to speak to, and of becoming prematurely an object of disgust himself, than in any other line. One day last spring, in town, I was in company with two men, striking instances of what I am talking of; Lord St Ives, whose father we all know to have been a country curate, without bread to eat; I was to give place to Lord St Ives, and a certain Admiral Baldwin, the most deplorable-looking personage you can imagine; his face the colour of mahogany, rough and rugged to the last degree; all lines and wrinkles, nine grey hairs of a side, and nothing but a dab of powder at top. 'In the name of heaven, who is that old fellow?' said I to a friend of mine who was standing near, (Sir Basil Morley). 'Old fellow!' cried Sir Basil, 'it is Admiral Baldwin. What do you take his age to be?' 'Sixty,' said I, 'or perhaps sixty-two.' 'Forty,' replied Sir Basil, 'forty, and no more.' Picture to yourselves my amazement; I shall not easily forget Admiral Baldwin. I never saw quite so wretched an example of what a sea-faring life can do; but to a degree, I know it is the same with them all: they are all knocked about, and exposed to every climate, and every weather, till they are not fit to be seen. It is a pity they are not knocked on the head at once, before they reach Admiral Baldwin's age."

Anne could not prevent a frown. This was not the case for *all* sailors. Her mind unwittingly pictured the features she favoured most and added the weathering that must surely mark them now. Wrinkles around the eyes from squinting into the sun; hair bleached and tossed by the elements. Anne's mouth went dry.

No, a diminished appearance would certainly not be the case for all sailors.

"Nay, Sir Walter," cried Mrs. Clay, "this is being severe indeed. Have a little mercy on the poor men. We are not all born to be handsome. The sea is no beautifier, certainly; sailors do grow old betimes; I have observed it; they soon lose the look of youth. But then, is not it the same with many other professions, perhaps most other? Soldiers, in active service, are not at all better off: and even in the quieter professions, there is a toil and a labour of the mind, if not of the body, which seldom leaves a man's looks to the natural effect of time. The lawyer plods, quite care-worn; the physician is up at all hours, and travelling in all weather; and even the clergyman—"she stopt a moment to consider what might do for the clergyman—"and even the clergyman, you know is obliged to go into infected rooms, and expose his health and looks to all the injury of a poisonous atmosphere. In fact, as I have long been convinced, though every profession is necessary and honourable in its turn, it is only the lot of those who are not obliged to follow any, who can live in a regular way, in the country, choosing their own hours, following their own pursuits, and living on their own property, without the torment of trying for more; it is only *their* lot, I say, to hold the blessings of health and a good appearance to the utmost: I know no other set of men but what lose something of their personableness when they cease to be quite young. Besides, sailors are so active that their bodies *greatly* benefit from it."

The last was said in a lecherous purr, and everyone in the room drew back from shock, Anne most of all. Had she not been thinking the same thing? To share such a thought with some one such as Mrs. Clay was alarming to say the least.

Mr. Shepherd chuckled awkwardly and quickly changed the subject back to the benefits of a sailor as *tenant*.

It seemed as if Mr. Shepherd, in this anxiety to bespeak Sir Walter's good will towards a naval officer as tenant, had been gifted with foresight; for the very first application for the house was from an Admiral Croft, with whom he shortly afterwards fell into company in attending the quarter sessions at Taunton; and indeed, he had received a hint of the Admiral from a London correspondent. By the report which he hastened over to Kellynch to make, Admiral Croft was a native of Somersetshire, who having acquired a very handsome fortune, was wishing to settle in his own country, and had come down to Taunton in order to look at some advertised places in that immediate neighbourhood, which, however, had not suited him; that accidentally hearing— (it was just as he had foretold, Mr. Shepherd observed, Sir Walter's concerns could not be kept a secret,)—accidentally hearing of the possibility of Kellynch Hall being to let, and understanding his (Mr. Shepherd's) connection with the owner, he had introduced himself to him in order to make particular inquiries, and had, in the course of a pretty long conference, expressed as strong an inclination for the place as a man who knew it only by description could feel; and given Mr. Shepherd, in his explicit account of himself, every proof of his being a most responsible, eligible tenant.

"And who is Admiral Croft?" was Sir Walter's cold suspicious inquiry.

Anne, who had been paying minimal attention to the conversation as she was again distracted by the exorbitant numbers of the Elliot family financial status on the sheet in front of her, suddenly gasped. When they turned to look at her, she coughed and waved her hand in the direction of her teacup. "Pardon," she said breathlessly. "I must have swallowed too much tea."

As the gentlemen returned to their conversation, Mr. Shepherd answered for his being of a gentleman's family, and mentioned a place; and Anne, her heart thundering in her throat and her mind eight years in the past, after the little pause which followed, added—

"He is a rear admiral of the white. He was in the Trafalgar action, and has been in the East Indies since; he was stationed there, I believe, several years."

"Then I take it for granted," observed Sir Walter, "that his face is about as orange as the cuffs and capes of my livery."

Mr. Shepherd hastened to assure him, that Admiral Croft was a very hale, hearty, well-looking man, a little weather-beaten, to be sure, but not much, and quite the gentleman in all his notions and behaviour; not likely to make the smallest difficulty about terms, only wanted a comfortable home, and to get into it as soon as possible; knew he must pay for his convenience; knew what rent a ready-furnished house of that consequence might fetch; should not have been surprised if Sir Walter had asked more; had inquired about the manor; would be glad of the deputation, certainly, but made no great point of it; said he sometimes took out a gun, but never killed; quite the gentleman.

Mr. Shepherd was eloquent on the subject; pointing out all the circumstances of the Admiral's family, which made him peculiarly desirable as a tenant. He was a married man, and without children; the very state to be wished for. A house was never taken good care of, Mr. Shepherd observed, without a lady: he did not know, whether furniture might not be in danger of suffering as much where there was no lady, as where there were many children. A lady, without a family, was the very best preserver of furniture in the world. He had seen Mrs. Croft, too; she was at Taunton with the admiral, and had been present almost all the time they were talking the matter over.

"And a very well-spoken, genteel, shrewd lady, she seemed to be," continued he; "asked more questions about the house, and terms, and taxes, than the Admiral himself, and seemed more conversant with business; and moreover, Sir Walter, I found she was not quite unconnected in this country, any more than her husband; that is to say, she is sister to a gentleman who did live amongst us once; she told me so herself: sister to the gentleman who lived a few years back at Monkford. Bless me! What was his name? At this moment I cannot recollect his name, though I have heard it so lately. Penelope, my dear, can you help me to the name of the gentleman who lived at Monkford: Mrs. Croft's brother?"

But Mrs. Clay was talking so eagerly with Miss Elliot, that she did not hear the appeal.

"I have no conception whom you can mean, Shepherd; I remember no gentleman resident at Monkford since the time of old Governor Trent."

"Bless me! How very odd! I shall forget my own name soon, I suppose. A name that I am so very well acquainted with; knew the gentleman so well by sight; seen him a hundred times; came to consult me once, I remember, about a trespass of one of his neighbours; farmer's man breaking into his orchard; wall torn down; apples stolen; caught in the fact; and afterwards, contrary to my judgement, submitted to an amicable compromise. Very odd indeed!"

After waiting another moment—

"You mean Mr. Wentworth, I suppose?" said Anne on an exhalation of pent-up breath.

Mr. Shepherd was all gratitude. No one had noticed the way Anne's voice caressed every syllable of that name.

"Wentworth was the very name! Mr. Wentworth was the very man. He had the curacy of Monkford, you know, Sir Walter, some time back, for two or three years. Came there about the year—5, I take it. You remember him, I am sure."

"Wentworth? Oh! Ay,—Mr. Wentworth, the curate of Monkford. You misled me by the term *gentleman*. I thought you were speaking of some man of property: Mr. Wentworth was nobody, I remember; quite unconnected; nothing to do with the Strafford family. One wonders how the names of many of our nobility become so common."

As Mr. Shepherd perceived that this connexion of the Crofts did them no service with Sir Walter, he mentioned it no more; returning, with all his zeal, to dwell on the circumstances more indisputably in their favour; their age, and number, and fortune; the high idea they had formed of Kellynch Hall, and extreme solicitude for the advantage of renting it; making it appear as if they ranked nothing beyond the happiness of being the tenants of Sir Walter Elliot: an extraordinary taste, certainly, could they have been supposed in the secret of Sir Walter's estimate of the dues of a tenant.

It succeeded, however; and though Sir Walter must ever look with an evil eye on anyone intending to inhabit that house, and think them infinitely too well off in being permitted to rent it on the highest terms, he was talked into allowing Mr. Shepherd to proceed in the treaty, and authorising him to wait on Admiral Croft, who still remained at Taunton, and fix a day for the house being seen.

Sir Walter was not very wise; but still he had experience enough of the world to feel, that a more unobjectionable tenant, in all essentials, than Admiral Croft bid fair to be, could hardly offer. So far went his understanding; and his vanity supplied a little additional soothing, in the Admiral's situation in life, which was just high enough, and not too high. "I have let my house to Admiral Croft," would sound extremely well; very much better than to any mere *Mr.*—; a *Mr.* (save, perhaps, some half dozen in the nation,) always needs a note of explanation. An admiral speaks his own consequence, and, at the same time, can never make a baronet look small. In all their dealings and intercourse, Sir Walter Elliot must ever have the precedence.

Nothing could be done without a reference to Elizabeth: but her inclination was growing so strong for a removal, that she was happy to have it fixed and expedited by a tenant at hand; and not a word to suspend decision was uttered by her.

Mr. Shepherd was completely empowered to act; and no sooner had such an end been reached, than Anne, who had been a most attentive listener to the whole, left the room, to seek the comfort of cool air for her flushed cheeks and to carry out a now necessary mission; and as she walked along a favourite grove, said, with a gentle sigh, "A few months more, and *he*, perhaps, may be walking here."

Her fingers passed over the bench where they had always met, and she knelt beside it to pull a box from the roots of the tree that had always sheltered them from prying eyes. The box would now be going with her. With a sigh, she settled the weight of the box on top of her thighs and steeled her courage. She could never touch it without opening it; could never open it without reading its contents; could never read its contents without despair.

She ran a finger across the initials carved in the lid: *F.W.* Slowly she opened the lid, and the aroma of old memories wafted upward. Countless letters lay inside, and she hesitated only a moment before reaching in and retrieving the one that lay on top. It was her favourite and the most read among its brethren for it contained the first declaration of his love.

The parchment trembled within her hand as she unfolded it, and she skimmed over the words in a familiar scrawl until she arrived at the very end—

Yours for ever,
Frederick

Chapter 4

He was not Mr. Wentworth, the former curate of Monkford, however suspicious appearances may be, but a Captain Frederick Wentworth, his brother, who being made commander in consequence of the action off St. Domingo, and not immediately employed, had come into Somersetshire, in the summer of 1806; and having no parent living, found a home for half a year at Monkford. He was, at that time, a remarkably fine young man, with a great deal of intelligence, spirit, and brilliancy; his looks and personality were unrivaled at every gathering at which he appeared. Every lady swooned over his wind-swept blonde hair and blue-green eyes, but at each event, he found himself staring over the heads of the misses who were vying for his attention at a diminutive girl with dark eyes.

He asked around quietly and discovered her name, and he could not help thinking Anne an extremely pretty girl; however, one mere conversation with her and he knew she was more than a pretty girl. Anne was gifted with gentleness, modesty, taste, and feeling. Half the sum of attraction, on either side, might have been enough, for he had nothing to do, and she had hardly anybody to love; but the encounter of such lavish recommendations could not fail. They were gradually acquainted; he made sure to seek her out at every dinner party thereafter for at least one conversation, though in his heart, he knew the conversations were too short. Before long, he desired her company more than anyone else's, and, once acquainted with this desire, he fell rapidly and deeply in love. He confessed his heart and sought her hand a very short time after first spotting her across a crowded ballroom, and she assured him she returned his love. It would be difficult to say which had seen highest perfection in the other, or which had been the happiest: she, in receiving his declarations and proposals, or he in having them accepted.

A short period of exquisite felicity followed.

Memories bombarded Anne as she sat beneath the tree with her box of letters.

Young Anne had loved young Frederick with a passion that she never could have guessed she would possess. After Anne agreed to marry him, they arranged to meet each other in the gardens of Kellynch Hall each afternoon. As they parted each day, Anne gifted Frederick with a kiss. He would trail the back of his index finger down her cheek, smile that smile that tilted upright more on the left side, lean in, and brush his lips across hers so sweetly and tenderly that it stole her breath. And though she loved these kisses and looked forward to them every day, she soon discovered that his innocent touch kindled a need within her that she had no way of containing and no idea how to quench.

One afternoon, perhaps a dozen sweet kisses into their afternoon interludes, one particular kiss that started off as sweet and innocent lasted but a moment before Frederick ventured to take matters one step further by tilting his head and licking at the seam of her lips. The move was so tentative that it was apparent he expected her to be shocked by his action; he was soon shocked himself.

Anne had never felt a more wonderful phenomenon than Frederick's tongue seeking entry into her mouth. She fisted her hands in the fabric of his jacket, pulled him even closer, and returned his tentative lick with a desperate one of her own. He made an incoherent noise deep within his throat, and in the next moment, her cautious lover disappeared. The large hands that had been trailing slowly down the slope of her back descended suddenly to the curve of her bottom where his fingers flexed, squeezing her tightly. He used this hold to pull her into his body even more, though she had not known they could be closer than they were. That was the moment she felt a sharp prodding to her stomach.

Anne gasped into Frederick's kiss, and he jerked away with harried apologies dripping from his glistening lips. But Anne refused to give up her hold on his jacket, and he was forced to either stop his retreat or tear the fabric from her fingers. Anne stared down through the space between their bodies and felt her eyes widen.

Frederick's fawn-coloured breeches barely contained a hard length that strained against the fabric so fiercely Anne wondered if it would rip. *Arousal*, Anne's brain supplied, and she realized she was staring at the evidence of his desire for her. Something molten unfurled deep within Anne's belly, and she heard a husky sound escape her parted lips.

"Oh, Anne," he whispered in a low, distraught voice. "Darling, I am so sorry." A few moments of awkward silence followed before he cleared his throat and with a self-conscious breath of laughter said, "I am trying to make it go away, but with you giving it so much attention, I haven't a prayer of succeeding, darling."

Like a scolded schoolgirl, Anne jerked her head up to meet his eyes. "Oh!" She felt blood stinging her cheeks. "I am not supposed to look at it, am I?"

That tilted smile of his made a broad appearance, and his hands, which had moved from her bottom to her upper arms when he had tried to step away from her, squeezed her gently as he tilted his head back, revealing a tantalizing corded length of throat, and emitted a deep rumble of laughter. His eyes met hers once again, brimming with amusement. "Anne, you can do anything to it that you want. Looking is the least licentious option."

"*Anything?*" Anne realized the breathless whisper had, indeed, come from her mouth instead of staying inside her head like she had intended when his smile lost its mirth and his fingers flexed again, this time almost painfully.

"What did you have in mind?" The words were so quiet as to almost not exist.

"May I—" Anne took a deep breath and forged ahead. "May I t-touch it?" Her focus had trailed down from his face as she stumbled over the words, and so she was looking at the *it* in question when she finished.

His arousal kicked up beneath the fabric of his breeches, and Anne felt her mouth go dry with absolute *want*.

Frederick's ragged intake of air sounded somewhere above her head, and then he trailed one of his hands down from her upper arm to tug her hand up to his lips. She focused on his face once again as he pressed a soft kiss to her fingertips. He seemed to steel himself, and then he placed her hand flat against the area near of the top button of his waistcoat. As his hand, now done with its duty, returned to grasp her upper arm, she felt muscles she did not know a man would possess flex beneath her fingers. She could not prevent an exploratory rotation of her hand, and the muscles she had just discovered rippled even more.

She looked at his face once again and noticed his Adam's apple bobbed up and down erratically. His lips were parted. His breaths were coming quicker than was usual, and his eyelids were lowered halfway.

She realized with a start that even this simple touch was affecting him greatly. Feeling a power that was both new and wonderful, Anne rotated her hand again, pointing her fingers downward, and slowly began to slide her palm down the plane of his abdomen.

His breathing increased in pace, and his lids lowered even more so that the lashes from top and bottom almost met.

Anne heard her own breathing increase, and she felt warmth swell at the apex of her thighs. Her fingers encountered the slight dip of his belly button, and then, right below it, the fabric of his breeches abruptly flared out. Her fingertips brushed against the blunt tip of his arousal, and he groaned sharp and deep and with such obvious pleasure that Anne dared to explore even further. She trailed her fingers down the outside of his breeches from the tip of his shaft and wrapt her hand around him as far as the fabric and his size would allow. She squeezed, and he made a noise that sounded close to a whimper.

It was so *hard*. She could not imagine how his body accommodated such a thing. "Does it hurt?" she asked in a whisper.

"*Yes.*"

She gasped, jerking her hand away. "I am sorry!"

He caught her hand and brought it back to the front of his breeches where, miraculously, his arousal had grown even harder. "Oh, Anne, it does not hurt that way." He pressed her fingers against him. "It *aches*," he said hoarsely. "For you."

She could understand that. The warm area between her thighs was now uncomfortably achy as well. Anne shifted restlessly on her feet, and she discovered that she was *wet* in the area that dully throbbed to the same rhythm as her erratic heartbeat.

"I ache, too," she murmured distractedly.

She heard his quick intake of air, and then the hand that was not holding her fingers against his arousal grabbed her free hand.

He intertwined their fingers. "Where, darling?"

Too desperate to be embarrassed, Anne guided their laced fingers to her lower belly. She did not have to guide him further.

Frederick slipped his fingers from hers and cupped her mound through her skirts. They both moaned. "So warm," he muttered almost unintelligibly.

And that was the last time either of them could string intelligent words together. He curved his fingers upward and brushed against a point of focus that shot through her. Anne swayed forward as her knees weakened, and Frederick scooped her against him with the hand that had been holding her fingers against his arousal.

He grunted softly, and then his lips descended upon hers. This was not the sweet and innocent kiss. This was not even the kiss where their tongues had lightly dueled. This was a full, sensual invasion of Anne's senses.

He thrust his tongue deeply into her mouth, sliding it against hers in a rhythm that Anne found made her even more mad for him. His fingers where he cupped her moved again, rubbing back and forth against the epicentre of her need. She moved her own fingers where they were surrounding his length, squeezing and releasing.

It was wonderful.

It was not enough.

She whimpered and moved her hand against him even faster. "More," she pled against his lips.

He made a noise of assent and lowered her to the grass without separating their lips or removing his hand from the area where she needed him most. As soon as she reclined, he covered her body with his own.

"*Yes*," she heard herself whisper in a voice she did not recognise through its desperation. Some instinct she could not identify had her raising her thighs on either side of his hips. His lower body sank into hers, and the length of his arousal pressed against her core.

She gripped his shoulders with fierce fingers. "Please!" She canted her hips against the length she craved more than her next breath of air.

He groaned long and low as he braced himself above her with one arm while the other moved to grab her skirts and pull them up.

Her heart exploded in joy as she realized that he was going to give her what she desired. He was going to love her. "Yes," she muttered in a rush. "Do it, please." Her fingers fumbled with the buttons of his breeches. She jerked at them so hard, she was sure she removed one or two.

As his arousal sprang into her hand, she felt his large, blunt fingers brush against the naked skin of her sex. "*Frederick*," she moaned sharply. "*Now!*"

"Anne—" He sounded in pain and his hips moved, thrusting his hardness through her grip. "We should not—"

A ragged sob sounded from Anne's chest. He was going to refuse her? She ached so badly. She writhed against his fingers and felt them spread her wetness over throbbing skin. "*Please.*"

"God forgive me," he moaned. His fingers replaced hers around his arousal, and he nudged her thighs even wider apart with his knees. She felt the tip of him brush against her entrance. "Love you so," he muttered just before thrusting into her. The sharp sting from his first enthusiastic entrance into her body made her gasp. He quickly fell forward, bracing himself on his elbows and cupping her face with both hands. He pressed a hurried kiss to her lips. "I h-have been told it will not hurt—" he gritted his teeth "—for long." He took three gulping breaths. "Anne, I cannot—" His earthy groan rent the air. "I cannot stop. *So tight.*"

He drew his hips back, and as the length within her retreated, pleasure lit in its wake. She gasped and clutched his firm rear end through the fabric of his breeches, trying to draw him back into her. "Do not stop!" she begged breathlessly.

"Never," he promised on an exhale as he thrust back into her. He withdrew again, just as quickly, and then surged back. The next moment, he fell preciously out of control. His thrusts lost all measure. He began moving within her far too quickly; even Anne in her inexperience knew that. His weight upon her was heavy, his hold almost too tight. His words of love were whispered breathlessly into her ear as he thrust himself into her over and over erratically—one moment too deep, the next too shallow.

He was a virgin, as well. The thought arrived amid the cacophony of pleasurable thoughts in Anne's head, and she knew in an instant that it was true. The knowledge caused a rush of moisture where they were joined, and he must have felt it for he cried out her name, and then he arched over her one final time. Heat spread in her womb as he jerked against her, and she felt so loved that tears stung her eyes. Then something even more wonderful occurred. The pleasure that had been building steadily reached some sort of peak as he spilled his seed within her. Flashes of light shot behind Anne's vision, and her back arched. Waves of ecstasy cascaded through her, wrenching a cry from her chest.

Frederick pulled his face from her neck to look at her with something akin to wonder spreading across his features. When she could finally breathe again, he leaned down slowly and pressed the softest of kisses to the corner of her mouth, never releasing her eyes.

"I cannot believe I was able to give you that," he whispered into the kiss.

She breathed a laugh. "Me either." She squeezed his bottom. "Want to give it to me again?"

His response faded into memory as Anne pulled herself from the past to look at the letter she held in her hands in the very spot where they had first consummated their love.

She had to smile to herself, even through the pain, as she remembered the details of that afternoon. It had been the most wondrous event of Anne's life. The period of her life to follow was the happiest she had ever experienced, and but a short one.

Troubles soon arose. Sir Walter, on being applied to, without actually withholding his consent, or saying it should never be, for it was obvious that he suspected them of doing exactly what they *had* been doing, gave it all the negative of great astonishment, great coldness, great silence, and a professed resolution of doing nothing for his daughter. He thought it a very degrading alliance; and Lady Russell, though with more tempered and pardonable pride, received it as a most unfortunate one.

Anne Elliot, with all her claims of birth, beauty, and mind, to throw herself away at nineteen; involve herself at nineteen in an engagement with a young man, who had nothing but himself to recommend him, and no hopes of attaining affluence, but in the chances of a most uncertain profession, and no connexions to secure even his farther rise in the profession, would be, indeed, a throwing away, which she grieved to think of! Anne Elliot, so young; known to so few, to be snatched off by a stranger without alliance or fortune; or rather sunk by him into a state of most wearing, anxious, youth-killing dependence! It must not be, if by any fair interference of friendship, any representations from one who had almost a mother's love, and mother's rights, it would be prevented.

Captain Wentworth had no fortune. He had been lucky in his profession; but spending freely, what had come freely, had realized nothing. But he was confident that he should soon be rich: full of life and ardour, he knew that he should soon have a ship, and soon be on a station that would lead to everything he wanted. He had always been lucky; he knew he should be so still. Such confidence, powerful in its own warmth, and bewitching in the wit which often expressed it, must have been enough for Anne; but Lady Russell saw it very differently. His sanguine temper, and fearlessness of mind, operated very differently on her. She saw in it but an aggravation of the evil. It only added a dangerous character to himself. He was brilliant, he was headstrong. Lady Russell had little taste for wit, and of anything approaching to imprudence a horror. She deprecated the connexion in every light.

Such opposition, as these feelings produced, was more than Anne could combat. Young and gentle as she was, it might yet have been possible to withstand her father's ill-will, though unsoftened by one kind word or look on the part of her sister; but Lady Russell, whom she had always loved and relied on, could not, with such steadiness of opinion, and such tenderness of manner, be continually advising her in vain. She was persuaded to believe the engagement a wrong thing: indiscreet, improper, hardly capable of success, and not deserving it. But it was not a merely selfish caution, under which she acted, in putting an end to it. Had she not imagined herself consulting his good, even more than her own, she could hardly have given him up. The belief of being prudent, and self-denying, principally for *his* advantage, was her chief consolation, under the misery of a parting, a final parting; and every consolation was required, for she had to encounter all the additional pain of opinions, on his side, totally unconvinced and unbending, and of his feeling himself ill used by so forced a relinquishment. He had left the country in consequence.

A few months had seen the beginning and the end of their acquaintance; but not with a few months ended Anne's share of suffering from it. Her attachment and regrets had, for a long time, clouded every enjoyment of youth, and an early loss of bloom and spirits had been their lasting effect.

More than seven years were gone since this little history of sorrowful interest had reached its close; and time had softened down much, perhaps nearly all of peculiar attachment to him, but she had been too dependent on time alone; no aid had been given in change of place (except in one visit to Bath soon after the rupture), or in any novelty or enlargement of society. No one had ever come within the Kellynch circle, who could bear a comparison with Frederick Wentworth, as he stood in her memory. No second attachment, the only thoroughly natural, happy, and sufficient cure, at her time of life, had been possible to the nice tone of her mind, the fastidiousness of her taste, in the small limits of the society around them. Nor had she been able to reconcile the fact that she was a ruined woman with the fact that many a man would overlook such a thing. She mentally used that excuse when the need arose, and she could not acknowledge that she could simply not consider another man for the very reason that her heart would never accept another man.

She had been solicited, when about two-and-twenty, to change her name, by the young man, who not long afterwards found a more willing mind in her younger sister; and Lady Russell had lamented her refusal; for Charles Musgrove was the eldest son of a man, whose landed property and general importance were second in that country, only to Sir Walter's, and of good character and appearance; and however Lady Russell might have asked yet for something more, while Anne was nineteen, she would have rejoiced to see her at twenty-two so respectably removed from the partialities and injustice of her father's house, and settled so permanently near herself. But in this case, Anne had left nothing for advice to do; and though Lady Russell, as satisfied as ever with her own discretion, never wished the past undone, she began now to have the anxiety which borders on hopelessness for Anne's being tempted, by some man of talents and independence, to enter a state for which she held her to be peculiarly fitted by her warm affections and domestic habits.

They knew not each other's opinion, either its constancy or its change, on the one leading point of Anne's conduct, for the subject was never alluded to; but Anne, at seven-and-twenty, thought very differently from what she had been made to think at nineteen. She did not blame Lady Russell, she did not blame herself for having been guided by her; but she felt that were any young person, in similar circumstances, to apply to her for counsel, they would never receive any of such certain immediate wretchedness, such uncertain future good.

She was persuaded that under every disadvantage of disapprobation at home, and every anxiety attending his profession, all their probable fears, delays, and disappointments, she should yet have been a happier woman in maintaining the engagement, than she had been in the sacrifice of it; and this, she fully believed, had the usual share, had even more than the usual share of all such solicitudes and suspense been theirs, without reference to the actual results of their case, which, as it happened, would have bestowed earlier prosperity than could be reasonably calculated on. All his sanguine expectations, all his confidence had been justified. His genius and ardour had seemed to foresee and to command his prosperous path. He had, very soon after their engagement ceased, got employ: and all that he had told her would follow, had taken place. He had distinguished himself, and early gained the other step in rank, and must now, by successive captures, have made a handsome fortune. She had only navy lists and newspapers for her authority, but she could not doubt his being rich; and, in favour of his constancy, she had no reason to believe him married.

How eloquent could Anne Elliot have been! how eloquent, at least, were her wishes on the side of early warm attachment, and a cheerful confidence in futurity, against that over-anxious caution which seems to insult exertion and distrust Providence! She had been forced into prudence in her youth, she learned romance as she grew older: the natural sequel of an unnatural beginning.

With all these circumstances, recollections and feelings, she could not hear that Captain Wentworth's sister was likely to live at Kellynch without a revival of former pain; and many a stroll, and many a sigh, were necessary to dispel the agitation of the idea. She often told herself it was folly, before she could harden her nerves sufficiently to feel the continual discussion of the Crofts and their business no evil. She was assisted, however, by that perfect indifference and apparent unconsciousness, among the only three of her own friends in the secret of the past, which seemed almost to deny any recollection of it.

She could do justice to the superiority of Lady Russell's motives in this, over those of her father and Elizabeth; she could honour all the better feelings of her calmness; but the general air of oblivion among them was highly important from whatever it sprung; and in the event of Admiral Croft's really taking Kellynch Hall, she rejoiced anew over the conviction which had always been most grateful to her, of the past being known to those three only among her connexions, by whom no syllable, she believed, would ever be whispered, and in the trust that among his, the brother only with whom he had been residing, had received any information of their short-lived engagement. That brother had been long removed from the country and being a sensible man, and, moreover, a single man at the time, she had a fond dependence on no human creature's having heard of it from him.

The sister, Mrs. Croft, had then been out of England, accompanying her husband on a foreign station, and her own sister, Mary, had been at school while it all occurred; and never admitted by the pride of some, and the delicacy of others, to the smallest knowledge of it afterwards.

With these supports, she hoped that the acquaintance between herself and the Crofts, which, with Lady Russell, still resident in Kellynch, and Mary fixed only three miles off, must be anticipated, need not involve any particular awkwardness.

Chapter 5

On the morning appointed for Admiral and Mrs. Croft's seeing Kellynch Hall, Anne found it most natural to take her almost daily walk to Lady Russell's, and keep out of the way till all was over; when she found it most natural to be sorry that she had missed the opportunity of seeing them.

This meeting of the two parties proved highly satisfactory, and decided the whole business at once. Each lady was previously well disposed for an agreement, and saw nothing, therefore, but good manners in the other; and with regard to the gentlemen, there was such an hearty good humour, such an open, trusting liberality on the Admiral's side, as could not but influence Sir Walter, who had besides been flattered into his very best and most polished behaviour by Mr. Shepherd's assurances of his being known, by report, to the Admiral, as a model of good breeding.

The house and grounds, and furniture, were approved, the Crofts were approved, terms, time, every thing, and every body, was right; and Mr. Shepherd's clerks were set to work, without there having been a single preliminary difference to modify of all that "This indenture sheweth."

Sir Walter, without hesitation, declared the Admiral to be the best-looking sailor he had ever met with, and went so far as to say, that if his own man might have had the arranging of his hair, he should not be ashamed of being seen with him any where; and the Admiral, with sympathetic cordiality, observed to his wife as they drove back through the park, "I thought we should soon come to a deal, my dear, in spite of what they told us at Taunton. The

Baronet will never set the Thames on fire, but there seems to be no harm in him."—reciprocal compliments, which would have been esteemed about equal.

The Crofts were to have possession at Michaelmas; and as Sir Walter proposed removing to Bath in the course of the preceding month, there was no time to be lost in making every dependent arrangement.

Lady Russell, convinced that Anne would not be allowed to be of any use, or any importance, in the choice of the house which they were going to secure, was very unwilling to have her hurried away so soon, and wanted to make it possible for her to stay behind till she might convey her to Bath herself after Christmas; but having engagements of her own which must take her from Kellynch for several weeks, she was unable to give the full invitation she wished, and Anne though dreading the possible heats of September in all the white glare of Bath, and grieving to forego all the influence so sweet and so sad of the autumnal months in the country, did not think that, everything considered, she wished to remain. It would be most right, and most wise, and, therefore must involve least suffering to go with the others.

Something occurred, however, to give her a different duty. Mary, often a little unwell, and always thinking a great deal of her own complaints, and always in the habit of claiming Anne when anything was the matter, was indisposed; and foreseeing that she should not have a day's health all the autumn, entreated, or rather required her, for it was hardly entreaty, to come to Uppercross Cottage, and bear her company as long as she should want her, instead of going to Bath.

"I cannot possibly do without Anne," was Mary's reasoning; and Elizabeth's reply was, "Then I am sure Anne had better stay, for nobody will want her in Bath."

To be claimed as a good, though in an improper style, is at least better than being rejected as no good at all; and Anne, glad to be thought of some use, glad to have anything marked out as a duty, and certainly not sorry to have the scene of it in the country, and her own dear country, readily agreed to stay.

This invitation of Mary's removed all Lady Russell's difficulties, and it was consequently soon settled that Anne should not go to Bath till Lady Russell took her, and that all the intervening time should be divided between Uppercross Cottage and Kellynch Lodge.

So far all was perfectly right; but Lady Russell was almost startled by the wrong of one part of the Kellynch Hall plan, when it burst on her, which was, Mrs. Clay's being engaged to go to Bath with Sir Walter and Elizabeth, as a most important and valuable assistant to the latter in all the business before her. Lady Russell was extremely sorry that such a measure should have been resorted to at all, wondered, grieved, and feared, and knew perfectly well that the woman was *not* going to Bath to be an assistant to *Elizabeth*; and the affront it contained to Anne, in Mrs. Clay's being of so much use, while Anne could be of none, was a very sore aggravation.

Anne herself was become hardened to such affronts; but she felt the imprudence of the arrangement quite as keenly as Lady Russell. With a great deal of quiet observation, and a knowledge, which she often wished less, of her father's character, she was sensible that results the most serious to his family from the intimacy were more than possible. She did not imagine that her father had at present an idea of the kind. Mrs. Clay had freckles, and a projecting tooth, and a clumsy wrist, which he was continually making severe remarks upon, in her absence; but she was young, and certainly altogether well-looking, and possessed, in an acute mind and assiduous pleasing manners, infinitely more dangerous attractions than any merely personal might have been. Anne was so impressed by the degree of their danger, that she could not excuse herself from trying to make it perceptible to her sister. She had little hope of success; but Elizabeth, who in the event of such a reverse would be so much more to be pitied than herself, should never, she thought, have reason to reproach her for giving no warning.

She spoke, and seemed only to offend. Elizabeth could not conceive how such an absurd suspicion should occur to her, and indignantly answered for each party's perfectly knowing their situation.

"Mrs. Clay," said she, warmly, "never forgets who she is; and as I am rather better acquainted with her sentiments than you can be, I can assure you, that upon the subject of marriage they are particularly nice, and that she reprobates all inequality of condition and rank more strongly than most people. And as to my father, I really should not have thought that he, who has kept himself single so long for our sakes, need be suspected now. If Mrs. Clay were a very beautiful woman, I grant you, it might be wrong to have her so much with me; not that anything in the world, I am sure, would induce my father to make a degrading match, but he might be rendered unhappy. But poor Mrs. Clay who, with all her merits, can never have been reckoned tolerably pretty, I really think poor Mrs. Clay may be staying here in perfect safety. One would imagine you had never heard my father speak of her personal misfortunes, though I know you must fifty times. That tooth of her's and those freckles. Freckles do not disgust me so very much as they do him. I have known a face not materially disfigured by a few, but he abominates them. You must have heard him notice Mrs. Clay's freckles."

"There is hardly any personal defect," replied Anne, "which an agreeable manner might not gradually reconcile one to. Elizabeth, I fear Mrs. Clay is going with you to be with our father. The way she looks at him sometimes—"

Elizabeth's head snapped around, and she pinned Anne with a narrowed glare. "I am sure I do not know what you mean."

Anne blushed. Elizabeth knew very well what Anne meant. Anne knew from the few times Elizabeth had confided to her in rare sisterly moments that Elizabeth herself was an expert at dallying with men while preserving her ultimate virtue. "Elizabeth, please." Anne looked at her hands clenched in her lap. "You know what I am saying."

"That Mrs. Clay and Father are *intimate*?" Elizabeth scoffed.

Anne blushed deeper. "I suspect that to be so, yes."

"I think very differently," answered Elizabeth, shortly; "an agreeable manner may set off handsome features, but can never alter plain ones. Father has much better taste than that. However, at any rate, as I have a great deal more at stake on this point than anybody else can have, I think it rather unnecessary in you to be advising me."

Anne had done; glad that it was over, and not absolutely hopeless of doing good. Elizabeth, though resenting the suspicion, might yet be made observant by it.

The last office of the four carriage-horses was to draw Sir Walter, Miss Elliot, and Mrs. Clay to Bath. The party drove off in very good spirits; Sir Walter prepared with condescending bows for all the afflicted tenantry and cottagers who might have had a hint to show themselves, and Anne walked up at the same time, in a sort of desolate tranquillity, to the Lodge, where she was to spend the first week.

Her friend was not in better spirits than herself. Lady Russell felt this break-up of the family exceedingly. Their respectability was as dear to her as her own, and a daily intercourse had become precious by habit. Her heart ached from Sir Walter's absence, however temporary it would be. It was painful to look upon their deserted grounds, and still worse to anticipate the new hands they were to fall into; and to escape the solitariness and the melancholy of so altered a village, and be out of the way when Admiral and Mrs. Croft first arrived, she had determined to make her own absence from home begin when she must give up Anne. Accordingly their removal was made together, and Anne was set down at Uppercross Cottage, in the first stage of Lady Russell's journey.

Uppercross was a moderate-sized village, which a few years back had been completely in the old English style, containing only two houses superior in appearance to those of the yeomen and labourers; the mansion of the squire, with its high walls, great gates, and old trees, substantial and unmodernized, and the compact, tight parsonage, enclosed in its own neat garden, with a vine and a pear-tree trained round its casements; but upon the marriage of the young 'squire, it had received the improvement of a farm-house elevated into a cottage, for his residence, and Uppercross Cottage, with its veranda, French windows, and other prettiness, was quite as likely to catch the traveller's eye as the more consistent and considerable aspect and premises of the Great House, about a quarter of a mile farther on.

Here Anne had often been staying. She knew the ways of Uppercross as well as those of Kellynch. The two families were so continually meeting, so much in the habit of running in and out of each other's house at all hours, that it was rather a surprise to her to find Mary alone; but being alone, her being unwell and out of spirits was almost a matter of course. Though better endowed than the elder sister, Mary had not Anne's understanding nor temper. While well, and happy, and properly attended to, she had great good humour and excellent spirits; but any indisposition sunk her completely. She had no resources for solitude; and inheriting a considerable share of the Elliot self-importance, was very prone to add to every other distress that of fancying herself neglected and ill-used. In person, she was inferior to both sisters, and had, even in her bloom, only reached the dignity of being "a fine girl." She was now lying on the faded sofa of the pretty little drawing-room, the once elegant furniture of which had been gradually growing shabby, under the influence of four summers and two children; and, on Anne's appearing, greeted her with—

"So, you are come at last! I began to think I should never see you. I am so ill I can hardly speak. I have not seen a creature the whole morning!"

"I am sorry to find you unwell," replied Anne. "You sent me such a good account of yourself on Thursday!"

"Yes, I made the best of it; I always do: but I was very far from well at the time; and I do not think I ever was so ill in my life as I have been all this morning: very unfit to be left alone, I am sure. Suppose I were to be seized of a sudden in some dreadful way, and not able to ring the bell! So, Lady Russell would not get out. I do not think she has been in this house three times this summer."

Anne said what was proper, and enquired after her husband. "Oh! Charles is out shooting. I have not seen him since seven o'clock. He would go, though I told him how ill I was. He said he should not stay out long; but he has never come back, and now it is almost one. I assure you, I have not seen a soul this whole long morning."

"You have had your little boys with you?"

"Yes, as long as I could bear their noise; but they are so unmanageable that they do me more harm than good. Little Charles does not mind a word I say, and Walter is growing quite as bad."

"Well, you will soon be better now," replied Anne, cheerfully. "You know I always cure you when I come. How are your neighbours at the Great House?"

"I can give you no account of them. I have not seen one of them to-day, except Mr. Musgrove, who just stopped and spoke through the window, but without getting off his horse; and though I told him how ill I was, not one of them have been near me. It did not happen to suit the Miss Musgroves, I suppose, and they never put themselves out of their way."

"You will see them yet, perhaps, before the morning is gone. It is early."

"I never want them, I assure you. They talk and laugh a great deal too much for me. Oh! Anne, I am so very unwell! It was quite unkind of you not to come on Thursday."

"My dear Mary, recollect what a comfortable account you sent me of yourself! You wrote in the cheerfullest manner, and said you were perfectly well, and in no hurry for me; and that being the case, you must be aware that my wish would be to remain with Lady Russell to the last: and besides what I felt on her account, I have really been so busy, have had so much to do, that I could not very conveniently have left Kellynch sooner."

"Dear me! what can *you* possibly have to do?"

"A great many things, I assure you. More than I can recollect in a moment; but I can tell you some. I have been making a duplicate of the catalogue of my father's books and pictures. I have been several times in the garden with Mackenzie, trying to understand, and make him understand, which of Elizabeth's plants are for Lady Russell. I have had all my own little concerns to arrange, books and music to divide, and all my trunks to repack, from not having understood in time what was intended as to the waggons: and one thing I have had to do, Mary, of a more trying nature: going to almost every house in the parish, as a sort of take-leave. I was told that they wished it. But all these things took up a great deal of time." Not to mention the box of memories she had needed to dig up. Her thoughts were just returning to the same scene she had relived while caressing Frederick's signature when her sister interrupted.

"Oh! well!" and after a moment's pause, "but you have never asked me one word about our dinner at the Pooles yesterday."

Anne sighed as her memory stalled right before Frederick's kiss. She turned her face toward her sister and smiled. "Did you go then? I have made no enquiries, because I concluded you must have been obliged to give up the party."

"Oh yes! I went. I was very well yesterday; nothing at all the matter with me till this morning. It would have been strange if I had not gone."

"I am very glad you were well enough, and I hope you had a pleasant party."

"Nothing remarkable. One always knows beforehand what the dinner will be, and who will be there; and it is so very uncomfortable not having a carriage of one's own. Mr. and Mrs. Musgrove took me, and we were so crowded! They are both so very large, and take up so much room; and Mr. Musgrove always sits forward. So, there was I, crowded into the back seat with Henrietta and Louise; and I think it very likely that my illness to-day may be owing to it."

A little further perseverance in patience and forced cheerfulness on Anne's side produced nearly a cure on Mary's. She could soon sit upright on the sofa, and began to hope she might be able to leave it by dinner-time. Then, forgetting to think of it, she was at the other end of the room, beautifying a nosegay; then, she ate her cold meat; and then she was well enough to propose a little walk.

"Where shall we go?" said she, when they were ready. "I suppose you will not like to call at the Great House before they have been to see you?"

"I have not the smallest objection on that account," replied Anne. "I should never think of standing on such ceremony with people I know so well as Mrs. and the Miss Musgroves."

"Oh! but they ought to call upon you as soon as possible. They ought to feel what is due to you as *my* sister. However, we may as well go and sit with them a little while, and when we have that over, we can enjoy our walk."

Anne had always thought such a style of intercourse highly imprudent; but she had ceased to endeavour to check it, from believing that, though there were on each side continual subjects of offence, neither family could now do without it. To the Great

House accordingly they went, to sit the full half hour in the old-fashioned square parlour, with a small carpet and shining floor, to which the present daughters of the house were gradually giving the proper air of confusion by a grand piano-forte and a harp, flower-stands and little tables placed in every direction. Oh! could the originals of the portraits against the wainscot, could the gentlemen in brown velvet and the ladies in blue satin have seen what was going on, have been conscious of such an overthrow of all order and neatness! The portraits themselves seemed to be staring in astonishment.

The Musgroves, like their houses, were in a state of alteration, perhaps of improvement. The father and mother were in the old English style, and the young people in the new. Mr. and Mrs. Musgrove were a very good sort of people; friendly and hospitable, not much educated, and not at all elegant. Their children had more modern minds and manners. There was a numerous family; but the only two grown up, excepting Charles, were Henrietta and Louisa, young ladies of nineteen and twenty, who had brought from school at Exeter all the usual stock of accomplishments, and were now like thousands of other young ladies, living to be fashionable, happy, and merry.

Their dress had every advantage, their faces were rather pretty, their spirits extremely good, their manner unembarrassed and pleasant; they were of consequence at home, and favourites abroad. Henrietta was sweet and shy with beautiful blonde hair and cornflower-blue eyes. Louisa had flame-red hair, emerald-green eyes, and a temperament that matched her hair. Both young ladies were shameless flirts, though innocent flirts all the same. Their interactions with men were a constant source of amusement to all who witnessed it. Anne always contemplated them as some of the happiest creatures of her acquaintance; but still, saved as we all are, by some comfortable feeling of superiority from wishing for the possibility of exchange, she would not have given up her own more elegant and cultivated mind for all their enjoyments; and envied them nothing but that seemingly perfect good understanding and agreement together, that good-humoured mutual affection, of which she had known so little herself with either of her sisters.

They were received with great cordiality. Nothing seemed amiss on the side of the Great House family, which was generally, as Anne very well knew, the least to blame. The half hour was chatted away pleasantly enough; and she was not at all surprised at the end of it, to have their walking party joined by both the Miss Musgroves, at Mary's particular invitation.

Chapter 6

Anne had not wanted this visit to Uppercross, to learn that a removal from one set of people to another, though at a distance of only three miles, will often include a total change of conversation, opinion, and idea. She had never been staying there before, without being struck by it, or without wishing that other Elliots could have her advantage in seeing how unknown, or unconsidered there, were the affairs which at Kellynch Hall were treated as of such general publicity and pervading interest; yet, with all this experience, she believed she must now submit to feel that another lesson, in the art of knowing our own nothingness beyond our own circle, was become necessary for her; for certainly, coming as she did, with a heart full of the subject which had been completely occupying both houses in Kellynch for many weeks, she had expected rather more curiosity and sympathy than she found in the separate but very similar remark of Mr. and Mrs. Musgrove: "So, Miss Anne, Sir Walter and your sister are gone; and what part of Bath do you think they will settle in?" and this, without much waiting for an answer; or in the young ladies' addition of, "I hope *we* shall be in Bath in the winter; but remember, papa, if we do go, we must be in a good situation: none of your Queen Squares for us!" or in the anxious supplement from Mary, of—"Upon my word, I shall be pretty well off, when you are all gone away to be happy at Bath!"

She could only resolve to avoid such self-delusion in future, and think with heightened gratitude of the extraordinary blessing of having one such truly sympathising friend as Lady Russell.

The Mr. Musgroves had their own game to guard, and to destroy, their own horses, dogs, and newspapers to engage them, and the females were fully occupied in all the other common subjects of housekeeping, neighbours, dress, dancing, and music. She acknowledged it to be very fitting, that every little social commonwealth should dictate its own matters of discourse; and hoped, ere long, to become a not unworthy member of the one she was now transplanted into. With the prospect of spending at least two months at Uppercross, it was highly incumbent on her to clothe her imagination, her memory, and all her ideas in as much of Uppercross as possible, and to forget Kellynch, the past, and all who that encompassed.

She had no dread of these two months. Mary was not so repulsive and unsisterly as Elizabeth, nor so inaccessible to all influence of hers; neither was there anything among the other component parts of the cottage inimical to comfort. She was always on friendly terms with her brother-in-law; and in the children, who loved her nearly as well, and respected her a great deal more than their mother, she had an object of interest, amusement, and wholesome exertion.

Charles Musgrove was civil and agreeable; in sense and temper he was undoubtedly superior to his wife, but not of powers, or conversation, or grace, to make the past, as they were connected together, at all a dangerous contemplation; though, at the same time, Anne could believe, with Lady Russell, that a more equal match might have greatly improved him; and that a woman of real understanding might have given more consequence to his character, and more usefulness, rationality, and elegance to his habits and pursuits. As it was, he did nothing with much zeal, but sport; and his time was otherwise trifled away, without benefit from books or anything else. He had very good spirits, which never seemed much affected by his wife's occasional lowness, bore with her unreasonableness sometimes to Anne's admiration, and upon the whole, though there was very often a little disagreement (in which she had sometimes more share than she wished, being appealed to by both parties), they might pass for a happily distant couple. This status was merely one of the reasons Anne had refused Charles when he had asked for her. Anne knew she would never have been satisfied with a happy distance between her and her husband. The very brief glimpse of passion she had experienced with—No. She stopped herself. She had just resolved to clothe her thoughts in Uppercross.

Charles and Mary were content. They were always perfectly agreed in the want of more money, and a strong inclination for a handsome present from his father; but here, as on most topics, he had the superiority, for while Mary thought it a great shame that such a present was not made, he always contended for his father's having many other uses for his money, and a right to spend it as he liked.

As to the management of their children, his theory was much better than his wife's, and his practice not so bad. "I could manage them very well, if it were not for Mary's interference," was what Anne often heard him say, and had a good deal of faith in; but when listening in turn to Mary's reproach of "Charles spoils the children so that I cannot get them into any order," she never had the smallest temptation to say, "Very true."

One of the least agreeable circumstances of her residence there was her being treated with too much confidence by all parties, and being too much in the secret of the complaints of each house. Known to have some influence with her sister, she was continually requested, or at least receiving hints to exert it, beyond what was practicable. "I wish you could persuade Mary not to be always fancying herself ill," was Charles's language; and, in an unhappy mood, thus spoke Mary: "I do believe if Charles were to see me dying, he would not think there was anything the matter with me. I am sure, Anne, if you would, you might persuade him that I really am very ill—a great deal worse than I ever own."

Mary's declaration was, "I hate sending the children to the Great House, though their grandmamma is always wanting to see them, for she humours and indulges them to such a degree, and gives them so much trash and sweet things, that they are sure to come back sick and cross for the rest of the day." And Mrs. Musgrove took the first opportunity of being alone with Anne, to say, "Oh! Miss Anne, I cannot help wishing Mrs. Charles had a little of your method with those children. They are quite different creatures with you! But to be sure, in general they are so spoilt! It is a pity you cannot put your sister in the way of managing them. They are as fine healthy children as ever were seen, poor little dears! without partiality; but Mrs. Charles knows no more how they should be treated—! Bless me! how troublesome they are sometimes. I assure you, Miss Anne, it prevents my wishing to see them at our house so often as I otherwise should. I believe Mrs. Charles is not quite pleased with my not inviting them oftener; but you know it is very bad to have children with one that one is obligated to be checking every moment; "don't do this," and "don't do that;" or that one can only keep in tolerable order by more cake than is good for them."

She had this communication, moreover, from Mary. "Mrs. Musgrove thinks all her servants so steady, that it would be high treason to call it in question; but I am sure, without exaggeration, that her upper house-maid and laundry-maid, instead of being in their business, are gadding about the village, all day long." When Anne did not react, she continued, "*With men*! I meet them wherever I go, always talking to some dark stranger or another; and I declare, I never go twice into my nursery without seeing something of them. If Jemima were not the trustiest, steadiest creature in the world, it would be enough to spoil her; for she tells me, they are always tempting her to take a walk with them." And on Mrs. Musgrove's side, it was, "I make a rule of never interfering in any of my daughter-in-law's concerns, for I know it would not do; but I shall tell *you*, Miss Anne, because you may be able to set things to rights, that I have no very good opinion of Mrs. Charles's nursery-maid: I hear strange stories of her; she is always upon the gad; and I suspect she uses this time to entertain a lover. Yes," she said when Anne raised her brows, "a *lover*. When does a nursery-maid have time for such a commitment as that?" Anne hid her smile behind her hand and nearly missed Mrs. Musgrove's next words. "And from my own knowledge, I can declare, she is such a fine-dressing lady, that she is enough to ruin any servants she comes near. Mrs. Charles quite swears by her, I know; but I just give you this hint, that you may be upon the watch; because, if you see anything amiss, you need not be afraid of mentioning it."

Again, it was Mary's complaint, that Mrs. Musgrove was very apt not to give her the precedence that was her due, when they dined at the Great House with other families; and she did not see any reason why she was to be considered so much at home as to lose her place. And one day when Anne was walking with only the Musgroves, one of them after talking of rank, people of rank, and jealousy of rank, said, "I have no scruple of observing to you, how nonsensical some persons are about their place, because all the world knows how easy and indifferent you are about it; but I wish anybody could give Mary a hint that it would be a great deal better if she were not so very tenacious, especially if she would not be always putting herself forward to take place of mamma. Nobody doubts her right to have precedence of mamma, but it would be more becoming in her not to be always insisting on it. It is not that mamma cares about it the least in the world, but I know it is taken notice of by many persons."

How was Anne to set all these matters to rights? She could do little more than listen patiently, soften every grievance, and excuse each to the other; give them all hints of the forbearance necessary between such near neighbours, make those hints broadest which were meant for her sister's benefit, and thank her stars that she had not married into such a mess herself.

In all other respects, her visit began and proceeded very well. Her own spirits improved by change of place and subject, by being removed three miles from Kellynch; Mary's ailments lessened by having a constant companion, and their daily intercourse with the other family, since there was neither superior affection, confidence, nor employment in the cottage, to be interrupted by it, was rather an advantage. It was certainly carried nearly as far as possible, for they met every morning, and hardly ever spent an evening asunder; but she believed they should not have done so well without the sight of Mr. and Mrs. Musgrove's respectable forms in the usual places, or without the talking, laughing, and singing of their daughters.

She played a great deal better than either of the Miss Musgroves, but having no voice, no knowledge of the harp, and no fond parents, to sit by and fancy themselves delighted, her performance was little thought of, only out of civility, or to refresh the others, as she was well aware. She knew that when she played she was giving pleasure only to herself; but this was no new sensation. Excepting one short period of her life, she had never, since the age of fourteen, never since the loss of her dear mother, known the happiness of being listened to, or encouraged by any just appreciation or real taste. There was a time, however, when one person had shown a particular interest in her music. He had sat beside her many a night, turning pages for her. When he remembered to, that is. More frequently, he used the opportunity to press against her shoulder to hip. He would lean in close, his breath caressing her cheek and sneaking down her neck and into her bodice. On nights he ventured to be even bolder, he would use the others' distraction in dancing to caress areas of Anne's body that his own hid from the others' view—a quick hand down her thigh, or a brush of the back of his fingers across her breast as he reached to turn a page.

He was never content until he had tantalized her to the point of a grievous error in the music. It had been the era she had most appreciated her music. In music she had been always used to feel alone in the world; with him by her side, she had not been. But that was in the past, and Mr. and Mrs. Musgrove's fond partiality for their own daughters' performance, and total indifference to any other person's, gave her much more pleasure for their sakes, than mortification for her own.

The party at the Great House was sometimes increased by other company. The neighbourhood was not large, but the Musgroves were visited by everybody, and had more dinner-parties, and more callers, more visitors by invitation and by chance, than any other family. They were more completely popular.

The girls were wild for dancing; and the evenings ended, occasionally, in an unpremeditated little ball. There was a family of cousins within a walk of Uppercross, in less affluent circumstances, who depended on the Musgroves for all their pleasures: they would come at any time, and help play at anything, or dance anywhere; and Anne, very much preferring the office of musician to a more active post, played country dances to them by the hour together; a kindness which always recommended her musical powers to the notice of Mr. and Mrs. Musgrove more than anything else, and often drew this compliment;—"Well done, Miss Anne! very well done indeed! Lord bless me! how those little fingers of yours fly about!"

So passed the first three weeks. Michaelmas came; and now Anne's heart must be in Kellynch again. A beloved home made over to others; all the precious rooms and furniture, groves, and prospects, beginning to own other eyes and other limbs! She could not think of much else on the 29th of September; and she had this sympathetic touch in the evening from Mary, who, on having occasion to note down the day of the month, exclaimed, "Dear me, is not this the day the Crofts were to come to Kellynch? I am glad I did not think of it before. How low it makes me!"

The Crofts took possession with true naval alertness, and were to be visited. Mary deplored the necessity for herself. "Nobody knew how much she should suffer. She should put it off as long as she could;" but was not easy till she had talked Charles into driving her over on an early day, and was in a very animated, comfortable state of imaginary agitation, when she came back. Anne had very sincerely rejoiced in there being no means of her going. She wished, however to see the Crofts, and was glad to be within when the visit was returned. They came: the master of the house was not at home, but the two sisters were together; and as it chanced that Mrs. Croft fell to the share of Anne, while the Admiral sat by Mary, and made himself very agreeable by his good-humoured notice of her little boys, she was well able to watch for a likeness, and if it failed her in the features, to catch it in the voice, or in the turn of sentiment and expression.

Mrs. Croft, though neither tall nor fat, had a squareness, uprightness, and vigour of form, which gave importance to her person. She had bright dark eyes, good teeth, and altogether an agreeable face; though her reddened and weather-beaten complexion, the consequence of her having been almost as much at sea as her husband, made her seem to have lived some years longer in the world than her real eight-and-thirty. She had Frederick's— *Captain Wentworth's*, she mentally corrected herself—hair and aquiline nose, and Anne had to remind herself not to stare, though she did not always succeed. Mrs. Croft caught her gaze more than once with a curious expression crossing those familiar features. It did not matter, however. Mrs. Croft was the most pleasant woman Anne had ever encountered and never questioned what had to be rather curious conduct on Anne's part. Her manners were open, easy, and decided, like one who had no distrust of herself, and no doubts of what to do; without any approach to coarseness, however, or any want of good humour. Anne gave her credit, indeed, for feelings of great consideration towards herself, in all that related to Kellynch, and it pleased her: especially, as she had satisfied herself in the very first half minute, in the instant even of introduction, that there was not the smallest symptom of any knowledge or suspicion on Mrs. Croft's side, to give a bias of any sort. She was quite easy on that head, and consequently full of strength and courage, till for a moment electrified by Mrs. Croft's suddenly saying,—

"It was you, and not your sister, I find, that my brother had the pleasure of being acquainted with, when he was in this country."

Anne hoped she had outlived the age of blushing; but the age of emotion she certainly had not. Oh, she could not bear it if her relationship with Fre—Captain Wentworth were discovered. She could not even remember to call him by his correct name! What would become of her and her tenuous hold on her emotions if the others began to question the past? Anne forced herself to respond in the positive though inside, her very centre rocked.

"Perhaps you may not have heard that he is married?" added Mrs. Croft.

Horror coursed through her, and Anne felt the blood flee her cheeks. "*No*," Anne whispered. It could not be.

Mrs. Croft mistook her response. "Yes, it is true! My oldest brother, happy at last."

Anne's hands unclenched within her lap, and relief so profound she nearly wept from it swept the horror away. She could now answer as she ought; and was happy to feel, when Mrs. Croft's words explained it to be Mr. Wentworth of whom she spoke, that she had said nothing which might not do for either brother. She immediately felt how reasonable it was, that Mrs. Croft should be thinking and speaking of Edward, and not of Frederick; and with shame at her own forgetfulness applied herself to the knowledge of their former neighbour's present state with proper interest.

The rest was all tranquillity; till, just as they were moving, she heard the Admiral say to Mary—

"We are expecting a brother of Mrs. Croft's here soon; I dare say you know him by name."

Regardless of the lesson she had just learned from assuming, Anne could not prevent the instinctual flare of hope that this news brought. She leaned forward eagerly, encouraging Admiral Croft to continue.

He was cut short by the eager attacks of the little boys, clinging to him like an old friend, and declaring he should not go; and being too much engrossed by proposals of carrying them away in his coat pockets, etcetera, to have another moment for finishing or recollecting what he had begun, Anne was left to persuade herself, as well as she could, that the same brother must still be in question. She could not, however, reach such a degree of certainty, as not to be anxious to hear whether anything had been said on the subject at the other house, where the Crofts had previously been calling.

The folks of the Great House were to spend the evening of this day at the Cottage; and it being now too late in the year for such visits to be made on foot, the coach was beginning to be listened for, when the youngest Miss Musgrove walked in. That she was coming to apologize, and that they should have to spend the evening by themselves, was the first black idea; and Mary was quite ready to be affronted, when Louisa made all right by saying, that she only came on foot, to leave more room for the harp, which was bringing in the carriage.

"And I will tell you our reason," she added, "and all about it. I am come on to give you notice, that papa and mamma are out of spirits this evening, especially mamma; she is thinking so much of poor Richard! And we agreed it would be best to have the harp, for it seems to amuse her more than the piano-forte. I will tell you why she is out of spirits. When the Crofts called this morning, (they called here afterwards, did not they?), they happened to say, that her brother, Captain Wentworth, is just returned to England,"— Anne's heart flipped within her chest—"or paid off, or something, and is coming to see them almost directly; and most unluckily it came into mamma's head, when they were gone, that Wentworth, or something very like it, was the name of poor Richard's captain at one time; I do not know when or where, but a great while before he died, poor fellow! And upon looking over his letters and things, she found it was so, and is perfectly sure that this must be the very man, and her head is quite full of it, and of poor Richard! So we must be as merry as we can, that she may not be dwelling upon such gloomy things."

The real circumstances of this pathetic piece of family history were, that the Musgroves had had the ill fortune of a very troublesome, hopeless son; and the good fortune to lose him before he reached his twentieth year; that he had been sent to sea because he was stupid and unmanageable on shore; that he had been very little cared for at any time by his family, though quite as much as he deserved; seldom heard of, and scarcely at all regretted, when the intelligence of his death abroad had worked its way to Uppercross, two years before.

He had, in fact, though his sisters were now doing all they could for him, by calling him "poor Richard," been nothing better than a thick-headed, unfeeling, unprofitable Dick Musgrove, who had never done anything to entitle himself to more than the abbreviation of his name, living or dead.

He had been several years at sea, and had, in the course of those removals to which all midshipmen are liable, and especially such midshipmen as every captain wishes to get rid of, been six months on board Captain Frederick Wentworth's frigate, the *Laconia*; and from the *Laconia* he had, under the influence of his captain, written the only two letters which his father and mother had ever received from him during the whole of his absence; that is to say, the only two disinterested letters; all the rest had been mere applications for money.

In each letter he had spoken well of his captain; but yet, so little were they in the habit of attending to such matters, so unobservant and incurious were they as to the names of men or ships, that it had made scarcely any impression at the time; and that Mrs. Musgrove should have been suddenly struck, this very day, with a recollection of the name of Wentworth, as connected with her son, seemed one of those extraordinary bursts of mind which do sometimes occur.

She had gone to her letters, and found it all as she supposed; and the re-perusal of these letters, after so long an interval, her poor son gone for ever, and all the strength of his faults forgotten, had affected her spirits exceedingly, and thrown her into greater grief for him than she had known on first hearing of his death. Mr. Musgrove was, in a lesser degree, affected likewise; and when they reached the cottage, they were evidently in want, first, of being listened to anew on this subject, and afterwards, of all the relief which cheerful companions could give them.

To hear them talking so much of Captain Wentworth, repeating his name so often, puzzling over past years, and at last ascertaining that it *might*, that it probably *would*, turn out to be the very same Captain Wentworth whom they recollected meeting, once or twice, after their coming back from Clifton—a very fine young man—but they could not say whether it was seven or eight years ago, was a new sort of trial to Anne's nerves. She found, however, that it was one to which she must inure herself. Since he actually was expected in the country, she must teach herself to be insensible on such points. And not only did it appear that he was expected, and speedily, but the Musgroves, in their warm gratitude for the kindness he had shewn poor Dick, and very high respect for his character, stamped as it was by poor Dick's having been six months under his care, and mentioning him in strong, though not perfectly well-spelt praise, as "a fine dashing fellow, only two perticular about the schoolmaster," were bent on introducing themselves, and seeking his acquaintance, as soon as they could hear of his arrival.

The resolution of doing so helped to form the comfort of their evening.

Chapter 7

A very few days more, and Captain Wentworth was known to be at Kellynch, and Mr. Musgrove had called on him, and come back warm in his praise, and he was engaged with the Crofts to dine at Uppercross, by the end of another week. It had been a great disappointment to Mr. Musgrove to find that no earlier day could be fixed, so impatient was he to shew his gratitude, by seeing Captain Wentworth under his own roof, and welcoming him to all that was strongest and best in his cellars. But a week must pass; only a week, in Anne's reckoning, and then, she supposed, they must meet; and soon she began to wish that she could feel secure even for a week, for she did not know what she would do the first time she saw him. Ages ago, when they were engaged, he had always picked her up and spun her around while laying a resounding kiss upon her lips as a greeting. That was obviously not going to happen when they first laid eyes on each other now, years later, when they were—Anne did not know what they were. With a sigh, she realized they may be enemies. Not on her part, of course, but she could not blame him for hating her.

Captain Wentworth made a very early return to Mr. Musgrove's civility, and she was all but calling there in the same half hour. She and Mary were actually setting forward for the Great House, where, as she afterwards learnt, they must inevitably have found him, when they were stopped by the eldest boy's being at that moment brought home in consequence of a bad fall. The child's situation put the visit entirely aside; but she could not hear of her escape with indifference, even in the midst of the serious anxiety which they afterwards felt on his account. The flare of relief carried with it a great deal of guilt that she would be able to find any positive emotion in her nephew's peril.

His collar-bone was found to be dislocated, and such injury received in the back, as roused the most alarming ideas. It was an afternoon of distress, and Anne had every thing to do at once; the apothecary to send for, the father to have pursued and informed, the mother to support and keep from hysterics, the servants to control, the youngest child to banish, and the poor suffering one to attend and soothe; besides sending, as soon as she recollected it, proper notice to the other house, which brought her an accession rather of frightened, enquiring companions, than of very useful assistants.

Her brother's return was the first comfort; he could take best care of his wife; and the second blessing was the arrival of the apothecary. Till he came and had examined the child, their apprehensions were the worse for being vague; they suspected great injury, but knew not where; but now the collar-bone was soon replaced, and though Mr. Robinson felt and felt, and rubbed, and looked grave, and spoke low words both to the father and the aunt, still they were all to hope the best, and to be able to part and eat their dinner in tolerable ease of mind; and then it was, just before they parted, that the two young aunts were able so far to digress from their nephew's state, as to give the information of Captain Wentworth's visit; staying five minutes behind their father and mother, to endeavour to express how perfectly delighted they were with him, how much handsomer, how infinitely more agreeable they thought him than any individual among their male acquaintance, who had been at all a favourite before. They raved over his blue eyes, and it took all of Anne's self-control not to correct them. Blue eyes? His eyes were not merely blue. And their description of his physique—broad and muscled—was not right either. Frederick had always been slender. Anne realized she had *again* called him by his Christian name in her thoughts and forced herself to pay attention to the excited Miss Musgroves.

The girls were saying how glad they had been to hear papa invite him to stay for dinner, how sorry when he said it was quite out of his power, and how glad again when he had promised in reply to papa and mamma's farther pressing invitations to come and dine with them on the morrow—actually on the morrow; and he had promised it in so pleasant a manner, as if he felt all the motive of their attention just as he ought. And in short, he had looked and said everything with such exquisite grace, that they could assure them all, their heads were both turned by him; and off they ran, quite as full of glee as of love, and apparently more full of Captain Wentworth than of little Charles. Anne felt a profound pang of sorrow within her chest that in her younger years might have been jealousy. Anne was too tired now to feel such a thing, and she could not blame them for their ardour. Anne had been their age when she had fallen head-over-heels in love with the handsome boy. How much easier it must be to fall in love with the handsome man.

The same story and the same raptures were repeated, when the two girls came with their father, through the gloom of the evening, to make enquiries; and Mr. Musgrove, no longer under the first uneasiness about his heir, could add his confirmation and praise, and hope there would be now no occasion for putting Captain Wentworth off, and only be sorry to think that the cottage party, probably, would not like to leave the little boy, to give him the meeting. "Oh no; as to leaving the little boy," both father and mother were in much too strong and recent alarm to bear the thought; and Anne, in the joy of the escape, could not help adding her warm protestations to theirs.

Charles Musgrove, indeed, afterwards, shewed more of inclination; "the child was going on so well, and he wished so much to be introduced to Captain Wentworth, that, perhaps, he might join them in the evening; he would not dine from home, but he might walk in for half an hour." But in this he was eagerly opposed by his wife, with "Oh! no, indeed, Charles, I cannot bear to have you go away. Only think if anything should happen?"

The child had a good night, and was going on well the next day. It must be a work of time to ascertain that no injury had been done to the spine; but Mr. Robinson found nothing to increase alarm, and Charles Musgrove began, consequently, to feel no necessity for longer confinement. The child was to be kept in bed and amused as quietly as possible; but what was there for a father to do? This was quite a female case, and it would be highly absurd in him, who could be of no use at home, to shut himself up. His father very much wished him to meet Captain Wentworth, and there being no sufficient reason against it, he ought to go; and it ended in his making a bold, public declaration, when he came in from shooting, of his meaning to dress directly, and dine at the other house.

"Nothing can be going on better than the child," said he; "so I told my father, just now, that I would come, and he thought me quite right. Your sister being with you, my love, I have no scruple at all. You would not like to leave him yourself, but you see I can be of no use. Anne will send for me if anything is the matter."

Husbands and wives generally understand when opposition will be vain. Mary knew, from Charles's manner of speaking, that he was quite determined on going, and that it would be of no use to teaze him. She said nothing, therefore, till he was out of the room, but as soon as there was only Anne to hear—

"So you and I are to be left to shift by ourselves, with this poor sick child; and not a creature coming near us all the evening! I knew how it would be. This is always my luck. If there is anything disagreeable going on men are always sure to get out of it, and Charles is as bad as any of them. Very unfeeling! I must say it is very unfeeling of him to be running away from his poor little boy.

Talks of his being going on so well! How does he know that he is going on well, or that there may not be a sudden change half an hour hence? I did not think Charles would have been so unfeeling. So here he is to go away and enjoy himself, and because I am the poor mother, I am not to be allowed to stir; and yet, I am sure, I am more unfit than anybody else to be about the child. My being the mother is the very reason why my feelings should not be tried. I am not at all equal to it. You saw how hysterical I was yesterday."

"But that was only the effect of the suddenness of your alarm—of the shock. You will not be hysterical again. I dare say we shall have nothing to distress us. I perfectly understand Mr. Robinson's directions, and have no fears; and indeed, Mary, I cannot wonder at your husband. Nursing does not belong to a man; it is not his province. A sick child is always the mother's property: her own feelings generally make it so." Anne certainly knew that if she could have been a mother, nothing would have ever separated her from her children, much less one of her children who was ill.

"I hope I am as fond of my child as any mother, but I do not know that I am of any more use in the sick-room than Charles, for I cannot be always scolding and teazing the poor child when it is ill; and you saw, this morning, that if I told him to keep quiet, he was sure to begin kicking about. I have not nerves for the sort of thing."

"But, could you be comfortable yourself, to be spending the whole evening away from the poor boy?"

"Yes; you see his papa can, and why should not I? Jemima is so careful; and she could send us word every hour how he was. I really think Charles might as well have told his father we would all come. I am not more alarmed about little Charles now than he is. I was dreadfully alarmed yesterday, but the case is very different to-day."

"Well," Anne looked at her lap, "if you do not think it too late to give notice for yourself, suppose you were to go, as well as your husband. Leave little Charles to my care." Anne dared to look at Mary. "Mr. and Mrs. Musgrove cannot think it wrong while I remain with him." Any worry Anne had over her motives being discovered for wanting to stay behind vanished as Mary's face lit.

"Are you serious?" cried Mary, her eyes brightening. "Dear me! that's a very good thought, very good, indeed. To be sure, I may just as well go as not, for I am of no use at home—am I? and it only harasses me. You, who have not a mother's feelings, are a great deal the properest person." Anne could not prevent a wince— motherhood had once been her greatest wish—but Mary did not notice. "You can make little Charles do anything; he always minds you at a word. It will be a great deal better than leaving him only with Jemima. Oh! I shall certainly go; I am sure I ought if I can, quite as much as Charles, for they want me excessively to be acquainted with Captain Wentworth, and I know you do not mind being left alone." Anne did not bother to correct her. "An excellent thought of yours, indeed, Anne. I will go and tell Charles, and get ready directly. You can send for us, you know, at a moment's notice, if anything is the matter; but I dare say there will be nothing to alarm you. I should not go, you may be sure, if I did not feel quite at ease about my dear child."

The next moment she was tapping at her husband's dressing-room door, and as Anne followed her up stairs, she was in time for the whole conversation, which began with Mary's saying, in a tone of great exultation—

"I mean to go with you, Charles, for I am of no more use at home than you are. If I were to shut myself up for ever with the child, I should not be able to persuade him to do anything he did not like. Anne will stay; Anne undertakes to stay at home and take care of him. It is Anne's own proposal, and so I shall go with you, which will be a great deal better, for I have not dined at the other house since Tuesday."

"This is very kind of Anne," was her husband's answer, "and I should be very glad to have you go; but it seems rather hard that she should be left at home by herself, to nurse our sick child."

Anne was now at hand to take up her own cause, and the sincerity of her manner being soon sufficient to convince him, where conviction was at least very agreeable, he had no farther scruples as to her being left to dine alone, though he still wanted her to join them in the evening, when the child might be at rest for the night, and kindly urged her to let him come and fetch her, but she was quite unpersuadable; and this being the case, she had ere long the pleasure of seeing them set off together in high spirits. They were gone, she hoped, to be happy, however oddly constructed such happiness might seem; as for herself, she was left with as many sensations of comfort, as were, perhaps, ever likely to be hers. She knew herself to be of the first utility to the child; and what was it to her if Frederick Wentworth were only half a mile distant, making himself agreeable to others?

She would have liked to know how he felt as to a meeting. Perhaps indifferent, if indifference could exist under such circumstances. He must be either indifferent or unwilling. Had he wished ever to see her again, he need not have waited till this time; he would have done what she could not but believe that in his place she should have done long ago, when events had been early giving him the independence which alone had been wanting.

Anne had not known she'd dozed off in her chair until a hand was roughly shaking her awake.

"Anne."

Even before she opened her eyes, she knew the man who owned that voice. His hand was warm on her shoulder, the fingers curling over her collarbone. Immediate need clenched within her belly.

Her eyes shot open, and Anne unerringly found his face.

The blue-green eyes were looking at her earnestly. His lips were parted.

"Frederick?"

His face relaxed and his hand against her shoulder softened, his fingers now feeling like a caress. "Anne, I had to see you."

Anne blinked sleep from her eyes, sure she was mishearing. "You are to be at dinner."

His lips tipped. "As were you." His fingers trailed lightly along her collarbone to skim up her neck. "I could wait no longer to see you."

Anne jerked to her feet and stepped away from his touch, sure any second that his fingers upon her skin would reduce her to a wanton mess. She held her hands out in front of her, palms toward him. "Please, Frederick—" Her speech tapered off. She was uncertain what to say—what to beg. *Go away* was probably not the correct thing to tell him, though she wished it with all of her being. She could not stand to be in the same room with him and not disgrace herself by doing something entirely untoward.

He stalked closer, paying no regard to her supplicating position or the fact that she backed further away from him, matching every one of his broad steps with a stumbling one of her own.

"*Anne.*" The word was a whisper and may as well have been a stroke of his hand across her stomach for how it quivered.

A whimper fell from her lips as he backed her out of her nephew's sick room and into the hall.

"Anne, I have perished for you," he said in a rumble, "every day for the last eight years."

Anne's back met the wall, and still, he kept coming. The heat from his body pressed into hers just before he stopped moving. He stood toe-to-toe with her and raised a broad hand to her face where he cradled her cheek within his palm.

Anne's breath left her in a sound akin to a sob.

"Shhh." He stepped even closer, pressing them hip-to-hip and breasts to chest. "All is well now." His thumb swept over her bottom lip. "I am here."

Her lips parted beneath his touch, and his thumb caressed the inside arch of her upper lip. He stared intently at her lips.

Something within Anne broke, and her need unleashed itself. She threw caution and to-morrow's consequences to the wind. "*Kiss me,*" she begged in a voice she barely recognised.

Fire flashed in his ocean-coloured eyes just before he lowered his head and replaced his thumb with an open-mouthed kiss.

Anne's gasp sucked his sigh into her lungs, and the silky slide of his lips against hers went straight to her head, rendering her dizzy.

He moaned harshly, and then pressed into her even further, crowding her into the wall. Every glorious inch of his body strained against hers. His flagrant arousal ground into her belly as he thrust his tongue into her mouth and wound his fingers into her hair.

She echoed his moan and dug her fingers into his coat, pulling him impossibly closer and rotating her hips so that she moved against his length.

"*Yes,*" he whispered into their kiss. "That's my Anne." He shoved a hand between the wall and her bottom and hauled her lower half so close it lay almost in between his thighs, whereupon he began thrusting against her in earnest.

Anne realized she was making a desperate mewling sound just as she felt air caress her bottom. The back of her skirts were raised. His fingers slid inside her drawers and down one rounded cheek before seeking the drenched area between her thighs. His forearm rippled across her bottom as he slipped two fingers into her sheath.

Anne cried out and thrust back into his hold, her slick body taking his fingers even further. Bliss spiraled up from his touch and straight to her heart. "Frederick," she half-sobbed, half-moaned into his dinner coat.

He leaned his head down to press kisses to her neck as he moved his fingers in and out of her body. He continued to thrust himself against her belly, and his breathing was becoming broken and now ended with a harsh whisper of her name on each exhale.

"Anne," he groaned desperately as he began to shake within her arms. "Oh, *Anne*." His body stiffened, and she could feel a spread of warmth against her stomach.

Her peak rose up suddenly and crashed down upon her. Her lips parted as she cried out, and her eyes shot open—

"Anne!" Mary cried as she shook her roughly. "Wake up, for heaven's sake. You must be having the worst night terror I have ever heard."

Anne sucked in an unsteady breath as her body struggled to discern reality. She blinked several times to discover that she was sitting in the chair beside her nephew's bed. Her sheath was still clenching and releasing around phantom fingers, and the shaking she had thought was Frederick's orgasm ceased when Mary released her and stepped back.

Anne only just prevented herself from clapping a hand over her mouth in mortification. Good heavens. What had she said in her sleep? Had she cried out as loudly as she thought she had?

"It is okay now," Mary said, looking at Anne with the barest modicum of concern. "We are here. No need to fear something from a dream."

Over Mary's shoulder, Anne's eyes found Charles's where he stood in the door to the sick room. One look at his raised brows and open mouth, and Anne realized Charles knew exactly what state Anne's body had been in when Mary woke her. The blood already staining Anne's cheeks grew even hotter, and she sought some way to direct attention away from herself. "H-how was your evening?" Even Anne could hear the husky quality to her voice, but Mary simply smiled broadly and launched into a rapid fall of words. After a slight hesitation and one more aghast perusal of Anne, Charles joined in.

Her brother and sister came back delighted with their new acquaintance, and their visit in general. There had been music, singing, talking, laughing, all that was most agreeable; charming manners in Captain Wentworth, no shyness or reserve; they seemed all to know each other perfectly, and he was coming the very next morning to shoot with Charles. Mary overlooked Anne's gasp completely, while Charles gazed sharply at her for a moment. When Anne waved Mary on, she continued. He was to come to breakfast, but not at the Cottage, though that had been proposed at first; but then he had been pressed to come to the Great House instead, and he seemed afraid of being in Mrs. Charles Musgrove's way, on account of the child, and therefore, somehow, they hardly knew how, it ended in Charles's being to meet him to breakfast at his father's.

Anne understood it. He wished to avoid seeing her. He had inquired after her, she found, slightly, as might suit a former slight acquaintance, seeming to acknowledge such as she had acknowledged, actuated, perhaps, by the same view of escaping introduction when they were to meet. Anne could not help but wonder how her name had sounded upon his lips. Had his voice deepened as he said her name as it used to when they were young? Had he called her Anne or Miss Elliot? Sorrow stabbed deeply as she realized that of course he would have called her Miss Elliot.

The morning hours of the Cottage were always later than those of the other house, and on the morrow the difference was so great that Mary and Anne were not more than beginning breakfast when Charles came in to say that they were just setting off, that he was come for his dogs, that his sisters were following with Captain Wentworth; his sisters meaning to visit Mary and the child, and Captain Wentworth proposing also to wait on her for a few minutes if not inconvenient; and though Charles had answered for the child's being in no such state as could make it inconvenient, Captain Wentworth would not be satisfied without his running on to give notice.

Mary, very much gratified by this attention, was delighted to receive him, while a thousand feelings rushed on Anne, of which this was the most consoling, that it would soon be over. And it was soon over. In two minutes after Charles's preparation, the others appeared; they were in the drawing-room. It took all of Anne's fortitude not to make some noise of dismay. Her Frederick—her sweet, slender, young Frederick—was gone. In his absence was a colossal man. As he stopped in the doorway to the drawing-room, his shoulders filled the space of the frame completely.

He was speaking to Mary, and while his attention was otherwise occupied, Anne felt it safe to quickly peruse how greatly his physique had changed in eight years. Not only were his shoulders broader than they had been, but the sleeves of his jacket strained around the bulge of his arms. His chest was enormous, swelling far out past his chin in great plains of muscle. The bigger dimensions of his shoulders and chest only served to emphasize how narrowly his stomach and hips tapered. His waistcoat hugged his body tightly, and Anne felt her mouth go dry at the powerful body such a cut of cloth only served to accentuate. His thighs bulged within his breeches, and rippled as he moved slightly in his conversation with Anne's sister. Suddenly, Henrietta and Louisa's description yesterday of his great strength and stature made a good deal more sense in the light of the evidence before her eyes.

He was much changed. And every fibre of Anne's body appreciated each and every glorious adjustment. He seemed to brace himself, and then he began to turn toward her. Anne quickly pulled her vision up from her unforgiveable scrutiny of his form to look at an area just over his shoulder. Her eye half met Captain Wentworth's, and the jolt to her system as those same blue-green eyes met hers was severe. Anne at once knew that, though his body had changed, he was still her Frederick. Anne corrected herself—not *her* Frederick at all. This was Captain Wentworth. His face remained passive. A bow, a curtsey passed; such trivial niceties that she could scarcely breathe without screaming. She stared at the wall as she tried to get a hold of her rioting emotions. She heard his voice; he talked to Mary, said all that was right, said something to the Miss Musgroves, enough to mark an easy footing; the room seemed full, full of persons and voices, but a few minutes ended it. Charles shewed himself at the window, all was ready, their visitor had bowed and was gone, never speaking a word to Anne and leaving the image of his well-muscled back flaring in Anne's memory. The Miss Musgroves were gone too, suddenly resolving to walk to the end of the village with the sportsmen: the room was cleared, and Anne might finish her breakfast as she could, which, as it turned out, was not at all. The food upon her plate grew cold.

"It is over! it is over!" she repeated to herself again and again, in nervous gratitude. "The worst is over!"

Mary talked, but she could not attend. She had seen him. They had met. They had been once more in the same room.

Soon, however, she began to reason with herself, and try to be feeling less. Eight years, almost eight years had passed, since all had been given up. How absurd to be resuming the agitation which such an interval had banished into distance and indistinctness! What might not eight years do? Events of every description, changes, alienations, removals—all, all must be comprised in it, and oblivion of the past—how natural, how certain too! It included nearly a third part of her own life.

Alas! with all her reasoning, she found, that to retentive feelings eight years may be little more than nothing.

Now, how were his sentiments to be read? Was this like wishing to avoid her? And the next moment she was hating herself for the folly which asked the question.

On one other question which perhaps her utmost wisdom might not have prevented, she was soon spared all suspense; for, after the Miss Musgroves had returned and finished their visit at the Cottage she had this spontaneous information from Mary:—

"Captain Wentworth is not very gallant by you, Anne, though he was so attentive to me. Henrietta asked him what he thought of you, when they went away, and he said, 'You were so altered he should not have known you again.'"

Anne's stomach heaved as though she would lose what little breakfast she had been able to manage. She covered her mouth with one hand and turned her face aside so that her sister would not see the glimmer of tears that now stung Anne's eyes. Mary had no feelings to make her respect her sister's in a common way, but she was perfectly unsuspicious of being inflicting any peculiar wound.

"Altered beyond his knowledge." Anne fully submitted, in silent, deep mortification. Shame burned hotly, and Anne remembered her reflection from the mirror this morning with despair: the tired shadows that bruised the hallows of her eyes, the lack of luster to her skin and hair, her drab clothing. She had barely been pretty before; she shuddered to think what she must be now. Was she—*ugly*? Doubtless it was so, and she could take no revenge, for he was enhanced, not altered for the worse. She had already acknowledged it to herself, and she could not think differently, let him think of her as he would. No: the years which had destroyed her youth and bloom had only given him a more glowing, manly, open look, in no respect lessening his personal advantages. Though his body had been different, she had seen the same Frederick Wentworth.

"So altered that he should not have known her again!" These were words which could not but dwell with her. Yet she soon began to rejoice that she had heard them. They were of sobering tendency; they allayed agitation; they composed, and consequently must make her happier. She, in her ugliness, was not worthy of such a handsome man, and the sooner she reconciled herself to that, the sooner the sting of his presence would lessen.

Frederick Wentworth had used such words, or something like them, but without an idea that they would be carried round to her. He had thought her wretchedly altered, and in the first moment of appeal, had spoken as he felt. The deep brown eyes that he had lost himself in many an afternoon in his youth were dull and lifeless. The hair that had shone in the sun, the hair that he had wrapt around his wrist so he could pull her head back and kiss her neck—that hair was pulled back severely, revealing every feature he had memorized and recalled over the years. Now those features were harsh and tired. And yet, the moment he had allowed himself to look at her, he had needed to stifle the flare of affection that surged through his body. His breeches had grown tight, of all things, to the point that he had had to shift restlessly while talking to Anne's sister to hide the evidence of burgeoning arousal. It was merely a habit of his body to react that way toward Anne. Soon enough, after enough discipline in her presence, Frederick was certain that his body would no longer betray him so.

Even though his body was confused, his mind was not. One thing was certain: He had not forgiven Anne Elliot. She had used him ill, deserted and disappointed him; Frederick shuddered to think of how long it took him to get over losing his virginity to a woman who had immediately abandoned him. He was half wounded, even still, and half appalled that such a thing actually mattered to him. He was more than aware that men gladly tossed away their virginity and cared little for how the lady regarded them afterwards. That Frederick's soul had been mortally hurt by Anne's careless handling of something that Frederick had valued so greatly was both debilitating and embarrassing, and one of his most closely guarded secrets. Her actions were unforgiveable and worse. She had shewn a feebleness of character in doing so horrible a thing, which his own decided, confident temper could not endure. She had given him up to oblige others. It had been the effect of over-persuasion. It had been weakness and timidity.

He had been most warmly attached to her, and had never seen a woman since whom he thought her equal; eight years had passed, and none could turn his head. He had not even been able to bring himself to be with another woman for something as simple and pressing as tending to the demanding needs associated with being a man. He had abstained for eight years, unable to shake the terrible feeling of rejection, and unwilling to face the possibility of a repeat of similar events. It had not been easy, and the strain had only grown, not abated over the years. He often feared he had a perversion in how often he had to seek privacy to give himself some ease. He had carefully avoided all female company; their presence had only made his ache worse even though he had genuinely felt no desire for any of the women he had encountered specifically. He had, however, listened raptly to the other sailors' ribald tales of bedroom escapades. He counted it as an important education, and he was fairly certain that he had a better-than-average idea of how to please a woman, except every time he imagined doing so, the only woman he could picture was Anne. But, except from some natural sensation of curiosity, he had no desire of meeting her again. Her power with him was gone for ever, or so he told himself each time her face flitted through his mind.

It was now his object to marry. He was more than tired of living the life of a monk, and he was certain he could ensure a different ending to his courtship this time by marrying the lady *before* the consummation. He was rich, and being turned on shore, fully intended to settle as soon as he could be properly tempted; actually looking round, ready to fall in love with all the speed which a clear head and a quick taste could allow. He had a theory that perhaps he had not desired any women before because he had not put the effort into it. He would do so now. He had a heart for either of the Miss Musgroves, if they could catch it; a heart, in short, for any pleasing young woman who came in his way, excepting Anne Elliot. This was his only secret exception, when he said to his sister, in answer to her suppositions:—

"Yes, here I am, Sophia, quite ready to make a foolish match. Anybody between fifteen and thirty may have me for asking. A little beauty, and a few smiles, and a few compliments to the navy, and I am a lost man. Should not this be enough for a sailor, who has had no society among women to make him nice?"

He said it, she knew, to be contradicted. His bright proud eye spoke the conviction that he was nice; and Anne Elliot was not out of his thoughts, when he more seriously described the woman he should wish to meet with. "A strong mind, with sweetness of manner," made the first and the last of the description.

"That is the woman I want," said he. "Something a little inferior I shall of course put up with, but it must not be much. If I am a fool, I shall be a fool indeed, for I have thought on the subject more than most men."

Chapter 8

From this time Captain Wentworth and Anne Elliot were repeatedly in the same circle. They were soon dining in company together at Mr. Musgrove's, for the little boy's state could no longer supply his aunt with a pretence for absenting herself; and this was but the beginning of other dinings and other meetings.

Whether former feelings were to be renewed must be brought to the proof; former times must undoubtedly be brought to the recollection of each; *they* could not but be reverted to; the year of their engagement could not but be named by him, in the little narratives or descriptions which conversation called forth. His profession qualified him, his disposition lead him, to talk; and "*That* was in the year six;" "*That* happened before I went to sea in the year six," occurred in the course of the first evening they spent together: and though his voice did not falter, and though she had no reason to suppose his eye wandering towards her while he spoke, Anne felt the utter impossibility, from her knowledge of his mind, that he could be unvisited by remembrance any more than herself. There were a great many things that had happened in the year six. They had met. He had kissed her for the first time, and then many times thereafter. They had daily spent time together. He had made love to her. She had broken his heart. Each time he mentioned the year six, these things ran through Anne's mind and a pang of real physical pain accompanied each memory. There must be the same immediate association of thought for him—she could not conceive it to be otherwise—though she was very far from conceiving it to be of equal pain.

They had no conversation together, no intercourse but what the commonest civility required. Once so much to each other! Now nothing! There *had* been a time, when of all the large party now filling the drawing-room at Uppercross, they would have found it most difficult to cease to speak to one another. With the exception, perhaps, of Admiral and Mrs. Croft, who seemed particularly attached and happy, (Anne could allow no other exceptions even among the married couples), there could have been no two hearts so open, no tastes so similar, no feelings so in unison, no countenances so beloved. And in the year six, while they would have talked at one of the gatherings, the tension between them would have mounted.

Frederick had had the most distracting habit of watching her lips intently as she spoke. It never failed to distract her fiercely. And then, of course, because his attention was so focused on her lips, she would wonder what *his* looked like as they moved around his words. She mused now that she could see why he had been so fascinated—she never appreciated a mouth's function as much as she did while watching Frederick talk. His full bottom lip was particularly enticing. And, villain that he was, he knew it and would worry it between his teeth while she stared, rendering her a complete simpleton in their conversation. Lord knew how many times utter nonsense fell from her mouth as she watched him bite into his bottom lip. Desire would curl within her belly, and she remembered many times during these public gatherings when he would have to cross one leg over the other, ankle to knee, to hide his own mounting desire. And then she would have something new to stare at. It wouldn't take long after that point; he could never stand to have her look at his arousal long without showing her exactly what her impertinence was doing to him. They would wait until everyone's attention was directed elsewhere, and then they would sneak off together to—well, anywhere that was nearby. Anne recalled a pantry and servants' quarters among the places they had slipped away to.

Even now, Anne's pulse fluttered at these long-cherished memories. Knowing they had minimal time before they were noticed as missing, these secret interludes were, of a necessity, short—and oh, so very sweet. In the pantry, he had sat upon a tower of bags of flour, hauling her into his lap while facing him, her knees on each side of his hips, and his arousal pressing deliciously just where she had needed it. They had ground together, him thrusting up against her, and her moving her hips under the direction of his almost-bruising hands. It had not taken long for either of them to finish, the excitement of possibly being discovered paired with the tinderbox and flame that they became whenever they touched, bringing them both to a quick—and rather loud, Anne remembered now with a smile—ending. The wonder of that moment had staid with her long after they had unwound themselves from each other and smoothed away the telltale indentions in the bags of flour to return to the party.

Now they were as strangers; nay, worse than strangers, for they could never become acquainted. It was a perpetual estrangement.

When he talked, she heard the same voice, and discerned the same mind. There was a very general ignorance of all naval matters throughout the party; and he was very much questioned, and especially by the two Miss Musgroves, who seemed hardly to have any eyes but for him, as to the manner of living on board, daily regulations, food, hours, etcetera, and their surprise at his accounts, at learning the degree of accommodation and arrangement which was practicable, drew from him some pleasant ridicule, which reminded Anne of the early days when she too had been ignorant, and she too had been accused of supposing sailors to be living on board without anything to eat, or any cook to dress it if there were, or any servant to wait, or any knife and fork to use.

From thus listening and thinking, she was roused by a whisper of Mrs. Musgrove's who, overcome by fond regrets, could not help saying—

"Ah! Miss Anne, if it had pleased Heaven to spare my poor son, I dare say he would have been just such another by this time."

Anne suppressed a smile, and listened kindly, while Mrs. Musgrove relieved her heart a little more; and for a few minutes, therefore, could not keep pace with the conversation of the others.

When she could let her attention take its natural course again, she found the Miss Musgroves just fetching the Navy List (their own navy list, the first that had ever been at Uppercross), and sitting down together to pore over it, with the professed view of finding out the ships that Captain Wentworth had commanded.

"Your first was the *Asp*, I remember; we will look for the *Asp*."

"You will not find her there. Quite worn out and broken up. I was the last man who commanded her. Hardly fit for service then. Reported fit for home service for a year or two, and so I was sent off to the West Indies."

The girls looked all amazement.

"The Admiralty," he continued, "entertain themselves now and then, with sending a few hundred men to sea, in a ship not fit to be employed. But they have a great many to provide for; and among the thousands that may just as well go to the bottom as not, it is impossible for them to distinguish the very set who may be least missed."

"Phoo! phoo!" cried the Admiral, "what stuff these young fellows talk! Never was a better sloop than the *Asp* in her day. For an old built sloop, you would not see her equal. Lucky fellow to get her! He knows there must have been twenty better men than himself applying for her at the same time. Lucky fellow to get anything so soon, with no more interest than his."

"I felt my luck, Admiral, I assure you;" replied Captain Wentworth, seriously. "I was as well satisfied with my appointment as you can desire. It was a great object with me at that time to be at sea; a very great object," his eyes flicked to Anne momentarily and then back to the Admiral, "I wanted to be doing something."

Anne felt that slight glance as though it were a blow to her heart. She turned aside so as to not accidentally see him look accusingly at her anymore. She would not survive another such instance.

"To be sure you did. What should a young fellow like you do ashore for half a year together? If a man had not a wife, he soon wants to be afloat again."

"But, Captain Wentworth," cried Louisa, "how vexed you must have been when you came to the *Asp*, to see what an old thing they had given you."

"I knew pretty well what she was before that day;" said he, smiling. "I had no more discoveries to make than you would have as to the fashion and strength of any old pelisse, which you had seen lent about among half your acquaintance ever since you could remember, and which at last, on some very wet day, is lent to yourself. Ah! she was a dear old *Asp* to me. She did all that I wanted. I knew she would. I knew that we should either go to the bottom together, or that she would be the making of me; and I never had two days of foul weather all the time I was at sea in her; and after taking privateers enough to be very entertaining, I had the good luck in my passage home the next autumn, to fall in with the very French frigate I wanted. I brought her into Plymouth; and here another instance of luck. We had not been six hours in the Sound, when a gale came on, which lasted four days and nights, and which would have done for poor old *Asp* in half the time; our touch with the Great Nation not having much improved our condition. Four-and-twenty hours later, and I should only have been a gallant Captain Wentworth, in a small paragraph at one corner of the newspapers; and being lost in only a sloop, nobody would have thought about me."

Against her will, her eyes returned to him as fear so stark it was debilitating coursed through Anne's veins. She hungrily scanned his form, reassuring herself that he was hearty and whole and in her presence, not at the bottom of the ocean. He had been nearly lost! She knew she certainly would have thought of him—for the rest of her life—had she seen such a horrific thing as the announcement of his untimely death in the paper. Anne's shudderings were to herself alone; but the Miss Musgroves could be as open as they were sincere, in their exclamations of pity and horror.

"And so then, I suppose," said Mrs. Musgrove, in a low voice, as if thinking aloud, "so then he went away to the *Laconia*, and there he met with our poor boy. Charles, my dear," (beckoning him to her), "do ask Captain Wentworth where it was he first met with your poor brother. I always forgot."

"It was at Gibraltar, mother, I know. Dick had been left ill at Gibraltar, with a recommendation from his former captain to Captain Wentworth."

"Oh! but, Charles, tell Captain Wentworth, he need not be afraid of mentioning poor Dick before me, for it would be rather a pleasure to hear him talked of by such a good friend."

Charles, being somewhat more mindful of the probabilities of the case, only nodded in reply, and walked away.

The girls were now hunting for the *Laconia*; and Captain Wentworth could not deny himself the pleasure of taking the precious volume into his own hands to save them the trouble, and once more read aloud the little statement of her name and rate, and present non-commissioned class, observing over it that she too had been one of the best friends man ever had.

"Ah! those were pleasant days when I had the *Laconia*! How fast I made money in her. A friend of mine and I had such a lovely cruise together off the Western Islands. Poor Harville, sister! You know how much he wanted money: worse than myself. He had a wife. Excellent fellow. I shall never forget his happiness. He felt it all, so much for her sake. I wished for him again the next summer, when I had still the same luck in the Mediterranean."

"And I am sure, Sir," said Mrs. Musgrove, "it was a lucky day for *us*, when you were put captain into that ship. *We* shall never forget what you did."

Her feelings made her speak low; and Captain Wentworth, hearing only in part, and probably not having Dick Musgrove at all near his thoughts, looked rather in suspense, and as if waiting for more.

"My brother," whispered one of the girls; "mamma is thinking of poor Richard."

"Poor dear fellow!" continued Mrs. Musgrove; "he was grown so steady, and such an excellent correspondent, while he was under your care! Ah! it would have been a happy thing, if he had never left you. I assure you, Captain Wentworth, we are very sorry he ever left you."

There was a momentary expression in Captain Wentworth's face at this speech, a certain glance of his bright eye, and curl of his handsome mouth, which convinced Anne, that instead of sharing in Mrs. Musgrove's kind wishes, as to her son, he had probably been at some pains to get rid of him; but it was too transient an indulgence of self-amusement to be detected by any who understood him less than herself; and then the unthinkable happened. He looked directly at her, his cool eyes taking on a heat she did not expect. His gaze roved her face slowly, and then he bit his bottom lip and raised one defiant eyebrow.

Anne gasped so loudly that everyone in the room turned to look at her.

Captain Wentworth's face blanked of all expression, and he looked upon her with nearly bored eyes.

"My dear," Mrs. Croft said solicitously with a soft tap of her hand upon Anne's back. "Are you quite all right?"

Anne coughed and squirmed restlessly in her seat as she offered up some excuse or other. It must have been sufficient, for everyone in the room rejoined their conversations. Captain Wentworth turned back to the Admiral and muttered something too low for her to hear. In another moment he was perfectly collected and serious, and almost instantly afterwards coming up to the sofa, on which she and Mrs. Musgrove were sitting, took a place by the latter, and entered into conversation with her, in a low voice, about her son, doing it with so much sympathy and natural grace, as shewed the kindest consideration for all that was real and unabsurd in the parent's feelings.

They were actually on the same sofa, for Mrs. Musgrove had most readily made room for him; they were divided only by Mrs. Musgrove. It was no insignificant barrier, indeed. Mrs. Musgrove was of a comfortable, substantial size, infinitely more fitted by nature to express good cheer and good humour, than tenderness and sentiment; and while the agitations of Anne's slender form, and pensive face, may be considered as very completely screened, Captain Wentworth should be allowed some credit for the self-command with which he attended to her large fat sighings over the destiny of a son, whom alive nobody had cared for.

Personal size and mental sorrow have certainly no necessary proportions. A large bulky figure has as good a right to be in deep affliction, as the most graceful set of limbs in the world. But, fair or not fair, there are unbecoming conjunctions, which reason will patronize in vain—which taste cannot tolerate—which ridicule will seize.

Despite her size, Mrs. Musgrove did not sufficiently screen him from Anne's vision. Anne's every sense was assaulted by Frederick's nearness. His voice, which had grown unexpectedly deeper in eight years, washed over Anne, and she was appalled to find goose bumps arising on the skin of her arms. She rubbed them brusquely in hopes that they would go away, but to no avail. And she did have a most uninterrupted view of his lips and how they moved slowly and almost lazily over the kind words he was saying to Mrs. Musgrove. And though he never once flicked his ocean eyes Anne's way during his conversation—from lack of want or from the impossibility of actually seeing her—Anne couldn't help but wonder if he had positioned himself in such a way that Anne would be forced to watch him as she had used to. And watch she did. His tongue slid over his teeth and bottom lip, and Anne's breasts puckered and grew heavy. She even found that her breathing was slightly laboured.

Anne was just beginning to become severely worried at her body's betrayal of her mind's ultimate goal of polite conduct around Captain Wentworth when the Admiral, after taking two or three refreshing turns about the room with his hands behind him, being called to order by his wife, now came up to Captain Wentworth, and without any observation of what he might be interrupting, thinking only of his own thoughts, began with—

"If you had been a week later at Lisbon, last spring, Frederick, you would have been asked to give a passage to Lady Mary Grierson and her daughters."

"Should I? I am glad I was not a week later then."

The Admiral abused him for his want of gallantry. He defended himself; though professing that he would never willingly admit any ladies on board a ship of his, excepting for a ball, or a visit, which a few hours might comprehend.

"But, if I know myself," said he, "this is from no want of gallantry towards them. It is rather from feeling how impossible it is, with all one's efforts, and all one's sacrifices, to make the accommodations on board such as women ought to have. There can be no want of gallantry, Admiral, in rating the claims of women to every personal comfort *high*, and this is what I do. I hate to hear of women on board, or to see them on board; and no ship under my command shall ever convey a family of ladies anywhere, if I can help it."

Anne was just staring at him with mouth open—when they had been engaged, they had planned for Anne to go everywhere with him, *especially* on his voyages—when this perplexing indictment upon her sex brought his sister upon him.

"Oh! Frederick! But I cannot believe it of you. All idle refinement! Women may be as comfortable on board, as in the best house in England. I believe I have lived as much on board as most women, and I know nothing superior to the accommodations of a man-of-war. I declare I have not a comfort or an indulgence about me, even at Kellynch Hall," (with a kind bow to Anne), "beyond what I always had in most of the ships I have lived in; and they have been five altogether. And the benefits of always being with the man you love—they are incomparable to anything else the world of comfort has to offer." The Admiral was standing just behind his wife now where she was seated in a chair beside where Anne sat on the sofa, his hand resting upon the back of the furniture. Anne saw him briefly skim the pad of his index finger down the back of his wife's neck, a move hidden from the rest of the gathering, and a corresponding shiver ran through Mrs. Croft's shoulders.

"Nothing to the purpose," replied her brother. "You were living with your husband, and were the only woman on board."

"But you, yourself, brought Mrs. Harville, her sister, her cousin, and three children, round from Portsmouth to Plymouth. Where was this superfine, extraordinary sort of gallantry of yours then?"

"All merged in my friendship, Sophia. I would assist any brother officer's wife that I could, and I would bring anything of Harville's from the world's end, if he wanted it. But do not imagine that I did not feel it an evil in itself."

"Depend upon it, they were all perfectly comfortable."

"I might not like them the better for that perhaps. Such a number of women and children have no *right* to be comfortable on board."

"My dear Frederick, you are talking quite idly. Pray, what would become of us poor sailors' wives, who often want to be conveyed to one port or another, after our husbands, if everybody had your feelings?"

"My feelings, you see, did not prevent my taking Mrs. Harville and all her family to Plymouth."

"But I hate to hear you talking so like a fine gentleman, and as if women were all fine ladies, instead of rational creatures. We none of us expect to be in smooth water all our days."

"Ah! my dear," said the Admiral, his voice at once deep and tender as he addressed his wife, "when he had got a wife, he will sing a different tune. When he is married, if we have the good luck to live to another war, we shall see him do as you and I, and a great many others, have done. We shall have him very thankful to anybody that will bring him his wife."

Mrs. Croft turned her face toward him, her expression utterly passionate and containing a flare of longing. "Ay, that we shall."

"Now I have done," cried Captain Wentworth. "When once married people begin to attack me with,—'Oh! you will think very differently, when you are married.' I can only say, 'No, I shall not;' and then they say again, 'Yes, you will,' and there is an end of it."

He got up and moved away.

"What a great traveller you must have been, ma'am!" said Mrs. Musgrove to Mrs. Croft.

"Pretty well, ma'am in the fifteen years of my marriage; though many women have done more. I have crossed the Atlantic four times, and have been once to the East Indies, and back again, and only once; besides being in different places about home: Cork, and Lisbon, and Gibraltar. But I never went beyond the Streights, and never was in the West Indies. We do not call Bermuda or Bahama, you know, the West Indies."

Mrs. Musgrove had not a word to say in dissent; she could not accuse herself of having ever called them anything in the whole course of her life.

"And I do assure you, ma'am," pursued Mrs. Croft, "that nothing can exceed the accommodations of a man-of-war; I speak, you know, of the higher rates. When you come to a frigate, of course, you are more confined; though any reasonable woman may be perfectly happy in one of them; and I can safely say, that the happiest part of my life has been spent on board a ship. While we were together, you know, there was nothing to be feared. Thank God! I have always been blessed with excellent health, and no climate disagrees with me. A little disordered always the first twenty-four hours of going to sea, but never knew what sickness was afterwards." She leaned forward a bit, and to Anne's left, Mrs. Musgrove did the same. Anne, crowded between two married women, felt an oncoming sense of dread as Mrs. Croft's eyes twinkled in the telltale marking of a woman about to divulge a confidence. "Speaking as one married woman to another," Mrs. Croft began in a low voice, as Anne fought the desperate desire to remind them that they were not *all* married women, "there are a great many—" she coughed delicately "—*advantages* to being with your man on his ship."

Mrs. Musgrove tittered, her fingers hovering over her lips, and Anne tried hard not to groan aloud as she wondered what she had done recently that would result in such punishment as this evening party was meting out. First, Frederick teasing her with his lips, and now this?

Mrs. Croft continued, "Men are very—hearty—upon the water. I tell you the truth, no amount of horses, much less *creature comforts*," she said these words with disgust, "could drag me away from the opportunity to be with him when he is so magnificent. Any discomfort travelling the sea brings is worth it. The only time I ever really suffered in body or mind, the only time that I ever fancied myself unwell, or had any ideas of danger, was the winter that I passed by myself at Deal, when the Admiral (*Captain* Croft then) was in the North Seas. I lived in perpetual fright at that time, and had all manner of imaginary complaints from not knowing what to do with myself, or when I should hear from him next; but as long as we could be together, nothing ever ailed me, and I never met with the smallest inconvenience."

"Aye, to be sure. Yes, indeed, oh yes! I am quite of your opinion, Mrs. Croft," was Mrs. Musgrove's hearty answer. "There is nothing so bad as a separation. I am quite of your opinion. *I* know what it is, for Mr. Musgrove always attends the assizes, and I am so glad when they are over, and he is safe back again." Mrs. Musgrove giggled again, a surprisingly youthful and delicate sound from one so rotund. "And there is nothing as glorious as a homecoming. The heart is not the *only* thing that absence makes grow, you know."

Now Anne did groan, a small, quiet sound, and both women snapped upright. Air rushed in to cool Anne's heated cheeks in the space that had been occupied by their close bodies.

"Oh, heavens!" Mrs. Musgrove exclaimed breathlessly. "Anne, dear, I quite forgot—

"Oh, she is fine," Mrs. Croft said with a shocking wink thrown in Anne's direction. "She is a grown woman."

Anne gaped in astonishment. No one had ever had that amount of confidence in Anne's capability to do anything, even if it was only confidence that Anne could handle ribald talk amongst matrons. Mrs. Croft's smile when Anne ventured her own shy curving of lips was brimming with friendship, and Anne felt a flare over her heart. This would have been her sister. What kind of woman might Anne have become if she had had the advantage of such an ally these past eight years?

The evening ended with dancing. On its being proposed, Anne offered her services, as usual; and though her eyes would sometimes fill with tears as she sat at the instrument, she was extremely glad to be employed, and desired nothing in return but to be unobserved.

It was a merry, joyous party, and no one seemed in higher spirits than Captain Wentworth. She felt that he had every thing to elevate him which general attention and deference, and especially the attention of all the young women, could do. The Miss Hayters, the females of the family of cousins already mentioned, were apparently admitted to the honour of being in love with him; and as for Henrietta and Louisa, they both seemed so entirely occupied by him, that nothing but the continued appearance of the most perfect good-will between themselves could have made it credible that they were not decided rivals. If he were a little spoilt by such universal, such eager admiration, who could wonder?

These were some of the thoughts which occupied Anne, while her fingers were mechanically at work, proceeding for half an hour together, equally without error, and without consciousness, for the spot beside her on the bench remained empty of distracting men. *Once* she felt that he was looking at herself, observing her altered features, perhaps, trying to trace in them the ruins of the face which had once charmed him; and *once* she knew that he must have spoken of her; she was hardly aware of it, till she heard the answer; but then she was sure of his having asked his partner whether Miss Elliot never danced? The answer was, "Oh, no; never; she has quite given up dancing. She had rather play. She is never tired of playing." Once, too, he spoke to her. She had left the instrument on the dancing being over, and he had sat down to try to make out an air which he wished to give the Miss Musgroves an idea of. Unintentionally she returned to that part of the room; he saw her, and, instantly rising, said, with studied politeness—

"I beg your pardon, madam, this is your seat;" and though she immediately drew back with a decided negative, he was not to be induced to sit down again.

Anne did not wish for more of such looks and speeches. His cold politeness, his ceremonious grace, were worse than anything.

As Frederick and the Crofts left the party that evening, he cursed himself soundly inside the carriage. His sister and her husband chatted happily where they nestled to the point of impropriety across from him. Frederick was left to look out the window and brood.

What the devil had possessed him to teaze Anne so by sitting across from her under the guise of talking to Mrs. Musgrove? Indeed, he had had no idea of his intentions until he found himself sitting beside the large woman, placing himself in a prime location for Anne to observe him. He knew she would watch him—no, he corrected himself—*hoped* is perhaps a better word. However, nothing could explain his earlier actions. He bit his lip—what in heaven's name had driven him to such depravity? Beyond simply being an ungentlemanly thing to do, it had been unkind. Over the years, women who learned of his self-imposed celibacy often teazed him physically: running their hands over his chest when no one was looking, brushing their breasts against him, some—the more bold—even fondling him. He had truly hated it. How dare he do such a thing to poor Anne, even if she did not want him any longer?

But his actions had not even been the worst thing that had happened to her this night. Frederick had discovered Anne to be even more neglected than she had been when they were young—and that was saying something. To put her to work at the piano-forte without any opportunity to engage in merry-making herself—

Was he the only one in the room who had had to force himself not to stare at the vacant space beside Anne as she played as though it were the brightest mark in the world? And he had nearly run aground on the rocks at her feet dozens of times. It had taken indomitable strength of will not to approach her and offer his services as page turner as he had used to.

No one paid her any mind, and, rather than such a thing passing his notice completely, Frederick had found himself becoming incensed. How did they not recognise such a treasure in their midst? It was true that she was no longer of value to Frederick himself, but for *them* to ignore her so—

It was not to be borne.

In the candlelight tonight, she had looked much as she had when he'd loved her. The flame had flickered over her hair, bringing out the highlights and lowlights of the glorious colour that was wound into a style that had not been as severe as the first time he had seen her after their long absence from each other. Frederick sighed and shifted in his seat as he remembered how delicately she had played tonight. Her fingers skipped over the keys at moments, and at others, they caressed the ivory. Her small forearms had rippled slightly with her movements, bringing to mind how they had done the same thing whilst she had worked a part of Frederick's body all those years ago. Her hair had not been the only thing to benefit from the candle perched on the instrument. Shadow and light had played across her entire body, casting enticing dark pools across the peaks and valleys of her bosom. The dip between her breasts had looked particularly warm, dark, and inviting. He could have slid his fingers into her bodice quite easily and stroked across the firm flesh, seeking—

Frederick broke off his line of thought with a violent curse as arousal swept through him so swiftly it nearly stole his breath. His shaft punched up against his breeches, and he scrambled to cross his legs as his sister and brother paused in their cooing at one another to look at him curiously. A quick glance at his lap and Frederick realized crossing his legs was not going to be enough. He tried as nonchalantly as possible to fold his hands across the most rebellious erection he had ever had and forced himself to meet his sister's eyes with a carefully innocent expression as she asked, "Are you quite all right, Frederick?"

His brother-in-law glanced down to where Frederick was trying, unsuccessfully, to hide his condition. The older man chuckled low and squeezed his wife a tad closer. "He's fine, love, let him be."

Frederick was blessed to have his unfortunate blush of horror go unnoticed by them both as the Admiral reclaimed his wife's attention through a loud smack of lips against her cheek. She turned to him in delight and continued whatever trivial lover's conversation she had been engaged in prior to Frederick's outburst.

As Frederick rode through the rest of the trip home in absolute discomfort, he once again vowed to devote his attention to the wife hunt. He apparently needed it more than he had guessed if he was lusting after Anne Elliot, the last woman he would ever marry.

Chapter 9

Captain Wentworth was come to Kellynch as to a home, to stay as long as he liked, being as thoroughly the object of the Admiral's fraternal kindness as of his wife's. He had intended, on first arriving, to proceed very soon into Shropshire, and visit the brother settled in that country, but the attractions of Uppercross induced him to put this off. There was so much of friendliness, and of flattery, and of everything most bewitching in his reception there; the old were so hospitable, the young so agreeable, that he could not but resolve to remain where he was, and take all the charms and perfections of Edward's wife upon credit a little longer. He was most certainly *not*, he reminded himself often, staying in Kellynch to be near Anne.

It was soon Uppercross with him almost every day. The Musgroves could hardly be more ready to invite than he to come, particularly in the morning, when he had no companion at home, for the Admiral and Mrs. Croft were generally out of doors together, interesting themselves in their new possessions, their grass, and their sheep, and dawdling about in a way not endurable to a third person—Frederick still had palpitations over the time he caught them making love against the side of the stables—or driving out in a gig, lately added to their establishment.

Hitherto there had been but one opinion of Captain Wentworth among the Musgroves and their dependencies. It was unvarying, warm admiration everywhere; but this intimate footing was not more than established, when a certain Charles Hayter returned among them, to be a good deal disturbed by it, and to think Captain Wentworth very much in the way.

Charles Hayter was the eldest of all the cousins, and a very amiable, pleasing young man, between whom and Henrietta there had been a considerable appearance of attachment previous to Captain Wentworth's introduction. He was in orders; and having a curacy in the neighbourhood, where residence was not required, lived at his father's house, only two miles from Uppercross. A short absence from home had left his fair one unguarded by his attentions at this critical period, and when he came back he had the pain of finding very altered manners, and of seeing Captain Wentworth.

Mrs. Musgrove and Mrs. Hayter were sisters. They had each had money, but their marriages had made a material difference in their degree of consequence. Mr. Hayter had some property of his own, but it was insignificant compared with Mr. Musgrove's; and while the Musgroves were in the first class of society in the country, the young Hayters would, from their parents' inferior, retired, and unpolished way of living, and their own defective education, have been hardly in any class at all, but for their connexion with Uppercross, this eldest son of course excepted, who had chosen to be a scholar and a gentleman, and who was very superior in cultivation and manners to all the rest.

The two families had always been on excellent terms, there being no pride on one side, and no envy on the other, and only such a consciousness of superiority in the Miss Musgroves, as made them pleased to improve their cousins. Charles's attentions to Henrietta had been observed by her father and mother without any disapprobation. "It would not be a great match for her; but if Henrietta liked him,"—and Henrietta *did* seem to like him. They were always found together on the property. As children, they had played with each other exclusively. As young adults, when they were found together, a springing apart was often the result. Mrs. Musgrove and Mrs. Hayter had laughed many a time over the look upon their children's faces whenever they were caught kissing in one of the rooms adjacent to the parlour. When Charles and Henrietta slipped off, their mothers exchanged a glance and a small smile, and then a handful of minutes later, one of them would go retrieve them, making sure to make a good deal of noise as they approached whatever room had a conspicuously closed door.

The two mothers might not have been so blasé about the liberties Charles and Henrietta were taking with each other had they known that, recently, the two had moved beyond kissing.

Knowing they would be caught post haste if they remained in the house, the two had taken to walking the countryside together. Such an activity afforded them a good deal more privacy, they discovered. In a copse of trees nearby, they had tentatively begun to explore one another's bodies—through their clothes, of course. Charles had insisted on this one nod to propriety. Their kisses were still the desperate, unpracticed embraces they had taken to in the house, as though they worried any moment they may be caught, irrational as the worry was, given their location. Now, however, their kisses were accompanied by fumbling hands and urgent squeezes that they were only beginning to discover brought the other person as much joy as themselves. In these moments, with Henrietta's sweet breath puffing against his neck and her breast filling his hand, Charles was sure he would never find more happiness with any other woman.

Henrietta fully thought so herself, before Captain Wentworth came; but from that time Cousin Charles had been very much forgotten.

Which of the two sisters was preferred by Captain Wentworth was as yet quite doubtful, as far as Anne's observation reached. Henrietta was perhaps the prettiest, Louisa had the higher spirits; and she knew not *now*, whether the more gentle or the more lively character were most likely to attract him.

Mr. and Mrs. Musgrove, either from seeing little, or from an entire confidence in the discretion of both their daughters, and of all the young men who came near them, seemed to leave everything to take its chance. There was not the smallest appearance of solicitude or remark about them in the Mansion-house; but it was different at the Cottage: the young couple there were more disposed to speculate and wonder; and Captain Wentworth had not been above four or five times in the Miss Musgroves' company, and Charles Hayter had but just reappeared, when Anne had to listen to the opinions of her brother and sister, as to *which* was the one liked best. Charles gave it for Louisa, Mary for Henrietta, but quite agreeing that to have him marry either could be extremely delightful.

Charles "had never seen a pleasanter man in his life; and from what he had once heard Captain Wentworth himself say, was very sure that he had not made less than twenty thousand pounds by the war. Here was a fortune at once; besides which, there would be the chance of what might be done in any future war; and he was sure Captain Wentworth was as likely a man to distinguish himself as any officer in the navy. Oh! it would be a capital match for either of his sisters."

Anne had to look away to hide her flare of disgust. *She* had loved him when he was poor.

"Upon my word it would," replied Mary. "Dear me! If he should rise to any very great honours! If he should ever be made a baronet! 'Lady Wentworth' sounds very well. That would be a noble thing, indeed, for Henrietta! She would take place of me then, and Henrietta would not dislike that. Sir Frederick and Lady Wentworth! It would be but a new creation, however, and I never think much of your new creations."

It suited Mary best to think Henrietta the one preferred on the very account of Charles Hayter, whose pretensions she wished to see put an end to. She looked down very decidedly upon the Hayters, and thought it would be quite a misfortune to have the existing connection between the families renewed—very sad for herself and her children.

"You know," said she, "I cannot think him at all a fit match for Henrietta; and considering the alliances which the Musgroves have made, she has no right to throw herself away. I do not think any young woman has a right to make a choice that may be disagreeable and inconvenient to the *principal* part of her family, and be giving bad connections to those who have not been used to them."

Anne's disgust morphed into hot anger. It was this attitude that had worked its persuasion upon her. It was the very reason she had parted from Frederick. Such attitudes were not only harmful to happiness, they were crass.

Mary continued, "And, pray, who is Charles Hayter? Nothing but a country curate. A most improper match for Miss Musgrove of Uppercross."

Her husband, however, would not agree with her here; for besides having a regard for his cousin, Charles Hayter was an eldest son, and he saw things as an eldest son himself.

"Now you are talking nonsense, Mary," was therefore his answer. "It would not be a *great* match for Henrietta, but Charles has a very fair chance, through the Spicers, of getting something from the Bishop in the course of a year or two; and you will please to remember, that he is the eldest son; whenever my uncle dies, he steps into very pretty property. The estate at Winthrop is not less than two hundred and fifty acres, besides the farm near Taunton, which is some of the best land in the country. I grant you, that any of them but Charles would be a very shocking match for Henrietta, and indeed it could not be; he is the only one that could be possible; but he is a very good-natured, good sort of a fellow; and whenever Winthrop comes into his hands, he will make a different sort of place of it, and live in a very different sort of way; and with that property, he will never be a contemptible man—good, freehold property. No, no; Henrietta might do worse than marry Charles Hayter; and if she has him, and Louisa can get Captain Wentworth, I shall be very well satisfied."

"Charles may say what he pleases," cried Mary to Anne, as soon as he was out of the room, "but it would be shocking to have Henrietta marry Charles Hayter; a very bad thing for *her*, and still worse for *me*; and therefore it is very much to be wished that Captain Wentworth may soon put him quite out of her head, and I have very little doubt that he has. She took hardly any notice of Charles Hayter yesterday. I wish you had been there to see her behaviour. She was never parted from Captain Wentworth's side and gazed up at him with great cow-eyes every moment of the time they were together. I swear, I even saw her touch his arm once or twice as she laughed. And as to Captain Wentworth's liking Louisa as well as Henrietta, it is nonsense to say so; for he certainly *does* like Henrietta a great deal the best. He never once shook Henrietta off yesterday. But Charles is so positive! I wish you had been with us yesterday, for then you might have decided between us; and I am sure you would have thought as I did, unless you had been determined to give it against me."

A dinner at Mr. Musgrove's had been the occasion when all these things should have been seen by Anne; but she had staid at home, under the mixed plea of a headache of her own, and some return of indisposition in little Charles. She was quite glad she had not witnessed such a spectacle as flirtatious touch. She had thought only of avoiding Captain Wentworth; but an escape from being appealed to as umpire was now added to the advantages of a quiet evening.

As to Captain Wentworth's views, she deemed it of more consequence that he should know his own mind early enough not to be endangering the happiness of either sister, or impeaching his own honour—something that had *used* to be the most important thing in the world to him—than that he should prefer Henrietta to Louisa, or Louisa to Henrietta. Either of them would, in all probability, make him an affectionate, good-humoured wife. With regard to Charles Hayter, she had delicacy which must be pained by any lightness of conduct in a well-meaning young woman, and a heart to sympathize in any of the sufferings it occasioned; but if Henrietta found herself mistaken in the nature of her feelings, the alternation could not be understood too soon.

Charles Hayter had met with much to disquiet and mortify him in his cousin's behaviour. She had too old a regard for him to be so wholly estranged as might in two meetings extinguish every past hope, and leave him nothing to do but to keep away from Uppercross: but there was such a change as became very alarming, when such a man as Captain Wentworth was to be regarded as the probable cause. He had been absent only two Sundays, and when they parted, had left her interested, even to the height of his wishes, in his prospect of soon quitting his present curacy, and obtaining that of Uppercross instead. At least, he had been certain she was highly interested. If a man could not tell such a thing by the impassioned sighs his love breathed into his ear while he caressed her body, what *could* he tell it by? It had then seemed the object nearest her heart, that Dr. Shirley, the rector, who for more than forty years had been zealously discharging all the duties of his office, but was now growing too infirm for many of them, should be quite fixed on engaging a curate; should make his curacy quite as good as he could afford, and should give Charles Hayter the promise of it.

The advantage of his having to come only to Uppercross, instead of going six miles another way; of his having, in every respect, a better curacy; of his belonging to their dear Dr. Shirley, and of dear, good Dr. Shirley's being relieved from the duty which he could no longer get through without most injurious fatigue, had been a great deal, even to Louisa, but had been almost everything to Henrietta. She had told him so in between feverish kisses. When he came back, alas! the zeal of the business was gone by. Louisa could not listen at all to his account of a conversation which he had just held with Dr. Shirley: she was at a window, looking out for Captain Wentworth; and even Henrietta had at best only a divided attention to give, and seemed to have forgotten all the former doubt and solicitude of the negotiation.

Her eyes had barely looked upon him as she had said distractedly, "Well, I am very glad indeed: but I always thought you would have it; I always thought you sure. It did not appear to me that—in short, you know, Dr. Shirley *must* have a curate, and you had secured his promise. Is he coming, Louisa?"

One morning, very soon after the dinner at the Musgroves, at which Anne had not been present, Captain Wentworth walked into the drawing-room at the Cottage, where were only herself and the little invalid Charles, who was lying on the sofa.

As soon as his gaze landed upon the sleeping boy and his former fiancé at the boy's side, his feet skidded to a stop. The noise of his boots scuffing upon the floor brought her dark head up with an almost audible snap. Her eyes widened as she saw him, and her lips parted. Without permission, Frederick's eyes narrowed in on the pretty pink flesh, which only grew more distracting as her abrupt nervousness at his presence manifested itself in a swift dart of her tongue across her bottom lip. The surprise of finding himself almost alone with Anne Elliot, deprived his manners of their usual composure: he started, and could only say, "I thought the Miss Musgroves had been here: Mrs. Musgrove told me I should find them here," before he walked to the window to recollect himself, and feel how he ought to behave. Old habits died hard. His body traitorously reminded him of what he *would* have done eight years ago upon finding Anne alone in a room. With meticulous attention to detail, his memory flowed through the times he had pressed her up against a wall, desperately pushing into her body with his own. The stolen kisses he had sneaked from her when no one was around had consisted of a furious plunging of his tongue into her warm mouth and an exultation in each of her hearty moans.

She spoke, interrupting his trip to the past quite effectively with a voice that wobbled. "They are up stairs with my sister: they will be down in a few moments, I dare say," was Anne's reply, in all the confusion that was natural; and if the child had not awakened and called her to come and do something for him, he suspected she would have been out of the room the next moment, and released Captain Wentworth as well as herself.

He continued at the window, his breath fogging up the glass in a quicker cadence than it should have; and after calmly and politely saying, "I hope the little boy is better," was silent.

She was obliged to kneel down by the sofa, and remain there to satisfy her patient; and thus they continued a few minutes as the awkwardness in the room billowed like ever-quickening smoke, when, to her very great satisfaction, she heard some other person crossing the little vestibule. She hoped, on turning her head, to see the master of the house; but it proved to be one much less calculated for making matters easy—Charles Hayter, probably not at all better pleased by the sight of Captain Wentworth than Captain Wentworth had been by the sight of Anne.

She only attempted to say, "How do you do? Will you not sit down? The others will be here presently."

Captain Wentworth, however, came from his window, apparently not ill-disposed for conversation; but Charles Hayter, who spared the Captain only one black look, soon put an end to his attempts by seating himself near the table, and taking up the newspaper; and, with a barely contained sigh, Captain Wentworth returned to his window.

Another minute brought another addition. The younger boy, a remarkable stout, forward child, of two years old, having got the door opened for him by some one without, made his determined appearance among them, and went straight to the sofa to see what was going on, and put in his claim to anything good that might be giving away.

There being nothing to eat, he could only have some play; and as his aunt would not let him tease his sick brother, he began to fasten himself upon her, as she knelt, in such a way that, busy as she was about Charles, she could not shake him off. She spoke to him, ordered, entreated, and insisted in vain. Once she did contrive to push him away, but the boy had the greater pleasure in getting upon her back again directly.

"Walter," said she, "get down this moment. You are extremely troublesome. I am very angry with you."

"Walter," cried Charles Hayter, "why do you not do as you are bid? Do not you hear your aunt speak? Come to me, Walter, come to cousin Charles."

But not a bit did Walter stir.

In another moment, however, she found herself in the state of being released from him; some one was taking him from her, though he had bent down her head so much, that his little sturdy hands were unfastened from around her neck, and he was resolutely borne away, before she knew that Captain Wentworth had done it.

He firmly placed Walter upon one hip and carried him over to the window where he had been keeping time since entering. A soft, low exchange occurred between the two of them, after which, Walter nodded his head exuberantly and looked quite contrite: his lower lip protruded further than the top, and his little eyes were swimming with tears when they found Anne's across the room.

"Sorry, Auntie," the small child said in a tremulous voice. "I be a gentleman now. Promise." His *r*s were softened *w*-sounds, and Anne's heart hitched within her chest when Captain Wentworth looked down at Walter with a soft, approving smile.

"Well done, sir," the Captain said to the boy alone, though his deep bass carried to where Anne sat. "Now, what gentlemanly exploits shall we get up to?"

The child shrugged shyly—an emotion Anne had never seen him exhibit.

"Every man should know how to navigate with a compass, wouldn't you say?" she offered quietly from her seat beside her sick nephew.

Frederick's eyes found hers, and the smile he still carried upon his handsome face from conversing with the child struck her through and through. His smile dimmed somewhat, but he nodded curtly just before turning back to Walter. "She is right, of course," he said while lowering the boy to the ground with one hand and reaching into his coat pocket with the other to produce a shiny, brass compass—the same one he had carried upon his person always when he had been Anne's. Frederick pulled the boy's hand up, placed the disc of metal within his hand, and leaned over to instruct him in its uses.

We would have made a good team, she thought as she looked upon them. *And he would have made a breathtaking father.*

Her sensations on the discovery of her wayward thoughts made her perfectly speechless. She could not even thank him for the rescue. She could only hang over little Charles, with most disordered feelings. His kindness in stepping forward to her relief, the manner, the quiet in which it had passed, the little particulars of the circumstance, with the conviction soon forced on her by the noise he was studiously making with the child, that he meant to avoid hearing her thanks, and rather sought to testify that her conversation was the last of his wants, produced such a confusion of varying, but very painful agitation, as she could not recover from, till enabled by the entrance of Mary and the Miss Musgroves to make over her little patient to their cares, and leave the room. She could not stay. It might have been an opportunity of watching the loves and jealousies of the four—they were now altogether; but she could stay for none of it. It was evident that Charles Hayter was not well inclined towards Captain Wentworth. She had a strong impression of his having said, in a vext tone of voice, after Captain Wentworth's interference, "You ought to have minded *me*, Walter; I told you not to teaze your aunt;" and could comprehend his regretting that Captain Wentworth should do what he ought to have done himself. But neither Charles Hayter's feelings, nor anybody's feelings, could interest her, till she had a little better arranged her own. She was ashamed of herself, quite ashamed of being so nervous, so overcome by such a trifle; she was even more ashamed by the brief but desperate wish that she had conceived all of those years ago. But so it was, and it required a long application of solitude and reflection to recover her.

Chapter 10

Other opportunities of making her observations could not fail to occur. Anne had soon been in company with all the four together often enough to have an opinion, though too wise to acknowledge as much at home, where she knew it would have satisfied neither husband nor wife; for while she considered Louisa to be rather the favourite, she could not but think, as far as she might dare to judge from memory and experience, that Captain Wentworth was not in love with either. When he had been in love with *her*, he had been unable to keep his eyes nor his hands to himself. He barely looked upon the young women. They were more in love with him; yet there it was not love. It was a little fever of admiration; but it might, probably must, end in love with some.

Charles Hayter seemed aware of being slighted, and yet Henrietta had sometimes the air of being divided between them. Anne longed for the power of representing to them all what they were about, and of pointing out some of the evils they were exposing themselves to. She did not attribute guile to any. It was the highest satisfaction to her to believe Captain Wentworth not in the least aware of the pain he was occasioning. There was no triumph, no pitiful triumph in his manner. He had, probably, never heard, and never thought of any claims of Charles Hayter. He was only wrong in accepting the attentions (for accepting must be the word) of two young women at once.

After a short struggle, however, Charles Hayter seemed to quit the field. Three days had passed without his coming once to Uppercross; a most decided change. He had even refused one regular invitation to dinner; and having been found on the occasion by Mr. Musgrove with some large books before him, Mr. and Mrs. Musgrove were sure all could not be right, and talked, with grave faces, of his studying himself to death. It was Mary's hope and belief that he had received a positive dismissal from Henrietta, and her husband lived under the constant dependence of seeing him to-morrow. Anne could only feel that Charles Hayter was wise.

One morning, about this time Charles Musgrove and Captain Wentworth being gone a-shooting together, as the sisters in the Cottage were sitting quietly at work, they were visited at the window by the sisters from the Mansion-house.

It was a very fine November day, and the Miss Musgroves came through the little grounds, and stopped for no other purpose than to say, that they were going to take a *long* walk, and therefore concluded Mary could not like to go with them; and when Mary immediately replied, with some jealousy at not being supposed a good walker, "Oh, yes, I should like to join you very much, I am very fond of a long walk;" Anne felt persuaded, by the looks of the two girls, that it was precisely what they did not wish, and admired again the sort of necessity which the family habits seemed to produce, of everything being to be communicated, and everything being to be done together, however undesired and inconvenient. She tried to dissuade Mary from going, but in vain; and that being the case, thought it best to accept the Miss Musgroves' much more cordial invitation to herself to go likewise, as she might be useful in turning back with her sister, and lessening the interference in any plan of their own.

"I cannot imagine why they should suppose I should not like a long walk," said Mary, as she went up stairs. "Everybody is always supposing that I am not a good walker; and yet they would not have been pleased, if we had refused to join them. When people come in this manner on purpose to ask us, how can one say no?"

Just as they were setting off, the gentlemen returned. They had taken out a young dog, who had spoilt their sport, and sent them back early. Their time and strength, and spirits, were, therefore, exactly ready for this walk, and they entered into it with pleasure. Could Anne have foreseen such a junction, she would have staid at home; but, from some feelings of interest and curiosity, she fancied now that it was too late to retract, and the whole six set forward together in the direction chosen by the Miss Musgroves, who evidently considered the walk as under their guidance.

Anne's object was, not to be in the way of anybody; and where the narrow paths across the fields made many separations necessary, to keep with her brother and sister. Her *pleasure* in the walk must arise from the exercise and the day, from the view of the last smiles of the year upon the tawny leaves, and withered hedges, and from repeating to herself some few of the thousand poetical descriptions extant of autumn, that season of peculiar and inexhaustible influence on the mind of taste and tenderness, that season which had drawn from every poet, worthy of being read, some attempt at description, or some lines of feeling. She occupied her mind as much as possible in such like musings and quotations; but it was not possible, that when within reach of Captain Wentworth's conversation with either of the Miss Musgroves, she should not try to hear it; yet she caught little very remarkable. It was mere lively chat, such as any young persons, on an intimate footing, might fall into. He was more engaged with Louisa than with Henrietta. Louisa certainly put more forward for his notice than her sister. This distinction appeared to increase, and there was one speech of Louisa's which struck her. After one of the many praises of the day, which were continually bursting forth, Captain Wentworth added:—

"What glorious weather for the Admiral and my sister! They meant to take a long drive this morning; perhaps we may hail them from some of these hills. They talked of coming into this side of the country. I wonder whereabouts they will upset to-day. Oh! it does happen very often, I assure you; but my sister makes nothing of it; she would as lieve be tossed out as not."

"Ah! You make the most of it, I know," cried Louisa, "but if it were really so, I should do just the same in her place. If I loved a man, as she loves the Admiral, I would always be with him, nothing should ever separate us, and I would rather be overturned by him, than driven safely by anybody else."

It was spoken with enthusiasm.

"Had you?" cried he, catching the same tone; "I honour you!" And there was silence between them for a little while.

Anne could not immediately fall into a quotation again. She felt Frederick's enthusiasm as a direct shot. He may as well have looked at her pointedly while honouring Louisa's loyalty. The sweet scenes of autumn were for a while put by, unless some tender sonnet, fraught with the apt analogy of the declining year, with declining happiness, and the images of youth and hope, and spring, all gone together, blessed her memory. She roused herself to say, as they struck by order into another path, "Is not this one of the ways to Winthrop?" But nobody heard, or, at least, nobody answered her.

Winthrop, however, or its environs—for young men are, sometimes to be met with, strolling about near home—was their destination; and after another half mile of gradual ascent through large enclosures, where the ploughs at work, and the fresh made path spoke the farmer counteracting the sweets of poetical despondence, and meaning to have spring again, they gained the summit of the most considerable hill, which parted Uppercross and Winthrop, and soon commanded a full view of the latter, at the foot of the hill on the other side.

Winthrop, without beauty and without dignity, was stretched before them an indifferent house, standing low, and hemmed in by the barns and buildings of a farm-yard.

Mary exclaimed, "Bless me! here is Winthrop. I declare I had no idea! Well now, I think we had better turn back; I am excessively tired."

Henrietta, conscious and ashamed, and seeing no cousin Charles walking along any path, or leaning against any gate, was ready to do as Mary wished; but "No!" said Charles Musgrove, and "No, no!" cried Louisa more eagerly, and taking her sister aside, seemed to be arguing the matter warmly.

Charles, in the meanwhile, was very decidedly declaring his resolution of calling on his aunt, now that he was so near; and very evidently, though more fearfully, trying to induce his wife to go too. But this was one of the points on which the lady shewed her strength; and when he recommended the advantage of resting herself a quarter of an hour at Winthrop, as she felt so tired, she resolutely answered, "Oh! no, indeed! walking up that hill again would do her more harm than any sitting down could do her good;" and, in short, her look and manner declared, that go she would not.

After a little succession of these sort of debates and consultations, it was settled between Charles and his two sisters, that he and Henrietta should just run down for a few minutes, to see their aunt and cousins, while the rest of the party waited for them at the top of the hill. Louisa seemed the principal arranger of the plan; and, as she went a little way with them, down the hill, still talking to Henrietta, Mary took the opportunity of looking scornfully around her, and saying to Captain Wentworth—

"It is very unpleasant, having such connexions! But, I assure you, I have never been in the house above twice in my life."

She received no other answer, than an artificial, assenting smile, followed by a contemptuous glance, as he turned away, which Anne perfectly knew the meaning of.

The brow of the hill, where they remained, was a cheerful spot: Louisa returned; and Mary, finding a comfortable seat for herself on the step of a stile, was very well satisfied so long as the others all stood about her; but when Louisa drew Captain Wentworth away, to try for a gleaning of nuts in an adjoining hedge-row, and they were gone by degrees quite out of sight and sound, Mary was happy no longer; she quarrelled with her own seat, was sure Louisa had got a much better somewhere, and nothing could prevent her from going to look for a better also. Anne had a sick feeling in the pit of her stomach as she tried to sit by quietly while Mary fussed. She had a suspicion that Louisa had drawn Captain Wentworth away to engage him in some sort of physical activity that might cement their courtship. She studiously ignored her own thoughts and tried to focus on her sister. Mary turned through the same gate the pair had walked through, but could not see them. The sick feeling grew stronger as Anne found a nice seat for Mary, on a dry sunny bank, under the hedge-row, in which she had no doubt of their still being, in some spot or other. Mary sat down for a moment, but it would not do; she was sure Louisa had found a better seat somewhere else, and she would go on till she overtook her.

Anne, really tired herself, was glad to sit down; and she very soon heard Captain Wentworth and Louisa in the hedge-row, behind her, as if making their way back along the rough, wild sort of channel, down the centre. Relief coursed through her at their casual tone of conversation that would have been very at odds with physical exertion of any kind. They were speaking as they drew near. Louisa's voice was the first distinguished. She seemed to be in the middle of some eager speech. What Anne first heard was—

"And so, I made her go. I could not bear that she should be frightened from the visit by such nonsense. What! would I be turned back from doing a thing that I had determined to do, and that I knew to be right, by the airs and interference of such a person, or of any person I may say? No, I have no idea of being so easily persuaded. When I have made up my mind, I have made it; and Henrietta seemed entirely to have made up hers to call at

Winthrop to-day; and yet, she was as near giving it up, out of nonsensical complaisance!"

With a heaviness to her heart, Anne thought how easy it was for Louisa to make such a claim when the only happiness she felt drawn to secure was her own.

Captain Wentworth interrupted Anne's thoughts. "She would have turned back then, but for you?"

"She would indeed. I am almost ashamed to say it."

"Happy for her, to have such a mind as yours at hand! After the hints you gave just now, which did but confirm my own observations, the last time I was in company with him, I need not affect to have no comprehension of what is going on. I see that more than a mere dutiful morning visit to your aunt was in question; and woe betide him, and her too, when it comes to things of consequence, when they are placed in circumstances requiring fortitude and strength of mind, if she have not resolution enough to resist idle interference in such a trifle as this. Your sister is an amiable creature; but yours is the character of decision and firmness, I see. If you value her conduct or happiness, infuse as much of your own spirit into her as you can. But this, no doubt, you have been always doing. It is the worst evil of too yielding and indecisive a character, that no influence over it can be depended on. You are never sure of a good impression being durable; everybody may sway it. Let those who would be happy be firm. Here is a nut," said he, catching one down from an upper bough, "to exemplify: a beautiful glossy nut, which, blessed with original strength, has outlived all the storms of autumn. Not a puncture, not a weak spot anywhere. This nut," he continued, with playful solemnity, "while so many of his brethren have fallen and been trodden under foot, is still in possession of all the happiness that a hazel nut can be supposed capable of." Then returning to his former earnest tone— "My first wish for all whom I am interested in, is that they should be firm. If Louisa Musgrove would be beautiful and happy in her November of life, she will cherish all her present powers of mind."

He had done, and was unanswered. It would have surprised Anne if Louisa could have readily answered such a speech: words of such interest, spoken with such serious warmth! She could imagine what Louisa was feeling.

He *must* be falling in love with her. And who would not? To be so young and so wise, only a year older than Anne had been when she had been persuaded to forego love for duty. For herself, Anne feared to move, lest she should be seen. While she remained, a bush of low rambling holly protected her, and they were moving on. Before they were beyond her hearing, however, Louisa spoke again.

"Mary is good-natured enough in many respects," said she; "but she does sometimes provoke me excessively, by her nonsense and pride—the Elliot pride. She has a great deal too much of the Elliot pride. We do so wish that Charles had married Anne instead. I suppose you know he wanted to marry Anne?"

After a moment's pause, Captain Wentworth said—

"Do you mean that she refused him?"

"Oh! yes; certainly."

"When did that happen?" His voice was curiously urgent. Anne was horrified that this was even coming to light.

"I do not exactly know, for Henrietta and I were at school at the time; but I believe about a year before he married Mary. I wish she had accepted him. We should all have liked her a great deal better; and papa and mamma always think it was her great friend Lady Russell's doing, that she did not. They think Charles might not be learned and bookish enough to please Lady Russell, and that therefore, she persuaded Anne to refuse him."

"I am sure she did," Captain Wentworth muttered venomously.

The sounds were retreating, and Anne distinguished no more. Her own emotions still kept her fixed. She had much to recover from, before she could move. The listener's proverbial fate was not absolutely hers; she had heard no evil of herself, but she had heard a great deal of very painful import. She saw how her own character was considered by Captain Wentworth, and there had been just that degree of feeling and curiosity about her in his manner which must give her extreme agitation.

As soon as she could, she went after Mary, and having found, and walked back with her to their former station, by the stile, felt some comfort in their whole party being immediately afterwards collected, and once more in motion together. Her spirits wanted the solitude and silence which only numbers could give.

Charles and Henrietta returned, bringing, as may be conjectured, Charles Hayter with them. The minutiae of the business Anne could not attempt to understand; even Captain Wentworth did not seem admitted to perfect confidence here; but that there had been a withdrawing on the gentleman's side, and a relenting on the lady's, and that they were now very glad to be together again, did not admit a doubt. Henrietta looked a little ashamed, but very well pleased;—Charles Hayter exceedingly happy: and they were devoted to each other almost from the first instant of their all setting forward for Uppercross. Anne, from her position at the back of the group, saw Charles Hayter touch Henrietta a dozen different times as they made progress: a pressing of his palm to the small of her back, a grabbing of her hand as she stepped over imaginary impediments. It was all so darling that Anne could not prevent a soft smile at the young man's exploits.

The smile faded, however, when Anne spied Louisa walking much too close to Captain Wentworth. Everything now marked out Louisa for Captain Wentworth; nothing could be plainer; and where many divisions were necessary, or even where they were not, they walked side by side nearly as much as the other two. In a long strip of meadow land, where there was ample space for all, they were thus divided, forming three distinct parties; and to that party of the three which boasted least animation, and least complaisance, Anne necessarily belonged. She joined Charles and Mary, and was tired enough to be very glad of Charles's other arm; but Charles, though in very good humour with her, was out of temper with his wife. Mary had shewn herself disobliging to him, and was now to reap the consequence, which consequence was his dropping her arm almost every moment to cut off the heads of some nettles in the hedge with his switch; and when Mary began to complain of it, and lament her being ill-used, according to custom, in being on the hedge side, while Anne was never incommoded on the other, he dropped the arms of both to hunt after a weasel which he had a momentary glance of, and they could hardly get him along at all.

This long meadow bordered a lane, which their footpath, at the end of it was to cross, and when the party had all reached the gate of exit, the carriage advancing in the same direction, which had been some time heard, was just coming up, and proved to be Admiral Croft's gig. He and his wife had taken their intended drive, and were returning home. Upon hearing how long a walk the young people had engaged in, they kindly offered a seat to any lady who might be particularly tired; it would save her a full mile, and they were going through Uppercross. The invitation was general, and generally declined. The Miss Musgroves were not at all tired, and Mary was either offended, by not being asked before any of the others, or what Louisa called the Elliot pride could not endure to make a third in a one horse chaise.

The walking party had crossed the lane, and were surmounting an opposite stile, and the Admiral was putting his horse in motion again, when Captain Wentworth cleared the hedge in a moment with an athletic leap that stretched his breeches across his backside most tantalizingly, to say something to his sister. The something might be guessed by its effects.

"Miss Elliot, I am sure *you* are tired," cried Mrs. Croft. "Do let us have the pleasure of taking you home. Here is excellent room for three, I assure you. If we were all like you, I believe we might sit four. You must, indeed, you must."

Anne was still in the lane; and though instinctively beginning to decline, she was not allowed to proceed. The Admiral's kind urgency came in support of his wife's; they would not be refused; they compressed themselves into the smallest possible space to leave her a corner. The sight of the small space only made Anne more frantic. She could not bear to inconvenience them so. She heard a rustle of clothing to her right, and Captain Wentworth, without saying a word, turned to her, and quietly obliged her to be assisted into the carriage.

"You can sit in the back without putting either of them out," he whispered lowly to her, somehow guessing the root behind her reticence. Without waiting for her response, his fingers grasped her elbow, and he began to steer her toward the back of the carriage. His fingers scorched her skin through the fabric of her dress, and Anne heard herself gasp as she tripped like a child over every rock and pebble in the road.

As it became apparent that Captain Wentworth was leading her to the small perch at the back of the carriage, Mrs. Croft objected. "Frederick, no. She will be horribly bounced around back there."

"She will be fine, sister," he said with a pointed look that had Mrs. Croft snapping her mouth shut in an almost comical fashion.

In the next moment, the carriage hid Frederick and Anne from the eyes of the rest of their party, and Anne felt the exhaustion—both emotional and physical—she had been holding at bay sweep through her without giving quarter. She nearly sagged within Frederick's grasp, and he must have instinctively known so, because his grip tightened slightly, and he moved closer to her side as though he intended to catch her should she fall.

They arrived at their destination, and Frederick's hand fell away. Anne felt an unwelcome wave of disappointment that was quickly cut off when he gripped her shoulders and turned her to face him.

Her breath stalled in her lungs as she looked up and up into his beautiful face to find his eyes serious and searching. They darted over every feature of Anne's face, pausing at her eyes, her nose, her mouth. The fingers upon her shoulders flexed, and his lips parted.

He was so close. All of Anne's surroundings faded away to be replaced by the magnificent presence that was Frederick Wentworth. His scent—that mix of open air, sunshine, and sea—had remained unchanged through the years, and it filled her lungs now that she'd ceased to breathe. She forced it from her lungs with a loud whoosh of air and studiously refused to take another breath, but now that his scent had been expelled, her other senses took over. His chest was so near, she could feel the heat of it wafting over her neck and the exposed skin above her bodice. She witnessed his Adam's apple bob up and down, and heard his breathing take on a labourious slant that only brought his chest swelling ever nearer as he seemed to struggle to take air.

Anne could no longer meet his eyes, and soon found herself staring at the hollow of his throat, a tantalizingly bare stretch of skin that was revealed by his scandalously loosened cravat. It was the most beautiful patch of skin she had ever seen, and the irrational desire to press her parted lips upon it nearly overtook her.

The fingers on her shoulders began to move. They headed downward, almost lovingly caressing her upper arms, before moving inward and grasping Anne around her ribcage. He squeezed gently. "Up you go," he whispered hoarsely, his voice so deep she could feel the vibrations in her own chest.

It was the only warning Anne had before the world moved as he lifted her effortlessly into the air to place her upon the small seat. Anne's hands flew up, seeking purchase, only to land upon Frederick's shoulders as they flexed and bulged beneath the slight burden of her weight. Her bottom landed softly upon the seat, and she was secure, but neither of them released the other.

They remained there for several heartbeats, his hands resting just beneath her breasts, hers upon his shoulders. Heat seemed to scorch from his touch straight into her heart, and she resisted as long as she could before she allowed her hands to explore the different layout of the muscles beneath her palms. Her fingers dug in slightly, and in response, Frederick's eyelids drooped in the most provocative fashion. His breaths increased even more, and he visibly hesitated a moment before the hands around her ribcage rotated. Anne was certain she was dreaming when she felt his thumbs firmly stroke the bottom swells of her breasts.

The area between Anne's thighs clenched with need, and she could not control the way her back arched into the caress, nor the wanton whimper that fell from her lips.

Captain Wentworth's eyes widened suddenly, and he dropped his hands from her body as though he had been burnt by the very fires of hell. He stepped back so quickly Anne nearly fell forward and off of the carriage when the shoulders she had been leaning on disappeared from beneath her hands. She scrambled to catch herself, and he did not even reach for her to make sure she staid safe.

His head jerked downward, and she heard him curse beneath his breath as he hurriedly moved his jacket around so that it hid the very obvious bulge marring the fall of fabric across the front of his breeches. Her flare of joy that she had brought him to such a state was abruptly cut off as his eyes met hers once more, this time carrying accusation. "Why do you keep doing this to me?" he muttered in a nearly lost voice.

Anne did not know what to say; did not know how she would even respond to such a thing. *She* do this to *him*? He was not the one squirming in uncomfortably damp drawers. Nevertheless, the people-pleasing side of her had her attempting apology. "I am—"

He cut her off with an impatient jerk of his head. "No," he said softly. "That was unfair of me." The harsh light in his eyes belied the words he forced from between taut lips. He looked to an area over her head and projected his voice. "She is secure."

Without another word, he turned to the side and stalked off. She heard a distant, sharp order to the horses from directly behind her, and then the carriage was lurching forward and swayed back and forth with the cadence of the horse. They crested the top of a hill, and she glimpsed the rigid contours of Captain Wentworth's back as he rejoined the party.

Conflicting emotions warred within her. Yes; he had done it. She was in the carriage, and felt that he had placed her there, that his will and his hands had done it, that she owed it to his perception of her fatigue, and his resolution to give her rest. She was very much affected by the view of his disposition towards her, which all these things made apparent. But then there was the other matter. It was the height of foolishness for them to have touched each other, even casually, for touch never staid casual with them; they both knew this. This little circumstance seemed the completion of all that had gone before. She understood him. He could not forgive her, but he could not be unfeeling.

Though condemning her for the past, and considering it with high and unjust resentment, though perfectly careless of her, and though becoming attached to another, still he could not see her suffer, without the desire of giving her relief; still he could not pass up the opportunity to touch her when it presented itself. It was a remainder of former sentiment; it was an impulse of pure, though unacknowledged friendship; it was a proof of his own warm and amiable heart; and undeniable proof that he was male, and therefore opportunistic when it came to the opposite sex, which she could not contemplate without emotions so compounded of pleasure and pain, that she knew not which prevailed, though if the devastated feeling within her was any indication, pain was rallying at the moment.

It was not long before her companions attempted to converse with her, and though Anne wished for the distraction with all of her being, her answers to the kindness and the remarks of her companions were at first unconsciously given. They had travelled half their way along the rough lane, before she was quite awake to what they said. She then found them talking of "Frederick."

"He certainly means to have one or other of those two girls, Sophy," said the Admiral; "but there is no saying which. He has been running after them, too, long enough, one would think, to make up his mind. Ay, this comes of the peace. If it were war now, he would have settled it long ago. We sailors, Miss Elliot, cannot afford to make long courtships in time of war. How many days was it, my dear, between the first time of my seeing you and our sitting down together in our lodgings at North Yarmouth?"

Anne had turned slightly in her seat to better hear the conversation that was muffled by the creaking of the carriage and by space, but her eye spied Admiral Croft's hand sneaking through the distance between him and his wife and tunneling beneath the blanket that lay in Mrs. Croft's lap. With a flash of amusement, jealousy, and slight embarrassment Anne quickly turned around again, but not before she saw Mrs. Croft press his hand closer for an instant before bringing it to her lips and then placing it back on the reins with a breathless, chiding laugh.

"We had better not talk about it, my dear," replied Mrs. Croft, pleasantly; "for if Miss Elliot were to hear how soon we came to an understanding, she would never be persuaded that we could be happy together. I had known you by character, however, long before."

"Well, and I had heard of you as a very pretty girl, and what were we to wait for besides? I do not like having such things so long in hand. I wish Frederick would spread a little more canvass, and bring us home one of these young ladies to Kellynch. Then there would always be company for them. And very nice young ladies they both are; I hardly know one from the other."

"Very good humoured, unaffected girls, indeed," said Mrs. Croft, in a tone of calmer praise, such as made Anne suspect that her keener powers might not consider either of them as quite worthy of her brother; "and a very respectable family. One could not be connected with better people." Mrs. Croft gasped, and Anne turned quickly to see what was the matter. "My dear Admiral, that post! we shall certainly take that post."

The Admiral scrambled to pull his hand back from where it had returned beneath Mrs. Croft's blanket, but she merely chuckled and grabbed the reins from her husband.

By coolly giving the reins a better direction herself they happily passed the danger; and by once afterwards judiciously putting out her hand they neither fell into a rut, nor ran foul of a dung-cart; and Anne, with some amusement at their style of driving that involved the Admiral touching his wife as much as possible while she chuckled and confidently steered the carriage, which she imagined no bad representation of the general guidance of their affairs, found herself safely deposited by them at the Cottage.

Chapter 11

The time now approached for Lady Russell's return: the day was even fixed; and Anne, being engaged to join her as soon as she was resettled, was looking forward to an early removal to Kellynch, and beginning to think how her own comfort was likely to be affected by it.

It would place her in the same village with Captain Wentworth, within half a mile of him; they would have to frequent the same church, and there must be intercourse between the two families. This was against her; but on the other hand, he spent so much of his time at Uppercross, that in removing thence she might be considered rather as leaving him behind, than as going towards him; and, upon the whole, she believed she must, on this interesting question, be the gainer, almost as certainly as in her change of domestic society, in leaving poor Mary for Lady Russell.

She wished it might be possible for her to avoid ever seeing Captain Wentworth at the Hall: those rooms had witnessed former meetings which would be brought too painfully before her. When her father and sister had been out, Frederick visited, and it had been novel to conduct their tête-à-têtes indoors rather than out beneath the tree in the garden. This fortuitous turn of events had happened very seldom—Anne could only remember two times, and she certainly would not have forgotten other occurrences—during the small amount of time they were engaged.

The first time had been the day after they first made love in the garden. Anne left a note for Frederick under their tree, and it was only moments after their scheduled meeting time that he showed up at the house as she had requested. The butler had barely maintained his decorum, going so far as to raise one shaggy, gray eyebrow at Anne as he had admitted the young man to the library, a place Anne knew they would be uninterrupted. Now, remembering back, Anne was sure she'd felt the sting of the servant's censure, but the only emotion that came to mind now was the overwhelming anticipation of being alone in the house with the man she loved. Frederick had waited impatiently for the butler to bow and exit the room; he had shifted back and forth on the balls of his feet. The click of the door closing reverberated through the room like a shot, and, instead of Frederick approaching her and kissing her senseless, as she had hoped he would do, he turned from her and marched to the library door.

With his face all but pressed into the polished wood of the doors, he spoke so softly she barely heard. "Am I here for the reason I think I am here?"

Anne's eyes devoured the back and shoulders she hoped to finally see bare; their breadth made her mouth water, but even lust could not overshadow the concern that flared when she noticed how stiff and hunched his shoulders were. The flare grew until Anne wondered with mortification if she had tacitly proposed they do something that Frederick found immoral to the extreme. The letter she had left for him had merely said, "Meet me at the house." However, the subtext had practically screamed its hidden addendum of what Anne planned to do with him there. She had thought he would be as excited as she—they had, after all, made love only the day before. Certainly her request to meet here was not so far off the path they had been traveling down. Perhaps he was having regrets? Or, perhaps, her request to make love again so quickly was evidence of a perversion?

Anne delayed responding as long as possible, as an unnamable sickness formed into a lump within her throat would not allow her to speak anyway. Her hands knotted in front of her, and she twisted her fingers brutally as she mentally searched for some way to get them out of this awkward situation. Why, oh why, had she been so forward?

She took so long that Frederick turned his face to the side, displaying the features she had come to love in glorious profile. He still did not look directly at her. "Anne?" he asked quietly.

The sound of her name, though quiet, caused Anne to jump. Suddenly, the words stuck in her throat tumbled out, tripping over one another in the space between them. "I am sorry—it was silly of me to suggest—of course you are right—I promise I am not wanton—"

At this last statement, Frederick finally reacted. He spun back toward her, his expression unreadable, though Anne was not certain it contained any denunciation. In fact, he looked quite—*affected*. "Anne, stop," he said in a low, deep voice before finally, *finally* smiling at her. "Darling, are you under the impression that I *disapprove* of a request to come to your home and lay my hands upon you?"

The air in the room was oppressive for the few heartbeats it took Anne's mind to engage and correctly interpret his words. "Y-You mean to say—that you do not?"

She barely got the words out of her mouth before Frederick was barreling across the library. He threw his arms around her and hauled her into his body so roughly, she would have stumbled and fallen had he not held her so securely. The next moment, his lips were upon hers, and he was thrusting his tongue through her teeth with a harsh moan. He probed her mouth with his tongue thoroughly, touching every part of her that he could reach with his hands, which seemed to be everywhere at once: grabbing her bottom to pull her lower body in so he could grind her belly against his rampant arousal, filling themselves with her breasts, threading their fingers through her hair.

He took her hand from where it clutched his jacket and placed her palm against the hard length pushing the front of his breeches.

With a hiss, he pulled back from their kiss. "Does that feel like disapproval to you?" he rumbled.

Anne sucked in a breath, hoping the air would help steady her wildly tilting world. "No," she breathed, experimenting with a small rotation of her hand. He gifted her with an approving groan and thrust his hips against her, grinding his erection even more against her hand. He placed a palm to each side of her face and stroked her cheeks with his thumbs. "You daft, beautiful woman," he whispered, his lips a hair's breadth from her own. "What would ever persuade you to think such a thing of me?"

It was hard to think through the distraction pressed into her hand, and the thumb that was now brushing her bottom lip, but Anne strove to answer him. "You were so—serious—and you would not look—Your back was to—I thought you were *leaving*."

"*Leave you?*" he asked, leaning in even closer to replace his thumb with a brief brush of his own lips. "Darling, I was praying for the strength to do just that in case I had misinterpreted your letter." His kissed her once more, this time pausing long enough to sweep his tongue against the roof of her mouth before continuing. "I could not believe I was so lucky as to have a woman who would want me again so soon."

Anne blushed furiously. So her desire for him *was* abnormal. She tried to pull away so she could hide her flaming cheeks and think of some excuse for her behaviour without the mind-altering effect of his touch, but Frederick refused to release her. His hands upon her cheeks flexed briefly, and he tilted her head up so she had no option but to look into his eyes. His gaze practically smoldered, and Anne felt an echo of heat within her womb as any nervousness and embarrassment fled completely.

"It took all of the strength I had not to set upon you as soon as the butler left." One of his hands left her face, and she next felt it in the small of her back. He pressed, pushing her into his body and eliminating the small space she had forced between them in her attempt to retreat. He groaned when her breasts crushed against his chest once more. She felt a fine tremor roll through him. "I want you so badly, Anne, I fear I will not be gentle."

A thrill of excitement shot up Anne's spine. "Then, do not be," she whispered.

His sea-coloured eyes darkened as though a storm approached, and Anne's body began to drip with want, but then he sighed and smiled, though the smile seemed forced. "Perhaps later. Now, I wish to savor you as I did not take the time to do yesterday."

His tone held a good heaping of self-reproach, and Anne leapt to correct him. "Everything about yesterday was perfect." Every unpracticed touch, every rough thrust, every eager kiss—they had all combined to create the perfect experience.

His smile softened. "I agree." His voice had deepened to the point that she felt it rumble through her body clear down to her toes. "And I promise to make to-day even better."

His grip upon her loosened, and then he lowered his head so slowly, Anne had more than enough time to anticipate his kiss. His lips were soft when they touched hers, and he drew in a long, uninterrupted breath, as though he were tasting her on his air. His embrace, though slack, was all-encompassing. One hand clutched her chin, holding her still and preventing her from taking their kiss beyond his control. His other arm wound around her back and up through her shoulder blades until it ended with his fingers massaging her nape. He parted his lips and teazed the seam of Anne's with his tongue.

Anne's body went absolutely liquid. Frederick's hand left her chin, and he caught her as her knees gave out, sweeping an arm behind her legs and pulling her into an embrace against his chest. He did all of this without taking his lips from hers, and Anne next gained cognitive thought to the discovery that he was carrying her across the library and lowering her to the sofa. Each movement he made was marked with languid passion, and she could not help but think that *savoring* definitely had its draw.

He broke the kiss to settle her upon the cushions of the sofa, seating her upright like a lady, with her back against the back of the sofa, and her feet upon the floor, and then he knelt in front of her.

His hands disappeared from her sight, and she felt a draft upon her ankle. He propped his fisted hands, full of her skirts, upon her knees and paused to give her a wry, endearingly crooked smile. "You will have to be quiet this time, dearest," he said with mock gravity. "We have already scandalized the poor butler to the point of quitting."

A bubble of pure happiness rose up in her chest and manifested itself in a breathless laugh. She *had* been rather noisy in the garden yesterday. "Are you quite sure that a gentleman would draw attention to such a thing?" she asked while leaning forward to place her hands upon his and pull them closer to her body, dragging her skirts up even more to reveal the length of her stocking-clad thighs to the point where the stockings stopped and her skin started.

He had been on the brink of a reply, his lips parted, and his eyes dancing with mirth, when he chanced a quick glance at her lap. His eyes met hers again, but quickly drained of anything but need. Slowly, so slowly, his eyes traveled down from her face to her lap once more, and she heard his shuddering intake of breath and saw his shoulders rise and fall quickly. Her gaze followed his, and she saw him release her skirts with one trembling hand, and cautiously drag the pad of his forefinger across the bare skin at the top of her thigh, causing a line of goose bumps to break out in the path of his finger.

Anne's breath forced its way from her lungs in a loud whoosh, but Frederick's focus never wavered. "How did I not take the time to look upon you properly?" he said so softly, Anne was sure he was talking to himself. His finger moved back over the field of goose bumps, and her skin tightened even more. "So beautiful," he whispered. "So soft."

He leaned forward, his chest propped against her knees, and pursed his swollen, full lips. He blew a stream of warm air across the skin he had been fondling, and with a moan, Anne arched her back and spread her knees without thought.

"Oh, *yes*, Anne," he said reverently as his upper body fell into the valley between her thighs. His hands gripped her hips and he rose up on his knees to kiss her once more. His fingers flexed on her flesh as he slowly rubbed his tongue against hers. Too soon, he ended the kiss. She moaned in protest, but his lips kissed the corner of her mouth, and then moved to her jaw, her ear, her neck, her collarbone.

A harsh moan erupted from Anne's lips as she threw her head back to allow him better access. His chuckle blew against the moist skin of her neck. "Shhh," he breathed into the hollow between her neck and shoulder before moving down to kiss the top of one breast where it strained above her bodice.

Anne clamped her lips closed, biting them so hard she worried she would draw blood, but she would not give him any cause to pause in what he was doing to her. She threaded her fingers through his hair and studiously schooled herself to be gentle and not pull, though she ached to do so with all of her heart.

He startled her when he moved beyond her breasts, pressing warm, open-mouthed kisses that scorched her skin through the fabric of her dress to her rib cage and stomach. It was not something she had expected, but it was so delicious, she did not wish to stop him. However, when his chin scratched against the exposed skin of her thigh, Anne grew alarmed.

"Frederick?" she asked breathlessly. She tugged at his hair gently, but the man would not budge.

"Shhh," he said again, his breath tickling her most private place through the inadequate barrier of her drawers. He shocked her even more when he leaned down further and pressed an almost chaste kiss to the top of her cleft through the soft, linen covering.

Anne could not breathe. Pleasure so intense she nearly peaked spiked through her entire body. Her lungs seized, and her fingers flexed once more in Frederick's hair, this time, she feared, too roughly, for he jerked beneath her hold.

"Shhh, darling," he said once more, pulling back slightly to give her a look that was probably meant to be censorious, but was too altered by lust to be very effective.

Anne moaned in protest, wishing with every fiber of her being that he would return his face to where it had just been. "I did not—"

Just then, the sound that Frederick had actually heard reached Anne's ears. The business-like clack of lady's shoes sounded from the hallway, and Anne heard Lady Russell in deep, loud conversation with the butler.

Anne gasped in horror as her eyes flew to the door of the library, but Frederick reacted much quicker. He jerked her skirts back down, the breeze their billowing caused blowing his blond hair back from his face. "Be calm," he admonished while scooting further back on his knees, and drawing one up, foot flat on the floor.

When the door flew open, Lady Russell and the disapproving butler were within its frame. Anne watch in mute suspense as Lady Russell's eyes roved them while a dark frown marred her brow, but she only saw Frederick down on one knee before Anne, her hands held between his, and an imploring look upon his face.

That was the moment Lady Russell learned of their betrothal. They never corrected her assumption that she had stumbled upon Frederick proposing with the knowledge that they had already been engaged for days. It would not have mattered any way. Lady Russell quickly and contemptuously escorted Frederick out, and then she began the constant litany of lectures on familial duty that had driven Anne to near madness.

The second time Frederick had visited the home while the family had been out ended much the same way save for two things: first, Lady Russell had caught them in obvious preparation to make love: Frederick's coat had been tossed aside in a pile on the floor, and his fingers had been deep inside Anne's body; and second, her lectures upon Anne increased in vehemence and piling on of guilt until she finally persuaded Anne to break the engagement by relaying the alarming news that Anne was more like her lecherous father than her saintly mother. Lady Russell could not have guessed how successful such a statement would be in convincing Anne to break from the man she loved so much, an act Anne had carried out the morning her courses appeared and ruined any remaining argument Anne knew could convince Lady Russell of the necessity of marrying Frederick.

These memories were bitter medicine, and Anne longed to keep from remembering them more often by prolonged absence from her former home; but she was yet more anxious for the possibility of Lady Russell and Captain Wentworth never meeting anywhere. For obvious reasons, they did not like each other, and no renewal of acquaintance now could do any good; and were Lady Russell to see them together, she might think that he had too much self-possession, and she too little. Or worse, she could wonder if they had lapsed into the indiscretions of her youth, and the lectures would recommence.

These points formed her chief solicitude in anticipating her removal from Uppercross, where she felt she had been stationed quite long enough. Her usefulness to little Charles would always give some sweetness to the memory of her two months' visit there, but he was gaining strength apace, and she had nothing else to stay for.

The conclusion of her visit, however, was diversified in a way which she had not at all imagined. Captain Wentworth, after being unseen and unheard of at Uppercross for two whole days, appeared again among them to justify himself by a relation of what had kept him away.

A letter from his friend, Captain Harville, having found him out at last, had brought intelligence of Captain Harville's being settled with his family at Lyme for the winter; of their being therefore, quite unknowingly, within twenty miles of each other. Captain Harville had never been in good health since a severe wound which he received two years before, and Captain Wentworth's anxiety to see him had determined him to go immediately to Lyme. He had been there for four-and-twenty hours. His acquittal was complete, his friendship warmly honoured, a lively interest excited for his friend, and his description of the fine country about Lyme so feelingly attended to by the party, that an earnest desire to see Lyme themselves, and a project for going thither was the consequence.

The young people were all wild to see Lyme. Captain Wentworth talked of going there again himself, it was only seventeen miles from Uppercross; though November, the weather was by no means bad; and, in short, Louisa, who was the most eager of the eager, having formed the resolution to go, and besides the pleasure of doing as she liked, being now armed with the idea of merit in maintaining her own way, bore down all the wishes of her father and mother for putting it off till summer; and to Lyme they were to go—Charles, Mary, Anne, Henrietta, Louisa, and Captain Wentworth.

The first heedless scheme had been to go in the morning and return at night; but to this Mr. Musgrove, for the sake of his horses, would not consent; and when it came to be rationally considered, a day in the middle of November would not leave much time for seeing a new place, after deducting seven hours, as the nature of the country required, for going and returning. They were, consequently, to stay the night there, and not to be expected back till the next day's dinner. This was felt to be a considerable amendment; and though they all met at the Great House at rather an early breakfast hour, and set off very punctually, it was so much past noon before the two carriages, Mr. Musgrove's coach containing the four ladies, and Charles's curricle, in which he drove Captain Wentworth, were descending the long hill into Lyme, and entering upon the still steeper street of the town itself, that it was very evident they would not have more than time for looking about them, before the light and warmth of the day were gone.

After securing accommodations, and ordering a dinner at one of the inns, the next thing to be done was unquestionably to walk directly down to the sea. They were come too late in the year for any amusement or variety which Lyme, as a public place, might offer. The rooms were shut up, the lodgers almost all gone, scarcely any family but of the residents left; and, as there is nothing to admire in the buildings themselves, the remarkable situation of the town, the principal street almost hurrying into the water, the walk to the Cobb, skirting round the pleasant little bay, which, in the season, is animated with bathing machines and company; the Cobb itself, its old wonders and new improvements, with the very beautiful line of cliffs stretching out to the east of the town, are what the stranger's eye will seek; and a very strange stranger it must be, who does not see charms in the immediate environs of Lyme, to make him wish to know it better. The scenes in its neighbourhood, Charmouth, with its high grounds and extensive sweeps of country, and still more, its sweet, retired bay, backed by dark cliffs, where fragments of low rock among the sands, make it the happiest spot for watching the flow of the tide, for sitting in unwearied contemplation; the woody varieties of the cheerful village of Up Lyme; and, above all, Pinny, with its green chasms between romantic rocks, where the scattered forest trees and orchards of luxuriant growth, declare that many a generation must have passed away since the first partial falling of the cliff prepared the ground for such a state, where a scene so wonderful and so lovely is exhibited, as may more than equal any of the resembling scenes of the far-famed Isle of Wight: these places must be visited, and visited again, to make the worth of Lyme understood.

The party from Uppercross passing down by the now deserted and melancholy looking rooms, and still descending, soon found themselves on the sea-shore; and lingering only, as all must linger and gaze on a first return to the sea, who ever deserved to look on it at all, proceeded towards the Cobb, equally their object in itself and on Captain Wentworth's account: for in a small house, near the foot of an old pier of unknown date, were the Harvilles settled. Captain Wentworth turned in to call on his friend; the others walked on, and he was to join them on the Cobb.

They were by no means tired of wondering and admiring; and not even Louisa seemed to feel that they had parted with Captain Wentworth long, when they saw him coming after them, with three companions, all well known already, by description, to be Captain and Mrs. Harville, and a Captain Benwick, who was staying with them.

Captain Benwick had some time ago been first lieutenant of the *Laconia*; and the account which Captain Wentworth had given of him, on his return from Lyme before, his warm praise of him as an excellent young man and an officer, whom he had always valued highly, which must have stamped him well in the esteem of every listener, had been followed by a little history of his private life, which rendered him perfectly interesting in the eyes of all the ladies. He had been engaged to Captain Harville's sister, and was now mourning her loss. They had been a year or two waiting for fortune and promotion. Fortune came, his prize-money as lieutenant being great; promotion, too, came at *last*; but Fanny Harville did not live to know it. She had died the preceding summer while he was at sea.

Captain Wentworth believed it impossible for man to be more attached to woman than poor Benwick had been to Fanny Harville, or to be more deeply afflicted under the dreadful change.

He considered his disposition as of the sort which must suffer heavily, uniting very strong feelings with quiet, serious, and retiring manners, and a decided taste for reading, and sedentary pursuits. To finish the interest of the story, the friendship between him and the Harvilles seemed, if possible, augmented by the event which closed all their views of alliance, and Captain Benwick was now living with them entirely. Captain Harville had taken his present house for half a year; his taste, and his health, and his fortune, all directing him to a residence inexpensive, and by the sea; and the grandeur of the country, and the retirement of Lyme in the winter, appeared exactly adapted to Captain Benwick's state of mind. The sympathy and good-will excited towards Captain Benwick was very great.

"And yet," said Anne to herself, as they now moved forward to meet the party, her eyes straying to the spectacularly built form of Captain Wentworth without her permission, "he has not, perhaps, a more sorrowing heart than I have. I cannot believe his prospects so blighted for ever. He is younger than I am; younger in feeling, if not in fact; younger as a man. He will rally again, and be happy with another."

They all met, and were introduced. Captain Harville was a tall, dark man, with a sensible, benevolent countenance; a little lame; and from strong features and want of health, looking much older than Captain Wentworth. Captain Benwick looked, and was, the youngest of the three, and, compared with either of them, a little man. He had a pleasing face and a melancholy air, just as he ought to have, and drew back from conversation.

Captain Harville, though not equalling Captain Wentworth in manners, was a perfect gentleman, unaffected, warm, and obliging. Mrs. Harville, a degree less polished than her husband, seemed, however, to have the same good feelings; and nothing could be more pleasant than their desire of considering the whole party as friends of their own, because the friends of Captain Wentworth, or more kindly hospitable than their entreaties for their all promising to dine with them. The dinner, already ordered at the inn, was at last, though unwillingly, accepted as a excuse; but they seemed almost hurt that Captain Wentworth should have brought any such party to Lyme, without considering it as a thing of course that they should dine with them.

There was so much attachment to Captain Wentworth in all this, and such a bewitching charm in a degree of hospitality so uncommon, so unlike the usual style of give-and-take invitations, and dinners of formality and display, that Anne felt her spirits not likely to be benefited by an increasing acquaintance among his brother-officers. "These would have been all my friends," was her thought; and she had to struggle against a great tendency to lowness.

On quitting the Cobb, they all went in-doors with their new friends, and found rooms so small as none but those who invite from the heart could think capable of accommodating so many. Anne had a moment's astonishment on the subject herself; but it was soon lost in the pleasanter feelings which sprang from the sight of all the ingenious contrivances and nice arrangements of Captain Harville, to turn the actual space to the best account, to supply the deficiencies of lodging-house furniture, and defend the windows and doors against the winter storms to be expected. The varieties in the fitting-up of the rooms, where the common necessaries provided by the owner, in the common indifferent plight, were contrasted with some few articles of a rare species of wood, excellently worked up, and with something curious and valuable from all the distant countries Captain Harville had visited, were more than amusing to Anne; connected as it all was with his profession, the fruit of its labours, the effect of its influence on his habits, the picture of repose and domestic happiness it presented, made it to her a something more, or less, than gratification.

Captain Harville was no reader; but he had contrived excellent accommodations, and fashioned very pretty shelves, for a tolerable collection of well-bound volumes, the property of Captain Benwick. His lameness prevented him from taking much exercise; but a mind of usefulness and ingenuity seemed to furnish him with constant employment within. He drew, he varnished, he carpentered, he glued; he made toys for the children; he fashioned new netting-needles and pins with improvements; and if everything else was done, sat down to his large fishing-net at one corner of the room.

Anne thought she left great happiness behind her when they quitted the house; and Louisa, by whom she found herself walking, burst forth into raptures of admiration and delight on the character of the navy; their friendliness, their brotherliness, their openness, their uprightness; protesting that she was convinced of sailors having more worth and warmth than any other set of men in England; that they only knew how to live, and they only deserved to be respected and loved.

They went back to dress and dine; and so well had the scheme answered already, that nothing was found amiss; though its being "so entirely out of season," and the "no thoroughfare of Lyme," and the "no expectation of company," had brought many apologies from the heads of the inn.

Anne found herself by this time growing so much more hardened to being in Captain Wentworth's company than she had at first imagined could ever be, that the sitting down to the same table with him now, and the interchange of the common civilities attending on it (they never got beyond), was become a mere nothing in comparison to the battle Anne did with her mind when she was alone. In his presence, while watching him smile and flirt with the girls around him, it was almost easier to forget him than in his absence.

The nights were too dark for the ladies to meet again till the morrow, but Captain Harville had promised them a visit in the evening; and he came, bringing his friend also, which was more than had been expected, it having been agreed that Captain Benwick had all the appearance of being oppressed by the presence of so many strangers. He ventured among them again, however, though his spirits certainly did not seem fit for the mirth of the party in general.

While Captains Wentworth and Harville led the talk on one side of the room, and by recurring to former days, supplied anecdotes in abundance to occupy and entertain the others, it fell to Anne's lot to be placed rather apart with Captain Benwick; and a very good impulse of her nature obliged her to begin an acquaintance with him. He was shy, and disposed to abstraction; but the engaging mildness of her countenance, and gentleness of her manners, soon had their effect; and Anne was well repaid the first trouble of exertion. He was evidently a young man of considerable taste in reading, though principally in poetry; and besides the persuasion of having given him at least an evening's indulgence in the discussion of subjects, which his usual companions had probably no concern in, she had the hope of being of real use to him in some suggestions as to the duty and benefit of struggling against affliction, which had naturally grown out of their conversation.

For, though shy, he did not seem reserved; it had rather the appearance of feelings glad to burst their usual restraints; and having talked of poetry, the richness of the present age, and gone through a brief comparison of opinion as to the first-rate poets, trying to ascertain whether *Marmion* or *The Lady of the Lake* were to be preferred, and how ranked the *Giaour* and *The Bride of Abydos*; and moreover, how the *Giaour* was to be pronounced, he showed himself so intimately acquainted with all the tenderest songs of the one poet, and all the impassioned descriptions of hopeless agony of the other; he repeated, with such tremulous feeling, the various lines which imaged a broken heart, or a mind destroyed by wretchedness, and looked so entirely as if he meant to be understood, that she ventured to hope he did not always read only poetry, and to say, that she thought it was the misfortune of poetry to be seldom safely enjoyed by those who enjoyed it completely; and that the strong feelings which alone could estimate it truly were the very feelings which ought to taste it but sparingly.

His looks shewing him not pained, but pleased with this allusion to his situation, she was emboldened to go on; and feeling in herself the right of seniority of mind, she ventured to recommend a larger allowance of prose in his daily study; and on being requested to particularize, mentioned such works of our best moralists, such collections of the finest letters, such memoirs of characters of worth and suffering, as occurred to her at the moment as calculated to rouse and fortify the mind by the highest precepts, and the strongest examples of moral and religious endurances.

Captain Benwick listened attentively, and seemed grateful for the interest implied; and though with a shake of the head, and sighs which declared his little faith in the efficacy of any books on grief like his, noted down the names of those she recommended, and promised to procure and read them.

Their conversation had just concluded when Anne raised her head, her lips tingling with the small smile she knew was curving their corners—she was so out of practice at smiling—when her gaze caught that of Captain Wentworth. He was glowering at her as he had not since being distracted by the presence of his dear friends in Lyme. His brows were lowered over his eyes so much that they cast those light orbs in complete darkness. His mouth was set in a grim line. However, as soon as Anne caught him staring, he seemed to shake himself. His mouth relaxed; his brows rose. He looked slightly chagrined and even ventured so far as to offer her a pained half-smile. He broke their eye contact and visibly forced his face into a relaxed expression, whereupon he turned to his right and engaged Louisa in animated conversation, and Anne knew she had been mentally dismissed. The sting of his actions lasted through the remainder of dinner.

When the evening was over, Anne could not but be amused at the idea of her coming to Lyme to preach patience and resignation to a young man whom she had never seen before; nor could she help fearing, on more serious reflection, that, like many other great moralists and preachers, she had been eloquent on a point in which her own conduct would ill bear examination.

She gave her excuses to the girls and took a quick turn around the lodging house to help clear her mind. It was ineffective at best. As she turned back to walk to her room, her thoughts were embroiled in the foolhardiness of allowing his cut at the dinner table to harm her. She was staring at her feet in the dim light, trying to ensure that she would not trip, and so she did not see the person who was leaning against the door to her room until it was too late. With a startled cry, Anne walked right into warm, towering man. She was walking so quickly that the sudden halt to her progress resulted in backward motion. Anne's arms were whirling, trying to find something to grab hold of to soften her inevitable fall when strong, capable hands gripped her arms and pulled her in until her face was crushed against a wide expanse of chest.

She gasped in shock, and the scent she knew better than any filled her lungs. In the panic of self-preservation, Anne jerked back and flung her arms to the side in hopes that she would dislodge his hands from her person.

He immediately removed them, and, contrarily, a small part of her heart protested. She roughly shoved that part aside and stared blankly upward where she knew his head must be, though she could not see it through the dark. "C-Captain Wentworth?"

The frightened quality of her voice irked her, and he obviously heard it, for he moved to the left slightly until a glimmer of light from her room's window illuminated the side of his face, casting familiar and yet unfamiliar features in light and shadow. He must have assumed the fear in her voice was caused by meeting a stranger in the dark. She felt relief that he had not guessed what she was truly afraid of was what she would do to the man whose identity she had known certainly upon her first breath. Even now, she feared she was swaying too close to him, seeking the comfort of his warmth when she was so very cold inside.

"Yes, it is me." His voice rumbled more deeply than ever, and Anne cursed the effect it had on her traitorous body. "I did not mean to frighten you."

She made some noise or other that she hoped portrayed it was nothing. It took all of her focus to maintain decorum.

He shifted impatiently, and she was reminded once again that this man before her hated her passionately. In an obvious bid to get whatever he was doing here over with, he began to speak in a rush. "I came to thank you for befriending Benwick."

Disappointment nearly crushed her. Was she to be thanked now for consorting with other men? "He is a good man," she offered lamely, hoping he would go away so she could retreat into her room to lick her wounds.

His ragged intake of air confused her. "Yes. He is." Several heartbeats of silence later, he continued, "I—that is to say—please be gentle with him. He is not ready for another broken heart."

Suddenly, his glower at the dinner table reappeared on the back of Anne's eyes. His anger now gained context, and with it, more hurt heaped upon her soul. "I would never hurt him," she nearly hissed. "And I do not seek more from him than friendship. Nor does he from me."

The resounding thud of one of his boots upon the plank walk was the only warning she had that he had moved. The next instant, his hands were upon her arms again, and he was pushing her backward. Her back met with the pillar across from her room, but he kept coming, crowding into her body with his own. She felt every inch of his body against hers, and she could not breathe through the panic and exhilaration that froze her lungs.

"Oh, thank God," she thought she heard him breathe, the words slipping by her ear with a ruffle of her hair. He pressed closer for an instant, and she felt his arousal growing slowly against her belly, but then his entire body stiffened.

"C-Captain Wentworth?" Anne ventured to ask.

With a muffled curse, Captain Wentworth wrenched himself away from her. Anne nearly stumbled forward with his sudden absence, and she watched in absolute confusion as the man who had just accosted her stomped away, his silhouette passing in front of her room's window and then disappearing into the night without another sound.

Chapter 12

Anne tossed and turned all night, Captain Wentworth's baffling actions playing and replaying through her mind, before finally rising earlier than normal. She was pleasantly surprised to find she was not alone when she returned from her morning ablutions; Henrietta was awake as well. Anne and Henrietta, finding themselves the earliest of the party, agreed to stroll down to the sea before breakfast. They went to the sands, to watch the flowing of the tide, which a fine south-easterly breeze was bringing in with all the grandeur which so flat a shore admitted. They praised the morning; gloried in the sea, which Anne could not help but inwardly compare in colour to a certain set of eyes; sympathized in the delight of the fresh-feeling breeze—and were silent; till Henrietta suddenly began again with—

"Oh! yes,—I am quite convinced that, with very few exceptions, the sea-air always does good. There can be no doubt of its having been of the greatest service to Dr. Shirley, after his illness, last spring twelve-month. He declares himself, that coming to Lyme for a month, did him more good than all the medicine he took; and, that being by the sea, always makes him feel young again. Now, I cannot help thinking it a pity that he does not live entirely by the sea. I do think he had better leave Uppercross entirely, and fix at Lyme. Do not you, Anne? Do not you agree with me, that it is the best thing he could do, both for himself and Mrs. Shirley? She has cousins here, you know, and many acquaintance, which would make it cheerful for her, and I am sure she would be glad to get to a place where she could have medical attendance at hand, in case of his having another seizure. Indeed I think it quite melancholy to have such excellent people as Dr. and Mrs. Shirley, who have been doing good all their lives, wearing out their last days in a place like Uppercross, where, excepting our family, they seem shut out from all the world. I wish his friends would propose it to him. I really think they ought. And, as to procuring a dispensation, there could be no difficulty at his time of life, and with his character. My only doubt is, whether anything could persuade him to leave his parish. He is so very strict and scrupulous in his notions; over-scrupulous I must say. Do not you think, Anne, it is being over-scrupulous? Do not you think it is quite a mistaken point of conscience, when a clergyman sacrifices his health for the sake of duties, which may be just as well performed by another person? And at Lyme too, only seventeen miles off, he would be near enough to hear, if people thought there was anything to complain of."

Anne smiled more than once to herself during this speech, and entered into the subject, as ready to do good by entering into the feelings of a young lady as of a young man, though here it was good of a lower standard, for what could be offered but general acquiescence? She said all that was reasonable and proper on the business; felt the claims of Dr. Shirley to repose as she ought; saw how very desirable it was that he should have some active, respectable young man, as a resident curate, and was even courteous enough to hint at the advantage of such resident curate's being married.

"I wish," said Henrietta, very well pleased with her companion, "I wish Lady Russell lived at Uppercross, and were intimate with Dr. Shirley. I have always heard of Lady Russell as a woman of the greatest influence with everybody! I always look upon her as able to persuade a person to anything! I am afraid of her, as I have told you before, quite afraid of her, because she is so very clever; but I respect her amazingly, and wish we had such a neighbour at Uppercross."

Anne was amused by Henrietta's manner of being grateful, and amused also that the course of events and the new interests of Henrietta's views should have placed her friend at all in favour with any of the Musgrove family; she had only time, however, for a general answer, and a wish that such another woman were at Uppercross, before all subjects suddenly ceased, on seeing Louisa and Captain Wentworth coming towards them. Captain Wentworth would not meet Anne's eyes this morning, and it was rather different from the other times he refused to meet her eyes, which was status quo as of late. This time, he seemed to have trouble keeping his eyes from her, and Anne could not help but wonder if he was wanting to apologize for or explain his behaviour. She certainly hoped so, as any illumination he could give to his actions last night would be welcome. However, it soon became apparent that they came also for a stroll till breakfast was likely to be ready; but Louisa recollecting, immediately afterwards that she had something to procure at a shop, invited them all to go back with her into the town. They were all at her disposal.

When they came to the steps, leading upwards from the beach, a gentleman, at the same moment preparing to come down, politely drew back, and stopped to give them way. They ascended and passed him; and as they passed, Anne's face caught his eye, and he looked at her with a degree of earnest admiration, which she could not be insensible of. She was looking remarkably well; her very regular, very pretty features, having the bloom and freshness of youth restored by the fine wind which had been blowing on her complexion, and by the animation of eye which it had also produced. It was evident that the gentleman, (completely a gentleman in manner) admired her exceedingly. Breaking from his efforts to avoid looking at her, Captain Wentworth looked round at her instantly in a way which shewed his noticing of it. He gave her a momentary glance, a glance of brightness, which seemed to say, "That man is struck with you, and even I, at this moment, see something like Anne Elliot again." And then the same thundercloud of an expression he'd worn while watching her and Captain Benwick converse last night made a reappearance. Anne wondered with a start if the emotion behind his expression could possibly be *jealousy*. But then she immediately dismissed the thought as rubbish. He jealous of her? When he had forced her to watch every flirtation between him and Louisa?

After attending Louisa through her business, and loitering about a little longer, they returned to the inn; and Anne, in passing afterwards quickly from her own chamber to their dining-room, had nearly run against the very same gentleman, as he came out of an adjoining apartment. She had before conjectured him to be a stranger like themselves, and determined that a well-looking groom, who was strolling about near the two inns as they came back, should be his servant. Both master and man being in mourning assisted the idea. It was now proved that he belonged to the same inn as themselves; and this second meeting, short as it was, also proved again by the gentleman's looks as his eyes swept over every bit of her front, that he thought hers very lovely, and by the readiness and propriety of his apologies as he leaned in close to bow, nearly brushing against her body, that he was a man of exceedingly good manners despite their close proximity, which could be blamed on the close quarters. He seemed about thirty, and though not as handsome as Captain Wentworth, had an agreeable person. Anne felt that she should like to know who he was.

They had nearly done breakfast, when the sound of a carriage, (almost the first they had heard since entering Lyme) drew half the party to the window. It was a gentleman's carriage, a curricle, but only coming round from the stable-yard to the front door; somebody must be going away. It was driven by a servant in mourning.

The word curricle made Charles Musgrove jump up that he might compare it with his own; the servant in mourning roused

Anne's curiosity, and the whole six were collected to look, by the time the owner of the curricle was to be seen issuing from the door amidst the bows and civilities of the household, and taking his seat, to drive off.

"Ah!" cried Captain Wentworth, instantly, and with half a glance at Anne, "it is the very man we passed."

The Miss Musgroves agreed to it; and having all kindly watched him as far up the hill as they could, they returned to the breakfast table. The waiter came into the room soon afterwards.

"Pray," said Captain Wentworth, immediately, his tone rough enough to snare a few curious stares from their party, "can you tell us the name of the gentleman who is just gone away?"

"Yes, Sir, a Mr. Elliot, a gentleman of large fortune, came in last night from Sidmouth. Dare say you heard the carriage, sir, while you were at dinner; and going on now for Crewkherne, in his way to Bath and London."

"Elliot!" Many had looked on each other, and many had repeated the name, before all this had been got through, even by the smart rapidity of a waiter.

"Bless me!" cried Mary; "it must be our cousin; it must be our Mr. Elliot, it must, indeed! Charles, Anne, must not it? In mourning, you see, just as our Mr. Elliot must be. How very extraordinary! In the very same inn with us! Anne, must not it be our Mr. Elliot? my father's next heir? Pray sir," turning to the waiter, "did not you hear, did not his servant say whether he belonged to the Kellynch family?"

"No, ma'am, he did not mention no particular family; but he said his master was a very rich gentleman, and would be a baronight some day."

"There! you see!" cried Mary in an ecstasy, "just as I said! Heir to Sir Walter Elliot! I was sure that would come out, if it was so. Depend upon it, that is a circumstance which his servants take care to publish, wherever he goes. But, Anne, only conceive how extraordinary! I wish I had looked at him more. I wish we had been aware in time, who it was, that he might have been introduced to us. What a pity that we should not have been introduced to each other! Do you think he had the Elliot countenance? I hardly looked at him, I was looking at the horses; but I think he had something of the Elliot countenance, I wonder the arms did not strike me! Oh! the great-coat was hanging over the panel, and hid the arms, so it did; otherwise, I am sure, I should have observed them, and the livery too; if the servant had not been in mourning, one should have known him by the livery."

"Putting all these very extraordinary circumstances together," said Captain Wentworth, "we must consider it to be the arrangement of Providence, that you should not be introduced to your cousin." His tone seemed curiously self-satisfied, and Anne wondered briefly what he would think had he known that though Anne and her cousin had not been introduced, they had indeed met again, and in the very same location that Captain Wentworth had confronted her just last evening. A small smile stretched Anne's lips.

When she could command Mary's attention, Anne quietly tried to convince her that their father and Mr. Elliot had not, for many years, been on such terms as to make the power of attempting an introduction at all desirable.

At the same time, however, it was a secret gratification to herself to have seen her cousin, and to know that the future owner of Kellynch was undoubtedly a gentleman, and had an air of good sense. She would not, upon any account, mention her having met with him the second time; luckily Mary did not much attend to their having passed close by him in their earlier walk, but she would have felt quite ill-used by Anne's having actually run against him in the passage, and received his very polite excuses, while she had never been near him at all; no, that cousinly little interview must remain a perfect secret.

"Of course," said Mary, "you will mention our seeing Mr. Elliot, the next time you write to Bath. I think my father certainly ought to hear of it; do mention all about him."

Anne avoided a direct reply, but it was just the circumstance which she considered as not merely unnecessary to be communicated, but as what ought to be suppressed. The offence which had been given her father, many years back, she knew; Elizabeth's particular share in it she suspected; and that Mr. Elliot's idea always produced irritation in both was beyond a doubt. Mary never wrote to Bath herself; all the toil of keeping up a slow and unsatisfactory correspondence with Elizabeth fell on Anne.

Breakfast had not been long over, when they were joined by Captain and Mrs. Harville and Captain Benwick; with whom they had appointed to take their last walk about Lyme. They ought to be setting off for Uppercross by one, and in the mean while were to be all together, and out of doors as long as they could.

Anne found Captain Benwick getting near her, as soon as they were all fairly in the street. Their conversation the preceding evening did not disincline him to seek her again; and they walked together some time, talking as before of Mr. Scott and Lord Byron, and still as unable as before, and as unable as any other two readers, to think exactly alike of the merits of either, till something occasioned an almost general change amongst their party, and instead of Captain Benwick, she had Captain Harville by her side.

"Miss Elliot," said he, speaking rather low, "you have done a good deed in making that poor fellow talk so much. I wish he could have such company oftener. It is bad for him, I know, to be shut up as he is; but what can we do? We cannot part."

"No," said Anne, "that I can easily believe to be impossible; but in time, perhaps—we know what time does in every case of affliction, and you must remember, Captain Harville, that your friend may yet be called a young mourner—only last summer, I understand."

"Ay, true enough," (with a deep sigh) "only June."

"And not known to him, perhaps, so soon."

"Not till the first week of August, when he came home from the Cape, just made into the *Grappler*. I was at Plymouth dreading to hear of him; he sent in letters, but the *Grappler* was under orders for Portsmouth. There the news must follow him, but who was to tell it? not I. I would as soon have been run up to the yard-arm. Nobody could do it, but that good fellow" (pointing to Captain Wentworth who stood a small distance away, his face raised to the wind that plastered his coat against his body.) "The *Laconia* had come into Plymouth the week before; no danger of her being sent to sea again. He stood his chance for the rest; wrote up for leave of absence, but without waiting the return, travelled night and day till he got to Portsmouth, rowed off to the *Grappler* that instant, and never left the poor fellow for a week. That's what he did, and nobody else could have saved poor James. You may think, Miss Elliot, whether he is dear to us!"

Anne did think on the question with perfect decision, and said as much in reply as her own feeling could accomplish, or as his seemed able to bear, for he was too much affected to renew the subject, and when he spoke again, it was of something totally different.

Mrs. Harville's giving it as her opinion that her husband would have quite walking enough by the time he reached home, determined the direction of all the party in what was to be their last walk; they would accompany them to their door, and then return and set off themselves. By all their calculations there was just time for this; but as they drew near the Cobb, there was such a general wish to walk along it once more, all were so inclined, and Louisa soon grew so determined, that the difference of a quarter of an hour, it was found, would be no difference at all; so with all the kind leave-taking, and all the kind interchange of invitations and promises which may be imagined, they parted from Captain and Mrs. Harville at their own door, and still accompanied by Captain

Benwick, who seemed to cling to them to the last, proceeded to make the proper adieus to the Cobb.

Anne found Captain Benwick again drawing near her. Lord Byron's "dark blue seas" could not fail of being brought forward by their present view, and she gladly gave him all her attention as long as attention was possible. It was soon drawn, perforce another way.

There was too much wind to make the high part of the new Cobb pleasant for the ladies, and they agreed to get down the steps to the lower, and all were contented to pass quietly and carefully down the steep flight, excepting Louisa; she must be jumped down them by Captain Wentworth. In all their walks, he had had to jump her from the stiles; the sensation was delightful to her. The hardness of the pavement for her feet, made him less willing upon the present occasion; he did it, however. She was safely down, and instantly, to show her enjoyment, ran up the steps to be jumped down again. He advised her against it, thought the jar too great; but no, he reasoned and talked in vain, she smiled and said, "I am determined I will:" he put out his hands; she was too precipitate by half a second, she fell on the pavement on the Lower Cobb, and was taken up lifeless! There was no wound, no blood, no visible bruise; but her eyes were closed, she breathed not, her face was like death. The horror of the moment to all who stood around!

Captain Wentworth, who had caught her up, knelt with her in his arms, looking on her with a face as pallid as her own, in an agony of silence. "She is dead! she is dead!" screamed Mary, catching hold of her husband, and contributing with his own horror to make him immoveable; and in another moment, Henrietta, sinking under the conviction, lost her senses too, and would have fallen on the steps, but for Captain Benwick and Anne, who caught and supported her between them.

"Is there no one to help me?" were the first words which burst from Captain Wentworth, in a tone of despair, and as if all his own strength were gone.

The catch in his voice tore through Anne. She turned desperately to Benwick. "Go to him, go to him," cried Anne, wishing with all her might that she was free to do so instead, "for heaven's sake go to him. I can support her myself. Leave me, and go to him. Rub her hands, rub her temples; here are salts; take them, take them."

Captain Benwick obeyed, and Charles at the same moment, disengaging himself from his wife, they were both with him; and Louisa was raised up and supported more firmly between them, and everything was done that Anne had prompted, but in vain; while Captain Wentworth, staggering against the wall for his support, met Anne's gaze with bloodshot, stricken eyes and exclaimed in the bitterest agony—

"Oh God! her father and mother!"

"A surgeon!" said Anne.

He caught the word; it seemed to rouse him at once, and saying only—"True, true, a surgeon this instant," was darting away, when Anne eagerly suggested—

"Captain Benwick, would not it be better for Captain Benwick? He knows where a surgeon is to be found."

Every one capable of thinking felt the advantage of the idea, and in a moment (it was all done in rapid moments) Captain Benwick had resigned the poor corpse-like figure entirely to the brother's care, and was off for the town with the utmost rapidity.

As to the wretched party left behind, it could scarcely be said which of the three, who were completely rational, was suffering most: Captain Wentworth, Anne, or Charles, who, really a very affectionate brother, hung over Louisa with sobs of grief, and could only turn his eyes from one sister, to see the other in a state as insensible, or to witness the hysterical agitations of his wife, calling on him for help which he could not give.

Anne, attending with all the strength and zeal, and thought, which instinct supplied, to Henrietta, still tried, at intervals, to suggest comfort to the others, tried to quiet Mary, to animate

Charles, to assuage the feelings of Captain Wentworth. Both seemed to look to her for directions.

"Anne, Anne," cried Charles, "What is to be done next? What, in heaven's name, is to be done next?"

Captain Wentworth's eyes were also turned towards her; she knew so without having to look at him for the heat that flared just below her skin.

"Had not she better be carried to the inn? Yes, I am sure: carry her gently to the inn."

"Yes, yes, to the inn," repeated Captain Wentworth, comparatively collected, and eager to be doing something. "I will carry her myself. Musgrove, take care of the others." Captain Wentworth cradled Louisa in his arms so gently and with such affection, rubbing a cheek against the top of her head, that Anne was momentarily stunned. She was distracted when Henrietta stirred. Anne turned her attention to Louisa's sister.

By this time the report of the accident had spread among the workmen and boatmen about the Cobb, and many were collected near them, to be useful if wanted, at any rate, to enjoy the sight of a dead young lady, nay, two dead young ladies, for it proved twice as fine as the first report. To some of the best-looking of these good people Henrietta was consigned, for, though partially revived, she was quite helpless; and in this manner, Anne walking by her side, and Charles attending to his wife, they set forward, treading back with feelings unutterable, the ground, which so lately, so very lately, and so light of heart, they had passed along.

They were not off the Cobb, before the Harvilles met them. Captain Benwick had been seen flying by their house, with a countenance which showed something to be wrong; and they had set off immediately, informed and directed as they passed, towards the spot. Shocked as Captain Harville was, he brought senses and nerves that could be instantly useful; and a look between him and his wife decided what was to be done. She must be taken to their house; all must go to their house; and await the surgeon's arrival there. They would not listen to scruples: he was obeyed; they were all beneath his roof; and while Louisa, under Mrs. Harville's direction, was conveyed up stairs, and given possession of her own bed, assistance, cordials, restoratives were supplied by her husband to all who needed them.

Louisa had once opened her eyes, but soon closed them again, without apparent consciousness. This had been a proof of life, however, of service to her sister; and Henrietta, though perfectly incapable of being in the same room with Louisa, was kept, by the agitation of hope and fear, from a return of her own insensibility. Mary, too, was growing calmer.

The surgeon was with them almost before it had seemed possible. They were sick with horror, while he examined; but he was not hopeless. The head had received a severe contusion, but he had seen greater injuries recovered from: he was by no means hopeless; he spoke cheerfully.

That he did not regard it as a desperate case, that he did not say a few hours must end it, was at first felt, beyond the hope of most; and the ecstasy of such a reprieve, the rejoicing, deep and silent, after a few fervent ejaculations of gratitude to Heaven had been offered, may be conceived.

The tone, the look, with which "Thank God!" was uttered by Captain Wentworth, Anne was sure could never be forgotten by her; nor the sight of him afterwards, as he sat near a table, leaning over it with folded arms and face concealed, as if overpowered by the various feelings of his soul, and trying by prayer and reflection to calm them. She remembered with shame that earlier this morning she had imagined him jealous of her interaction with Benwick. He was obviously in love with the young woman.

Louisa's limbs had escaped. There was no injury but to the head.

It now became necessary for the party to consider what was best to be done, as to their general situation. They were now able to speak to each other and consult. That Louisa must remain where she was, however distressing to her friends to be involving the Harvilles in such trouble, did not admit a doubt. Her removal was impossible. The Harvilles silenced all scruples; and, as much as they could, all gratitude. They had looked forward and arranged everything before the others began to reflect. Captain Benwick must give up his room to them, and get another bed elsewhere; and the whole was settled. They were only concerned that the house could accommodate no more; and yet perhaps, by "putting the children away in the maid's room, or swinging a cot somewhere," they could hardly bear to think of not finding room for two or three besides, supposing they might wish to stay; though, with regard to any attendance on Miss Musgrove, there need not be the least uneasiness in leaving her to Mrs. Harville's care entirely. Mrs. Harville was a very experienced nurse, and her nursery-maid, who had lived with her long, and gone about with her everywhere, was just such another. Between these two, she could want no possible attendance by day or night. And all this was said with a truth and sincerity of feeling irresistible.

Charles, Henrietta, and Captain Wentworth were the three in consultation, and for a little while it was only an interchange of perplexity and terror. "Uppercross, the necessity of some one's going to Uppercross; the news to be conveyed; how it could be broken to Mr. and Mrs. Musgrove; the lateness of the morning; an hour already gone since they ought to have been off; the impossibility of being in tolerable time." At first, they were capable of nothing more to the purpose than such exclamations; but, after a while, Captain Wentworth, exerting himself, said—

"We must be decided, and without the loss of another minute. Every minute is valuable. Some one must resolve on being off for Uppercross instantly. Musgrove, either you or I must go."

Charles agreed, but declared his resolution of not going away. He would be as little incumbrance as possible to Captain and Mrs. Harville; but as to leaving his sister in such a state, he neither ought, nor would. So far it was decided; and Henrietta at first declared the same. She, however, was soon persuaded to think differently. The usefulness of her staying! She who had not been able to remain in Louisa's room, or to look at her, without sufferings which made her worse than helpless! She was forced to acknowledge that she could do no good, yet was still unwilling to be away, till, touched by the thought of her father and mother, she gave it up; she consented, she was anxious to be at home.

The plan had reached this point, when Anne, coming quietly down from Louisa's room, could not but hear what followed, for the parlour door was open.

"Then it is settled, Musgrove," cried Captain Wentworth, "that you stay, and that I take care of your sister home. But as to the rest, as to the others, if one stays to assist Mrs. Harville, I think it need be only one. Mrs. Charles Musgrove will, of course, wish to get back to her children; but if Anne will stay, no one so proper, so capable as Anne."

She paused a moment to recover from the emotion of hearing herself so spoken of. She was perched between elation and despair: Did he wish her to stay so she would be far, far away from him? Or did he wish her to stay because he had the uttermost faith in her ability to maintain a level head in the midst of tragedy? Neither reason pointed to a feeling of warmth on his part for anyone other than Louisa. The other two warmly agreed with what he said, and Anne then appeared.

"You will stay, I am sure; you will stay and nurse her;" cried he, turning to her and speaking with a glow, and yet a gentleness, which seemed almost restoring the past. She coloured deeply, and he recollected himself and moved away. She expressed herself most willing, ready, happy to remain. "It was what she had been thinking of, and wishing to be allowed to do. A bed on the floor in

Louisa's room would be sufficient for her, if Mrs. Harville would but think so."

One thing more, and all seemed arranged. Though it was rather desirable that Mr. and Mrs. Musgrove should be previously alarmed by some share of delay; yet the time required by the Uppercross horses to take them back, would be a dreadful extension of suspense; and Captain Wentworth proposed, and Charles Musgrove agreed, that it would be much better for him to take a chaise from the inn, and leave Mr. Musgrove's carriage and horses to be sent home the next morning early, when there would be the farther advantage of sending an account of Louisa's night.

Captain Wentworth now hurried off to get everything ready on his part, and to be soon followed by the two ladies. When the plan was made known to Mary, however, there was an end of all peace in it. She was so wretched and so vehement, complained so much of injustice in being expected to go away instead of Anne; Anne, who was nothing to Louisa, while she was her sister, and had the best right to stay in Henrietta's stead! Why was not she to be as useful as Anne? And to go home without Charles, too, without her husband! No, it was too unkind. And in short, she said more than her husband could long withstand, and as none of the others could oppose when he gave way, there was no help for it; the change of Mary for Anne was inevitable.

Anne had never submitted more reluctantly to the jealous and ill-judging claims of Mary; but so it must be, and they set off for the town, Charles taking care of his sister, and Captain Benwick attending to her. She gave a moment's recollection, as they hurried along, to the little circumstances which the same spots had witnessed earlier in the morning. There she had listened to Henrietta's schemes for Dr. Shirley's leaving Uppercross; farther on, she had first seen Mr. Elliot; a moment seemed all that could now be given to any one but Louisa, or those who were wrapt up in her welfare.

Captain Benwick was most considerately attentive to her; and, united as they all seemed by the distress of the day, she felt an increasing degree of good-will towards him, and a pleasure even in thinking that it might, perhaps, be the occasion of continuing their acquaintance.

Captain Wentworth was on the watch for them, and a chaise and four in waiting, stationed for their convenience in the lowest part of the street; but his evident surprise and vexation at the substitution of one sister for the other, the change in his countenance, the astonishment, the expressions begun and suppressed, with which Charles was listened to, made but a mortifying reception of Anne; or must at least convince her that she was valued only as she could be useful to Louisa.

She endeavoured to be composed, and to be just. Without emulating the feelings of an Emma towards her Henry, she would have attended on Louisa with a zeal above the common claims of regard, for his sake; and she hoped he would not long be so unjust as to suppose she would shrink unnecessarily from the office of a friend.

In the mean while she was in the carriage. He had handed them both in, and placed himself between them; and in this manner, under these circumstances, full of astonishment and emotion to Anne, she quitted Lyme. How the long stage would pass; how it was to affect their manners; what was to be their sort of intercourse, she could not foresee. Anne pressed herself as far against the side of the carriage as the unforgiving wall would allow, and still she could not escape the heat of Captain Wentworth's body, or the familiar smell of his skin. But if she was worried that he would suffer from similar experiences, his conduct could not have proven her more wrong. It was all quite natural. He was devoted to Henrietta; always turning towards her; and when he spoke at all, always with the view of supporting her hopes and raising her spirits. In general, his voice and manner were studiously calm. To spare Henrietta from agitation seemed the governing principle. Once only, when she had been grieving over the last ill-judged, ill-fated walk to the Cobb, bitterly lamenting that it ever had been thought of, he burst forth, as if wholly overcome—

"Don't talk of it, don't talk of it," he cried. "Oh God! that I had not given way to her at the fatal moment! Had I done as I ought! But so eager and so resolute! Dear, sweet Louisa!"

Anne wondered whether it ever occurred to him now, to question the justness of his own previous opinion as to the universal felicity and advantage of firmness of character; and whether it might not strike him that, like all other qualities of the mind, it should have its proportions and limits. She thought it could scarcely escape him to feel that a persuadable temper might sometimes be as much in favour of happiness as a very resolute character.

They got on fast. Anne was astonished to recognise the same hills and the same objects so soon. Their actual speed, heightened by some dread of the conclusion, made the road appear but half as long as on the day before. It was growing quite dusk, however, before they were in the neighbourhood of Uppercross, and there had been total silence among them for some time, Henrietta leaning back in the corner, with a shawl over her face, giving the hope of her having cried herself to sleep; when, as they were going up their last hill, Anne found herself all at once addressed by Captain Wentworth. He turned toward her slowly and looked at her from the corners of his eyes rather than head-on. Even in this, he tried to refrain from direct contact with her. In a low, cautious voice, he said:—

"I have been considering what we had best do. She must not appear at first. She could not stand it. I have been thinking whether you had not better remain in the carriage with her, while I go in and break it to Mr. and Mrs. Musgrove. Do you think this is a good plan?"

She did: he was satisfied, and said no more. But the remembrance of the appeal remained a pleasure to her, as a proof of friendship, and of deference for her judgement, a great pleasure; she worked hard to convince herself that the pleasure of his friendship was enough, and when it became a sort of parting proof, its value did not lessen.

When the distressing communication at Uppercross was over, and he had seen the father and mother quite as composed as could be hoped, and the daughter all the better for being with them, he announced his intention of returning in the same carriage to Lyme; and when the horses were baited, he was off, thanking God that, this time, the carriage held only himself. He drew a massive breath through his teeth, the hissing sound bringing him a measure of comfort that was immediately canceled out by the scent that filled his nostrils.

"Devil take it!" he swore violently beneath his breath. Her scent *still* pervaded the carriage! Would he *never* be free of her? Was it not enough that he had had to ride beside her for hours, literally pressed against the warm, soft curve of her hip? He had tried in vain to distract himself from her close proximity by talking constantly with Henrietta, and it had done nothing—*nothing*—that it was supposed to do. He had remained hyper-aware of Anne's presence each second of the eternal carriage ride to Uppercross. His elbow even had the audacity to brush against the side of her breast—*more* than once! And now, when he was finally alone, she still haunted him? It was too much.

In a fit of anger, he smacked his palms against the leather of the seat on either side of his thighs. While the sound of the slap reverberated around the close space, Frederick froze. Slowly, he turned his head to the right and allowed his eyes to drift down to the seat. His right hand was planted in a bundle of canary yellow fabric. He watched as his hand clenched, fisting the cloth, and he realized that he was staring at a lady's shawl—but *not* the shawl that Henrietta had slept beneath.

With a sense of foreboding, Frederick raised the shawl to his face, and before he could bury his nose in it, the overwhelming scent of *Anne* filled his being.

A harsh groan erupted from his chest, and the knowledge that he no longer had to be strong—was no longer in her presence—overwhelmed him with dark purpose. He gripped the shawl in both hands and allowed himself the pleasure of languishing in her essence. The soft fabric caught in the day's growth of beard that marred his usually pristinely groomed jaw, and the contrast of rough to smooth shot straight through his body and down to his cock.

And just like that, the horrors of the day, the tension of the carriage ride, the sharp edge of heartbreak—all drifted away as Frederick's world narrowed down to one canary yellow bit of cloth and seldom-visited, happy memories of the past.

"*Anne.*" The rough use of her name would have startled him had he the mental capacity to recognise he had spoken at all. His mind was embroiled with images of Anne's skin dappled beneath the checkered shade of their tree; Anne's sighs as he entered her body, filling her between her thighs; Anne's soft hands as they touched every inch of him; Anne's face as she reached her ultimate pleasure.

His every thought, his every sense, was Anne.

He closed his eyes; his head fell back. The smooth, cool fabric of Anne's shawl moved from his face to his neck. He rubbed it against the column of his throat with one hand while the other began to jerk recklessly at the fall of his breeches.

The feeling of the night's cool air caressing his erection was enough to pull him from the haze of his thoughts—but only long enough for his mind to ponder if he was truly depraved enough to do what he was about to do. In the next moment, he was swept back into the past, and the shawl made its final journey from his chest down to his lap.

Without another thought, Frederick wrapt Anne's shawl around his throbbing cock, and squeezed his fist. His hiss of pleasure was loud and primal, and he did not pause even a moment before moving his fist up the length of his erection, passing the cool satin over the angry, aching head.

His hips surged up from the seat, thrusting into his grip and starting a series of uncontrollable movements. His left hand belted out to the side, and his palm squeaked against the frosty, cold glass of the carriage window while his right hand kicked up the pace, working his cock at an unforgiving, brutal speed. His hips continued to surge and retreat, and he had to raise one leg, bending it at the knee, to brace his foot on the opposing carriage wall.

The cool fabric had quickly warmed to skin temperature from Frederick's handling of it, and his addled mind recognised it as almost—*almost*—as good as Anne's actual touch had been. His neck bent back at an awkward angle as his head thumped against the seat behind him, and he realized in that moment that he was breathing so sporadically that stars were dancing behind his eyes. He forced himself to close the mouth that was gasping at air and breath through his nose, but that action only brought more of her scent, which was wafting from the shawl even more now from friction and heat, to his senses.

A brilliant flash of light erupted behind Frederick's closed eyes, and with a hoarse shout, he ejaculated into the warm fabric of Anne's shawl. His hips continued to jerk from the seat, wringing more from his body than he had ever had to give before. What felt like hours later, his body finally stilled; his breathing began to slow. And with his body's return to calm, Frederick's mind returned to clarity.

He looked down at his lap in horror: his hand still fisted Anne's shawl around his faltering arousal. A spread of his spent passion marred the delicate fabric obscenely.

Good God, what had he done? He wrenched his body upright and unceremoniously dropped the offending shawl to the floor of the carriage to shove his semi-erect penis back into his breeches brutally.

To-day of all days, the day he had caused physical harm to the lady he had been—well, *courting* was a bit of a stretch—he had sunk so low as to defile poor Anne with such horrible actions.

Some dim region of his mind sought to bring to his attention that his concern in this moment was not for what Louisa would have thought had she known of his actions, but what Anne—the woman he should be forgetting—would have thought.

Frederick refused to acknowledge that voice. Instead, he focused all of his mental faculties on trying to find the motive behind his unforgiveable behaviour.

Stress—that had to be it. To-day had not been an easy day. And lately, Frederick had needed to seek release more frequently than he had in the past. The idea of finally seeking a wife, of finally breaking his period of self-imposed celibacy—had excited his system to the extreme.

With a sigh of relief, he realized that all of those things could have contributed to the actions Frederick had just taken. He was merely a man, after all. His body needed certain things, and that he had used Anne's shawl and Anne's memory to achieve them meant nothing—certainly not that he was still in love with her.

No. Certainly not.

(End of volume one.)

Chapter 13

The remainder of Anne's time at Uppercross, comprehending only two days, was spent entirely at the Mansion House; and she had the satisfaction of knowing herself extremely useful there, both as an immediate companion, and as assisting in all those arrangements for the future, which, in Mr. and Mrs. Musgrove's distressed state of spirits, would have been difficulties.

They had an early account from Lyme the next morning. Louisa was much the same. No symptoms worse than before had appeared. Charles came a few hours afterwards, to bring a later and more particular account. He was tolerably cheerful. A speedy cure must not be hoped, but everything was going on as well as the nature of the case admitted. In speaking of the Harvilles, he seemed unable to satisfy his own sense of their kindness, especially of Mrs. Harville's exertions as a nurse. "She really left nothing for Mary to do. He and Mary had been persuaded to go early to their inn last night. Mary had been hysterical again this morning. When he came away, she was going to walk out with Captain Benwick, which, he hoped, would do her good. He almost wished she had been prevailed on to come home the day before; but the truth was, that Mrs. Harville left nothing for anybody to do."

Charles was to return to Lyme the same afternoon, and his father had at first half a mind to go with him, but the ladies could not consent. It would be going only to multiply trouble to the others, and increase his own distress; and a much better scheme followed and was acted upon. A chaise was sent for from Crewkherne, and Charles conveyed back a far more useful person in the old nursery-maid of the family, one who having brought up all the children, and seen the very last, the lingering and long-petted Master Harry, sent to school after his brothers, was now living in her deserted nursery to mend stockings and dress all the blains and bruises she could get near her, and who, consequently, was only too happy in being allowed to go and help nurse dear Miss Louisa. Vague wishes of getting Sarah thither, had occurred before to Mrs. Musgrove and Henrietta; but without Anne, it would hardly have been resolved on, and found practicable so soon.

They were indebted, the next day, to Charles Hayter, for all the minute knowledge of Louisa, which it was so essential to obtain every twenty-four hours. He made it his business to go to Lyme, and his account was still encouraging. The intervals of sense and consciousness were believed to be stronger. Every report agreed in Captain Wentworth's appearing fixed in Lyme.

Anne was to leave them on the morrow, an event which they all dreaded. "What should they do without her? They were wretched comforters for one another." And so much was said in this way, that Anne thought she could not do better than impart among them the general inclination to which she was privy, and persuaded them all to go to Lyme at once. She had little difficulty; it was soon determined that they would go; go to-morrow, fix themselves at the inn, or get into lodgings, as it suited, and there remain till dear Louisa could be moved. They must be taking off some trouble from the good people she was with; they might at least relieve Mrs. Harville from the care of her own children; and in short, they were so happy in the decision, that Anne was delighted with what she had done, and felt that she could not spend her last morning at Uppercross better than in assisting their preparations, and sending them off at an early hour, though her being left to the solitary range of the house with all of her conflicting thoughts of Frederick—Captain Wentworth—as her only companions was the consequence.

She was the last, excepting the little boys at the cottage, she was the very last, the only remaining one of all that had filled and animated both houses, of all that had given Uppercross its cheerful character. A few days had made a change indeed!

If Louisa recovered, it would all be well again. More than former happiness would be restored. There could not be a doubt, to her mind there was none, of what would follow her recovery. A few months hence, and the room now so deserted, occupied but by her silent, pensive self, might be filled again with all that was happy and gay, all that was glowing and bright in prosperous love, all that was most unlike Anne Elliot!

An hour's complete leisure for such reflections as these, on a dark November day, a small thick rain almost blotting out the very few objects ever to be discerned from the windows, was enough to make the sound of Lady Russell's carriage exceedingly welcome; and yet, though desirous to be gone, she could not quit the Mansion House, or look an adieu to the Cottage, with its black, dripping and comfortless veranda, or even notice through the misty glasses the last humble tenements of the village, without a saddened heart. Scenes had passed in Uppercross which made it precious. It stood the record of many sensations of pain, once severe, but now softened; and of some instances of relenting feeling, some breathings of friendship and reconciliation, which could never be looked for again, and which could never cease to be dear. She left it all behind her, all but the recollection that such things had been.

Anne had never entered Kellynch since her quitting Lady Russell's house in September. It had not been necessary, and the few occasions of its being possible for her to go to the Hall she had contrived to evade and escape from. Her first return was to resume her place in the modern and elegant apartments of the Lodge, and to gladden the eyes of its mistress.

There was some anxiety mixed with Lady Russell's joy in meeting her. She knew who had been frequenting Uppercross.

But happily, either Anne was improved in plumpness and looks, or Lady Russell fancied her so; and Anne, in receiving her compliments on the occasion, had the amusement of connecting them with the silent admiration of her cousin, and of hoping that she was to be blessed with a second spring of youth and beauty.

When they came to converse, she was soon sensible of some mental change. The subjects of which her heart had been full on leaving Kellynch, and which she had felt slighted, and been compelled to smother among the Musgroves, were now become but of secondary interest. She had lately lost sight even of her father and sister and Bath. Their concerns had been sunk under those of Uppercross; and when Lady Russell reverted to their former hopes and fears, and spoke her satisfaction in the house in Camden Place, which had been taken, and her regret that Mrs. Clay should still be with them, Anne would have been ashamed to have it known how much more she was thinking of Lyme and Louisa Musgrove, and all her acquaintance there; how much more interesting to her was the home and the friendship of the Harvilles and Captain Benwick, than her own father's house in Camden Place, or her own sister's intimacy with Mrs. Clay. She was actually forced to exert herself to meet Lady Russell with anything like the appearance of equal solicitude, on topics which had by nature the first claim on her.

There was a little awkwardness at first in their discourse on another subject. They must speak of the accident at Lyme. Lady Russell had not been arrived five minutes the day before, when a full account of the whole had burst on her; but still it must be talked of, she must make enquiries, she must regret the imprudence, lament the result, and Captain Wentworth's name must be mentioned by both. Anne was conscious of not doing it so well as Lady Russell. She could not speak the name, and look straight forward to Lady Russell's eye, till she had adopted the expedient of telling her briefly what she thought of the attachment between him and Louisa. When this was told, his name distressed her no longer.

Lady Russell had only to listen composedly, and wish them happy, but internally her heart revelled in angry pleasure, in pleased contempt, that the man who at twenty-three had seemed to understand somewhat of the value of an Anne Elliot, should, eight years afterwards, be charmed by a Louisa Musgrove.

The first three or four days passed most quietly, with no circumstance to mark them excepting the receipt of a note or two from Lyme, which found their way to Anne, she could not tell how, and brought a rather improving account of Louisa. At the end of that period, Lady Russell's politeness could repose no longer, and the fainter self-threatenings of the past became in a decided tone, "I must call on Mrs. Croft; I really must call upon her soon. Anne, have you courage to go with me, and pay a visit in that house? It will be some trial to us both."

Anne did not shrink from it; on the contrary, she truly felt as she said, in observing—

"I think you are very likely to suffer the most of the two; your feelings are less reconciled to the change than mine. By remaining in the neighbourhood, I am become inured to it."

She could have said more on the subject; for she had in fact so high an opinion of the Crofts, and considered her father so very fortunate in his tenants, felt the parish to be so sure of a good example, and the poor of the best attention and relief, that however sorry and ashamed for the necessity of the removal, she could not but in conscience feel that they were gone who deserved not to stay, and that Kellynch Hall had passed into better hands than its owners'. These convictions must unquestionably have their own pain, and severe was its kind; but they precluded that pain which Lady Russell would suffer in entering the house again, and returning through the well-known apartments.

In such moments Anne had no power of saying to herself, "These rooms ought to belong only to us. Oh, how fallen in their destination! How unworthily occupied! An ancient family to be so driven away! Strangers filling their place!" No, except when she thought of her mother, and remembered where she had been used to sit and preside, she had no sigh of that description to heave.

Mrs. Croft always met her with a kindness which gave her the pleasure of fancying herself a favourite, and on the present occasion, receiving her in that house, there was particular attention.

The sad accident at Lyme was soon the prevailing topic, and on comparing their latest accounts of the invalid, it appeared that each lady dated her intelligence from the same hour of yestermorn; that Captain Wentworth had been in Kellynch yesterday (the first time since the accident), had brought Anne the last note, which she had not been able to trace the exact steps of; had staid a few hours and then returned again to Lyme, and without any present intention of quitting it any more. He had enquired after her, she found, particularly; had expressed his hope of Miss Elliot's not being the worse for her exertions, and had spoken of those exertions as great. This was handsome, and gave her more pleasure than almost anything else could have done.

As to the sad catastrophe itself, it could be canvassed only in one style by a couple of steady, sensible women, whose judgements had to work on ascertained events; and it was perfectly decided that it had been the consequence of much thoughtlessness and much imprudence; that its effects were most alarming, and that it was frightful to think, how long Miss Musgrove's recovery might yet be doubtful, and how liable she would still remain to suffer from the concussion hereafter! The Admiral wound it up summarily by exclaiming—

"Ay, a very bad business indeed. A new sort of way this, for a young fellow to be making love, by breaking his mistress's head, is not it, Miss Elliot? This is breaking a head and giving a plaster, truly!"

Admiral Croft's manners were not quite of the tone to suit Lady Russell, but they delighted Anne, though his hastily spoken words brought to mind a head of Anne's that Captain Wentworth had indeed broken—an act that still brought Anne great pleasure in each remembrance. Admiral Croft's goodness of heart and simplicity of character were irresistible.

"Now, this must be very bad for you," said he, suddenly rousing from a little reverie, "to be coming and finding us here. I had not recollected it before, I declare, but it must be very bad. But now, do not stand upon ceremony. Get up and go over all the rooms in the house if you like it."

Unbidden, the image of the library came to mind. "Another time, Sir, I thank you, not now," Anne said rather too quickly.

"Well, whenever it suits you. You can slip in from the shrubbery at any time; and there you will find we keep our umbrellas hanging up by that door. A good place is not it? But," (checking himself), "you will not think it a good place, for yours were always kept in the butler's room. Ay, so it always is, I believe. One man's ways may be as good as another's, but we all like our own best. And so you must judge for yourself, whether it would be better for you to go about the house or not."

Anne, finding she might decline it, did so, very gratefully.

"We have made very few changes either," continued the Admiral, after thinking a moment. "Very few. We told you about the laundry-door, at Uppercross. That has been a very great improvement. The wonder was, how any family upon earth could bear with the inconvenience of its opening as it did, so long! You will tell Sir Walter what we have done, and that Mr. Shepherd thinks it the greatest improvement the house ever had. Indeed, I must do ourselves the justice to say, that the few alterations we have made have been all very much for the better. My wife should have the credit of them, however. I have done very little besides sending away some of the large looking-glasses from my dressing-room, which was your father's. A very good man, and very much the gentleman I am sure: but I should think, Miss Elliot," (looking with serious reflection), "I should think he must be rather a dressy man for his time of life. Such a number of looking-glasses! oh Lord! there was no getting away from one's self. So I got Sophy to lend me a hand, and we soon shifted their quarters; and now I am quite snug, with my little shaving glass in one corner, and another great thing that I never go near."

Anne, amused in spite of herself, was rather distressed for an answer, and the Admiral, fearing he might not have been civil enough, took up the subject again, to say—

"The next time you write to your good father, Miss Elliot, pray give him my compliments and Mrs. Croft's, and say that we are settled here quite to our liking, and have no fault at all to find with the place. The breakfast-room chimney smokes a little, I grant you, but it is only when the wind is due north and blows hard, which may not happen three times a winter. And take it altogether, now that we have been into most of the houses hereabouts and can judge, there is not one that we like better than this. Pray say so, with my compliments. He will be glad to hear it."

Lady Russell and Mrs. Croft were very well pleased with each other: but the acquaintance which this visit began was fated not to proceed far at present; for when it was returned, the Crofts announced themselves to be going away for a few weeks, to visit their connexions in the north of the county, and probably might not be at home again before Lady Russell would be removing to Bath.

So ended all danger to Anne of meeting Captain Wentworth at Kellynch Hall, or of seeing him in company with her friend. Everything was safe enough, and she smiled over the many anxious feelings she had wasted on the subject.

Chapter 14

Though Charles and Mary had remained at Lyme much longer after Mr. and Mrs. Musgrove's going than Anne conceived they could have been at all wanted, they were yet the first of the family to be at home again; and as soon as possible after their return to Uppercross they drove over to the Lodge. They had left Louisa beginning to sit up; but her head, though clear, was exceedingly weak, and her nerves susceptible to the highest extreme of tenderness; and though she might be pronounced to be altogether doing very well, it was still impossible to say when she might be able to bear the removal home; and her father and mother, who must return in time to receive their younger children for the Christmas holidays, had hardly a hope of being allowed to bring her with them.

They had been all in lodgings together. Mrs. Musgrove had got Mrs. Harville's children away as much as she could, every possible supply from Uppercross had been furnished, to lighten the inconvenience to the Harvilles, while the Harvilles had been wanting them to come to dinner every day; and in short, it seemed to have been only a struggle on each side as to which should be most disinterested and hospitable.

Mary had had her evils; but upon the whole, as was evident by her staying so long, she had found more to enjoy than to suffer. Charles Hayter had been at Lyme oftener than suited her; and when they dined with the Harvilles there had been only a maid-servant to wait, and at first Mrs. Harville had always given Mrs. Musgrove precedence; but then, she had received so very handsome an apology from her on finding out whose daughter she was, and there had been so much going on every day, there had been so many walks between their lodgings and the Harvilles, and she had got books from the library, and changed them so often, that the balance had certainly been much in favour of Lyme. She had been taken to Charmouth too, and she had bathed, and she had gone to church, and there were a great many more people to look at in the church at Lyme than at Uppercross; and all this, joined to the sense of being so very useful, had made really an agreeable fortnight.

Anne enquired after Captain Benwick, Mary's face was clouded directly. Charles laughed.

"Oh! Captain Benwick is very well, I believe, but he is a very odd young man. I do not know what he would be at. We asked him to come home with us for a day or two: Charles undertook to give him some shooting, and he seemed quite delighted, and, for my part, I thought it was all settled; when behold! on Tuesday night, he made a very awkward sort of excuse; 'he never shot' and he had 'been quite misunderstood,' and he had promised this and he had promised that, and the end of it was, I found, that he did not mean to come. I suppose he was afraid of finding it dull; but upon my word I should have thought we were lively enough at the Cottage for such a heart-broken man as Captain Benwick."

Charles laughed again and said, "Now Mary, you know very well how it really was. It was all your doing," (turning to Anne.) "He fancied that if he went with us, he should find you close by: he fancied everybody to be living in Uppercross; and when he discovered that Lady Russell lived three miles off, his heart failed him, and he had not courage to come. That is the fact, upon my honour, Mary knows it is."

But Mary did not give into it very graciously, whether from not considering Captain Benwick entitled by birth and situation to be in love with an Elliot, or from not wanting to believe Anne a greater attraction to Uppercross than herself, must be left to be guessed. Anne's good-will, however, was not to be lessened by what she heard. She boldly acknowledged herself flattered, and continued her enquiries.

"Oh! he talks of you," cried Charles, "in such terms—" Mary interrupted him. "I declare, Charles, I never heard him mention Anne twice all the time I was there. I declare, Anne, he never talks of you at all."

"No," admitted Charles, "I do not know that he ever does, in a general way; but however, it is a very clear thing that he admires you exceedingly. His head is full of some books that he is reading upon your recommendation, and he wants to talk to you about them; he has found out something or other in one of them which he thinks—oh! I cannot pretend to remember it, but it was something very fine—I overheard him telling Henrietta all about it; and then 'Miss Elliot' was spoken of in the highest terms! Now Mary, I declare it was so, I heard it myself, and you were in the other room. 'Elegance, sweetness, beauty.' Oh! there was no end of Miss Elliot's charms."

"And I am sure," cried Mary, warmly, "it was a very little to his credit, if he did. Miss Harville only died last June. Such a heart is very little worth having; is it, Lady Russell? I am sure you will agree with me."

"I must see Captain Benwick before I decide," said Lady Russell, smiling.

"And that you are very likely to do very soon, I can tell you, ma'am," said Charles. "Though he had not nerves for coming away with us, and setting off again afterwards to pay a formal visit here, he will make his way over to Kellynch one day by himself, you may depend on it. I told him the distance and the road, and I told him of the church's being so very well worth seeing; for as he has a taste for those sort of things, I thought that would be a good excuse, and he listened with all his understanding and soul; and I am sure from his manner that you will have him calling here soon. So, I give you notice, Lady Russell."

"Any acquaintance of Anne's will always be welcome to me," was Lady Russell's kind answer.

"Oh! as to being Anne's acquaintance," said Mary, "I think he is rather my acquaintance, for I have been seeing him every day this last fortnight."

"Well, as your joint acquaintance, then, I shall be very happy to see Captain Benwick."

"You will not find anything very agreeable in him, I assure you, ma'am. He is one of the dullest young men that ever lived. He has walked with me, sometimes, from one end of the sands to the other, without saying a word. He is not at all a well-bred young man. I am sure you will not like him."

"There we differ, Mary," said Anne. "I think Lady Russell would like him. I think she would be so much pleased with his mind, that she would very soon see no deficiency in his manner."

"So do I, Anne," said Charles. "I am sure Lady Russell would like him. He is just Lady Russell's sort. Give him a book, and he will read all day long."

"Yes, that he will!" exclaimed Mary, tauntingly. "He will sit poring over his book, and not know when a person speaks to him, or when one drop's one's scissors, or anything that happens. Do you think Lady Russell would like that?"

Lady Russell could not help laughing. "Upon my word," said she, "I should not have supposed that my opinion of any one could have admitted of such difference of conjecture, steady and matter of fact as I may call myself. I have really a curiosity to see the person who can give occasion to such directly opposite notions. I wish he may be induced to call here. And when he does, Mary, you may depend upon hearing my opinion; but I am determined not to judge him beforehand."

"You will not like him, I will answer for it."

Lady Russell began talking of something else, but Anne's mind was snared by one thing: Captain Benwick had feelings for her.

It was difficult to believe. It had been ages since Anne had thought of herself as pretty or desirable. In fact, Captain Wentworth's callous comment upon seeing her for the first time in eight years was proof enough of her deteriorating beauty, if, indeed, she'd ever possessed beauty at all. Some distant corner of her mind often wondered if Captain Wentworth had only thought her beautiful because she allowed him to do things to her body that a young man would appreciate so greatly that he may find *any* woman who granted him such boons beautiful. Watching him woo Louisa had solidified this suspicion; Louisa was young and beautiful in a way that Anne highly doubted she had ever managed to be.

Anne was watching every chance at future happiness in love wilt away. It had been years since Captain Wentworth was an option for her happiness, but some part of her had held onto hope. Now that it was more than clear that Anne was a *friend*—if that—and Anne had to wonder, *could* she love another man?

Captain Benwick was certainly handsome. In fact, one might say he was more classically handsome than Captain Wentworth, whose unconventionally sun-bleached hair and excess of muscle more than likely labeled him as a labourer rather than a gentleman. Captain Benwick possessed the slight stature of a man of leisure and the dark, brooding features of a poet. His black hair was perhaps a bit too long, but it curled about his face in a way that drew attention to his dark, nearly black eyes.

Captain Benwick was a beautiful man. Any woman would be lucky to catch his eye.

While Lady Russell droned on about something Anne could not track, Anne forced herself to close her eyes and imagine Captain Benwick. Could she allow him to lay his hands upon her as Captain Wentworth had done?

Anne studiously pushed aside the images of blond hair and rippling muscles that the man's name never failed to draw forth whenever she thought it. Instead, she pictured Berwick's hands: pale, steady, finely boned. Anne had no trouble imagining those hands reaching toward her to tuck a curl behind her ear and trail a finger down her cheek. His poet's soul would lead him to take such actions, and the imagining of them was quite pleasant.

However, when Anne tried to imagine that finger trailing further than her cheek, to brush across the top of her breasts, her traitorous mind immediately replaced Benwick's almost delicate hands with the tan, rough hands of Captain Wentworth. The feeling of what his calloused fingers had felt like against her delicate skin thoroughly displaced Benwick from her thoughts so violently that Anne nearly gasped aloud at remembered sensations: Frederick's fingers inside her sheath; his tongue dipping into the hallow of her throat; the sound he made deep within his chest when he completed; the way he looked at her when *she* completed, his eyes fixed, soft and loving, upon her face.

At this thought, a small sound *did* escape Anne. As she made an excuse to placate the two women who stared at her curiously, Anne knew she could never allow Captain Benwick to touch her. The mere thought of calling him by his given name—*James*—in a fit of passion almost sent her into riots of hysterical giggles. Captain Benwick felt akin to a brother; had Anne been fortunate enough to have one, she imagined he would be something like him. Unfortunately, Anne could think of no one she would allow to touch her but Frederick—*Captain Wentworth*.

Anne was praying her blush was not noticeable, when she noticed Mary spoke with animation of their meeting with, or rather missing, Mr. Elliot so extraordinarily.

"He is a man," said Lady Russell, "whom I have no wish to see. His declining to be on cordial terms with the head of his family, has left a very strong impression in his disfavour with me."

This decision checked Mary's eagerness, and stopped her short in the midst of the Elliot countenance.

With regard to Captain Wentworth, though Anne hazarded no enquiries, there was voluntary communication sufficient. His spirits had been greatly recovering lately as might be expected. As Louisa improved, he had improved, and he was now quite a different creature from what he had been the first week. He had not seen Louisa; and was so extremely fearful of any ill consequence to her from an interview, that he did not press for it at all; and, on the contrary, seemed to have a plan of going away for a week or ten days, till her head was stronger. He had talked of going down to Plymouth for a week, and wanted to persuade Captain Benwick to go with him; but, as Charles maintained to the last, Captain Benwick seemed much more disposed to ride over to Kellynch. Anne found this odd; the one time she had been ill while she and Captain Wentworth had been together, he had pressed to be at her side every minute. Lady Russell had ensured he did not have access to her, but his desire to be with her had been begrudgingly relayed. Perhaps his feelings for Louisa were *so* strong that he could not abide seeing her ill?

There can be no doubt that Lady Russell and Anne were both occasionally thinking of Captain Benwick, from this time. Lady Russell could not hear the door-bell without feeling that it might be his herald; nor could Anne return from any stroll of solitary indulgence in her father's grounds, or any visit of charity in the village, without wondering whether she might see him or hear of him, and how she could be kind while simultaneously discouraging him from an attachment to her of any sort. Captain Benwick came not, however. He was either less disposed for it than Charles had imagined, or he was too shy; and after giving him a week's indulgence, Lady Russell determined him to be unworthy of the interest which he had been beginning to excite.

The Musgroves came back to receive their happy boys and girls from school, bringing with them Mrs. Harville's little children, to improve the noise of Uppercross, and lessen that of Lyme.

Henrietta remained with Louisa; but all the rest of the family were again in their usual quarters.

Lady Russell and Anne paid their compliments to them once, when Anne could not but feel that Uppercross was already quite alive again. Though neither Henrietta, nor Louisa, nor Charles Hayter, nor Captain Wentworth were there, the room presented as strong a contrast as could be wished to the last state she had seen it in.

Immediately surrounding Mrs. Musgrove were the little Harvilles, whom she was sedulously guarding from the tyranny of the two children from the Cottage, expressly arrived to amuse them. On one side was a table occupied by some chattering girls, cutting up silk and gold paper; and on the other were tressels and trays, bending under the weight of brawn and cold pies, where riotous boys were holding high revel; the whole completed by a roaring Christmas fire, which seemed determined to be heard, in spite of all the noise of the others. Anne took this in and felt a sharp pang to her heart. How she loved children. The possibility that she would never have her own was great, but even if she could, she could not imagine giving birth to any child that did not have sea foam green eyes or blonde hair.

Charles and Mary also came in, of course, during their visit, and Mr. Musgrove made a point of paying his respects to Lady Russell, and sat down close to her for ten minutes, talking with a very raised voice, but from the clamour of the children on his knees, generally in vain. It was a fine family-piece.

Anne, judging from her own temperament, would have deemed such a domestic hurricane a bad restorative of the nerves, which Louisa's illness must have so greatly shaken. But Mrs. Musgrove, who got Anne near her on purpose to thank her most cordially, again and again, for all her attentions to them, concluded a short recapitulation of what she had suffered herself by observing, with a happy glance round the room, that after all she had gone through, nothing was so likely to do her good as a little quiet cheerfulness at home.

Louisa was now recovering apace. Her mother could even think of her being able to join their party at home, before her brothers and sisters went to school again. The Harvilles had promised to come with her and stay at Uppercross, whenever she returned. Captain Wentworth was gone, for the present, to see his brother in Shropshire.

"I hope I shall remember, in future," said Lady Russell, as soon as they were reseated in the carriage, "not to call at Uppercross in the Christmas holidays."

Everybody has their taste in noises as well as in other matters; and sounds are quite innoxious, or most distressing, by their sort rather than their quantity. When Lady Russell not long afterwards, was entering Bath on a wet afternoon, and driving through the long course of streets from the Old Bridge to Camden Place, amidst the dash of other carriages, the heavy rumble of carts and drays, the bawling of newspapermen, muffin-men and milkmen, and the ceaseless clink of pattens, she made no complaint. No, these were noises which belonged to the winter pleasures; her spirits rose under their influence; and like Mrs. Musgrove, she was feeling, though not saying, that after being long in the country, nothing could be so good for her as a little quiet cheerfulness.

Anne did not share these feelings. She persisted in a very determined, though very silent disinclination for Bath; caught the first dim view of the extensive buildings, smoking in rain, without any wish of seeing them better; felt their progress through the streets to be, however disagreeable, yet too rapid; for who would be glad to see her when she arrived? And looked back, with fond regret, to the bustles of Uppercross and the seclusion of Kellynch.

Elizabeth's last letter had communicated a piece of news of some interest. Mr. Elliot was in Bath. He had called in Camden Place; had called a second time, a third; had been pointedly attentive.

If Elizabeth and her father did not deceive themselves, had been taking much pains to seek the acquaintance, and proclaim the value of the connection, as he had formerly taken pains to shew neglect. This was very wonderful if it were true; and Lady Russell was in a state of very agreeable curiosity and perplexity about Mr. Elliot, already recanting the sentiment she had so lately expressed to Mary, of his being "a man whom she had no wish to see." She had a great wish to see him. If he really sought to reconcile himself like a dutiful branch, he must be forgiven for having dismembered himself from the paternal tree.

Anne was not animated to an equal pitch by the circumstance, but she felt, with a shy smile to herself, that she would rather see Mr. Elliot again than not, which was more than she could say for many other persons in Bath.

She was put down in Camden Place; and Lady Russell then drove to her own lodgings, in Rivers Street.

Chapter 15

Sir Walter had taken a very good house in Camden Place, a lofty dignified situation, such as becomes a man of consequence; and both he and Elizabeth were settled there, much to their satisfaction.

Anne entered it with a sinking heart, anticipating an imprisonment of many months, and anxiously saying to herself, "Oh! when shall I leave you again?" A degree of unexpected cordiality, however, in the welcome she received, did her good. Her father and sister were glad to see her, for the sake of shewing her the house and furniture, and met her with kindness. Her making a fourth, when they sat down to dinner, was noticed as an advantage.

Mrs. Clay was very pleasant, and very smiling, but her courtesies and smiles were more a matter of course. Anne had always felt that she would pretend what was proper on her arrival, but the complaisance of the others was unlooked for. They were evidently in excellent spirits, and she was soon to listen to the causes. They had no inclination to listen to her. After laying out for some compliments of being deeply regretted in their old neighbourhood, which Anne could not pay, they had only a few faint enquiries to make, before the talk must be all their own. Uppercross excited no interest, Kellynch very little: it was all Bath.

They had the pleasure of assuring her that Bath more than answered their expectations in every respect. Their house was undoubtedly the best in Camden Place; their drawing-rooms had many decided advantages over all the others which they had either seen or heard of, and the superiority was not less in the style of the fitting-up, or the taste of the furniture. Their acquaintance was exceedingly sought after. Everybody was wanting to visit them. They had drawn back from many introductions, and still were perpetually having cards left by people of whom they knew nothing.

Here were funds of enjoyment. Could Anne wonder that her father and sister were happy? She might not wonder, but she must sigh that her father should feel no degradation in his change, should see nothing to regret in the duties and dignity of the resident landholder, should find so much to be vain of in the littlenesses of a town; and she must sigh, and smile, and wonder too, as Elizabeth threw open the folding-doors and walked with exultation from one drawing-room to the other, boasting of their space; at the possibility of that woman, who had been mistress of Kellynch Hall, finding extent to be proud of between two walls, perhaps thirty feet asunder.

But this was not all which they had to make them happy. They had Mr. Elliot too. Anne had a great deal to hear of Mr. Elliot. He was not only pardoned, they were delighted with him. He had been in Bath about a fortnight; (he had passed through Bath in November, in his way to London, when the intelligence of Sir Walter's being settled there had of course reached him, though only twenty-four hours in the place, but he had not been able to avail himself of it;) but he had now been a fortnight in Bath, and his first object on arriving, had been to leave his card in Camden Place, following it up by such assiduous endeavours to meet, and when they did meet, by such great openness of conduct, such readiness to apologize for the past, such solicitude to be received as a relation again, that their former good understanding was completely re-established.

They had not a fault to find in him. He had explained away all the appearance of neglect on his own side. It had originated in misapprehension entirely. He had never had an idea of throwing himself off; he had feared that he was thrown off, but knew not why, and delicacy had kept him silent. Upon the hint of having spoken disrespectfully or carelessly of the family and the family honours, he was quite indignant. He, who had ever boasted of being an Elliot, and whose feelings, as to connection, were only too strict to suit the unfeudal tone of the present day. He was astonished, indeed, but his character and general conduct must refute it. He could refer Sir Walter to all who knew him; and certainly, the pains he had been taking on this, the first opportunity of reconciliation, to be restored to the footing of a relation and heir-presumptive, was a strong proof of his opinions on the subject.

The circumstances of his marriage, too, were found to admit of much extenuation. This was an article not to be entered on by himself; but a very intimate friend of his, a Colonel Wallis, a highly respectable man, perfectly the gentleman, (and not an ill-looking man, Sir Walter added), who was living in very good style in Marlborough Buildings, and had, at his own particular request, been admitted to their acquaintance through Mr. Elliot, had mentioned one or two things relative to the marriage, which made a material difference in the discredit of it.

Colonel Wallis had known Mr. Elliot long, had been well acquainted also with his wife, had perfectly understood the whole story. She was certainly not a woman of family, but well educated, accomplished, rich, and excessively in love with his friend. There had been the charm. She had sought him. Without that attraction, not all her money would have tempted Elliot, and Sir Walter was, moreover, assured of her having been a very fine woman. Here was a great deal to soften the business. A very fine woman with a large fortune, in love with him! Sir Walter seemed to admit it as complete apology; and though Elizabeth could not see the circumstance in quite so favourable a light, she allowed it be a great extenuation.

Mr. Elliot had called repeatedly, had dined with them once, evidently delighted by the distinction of being asked, for they gave no dinners in general; delighted, in short, by every proof of cousinly notice, and placing his whole happiness in being on intimate terms in Camden Place.

Anne listened, but without quite understanding it. Allowances, large allowances, she knew, must be made for the ideas of those who spoke. She heard it all under embellishment. All that sounded extravagant or irrational in the progress of the reconciliation might have no origin but in the language of the relators. Still, however, she had the sensation of there being something more than immediately appeared, in Mr. Elliot's wishing, after an interval of so many years, to be well received by them. In a worldly view, he had nothing to gain by being on terms with Sir Walter; nothing to risk by a state of variance. In all probability he was already the richer of the two, and the Kellynch estate would as surely be his hereafter as the title. A sensible man, and he had looked like a *very* sensible man, why should it be an object to him? She could only offer one solution; it was, perhaps, for Elizabeth's sake. There might really have been a liking formerly, though convenience and accident had drawn him a different way; and now that he could afford to please himself, he might mean to pay his addresses to her. Elizabeth was certainly very handsome, with well-bred, elegant manners, and her character might never have been penetrated by Mr. Elliot, knowing her but in public, and when very young himself. Everyone who had witnessed Mr. Elliot's interaction with Anne and fancied him half in love with her had obviously been mistaken. Why else would he be here paying court to Elizabeth, who was a much prettier catch than Anne? How her temper and understanding might bear the investigation of his present keener time of life was another concern and rather a fearful one. Most earnestly did she wish that he might not be too nice, or too observant if Elizabeth were his object; and that Elizabeth was disposed to believe herself so, and that her friend Mrs. Clay was encouraging the idea, seemed apparent by a glance or two between them, while Mr. Elliot's frequent visits were talked of.

Anne mentioned the glimpses she had had of him at Lyme, but without being much attended to. "Oh! yes, perhaps, it had been Mr. Elliot. They did not know. It might be him, perhaps." They could not listen to her description of him. They were describing him themselves; Sir Walter especially. He did justice to his very gentlemanlike appearance, his air of elegance and fashion, his good shaped face, his sensible eye; but, at the same time, "must lament his being very much under-hung, a defect which time seemed to have increased; nor could he pretend to say that ten years had not altered almost every feature for the worse. Mr. Elliot appeared to think that he (Sir Walter) was looking exactly as he had done when they last parted;" but Sir Walter had "not been able to return the compliment entirely, which had embarrassed him. He did not mean to complain, however. Mr. Elliot was better to look at than most men, and he had no objection to being seen with him anywhere."

Anne remembered him similarly. He *was* better to look at than most men, though not as handsome as some. In fact, Anne could think of only one man who surpassed him in looks, and she had to acknowledge that she may be biased in that comparison.

Mr. Elliot, and his friends in Marlborough Buildings, were talked of the whole evening. "Colonel Wallis had been so impatient to be introduced to them! and Mr. Elliot so anxious that he should!" and there was a Mrs. Wallis, at present known only to them by description, as she was in daily expectation of her confinement; but Mr. Elliot spoke of her as "a most charming woman, quite worthy of being known in Camden Place," and as soon as she recovered they were to be acquainted. Sir Walter thought much of Mrs. Wallis; she was said to be an excessively pretty woman, beautiful. He longed to see her. He hoped she might make some amends for the many very plain faces he was continually passing in the streets. The worst of Bath was the number of its plain women. He did not mean to say that there were no pretty women, but the number of the plain was out of all proportion. He had frequently observed, as he walked, that one handsome face would be followed by thirty, or five-and-thirty frights; and once, as he had stood in a shop on Bond Street, he had counted eighty-seven women go by, one after another, without there being a tolerable face among them. It had been a frosty morning, to be sure, a sharp frost, which hardly one woman in a thousand could stand the test of. But still, there certainly were a dreadful multitude of ugly women in Bath; and as for the men! they were infinitely worse. Such scarecrows as the streets were full of! It was evident how little the women were used to the sight of anything tolerable, by the effect which a man of decent appearance produced. He had never walked anywhere arm-in-arm with Colonel Wallis (who was a fine military figure, though sandy-haired) without observing that every woman's eye was upon him; every woman's eye was sure to be upon Colonel Wallis. Modest Sir Walter! He was not allowed to escape, however. His daughter and Mrs. Clay united in hinting that Colonel Wallis's companion might have as good a figure as Colonel Wallis, and certainly was not sandy-haired.

"How is Mary looking?" said Sir Walter, in the height of his good humour. "The last time I saw her she had a red nose, but I hope that may not happen every day."

"Oh! no, that must have been quite accidental. In general she has been in very good health and very good looks since Michaelmas."

"If I thought it would not tempt her to go out in sharp winds, and grow coarse, I would send her a new hat and pelisse."

Anne was considering whether she should venture to suggest that a gown, or a cap, would not be liable to any such misuse, when a knock at the door suspended everything. A knock at the door! and so late! It was ten o'clock. Could it be Mr. Elliot? They knew he was to dine in Lansdown Crescent. It was possible that he might stop in his way home to ask them how they did. They could think of no one else. Mrs. Clay decidedly thought it Mr. Elliot's knock. Mrs. Clay was right. With all the state which a butler and foot-boy could give, Mr. Elliot was ushered into the room.

His broad form filled the doorway, and he seemed to pose before walking toward them all. The muscles of his thighs flexed beneath the tight fabric of his breeches, and he strolled through the room with languid, sensual grace. His dark, decadent eyes were nearly hidden by his lowered lids and lush lashes, and his black hair, cut to the height of fashion, curled around his collar. He spotted Anne first, and a slow smile spread his lips with an almost teasing expression; in a moment, his eyes had devoured Anne from the top of her head to the tips of her toes. Then, just as quickly, his eyes darted away and looked upon Sir Walter and Elizabeth. Anne wondered if she had imagined his hungry perusal of her body, but foreboding swept her body in the wake of his gaze, and she knew that her mind had not imagined it.

It was the same, the very same man, with no difference but of dress. Anne drew a little back, utterly ashamed that she had once entertained the notion that he found her desirable. He was nearly perfection, and his every movement was cultivated to be suggestive. She looked at her lap, trying desperately to displace the misbegotten notion that he had wanted her while the others received his compliments, and her sister his apologies for calling at so unusual an hour, but "he could not be so near without wishing to know that neither she nor her friend had taken cold the day before," etcetera etcetera; which was all as politely done, and as politely taken, as possible, but her part must follow then. Sir Walter talked of his youngest daughter; "Mr. Elliot must give him leave to present him to his youngest daughter" (there was no occasion for remembering Mary); and Anne, smiling and blushing, very becomingly shewed to Mr. Elliot the pretty features which he had by no means forgotten, and instantly saw, with amusement at his little start of surprise, that he had not been at all aware of who she was. He looked completely astonished, but not more astonished than pleased; his eyes brightened! and with the most perfect alacrity he welcomed the relationship, alluded to the past, and entreated to be received as an acquaintance already. He was quite as good-looking as he had appeared at Lyme, his countenance improved by speaking, and his manners were so exactly what they ought to be, so polished, so easy, so particularly agreeable, that she could compare them in excellence to only one person's manners. They were not the same, but they were, perhaps, equally good.

He sat down with them, and improved their conversation very much. There could be no doubt of his being a sensible man. Ten minutes were enough to certify that. His tone, his expressions, his choice of subject, his knowing where to stop; it was all the operation of a sensible, discerning mind.

As soon as he could, he moved from the chair where he sat solitarily and took a seat beside Anne. As the others looked on in shock, he began to talk to her of Lyme, wanting to compare opinions respecting the place, but especially wanting to speak of the circumstance of their happening to be guests in the same inn at the same time; to give his own route, understand something of hers, and regret that he should have lost such an opportunity of paying his respects to her. She gave him a short account of her party and business at Lyme.

At this point, they lost the attention of Sir Walter, Elizabeth, and Mrs. Clay, who could not be bothered with Anne's dreary recounting of her experience in Lyme. They turned to each other in conversation, and Mr. Elliot shifted in his seat, landing closer to Anne, seemingly for the purpose of better being able to hear her. His regret increased as he listened. He had spent his whole solitary evening in the room adjoining theirs; had heard voices, mirth continually; thought they must be a most delightful set of people, longed to be with them, but certainly without the smallest suspicion of his possessing the shadow of a right to introduce himself. If he had but asked who the party were! The name of Musgrove would have told him enough.

They were innocent enough comments, but Anne found herself quite short of breath. There was something in Mr. Elliot's delivery. He talked of being in the room adjacent to hers as though he had spent the entire night listening for her every move in bed. As though he had taken great pleasure in being next to a room full of young women. Anne was startled to find that he seemed to be playing some sort of *game*. Her heart raced. Was she mistaken, or had he leaned closer and closer to her as he talked? His voice was certainly pitched lower. It neared a purr, and Anne feared she would react.

From the corner of her eye, she saw her father and sister turn toward them, and their conversation petered out completely until their silence penetrated the cocoon surrounding Anne and Mr. Elliot. With a sharp laugh, Mr. Elliot tossed his head back jovially, and when he again looked at her, he was an appropriate distance away from her. He smiled broadly and continued the conversation. "Well, it would serve to cure him of an absurd practice of never asking a question at an inn, which he had adopted, when quite a young man, on the principal of its being very ungenteel to be curious.

"The notions of a young man of one or two and twenty," said he, "as to what is necessary in manners to make him quite the thing, are more absurd, I believe, than those of any other set of beings in the world. The folly of the means they often employ is only to be equalled by the folly of what they have in view."

But he must not be addressing his reflections to Anne alone: he knew it; he was soon diffused again among the others, and it was only at intervals that he could return to Lyme.

His enquiries, however, produced at length an account of the scene she had been engaged in there, soon after his leaving the place. Having alluded to "an accident," he must hear the whole. When he questioned, Sir Walter and Elizabeth began to question also, but the difference in their manner of doing it could not be unfelt. She could only compare Mr. Elliot to Lady Russell, in the wish of really comprehending what had passed, and in the degree of concern for what she must have suffered in witnessing it.

He staid an hour with them. The elegant little clock on the mantel-piece had struck "eleven with its silver sounds," and the watchman was beginning to be heard at a distance telling the same tale, before Mr. Elliot or any of them seemed to feel that he had been there long.

Mr. Elliot rose to his feet quite abruptly. "Oh, forgive me," he said, bowing slightly to all of them as a whole. "I fear I have overstaid my welcome." Amid a cacophony of protest to such a statement, he smiled charmingly and turned to Anne. "Cousin, would you escort me to the door? I have just one more question about Lyme."

The cacophony in the room settled just as suddenly as it had started. Sir Walter, Elizabeth, and Mrs. Clay all turned their heads as one to look at Anne with wide, blinking eyes. They brought to mind a trio of owls, and, hiding a smile, Anne rose to her feet. "Of course," she said, mirth finding its way unbidden into her words.

The clutch of night fowl continued to watch them as Mr. Elliot and Anne left the drawing room and walked to the front door. Anne turned her face toward Mr. Elliot, assuming he would ask his question right away, only to find she was staring at his well-formed profile. They walked in silence to the front door, and Anne could not help but feel the weight of awkwardness. She had imagined this handsome man halfway in love with her, and she was no fool: her father and sister would certainly interpret Mr. Elliot's request to speak to Anne alone as an indicant of his favour.

She stifled a sigh. That would be difficult to demystify, but demystify she must. It would not do for them to imagine her paired with Mr. Elliot; she was certainly not who he would have in mind when considering a bride.

They arrived at the door, and Anne knew she must speak. "Your question, Mr. Elliot?"

Rather than ask a question, Mr. Elliot turned to the dutiful butler who stood poised to open the door. "That will be all, thank you," Mr. Elliot said to the poor man who looked back and forth between Anne and the guest who had dared dismiss him before bowing curtly and leaving them alone.

Anne fought the desire to swallow loudly, knowing that would not be ladylike.

"I fear I had no question, Miss Elliot," Mr. Elliot said taking a step toward her. "I merely wanted to speak to you without the gawking of your father and sister." Anne took a step back as he advanced, and he continued to follow. "Forgive me for being dishonest?" he asked with a sly wink.

Now, Anne *did* swallow, and it echoed in her head like a gong. What, exactly, was he about? It was behaviour like this that led others to believe he fancied her. In fact, it was hard for Anne to remember why she had thought such a notion absurd herself mere moments ago when he leaned in close.

"I wished to tell you how happy I am to see you again," he whispered.

He was close enough that his breath, scented with mint, fanned across her face. Anne watched in fascination as his dark eyes grew even darker as his pupil expanded to eat up the rich, chocolate colour. His gaze fell to her lips, and Anne felt them part traitorously.

If any space remained between them, he quickly closed it, taking a small step forward so that the lapels of his jacket brushed against her breasts. The mint of his breath was overshadowed by the male scent of him.

She saw his arm rise out of the corner of her eye, and every muscle in her body tensed as she anticipated being touched.

But the touch never came. His arm fell back to his side at the same time that he took a step back from her, and Anne noticed with astonishment that the hand he had raised now clutched his cane and hat.

Mortification stung her cheeks. She had imagined him ready to kiss her, and he had merely been reaching for his personal items from the stand to her right.

She darted out of the way as Mr. Elliot reached forward to grasp the doorknob, not willing to let herself imagine any more untoward slant to his innocent actions.

She was staring at the floor when he spoke. "Thank you for seeing me out, Miss Elliot."

"T-the pleasure was all mine," Anne managed to stutter.

A breathless laugh sounded above her head, and, without her consent, Anne's gaze locked upon his handsome face. Those dark eyes of his stroked every plane of her body before returning to her face. "Oh, I sincerely doubt that."

And before she could puzzle out a proper interpretation of his words—he was in love with *Elizabeth*—he was gone.

As she returned to the drawing room in a near trance, Anne felt a smile stretch her cheeks despite her constant self-reminders that Mr. Elliot was not interested in *her*. Unbidden, flattery lit through her. She could not have supposed it possible that her first evening in Camden Place could have passed so well!

Chapter 16

There was one point which Anne, on returning to her family, would have been more thankful to ascertain even than Mr. Elliot's being in love with Elizabeth, which was, her father's not being in love with Mrs. Clay; and she was very far from easy about it, when she had been at home a few hours.

On going down to breakfast the next morning, she found there had just been a decent pretence on the lady's side of meaning to leave them. The sound of Mrs. Clay cooing and Sir Walter's vehement objection reached Anne just before she entered the room, fortuitously stopping Anne in the hall. Had Anne been more lost in her thoughts, she would have entered the breakfast room and witnessed what certain sounds indicated was a quickly developing tryst between Mrs. Clay and Anne's father.

Sir Walter's low, hoarse chuckle was accompanied by a screech of his chair across the floor, and Anne instinctually knew Mrs. Clay was placing herself in Sir Walter's lap. The obvious sound of sloppy kisses filtered out into the hall. With a horrified gasp, Anne wondered what she should do. If she were to behave properly and encourage proper behaviour in her family, she should enter the room and put a stop to whatever was going on in there immediately.

However, Anne could not force herself to witness her father in a compromising position, and when Sir Walter's harsh groan reverberated down the hall, Anne abandoned all pretence and spun on her heel to retreat. Anne meant to escape up the stairs to her room, but she saw Elizabeth trouncing down them, humming a tune that sounded suspiciously like a bawdy song.

The sounds within the breakfast room halted as Elizabeth's humming grew louder, and Anne adjusted her path of flight accordingly and slipped into the nearby drawing room. After waiting a few moments to steel her nerves and allow her family to settle in, Anne left the drawing room and headed into breakfast. But just outside the door, their conversation reached Anne. She could imagine Mrs. Clay to have said, that "now Miss Anne was come, she could not suppose herself at all wanted;" for Elizabeth was replying in a sort of whisper, "That must not be any reason, indeed. I assure you I feel it none. She is nothing to me, compared with you;" and she was in full time to hear her father say, "My dear madam, this must not be. As yet, you have seen nothing of Bath. You have been here only to be useful. You must not run away from us now. You must stay to be acquainted with Mrs. Wallis, the beautiful Mrs. Wallis. To your fine mind, I well know the sight of beauty is a real gratification."

He spoke and looked so much in earnest, that Anne was not surprised to see Mrs. Clay stealing a glance at Elizabeth and herself, no doubt to check if either of them suspected her of fornicating with their father. Her countenance, perhaps, might express some watchfulness; but the praise of the fine mind did not appear to excite a thought in her sister. The lady could not but yield to such joint entreaties, and promise to stay.

In the course of the same morning, Anne and her father chancing to be alone together, he began to compliment her on her improved looks; he thought her "less thin in her person, in her cheeks; her skin, her complexion, greatly improved; clearer, fresher. Had she been using any thing in particular?" "No, nothing." "Merely Gowland," he supposed. "No, nothing at all." "Ha! he was surprised at that;" and added, "certainly you cannot do better than to continue as you are; you cannot be better than well; or I should recommend Gowland, the constant use of Gowland, during the spring months. Mrs. Clay has been using it at my recommendation, and you see what it has done for her. You see how it has carried away her freckles."

If Elizabeth could but have heard this! Such personal praise might have struck her, especially as it did not appear to Anne that the freckles were at all lessened. But everything must take its chance. The evil of a marriage would be much diminished, if Elizabeth were also to marry. As for herself, she might always command a home with Lady Russell.

Lady Russell's composed mind and polite manners were put to some trial on this point, in her intercourse in Camden Place. The sight of Mrs. Clay in such favour, and of Anne so overlooked, was a perpetual provocation to her there; and vexed her as much when she was away, as a person in Bath who drinks the water, gets all the new publications, and has a very large acquaintance, has time to be vexed.

As Mr. Elliot became known to her, she grew more charitable, or more indifferent, towards the others. His manners were an immediate recommendation; and on conversing with him she found the solid so fully supporting the superficial, that she was at first, as she told Anne, almost ready to exclaim, "Can this be Mr. Elliot?" and could not seriously picture to herself a more agreeable or estimable man. Everything united in him; good understanding, correct opinions, knowledge of the world, and a warm heart. He had strong feelings of family attachment and family honour, without pride or weakness; he lived with the liberality of a man of fortune, without display; he judged for himself in everything essential, without defying public opinion in any point of worldly decorum. He was steady, observant, moderate, candid; never run away with by spirits or by selfishness, which fancied itself strong feeling; and yet, with a sensibility to what was amiable and lovely, and a value for all the felicities of domestic life, which characters of fancied enthusiasm and violent agitation seldom really possess. She was sure that he had not been happy in marriage. Colonel Wallis said it, and Lady Russell saw it; but it had been no unhappiness to sour his mind, nor (she began pretty soon to suspect) to prevent his thinking of a second choice. Her satisfaction in Mr. Elliot outweighed all the plague of Mrs. Clay.

It was now some years since Anne had begun to learn that she and her excellent friend could sometimes think differently; and it did not surprise her, therefore, that Lady Russell should see nothing suspicious or inconsistent, nothing to require more motives than appeared, in Mr. Elliot's great desire of a reconciliation. In Lady Russell's view, it was perfectly natural that Mr. Elliot, at a mature time of life, should feel it a most desirable object, and what would very generally recommend him among all sensible people, to be on good terms with the head of his family; the simplest process in the world of time upon a head naturally clear, and only erring in the heyday of youth. Anne presumed, however, still to smile about it, and at last, because Anne needed reminding as well, to mention "Elizabeth." Lady Russell listened, and looked, and made only this cautious reply:—"Elizabeth! very well; time will explain."

It was a reference to the future, which Anne, after a little observation, felt she must submit to. She could determine nothing at present. In that house Elizabeth must be first; and she was in the habit of such general observance as "Miss Elliot," that any particularity of attention seemed almost impossible. Mr. Elliot, too, it must be remembered, had not been a widower seven months. A little delay on his side might be very excusable. In fact, Anne could never see the crape round his hat, without fearing that she was the inexcusable one, in attributing to him such imaginations; for though his marriage had not been very happy, still it had existed so many years that she could not comprehend a very rapid recovery from the awful impression of its being dissolved.

However it might end, he was without any question their pleasantest acquaintance in Bath: she saw nobody equal to him; and it was a great indulgence now and then to talk to him about

Lyme, which he seemed to have as lively a wish to see again, and to see more of, as herself. They went through the particulars of their first meeting a great many times. He gave her to understand that he had looked at her with some earnestness. She knew it well; and she remembered another person's look also.

They did not always think alike. His value for rank and connexion she perceived was greater than hers. It was not merely complaisance, it must be a liking to the cause, which made him enter warmly into her father and sister's solicitudes on a subject which she thought unworthy to excite them. The Bath paper one morning announced the arrival of the Dowager Viscountess Dalrymple, and her daughter, the Honourable Miss Carteret; and all the comfort of No.—, Camden Place, was swept away for many days; for the Dalrymples (in Anne's opinion, most unfortunately) were cousins of the Elliots; and the agony was how to introduce themselves properly.

Anne had never seen her father and sister before in contact with nobility, and she must acknowledge herself disappointed. She had hoped better things from their high ideas of their own situation in life, and was reduced to form a wish which she had never foreseen; a wish that they had more pride; for "our cousins Lady Dalrymple and Miss Carteret;" "our cousins, the Dalrymples," sounded in her ears all day long.

Sir Walter had once been in company with the late viscount, but had never seen any of the rest of the family; and the difficulties of the case arose from there having been a suspension of all intercourse by letters of ceremony, ever since the death of that said late viscount, when, in consequence of a dangerous illness of Sir Walter's at the same time, there had been an unlucky omission at Kellynch. No letter of condolence had been sent to Ireland. The neglect had been visited on the head of the sinner; for when poor Lady Elliot died herself, no letter of condolence was received at Kellynch, and, consequently, there was but too much reason to apprehend that the Dalrymples considered the relationship as closed. How to have this anxious business set to rights, and be admitted as cousins again, was the question: and it was a question which, in a more rational manner, neither Lady Russell nor Mr. Elliot thought unimportant. "Family connexions were always worth preserving, good company always worth seeking; Lady Dalrymple had taken a house, for three months, in Laura Place, and would be living in style. She had been at Bath the year before, and Lady Russell had heard her spoken of as a charming woman. It was very desirable that the connexion should be renewed, if it could be done, without any compromise of propriety on the side of the Elliots."

Sir Walter, however, would choose his own means, and at last wrote a very fine letter of ample explanation, regret, and entreaty, to his right honourable cousin. Neither Lady Russell nor Mr. Elliot could admire the letter; but it did all that was wanted, in bringing three lines of scrawl from the Dowager Viscountess. "She was very much honoured, and should be happy in their acquaintance." The toils of the business were over, the sweets began. They visited in Laura Place, they had the cards of Dowager Viscountess Dalrymple, and the Honourable Miss Carteret, to be arranged wherever they might be most visible: and "Our cousins in Laura Place,"—"Our cousin, Lady Dalrymple and Miss Carteret," were talked of to everybody.

Anne was ashamed. Had Lady Dalrymple and her daughter even been very agreeable, she would still have been ashamed of the agitation they created, but they were nothing. There was no superiority of manner, accomplishment, or understanding. Lady Dalrymple had acquired the name of "a charming woman," because she had a smile and a civil answer for everybody. Miss Carteret, with still less to say, was so plain and so awkward, that she would never have been tolerated in Camden Place but for her birth.

Lady Russell confessed she had expected something better; but yet "it was an acquaintance worth having;" and when Anne ventured to speak her opinion of them to Mr. Elliot, he agreed to their being nothing in themselves, but still maintained that, as a family connexion, as good company, as those who would collect good company around them, they had their value. Anne smiled and said,

"My idea of good company, Mr. Elliot, is the company of clever, well-informed people, who have a great deal of conversation; that is what I call good company."

"You are mistaken," said he gently, lowering his voice and forcing the conversation to take an intimate turn, "that is not good company; that is the best. Good company requires only birth, education, and manners, and with regard to education is not very nice. Birth and good manners are essential; but a little learning is by no means a dangerous thing in good company; on the contrary, it will do very well. My cousin Anne shakes her head. She is not satisfied. She is fastidious. My dear cousin" (sitting down by her so close their knees brushed), "you have a better right to be fastidious than almost any other woman I know; but will it answer? Will it make you happy? Will it not be wiser to accept the society of those good ladies in Laura Place, and enjoy all the advantages of the connexion as far as possible? You may depend upon it, that they will move in the first set in Bath this winter, and as rank is rank, your being known to be related to them will have its use in fixing your family (*our* family let me say) in that degree of consideration which we must all wish for."

"Yes," sighed Anne, trying to expel his overwhelming scent—not at all the clean scent she preferred—from her lungs, "we shall, indeed, be known to be related to them!" then recollecting herself, and not wishing to be answered, she added, "I certainly do think there has been by far too much trouble taken to procure the acquaintance. I suppose" (smiling) "I have more pride than any of you; but I confess it does vex me, that we should be so solicitous to have the relationship acknowledged, which we may be very sure is a matter of perfect indifference to them."

Mr. Elliot's smile broadened, and she did not object when he leaned closer to say, "Pardon me, dear cousin, you are unjust in your own claims. In London, perhaps, in your present quiet style of living, it might be as you say: but in Bath; Sir Walter Elliot and his family will always be worth knowing: always acceptable as acquaintance."

Had Anne imagined the brush of his shoulder against hers when he talked of *family*? Her every sense was so overcome by his presence that she could scarcely breathe. "Well," said Anne, "I certainly am proud, too proud to enjoy a welcome which depends so entirely upon place."

"I love your indignation," said he, placing a peculiar emphasis on the word *love*; "it is very natural. But here you are in Bath, and the object is to be established here with all the credit and dignity which ought to belong to Sir Walter Elliot. You talk of being proud; I am called proud, I know, and I shall not wish to believe myself otherwise; for our pride, if investigated, would have the same object, I have no doubt, though the kind may seem a little different. In one point, I am sure, my dear cousin," (he continued, speaking lower, though there was no one else in the room, a fact that was blaring itself through Anne's mind) "in one point, I am sure, we must feel alike. We must feel that every addition to your father's society, among his equals or superiors, may be of use in diverting his thoughts from those who are beneath him."

He looked, as he spoke, to the seat which Mrs. Clay had been lately occupying: a sufficient explanation of what he particularly meant; and though Anne could not believe in their having the same sort of pride, she was pleased with him for not liking Mrs. Clay; and her conscience admitted that his wishing to promote her father's getting great acquaintance was more than excusable in the view of defeating her.

Mr. Elliot's gaze shifted in expression when it returned to Anne's face, and he took on an intent look that stalled Anne's heart within her chest. She realized that they sat far too close for propriety, that they had been whispering like lovers with a secret, and that the side of his body was pressed into the entirety of Anne's. The knowledge that they were alone again presented itself to her, and Anne fought to remember that Mr. Elliot was for *Elizabeth*, not her.

Mr. Elliot's lips parted, and every fibre of Anne's body clenched as she waited for what he would say—half flattered that it would be a declaration, half terrified for the same reason.

The sounds of Mrs. Clay and Elizabeth chatting gaily entered the room a moment before they did, and in that moment, Mr. Elliot quickly drew away from her, pressing into the side of the sofa instead of the side of his cousin with such ease that Anne wondered if she had invented his closeness. He greeted his cousin jovially and entered into light-hearted conversation with the two women while Anne fought to remind herself that she thought far too much of simple, friendly actions.

Chapter 17

While Sir Walter and Elizabeth were assiduously pushing their good fortune in Laura Place, Anne was renewing an acquaintance of a very different description.

She had called on her former governess, and had heard from her of there being an old school-fellow in Bath, who had the two strong claims on her attention of past kindness and present suffering. Miss Hamilton, now Mrs. Smith, had shewn her kindness in one of those periods of her life when it had been most valuable. Anne had gone unhappy to school, grieving for the loss of a mother whom she had dearly loved, feeling her separation from home, and suffering as a girl of fourteen, of strong sensibility and not high spirits, must suffer at such a time; and Miss Hamilton, three years older than herself, but still from the want of near relations and a settled home, remaining another year at school, had been useful and good to her in a way which had considerably lessened her misery, and could never be remembered with indifference.

Miss Hamilton had left school, had married not long afterwards, was said to have married a man of fortune, and this was all that Anne had known of her, till now that their governess's account brought her situation forward in a more decided but very different form.

She was a widow and poor. Her husband had been extravagant; and at his death, about two years before, had left his affairs dreadfully involved. She had had difficulties of every sort to contend with, and in addition to these distresses had been afflicted with a severe rheumatic fever, which, finally settling in her legs, had made her for the present a cripple. She had come to Bath on that account, and was now in lodgings near the hot baths, living in a very humble way, unable even to afford herself the comfort of a servant, and of course almost excluded from society.

Their mutual friend answered for the satisfaction which a visit from Miss Elliot would give Mrs. Smith, and Anne therefore lost no time in going. She mentioned nothing of what she had heard, or what she intended, at home. It would excite no proper interest there. She only consulted Lady Russell, who entered thoroughly into her sentiments, and was most happy to convey her as near to Mrs. Smith's lodgings in Westgate Buildings, as Anne chose to be taken.

The visit was paid, their acquaintance re-established, their interest in each other more than re-kindled. The first ten minutes had its awkwardness and its emotion. Twelve years were gone since they had parted, and each presented a somewhat different person from what the other had imagined. Twelve years had changed Anne from the blooming, silent, unformed girl of fifteen, to the elegant little woman of seven-and-twenty, with every beauty except bloom, and with manners as consciously right as they were invariably gentle; and twelve years had transformed the fine-looking, well-grown Miss Hamilton, in all the glow of health and confidence of superiority, into a poor, infirm, helpless widow, receiving the visit of her former *protégée* as a favour; but all that was uncomfortable in the meeting had soon passed away, and left only the interesting charm of remembering former partialities and talking over old times.

Anne found in Mrs. Smith the good sense and agreeable manners which she had almost ventured to depend on, and a disposition to converse and be cheerful beyond her expectation. Neither the dissipations of the past—and she had lived very much in the world—nor the restrictions of the present, neither sickness nor sorrow seemed to have closed her heart or ruined her spirits.

In the course of a second visit she talked with great openness, and Anne's astonishment increased. She could scarcely imagine a more cheerless situation in itself than Mrs. Smith's. She had been very fond of her husband: she had buried him. She had been used to affluence: it was gone. She had no child to connect her with life and happiness again, no relations to assist in the arrangement of perplexed affairs, no health to make all the rest supportable. Her accommodations were limited to a noisy parlour, and a dark bedroom behind, with no possibility of moving from one to the other without assistance, which there was only one servant in the house to afford, and she never quitted the house but to be conveyed into the warm bath. Yet, in spite of all this, Anne had reason to believe that she had moments only of languor and depression, to hours of occupation and enjoyment. How could it be? She watched, observed, reflected, and finally determined that this was not a case of fortitude or of resignation only. A submissive spirit might be patient, a strong understanding would supply resolution, but here was something more; here was that elasticity of mind, that disposition to be comforted, that power of turning readily from evil to good, and of finding employment which carried her out of herself, which was from nature alone. It was the choicest gift of Heaven; and Anne viewed her friend as one of those instances in which, by a merciful appointment, it seems designed to counterbalance almost every other want.

There had been a time, Mrs. Smith told her, when her spirits had nearly failed. She could not call herself an invalid now, compared with her state on first reaching Bath. Then she had, indeed, been a pitiable object; for she had caught cold on the journey, and had hardly taken possession of her lodgings before she was again confined to her bed and suffering under severe and constant pain; and all this among strangers, with the absolute necessity of having a regular nurse, and finances at that moment particularly unfit to meet any extraordinary expense. She had weathered it, however, and could truly say that it had done her good. It had increased her comforts by making her feel herself to be in good hands. She had seen too much of the world, to expect sudden or disinterested attachment anywhere, but her illness had proved to her that her landlady had a character to preserve, and would not use her ill; and she had been particularly fortunate in her nurse, as a sister of her landlady, a nurse by profession, and who had always a home in that house when unemployed, chanced to be at liberty just in time to attend her.

"And she," said Mrs. Smith, "besides nursing me most admirably, has really proved an invaluable acquaintance. As soon as I could use my hands she taught me to knit, which has been a great amusement; and she put me in the way of making these little thread-cases, pin-cushions and card-racks, which you always find me so busy about, and which supply me with the means of doing a little good to one or two very poor families in this neighbourhood. She had a large acquaintance, of course professionally, among those who can afford to buy, and she disposes of my merchandise. She always takes the right time for applying. Everybody's heart is open, you know, when they have recently escaped from severe pain, or are recovering the blessing of health, and Nurse Rooke thoroughly understands when to speak. She is a shrewd, intelligent, sensible woman. Hers is a line for seeing human nature; and she has a fund of good sense and observation, which, as a companion, make her infinitely superior to thousands of those who having only received 'the best education in the world,' know nothing worth attending to. Call it gossip, if you will, but when Nurse Rooke has half an hour's leisure to bestow on me, she is sure to have something to relate that is entertaining and profitable: something that makes one know one's species better. One likes to hear what is going on, to be au fait as to the newest modes of being trifling and silly. To me, who live so much alone, her conversation, I assure you, is a treat."

Anne, far from wishing to cavil at the pleasure, replied, "I can easily believe it. Women of that class have great opportunities, and if they are intelligent may be well worth listening to. Such varieties of human nature as they are in the habit of witnessing! And it is not merely in its follies, that they are well read; for they see it occasionally under every circumstance that can be most interesting or affecting. What instances must pass before them of ardent, disinterested, self-denying attachment, of heroism, fortitude, patience, resignation: of all the conflicts and all the sacrifices that ennoble us most. A sick chamber may often furnish the worth of volumes."

"Yes," said Mrs. Smith more doubtingly, "sometimes it may, though I fear its lessons are not often in the elevated style you describe. Here and there, human nature may be great in times of trial; but generally speaking, it is its weakness and not its strength that appears in a sick chamber: it is selfishness and impatience rather than generosity and fortitude, that one hears of. There is so little real friendship in the world! and unfortunately" (speaking low and tremulously) "there are so many who forget to think seriously till it is almost too late."

Anne saw the misery of such feelings. The husband had not been what he ought, and the wife had been led among that part of mankind which made her think worse of the world than she hoped it deserved. It was but a passing emotion however with Mrs. Smith; she shook it off, and soon added in a different tone—

"I do not suppose the situation my friend Mrs. Rooke is in at present, will furnish much either to interest or edify me. She is only nursing Mrs. Wallis of Marlborough Buildings; a mere pretty, silly, expensive, fashionable woman, I believe; and of course will have nothing to report but of lace and finery. I mean to make my profit of Mrs. Wallis, however. She has plenty of money, and I intend she shall buy all the high-priced things I have in hand now."

Anne had called several times on her friend, before the existence of such a person was known in Camden Place. At last, it became necessary to speak of her. Sir Walter, Elizabeth and Mrs. Clay, returned one morning from Laura Place, with a sudden invitation from Lady Dalrymple for the same evening, and Anne was already engaged, to spend that evening in Westgate Buildings. She was not sorry for the excuse. They were only asked, she was sure, because Lady Dalrymple being kept at home by a bad cold, was glad to make use of the relationship which had been so pressed on her; and she declined on her own account with great alacrity—"She was engaged to spend the evening with an old schoolfellow." They were not much interested in anything relative to Anne; but still there were questions enough asked, to make it understood what this old schoolfellow was; and Elizabeth was disdainful, and Sir Walter severe.

"Westgate Buildings!" said he, "and who is Miss Anne Elliot to be visiting in Westgate Buildings? A Mrs. Smith. A widow Mrs. Smith; and who was her husband? One of five thousand Mr. Smiths whose names are to be met with everywhere. And what is her attraction? That she is old and sickly. Upon my word, Miss Anne Elliot, you have the most extraordinary taste! Everything that revolts other people, low company, paltry rooms, foul air, disgusting associations are inviting to you. But surely you may put off this old lady till to-morrow: she is not so near her end, I presume, but that she may hope to see another day. What is her age? Forty?"

"No, sir, she is not one-and-thirty; but I do not think I can put off my engagement, because it is the only evening for some time which will at once suit her and myself. She goes into the warm bath to-morrow, and for the rest of the week, you know, we are engaged."

"But what does Lady Russell think of this acquaintance?" asked Elizabeth.

As though Anne could have no relationship without the express approval of Lady Russell? "She sees nothing to blame in it," replied Anne, a bit more severely than she had intended; "on the contrary, she approves it, and has generally taken me when I have called on Mrs. Smith."

If they noticed Anne's vehement response, it did not show. "Westgate Buildings must have been rather surprised by the appearance of a carriage drawn up near its pavement," observed Sir Walter. "Sir Henry Russell's widow, indeed, has no honours to distinguish her arms, but still it is a handsome equipage, and no doubt is well known to convey a Miss Elliot. A widow Mrs. Smith lodging in Westgate Buildings! A poor widow barely able to live, between thirty and forty; a mere Mrs. Smith, an every-day Mrs. Smith, of all people and all names in the world, to be the chosen friend of Miss Anne Elliot, and to be preferred by her to her own family connections among the nobility of England and Ireland! Mrs. Smith! Such a name!"

Mrs. Clay, who had been present while all this passed, now thought it advisable to leave the room, and Anne could have said much, and did long to say a little in defense of *her* friend's not very dissimilar claims to theirs, but her sense of personal respect to her father prevented her. She made no reply. She left it to himself to recollect, that Mrs. Smith was not the only widow in Bath between thirty and forty, with little to live on, and no surname of dignity.

Anne kept her appointment; the others kept theirs, and of course she heard the next morning that they had had a delightful evening. She had been the only one of the set absent, for Sir Walter and Elizabeth had not only been quite at her ladyship's service themselves, but had actually been happy to be employed by her in collecting others, and had been at the trouble of inviting both Lady Russell and Mr. Elliot; and Mr. Elliot had made a point of leaving Colonel Wallis early, and Lady Russell had fresh arranged all her evening engagements in order to wait on her. Anne had the whole history of all that such an evening could supply from Lady Russell. To her, its greatest interest must be, in having been very much talked of between her friend and Mr. Elliot; in having been wished for, regretted, and at the same time honoured for staying away in such a cause. Her kind, compassionate visits to this old schoolfellow, sick and reduced, seemed to have quite delighted Mr. Elliot. He thought her a most extraordinary young woman; in her temper, manners, mind, a model of female excellence. He could meet even Lady Russell in a discussion of her merits; and Anne could not be given to understand so much by her friend, could not know herself to be so highly rated by a sensible man, without many of those agreeable sensations which her friend meant to create.

Lady Russell was now perfectly decided in her opinion of Mr. Elliot. She was as much convinced of his meaning to gain Anne in time as of his deserving her, and was beginning to calculate the number of weeks which would free him from all the remaining restraints of widowhood, and leave him at liberty to exert his most open powers of pleasing. She would not speak to Anne with half the certainty she felt on the subject, she would venture on little more than hints of what might be hereafter, of a possible attachment on his side, of the desirableness of the alliance, supposing such attachment to be real and returned. Anne heard her, and made no violent exclamations; she only smiled, blushed, and gently shook her head. Anne had continuously reminded herself that Mr. Elliot was interested in Elizabeth, and she dare not allow that opinion to waver now.

"I am no match-maker, as you well know," said Lady Russell, "being much too well aware of the uncertainty of all human events and calculations. I only mean that if Mr. Elliot should some time hence pay his addresses to you, and if you should be disposed to accept him, I think there would be every possibility of your being happy together. A most suitable connection everybody must consider it, but I think it might be a very happy one."

"Mr. Elliot is an exceedingly agreeable man, and in many respects I think highly of him," said Anne, thinking of his dark good looks and the warm fan of mint-scented breath: features so different from the ones she craved; "but we should not suit."

Lady Russell let this pass, and only said in rejoinder, "I own that to be able to regard you as the future mistress of Kellynch, the future Lady Elliot, to look forward and see you occupying your dear mother's place, succeeding to all her rights, and all her popularity, as well as to all her virtues, would be the highest possible gratification to me. You are your mother's self in countenance and disposition; and if I might be allowed to fancy you such as she was, in situation and name, and home, presiding and blessing in the same spot, and only superior to her in being more highly valued! My dearest Anne, it would give me more delight than is often felt at my time of life!"

Anne was obliged to turn away, to rise, to walk to a distant table, and, leaning there in pretended employment, try to subdue the feelings this picture excited. For a few moments her imagination and her heart were bewitched. She was half-convinced that Mr. Elliot did not mean to marry Elizabeth, and the feeling inspired a great deal of conflict. The idea of becoming what her mother had been; of having the precious name of "Lady Elliot" first revived in herself; of being restored to Kellynch, calling it her home again, her home for ever, was a charm which she could not immediately resist. And it would not be a hardship to be the woman Mr. Elliot took to his marriage bed. True, he did not excite her as Captain Wentworth had, but he certainly excited her more than any other man had. He certainly did not feel as though he were her brother, like Captain Benwick. Lady Russell said not another word, willing to leave the matter to its own operation; and believing that, could Mr. Elliot at that moment with propriety have spoken for himself!—she believed, in short, what Anne did not believe. The same image of Mr. Elliot speaking for himself brought Anne to composure again. The charm of Kellynch and of "Lady Elliot" all faded away. She never could accept him. And it was not only that her feelings were still adverse to any man save one; her judgement, on a serious consideration of the possibilities of such a case was against Mr. Elliot.

Though they had now been acquainted a month, she could not be satisfied that she really knew his character. That he was a sensible man, an agreeable man, that he talked well, professed good opinions, seemed to judge properly and as a man of principle, this was all clear enough. He certainly knew what was right, nor could she fix on any one article of moral duty evidently transgressed; but yet she would have been afraid to answer for his conduct. She distrusted the past, if not the present. For one thing, his ambiguous treatment of the two elder Elliot sisters was curious and not something Anne was inclined to forgive. If he had meant to pursue Anne, why spend time with Elizabeth? Perhaps that could be overlooked due to the fact that he stopped seeking out Elizabeth once Anne arrived in Bath. However, the names which occasionally dropt of former associates, the allusions to former practices and pursuits, suggested suspicions not favourable of what he had been. She saw that there had been bad habits; that Sunday travelling had been a common thing; that there had been a period of his life (and probably not a short one) when he had been, at least, careless in all serious matters; and, though he might now think very differently, who could answer for the true sentiments of a clever, cautious man, grown old enough to appreciate a fair character? How could it ever be ascertained that his mind was truly cleansed?

Mr. Elliot was rational, discreet, polished, but he was not open. There was never any burst of feeling, any warmth of indignation or delight, at the evil or good of others. This, to Anne, was a decided imperfection. Her early impressions were incurable. She prized the frank, the open-hearted, the eager character beyond all others. Warmth and enthusiasm did captivate her still. She felt that she could so much more depend upon the sincerity of those who sometimes looked or said a careless or a hasty thing, than of those whose presence of mind never varied, whose tongue never slipped.

Mr. Elliot was too generally agreeable. Various as were the tempers in her father's house, he pleased them all. He endured too well, stood too well with every body. He had spoken to her with some degree of openness of Mrs. Clay; had appeared completely to see what Mrs. Clay was about, and to hold her in contempt; and yet Mrs. Clay found him as agreeable as any body.

Lady Russell saw either less or more than her young friend, for she saw nothing to excite distrust. She could not imagine a man more exactly what he ought to be than Mr. Elliot; nor did she ever enjoy a sweeter feeling than the hope of seeing him receive the hand of her beloved Anne in Kellynch church, in the course of the following autumn.

Chapter 18

It was the beginning of February; and Anne, having been a month in Bath, was growing very eager for news from Uppercross and Lyme. She wanted to hear much more than Mary had communicated. It was three weeks since she had heard at all. She only knew that Henrietta was at home again; and that Louisa, though considered to be recovering fast, was still in Lyme; and she was thinking of them all very intently one evening, when a thicker letter than usual from Mary was delivered to her; and, to quicken the pleasure and surprise, with Admiral and Mrs. Croft's compliments.

The Crofts must be in Bath! A circumstance to interest her. They were people whom her heart turned to very naturally.

"What is this?" cried Sir Walter. "The Crofts have arrived in Bath? The Crofts who rent Kellynch? What have they brought you?"

"A letter from Uppercross Cottage, Sir."

"Oh! those letters are convenient passports. They secure an introduction. I should have visited Admiral Croft, however, at any rate. I know what is due to my tenant."

Anne could listen no longer; she could not even have told how the poor Admiral's complexion escaped; her letter engrossed her. It had been begun several days back.

"February 1st.

"My dear Anne,—I make no apology for my silence, because I know how little people think of letters in such a place as Bath. You must be a great deal too happy to care for Uppercross, which, as you well know, affords little to write about. We have had a very dull Christmas; Mr. and Mrs. Musgrove have not had one dinner party all the holidays. I do not reckon the Hayters as anybody. The holidays, however, are over at last: I believe no children ever had such long ones. I am sure I had not. The house was cleared yesterday, except of the little Harvilles; but you will be surprised to hear they have never gone home. Mrs. Harville must be an odd mother to part with them so long. I do not understand it. They are not at all nice children, in my opinion; but Mrs. Musgrove seems to like them quite as well, if not better, than her grandchildren. What dreadful weather we have had! It may not be felt in Bath, with your nice pavements; but in the country it is of some consequence. I have not had a creature call on me since the second week in January, except Charles Hayter, who had been calling much oftener than was welcome. Between ourselves, I think it a great pity Henrietta did not remain at Lyme as long as Louisa; it would have kept her a little out of his way. The carriage is gone to-day, to bring Louisa and the Harvilles to-morrow. We are not asked to dine with them, however, till the day after, Mrs. Musgrove is so afraid of her being fatigued by the journey, which is not very likely, considering the care that will be taken of her; and it would be much more convenient to me to dine there to-morrow. I am glad you find Mr. Elliot so agreeable, and wish I could be acquainted with him too; but I have my usual luck: I am always out of the way when any thing desirable is going on; always the last of my family to be noticed. What an immense time Mrs. Clay has been staying with Elizabeth! Does she never mean to go away? But perhaps if she were to leave the room vacant, we might not be invited. Let me know what you think of this. I do not expect my children to be asked, you know. I can leave them at the Great House very well, for a month or six weeks. I have this moment heard that the Crofts are going to Bath almost immediately; they think the Admiral gouty. Charles heard it quite by chance; they have not had the civility to give me any notice, or of offering to take anything. I do not think they improve at all as neighbours. We see nothing of them, and this is really an instance of gross inattention. Charles joins me in love, and everything proper. Yours affectionately,

"Mary M—.

"I am sorry to say that I am very far from well; and Jemima has just told me that the butcher says there is a bad sore-throat very much about. I dare say I shall catch it; and my sore-throats, you know, are always worse than anybody's."

So ended the first part, which had been afterwards put into an envelope, containing nearly as much more.

"I kept my letter open, that I might send you word how Louisa bore her journey, and now I am extremely glad I did, having a great deal to add. In the first place, I had a note from Mrs. Croft yesterday, offering to convey anything to you; a very kind, friendly note indeed, addressed to me, just as it ought; I shall therefore be able to make my letter as long as I like. The Admiral does not seem very ill, and I sincerely hope Bath will do him all the good he wants. I shall be truly glad to have them back again. Our neighbourhood cannot spare such a pleasant family. But now for Louisa. I have something to communicate that will astonish you not a little. She and the Harvilles came on Tuesday very safely, and in the evening we went to ask her how she did, when we were rather surprised not to find Captain Benwick of the party, for he had been invited as well as the Harvilles; and what do you think was the reason? Neither more nor less than his being in love with Louisa, and not choosing to venture to Uppercross till he had had an answer from Mr. Musgrove; for it was all settled between him and her before she came away, and he had written to her father by Captain Harville. True, upon my honour! Are not you astonished? I shall be surprised at least if you ever received a hint of it, for I never did. Mrs. Musgrove protests solemnly that she knew nothing of the matter. We are all very well pleased, however, for though it is not equal to her marrying Captain Wentworth, it is infinitely better than Charles Hayter; and Mr. Musgrove has written his consent, and Captain Benwick is expected to-day. Mrs. Harville says her husband feels a good deal on his poor sister's account; but, however, Louisa is a great favourite with both. Indeed, Mrs.

Harville and I quite agree that we love her the better for having nursed her. Charles wonders what Captain Wentworth will say; but if you remember, I never thought him attached to Louisa; I never could see anything of it. And this is the end, you see, of Captain Benwick's being supposed to be an admirer of yours. How Charles could take such a thing into his head was always incomprehensible to me. I hope he will be more agreeable now. Certainly not a great match for Louisa Musgrove, but a million times better than marrying among the Hayters."

Mary need not have feared her sister's being in any degree prepared for the news. She had never in her life been more astonished. Captain Benwick and Louisa Musgrove! It was almost too wonderful for belief, and it was with the greatest effort that she could remain in the room, preserve an air of calmness, and answer the common questions of the moment. Happily for her, they were not many. Sir Walter wanted to know whether the Crofts travelled with four horses, and whether they were likely to be situated in such a part of Bath as it might suit Miss Elliot and himself to visit in; but had little curiosity beyond.

"How is Mary?" said Elizabeth; and without waiting for an answer, "And pray what brings the Crofts to Bath?"

"They come on the Admiral's account. He is thought to be gouty."

"Gout and decrepitude!" said Sir Walter. "Poor old gentleman."

"Have they any acquaintance here?" asked Elizabeth.

"I do not know; but I can hardly suppose that, at Admiral Croft's time of life, and in his profession, he should not have many acquaintance in such a place as this."

"I suspect," said Sir Walter coolly, "that Admiral Croft will be best known in Bath as the renter of Kellynch Hall. Elizabeth, may we venture to present him and his wife in Laura Place?"

"Oh, no! I think not. Situated as we are with Lady Dalrymple, cousins, we ought to be very careful not to embarrass her with acquaintance she might not approve. If we were not related, it would not signify; but as cousins, she would feel scrupulous as to any proposal of ours. We had better leave the Crofts to find their own level. There are several odd-looking men walking about here, who, I am told, are sailors. The Crofts will associate with them."

This was Sir Walter and Elizabeth's share of interest in the letter; when Mrs. Clay had paid her tribute of more decent attention, in an enquiry after Mrs. Charles Musgrove, and her fine little boys, Anne was at liberty.

In her own room, she tried to comprehend it. Well might Charles wonder how Captain Wentworth would feel! Perhaps he had quitted the field, had given Louisa up, had ceased to love, had found he did not love her. She could not endure the idea of treachery or levity, or anything akin to ill usage between him and his friend. She could not endure that such a friendship as theirs should be severed unfairly.

Captain Benwick and Louisa Musgrove! The high-spirited, joyous-talking Louisa Musgrove, and the dejected, thinking, feeling, reading, Captain Benwick, seemed each of them everything that would not suit the other. Their minds most dissimilar! Where could have been the attraction? The answer soon presented itself. It had been in situation. They had been thrown together several weeks; they had been living in the same small family party: since Henrietta's coming away, they must have been depending almost entirely on each other, and Louisa, just recovering from illness, had been in an interesting state, and Captain Benwick was not inconsolable. It was a situation that contained the perfect elements for a great eruption.

Anne's musings here were more than accurate. As it turned out, Captain Benwick was alarmed by the level of panic coursing through him as he abided in the same house with the ailing Louisa. He had been so far away from his own Fanny when she had been ill; it seemed obscene that he was so close in proximity now to a woman who meant next to nothing to him. Would that he could have switched positions in time and been with Fanny at the end.

He spent several days embroiled in these dark thoughts to such a point that he began to resent Louisa. These feelings drove him to sit for several hours each day in the chair that graced the corner of her sick room. There, he would prop his head up with one hand, rubbing his throbbing temple with shaking fingers, as he glared at the woman who dared claim the honour of having everyone she loved near when the one he had loved had been denied the same sad pleasure.

But the longer he sat and watched Louisa, the more it became apparent that she was healing. Before his eyes, her sallow skin gained colour and health. And then he began to notice her beauty: the way her flame-red hair spread out on her pillow; the delicate features of her face; the elegant slope of her neck; even, God forgive him, the way her breasts rose and fell with her slow, deep breaths.

When her green eyes opened for the first time, it was Captain Benwick who witnessed her return to consciousness. She had blinked her eyes once or twice as she tried to focus upon him, but when she realized who was in the room with her, she smiled beautifully at him and offered a simple, breathless, "Hello."

With that word, Captain Benwick fell deeply, desperately in love. He continued to sit in her room with her each day—reading to her from his favourite poets when she was awake, watching over her when she slept. But the chair that sat in the corner slowly edged forward over time until Captain Benwick conducted these activities with his knees pressed against her bed, and her warm, soft fingers covered by his hand.

The others in the house observed the change in Louisa and Benwick with smiles and raised eyebrows, and if the dangers of a young man wooing a young woman whilst a bed was in the room escaped their worry, such an oversight was remedied one day when Mrs. Harville was bringing the two their lunch. She discovered Captain Benwick absent from his chair and instead, stretched out atop Louisa in her bed. The young woman's hands were scandalously placed upon Captain Benwick's rump, and *his* hands were tunneling beneath Louisa's nightgown.

Mrs. Harville's shriek nearly brought down the roof, and it certainly brought her husband, who arrived as quickly as his injury would allow. It took Captain Harville but a moment to discern what had happened when he spied a chagrined Captain Benwick standing beside the bed in rumpled clothes and a young Louisa in bed with swollen lips and whisker burn on her cheeks. Captain Harville had chuckled, earning a sharp, rebuking glare from his wife, and they had both insisted that Captain Benwick marry Louisa right away, a notion that both young people readily agreed with.

And if Captain Benwick thought a moment beyond Louisa's *hello* about Anne Elliot, the woman he imagined he might be falling in love with, it was only with the warm regard of a friend. His romantic interest in her was a point which Anne had not been able to avoid suspecting before; and instead of drawing the same conclusion as Mary, from the present course of events, they served only to confirm the idea of his having felt some dawning of tenderness toward herself. She did not mean, however, to derive much more from it to gratify her vanity, than Mary might have allowed. She was persuaded that any tolerably pleasing young woman who had listened and seemed to feel for him would have received the same compliment. He had an affectionate heart. He must love somebody.

She saw no reason against their being happy. Louisa had fine naval fervour to begin with, and they would soon grow more alike. He would gain cheerfulness, and she would learn to be an enthusiast for Scott and Lord Byron; nay, that was probably learnt already; of course they had fallen in love over poetry. The idea of Louisa Musgrove turned into a person of literary taste, and sentimental reflection was amusing, but she had no doubt of its being so. The day at Lyme, the fall from the Cobb, might influence her health, her nerves, her courage, her character to the end of her life, as thoroughly as it appeared to have influenced her fate.

The conclusion of the whole was, that if the woman who had been sensible of Captain Wentworth's merits could be allowed to prefer another man, there was nothing in the engagement to excite lasting wonder; and if Captain Wentworth lost no friend by it, certainly nothing to be regretted. No, it was not regret which made Anne's heart beat in spite of herself, and brought the colour into her cheeks when she thought of Captain Wentworth unshackled and free. She had some feelings which she was ashamed to investigate. They were too much like joy, senseless joy!

She longed to see the Crofts; but when the meeting took place, it was evident that no rumour of the news had yet reached them. The visit of ceremony was paid and returned; and Louisa Musgrove was mentioned, and Captain Benwick, too, without even half a smile.

The Crofts had placed themselves in lodgings in Gay Street, perfectly to Sir Walter's satisfaction. He was not at all ashamed of the acquaintance, and did, in fact, think and talk a great deal more about the Admiral, than the Admiral ever thought or talked about him.

The Crofts knew quite as many people in Bath as they wished for, and considered their intercourse with the Elliots as a mere matter of form, and not in the least likely to afford them any pleasure. They brought with them their country habit of being almost always together. He was ordered to walk to keep off the gout, and Mrs. Croft seemed to go shares with him in everything, and to walk for her life to do him good. Anne saw them wherever she went. Lady Russell took her out in her carriage almost every morning, and she never failed to think of them, and never failed to see them. Knowing their feelings as she did, it was a most attractive picture of happiness to her. She always watched them as long as she could, delighted to fancy she understood what they might be talking of, as they walked along in happy independence, or equally delighted to see the Admiral's hearty shake of the hand when he encountered an old friend, and observe their eagerness of conversation when occasionally forming into a little knot of the navy, Mrs. Croft looking as intelligent and keen as any of the officers around her.

Anne was too much engaged with Lady Russell to be often walking herself; but it so happened that one morning, about a week or ten days after the Croft's arrival, it suited her best to leave her friend, or her friend's carriage, in the lower part of the town, and return alone to Camden Place, and in walking up Milsom Street she had the good fortune to meet with the Admiral. He was standing by himself at a printshop window, with his hands behind him, in earnest contemplation of some print, and she not only might have passed him unseen, but was obliged to touch as well as address him before she could catch his notice. When he did perceive and acknowledge her, however, it was done with all his usual frankness and good humour. "Ha! is it you? Thank you, thank you. This is treating me like a friend. Here I am, you see, staring at a picture. I can never get by this shop without stopping. But what a thing here is, by way of a boat! Do look at it. Did you ever see the like? What queer fellows your fine painters must be, to think that anybody would venture their lives in such a shapeless old cockleshell as that? And yet here are two gentlemen stuck up in it mightily at their ease, and looking about them at the rocks and mountains, as if they were not to be upset the next moment, which they certainly must be. I wonder where that boat was built!" (laughing heartily); "I would not venture over a horsepond in it. Well," (turning away), "now, where are you bound? Can I go anywhere for you, or with you? Can I be of any use?"

"None, I thank you, unless you will give me the pleasure of your company the little way our road lies together. I am going home."

"That I will, with all my heart, and farther, too. Yes, yes we will have a snug walk together, and I have something to tell you as we go along. There, take my arm; that's right; I do not feel comfortable if I have not a woman there. Lord! what a boat it is!" taking a last look at the picture, as they began to be in motion.

"Did you say that you had something to tell me, sir?"

"Yes, I have, presently. But here comes a friend, Captain Brigden; I shall only say, 'How d'ye do?' as we pass, however. I shall not stop. 'How d'ye do?' Brigden stares to see anybody with me but my wife. She, poor soul, is tied by the leg. She has a blister on one of her heels, as large as a three-shilling piece. If you look across the street, you will see Admiral Brand coming down and his brother. Shabby fellows, both of them! I am glad they are not on this side of the way. Sophy cannot bear them. They played me a pitiful trick once: got away with some of my best men. I will tell you the whole story another time. There comes old Sir Archibald Drew and his grandson. Look, he sees us; he kisses his hand to you; he takes you for my wife. Ah! the peace has come too soon for that younker. Poor old Sir Archibald! How do you like Bath, Miss Elliot? It suits us very well. We are always meeting with some old friend or other; the streets full of them every morning; sure to have plenty of chat; and then we get away from them all, and shut ourselves in our lodgings, and draw in our chairs, and are snug as if we were at Kellynch, ay, or as we used to be even at North Yarmouth and Deal. We do not like our lodgings here the worse, I can tell you, for putting us in mind of those we first had at North Yarmouth. The wind blows through one of the cupboards just in the same way."

When they were got a little farther, Anne ventured to press again for what he had to communicate. She hoped when clear of Milsom Street to have her curiosity gratified; but she was still obliged to wait, for the Admiral had made up his mind not to begin till they had gained the greater space and quiet of Belmont; and as she was not really Mrs. Croft, she must let him have his own way. As soon as they were fairly ascending Belmont, he began—

"Well, now you shall hear something that will surprise you. But first of all, you must tell me the name of the young lady I am going to talk about. That young lady, you know, that we have all been so concerned for. The Miss Musgrove, that all this has been happening to. Her Christian name: I always forget her Christian name."

Anne had been ashamed to appear to comprehend so soon as she really did; but now she could safely suggest the name of "Louisa."

"Ay, ay, Miss Louisa Musgrove, that is the name. I wish young ladies had not such a number of fine Christian names. I should never be out if they were all Sophys, or something of that sort. Well, this Miss Louisa, we all thought, you know, was to marry Frederick. He was courting her week after week. The only wonder was, what they could be waiting for, till the business at Lyme came; then, indeed, it was clear enough that they must wait till her brain was set to right. But even then there was something odd in their way of going on. Instead of staying at Lyme, he went off to Plymouth, and then he went off to see Edward. When we came back from Minehead he was gone down to Edward's, and there he has been ever since. We have seen nothing of him since November. Even Sophy could not understand it. But now, the matter has taken the strangest turn of all; for this young lady, the same Miss Musgrove, instead of being to marry Frederick, is to marry James Benwick. You know James Benwick."

"A little. I am a little acquainted with Captain Benwick."

"Well, she is to marry him. Nay, most likely they are married already, for I do not know what they should wait for."

"I thought Captain Benwick a very pleasing young man," said Anne, "and I understand that he bears an excellent character."

"Oh! yes, yes, there is not a word to be said against James Benwick. He is only a commander, it is true, made last summer, and these are bad times for getting on, but he has not another fault that I know of. An excellent, good-hearted fellow, I assure you; a very active, zealous officer too, which is more than you would think for, perhaps, for that soft sort of manner does not do him justice."

"Indeed you are mistaken there, sir; I should never augur want of spirit from Captain Benwick's manners. I thought them particularly pleasing, and I will answer for it, they would generally please."

"Well, well, ladies are the best judges; but James Benwick is rather too piano for me; and though very likely it is all our partiality, Sophy and I cannot help thinking Frederick's manners better than his. There is something about Frederick more to our taste."

Anne was caught. She had only meant to oppose the too common idea of spirit and gentleness being incompatible with each other, not at all to represent Captain Benwick's manners as the very best that could possibly be, much less better than Frederick's—Captain Wentworth's; and, after a little hesitation, she was beginning to say, "I was not entering into any comparison of the two friends," but the Admiral interrupted her with—

"And the thing is certainly true. It is not a mere bit of gossip. We have it from Frederick himself. His sister had a letter from him yesterday, in which he tells us of it, and he had just had it in a letter from Harville, written upon the spot, from Uppercross. I fancy they are all at Uppercross."

This was an opportunity which Anne could not resist; she said, therefore, "I hope, Admiral, I hope there is nothing in the style of Captain Wentworth's letter to make you and Mrs. Croft particularly uneasy. It did seem, last autumn, as if there were an attachment between him and Louisa Musgrove; but I hope it may be understood to have worn out on each side equally, and without violence. I hope his letter does not breathe the spirit of an ill-used man."

"Not at all, not at all; there is not an oath or a murmur from beginning to end."

Anne looked down to hide her smile.

"No, no; Frederick is not a man to whine and complain; he has too much spirit for that. If the girl likes another man better, it is very fit she should have him."

"Certainly. But what I mean is, that I hope there is nothing in Captain Wentworth's manner of writing to make you suppose he thinks himself ill-used by his friend, which might appear, you know, without its being absolutely said. I should be very sorry that such a friendship as has subsisted between him and Captain Benwick should be destroyed, or even wounded, by a circumstance of this sort."

"Yes, yes, I understand you. But there is nothing at all of that nature in the letter. He does not give the least fling at Benwick; does not so much as say, 'I wonder at it, I have a reason of my own for wondering at it.' No, you would not guess, from his way of writing, that he had ever thought of this Miss (what's her name?) for himself. He very handsomely hopes they will be happy together; and there is nothing very unforgiving in that, I think."

Anne did not receive the perfect conviction which the Admiral meant to convey, but it would have been useless to press the enquiry farther. She therefore satisfied herself with common-place remarks or quiet attention, and the Admiral had it all his own way.

"Poor Frederick!" said he at last. "Now he must begin all over again with somebody else. I think we must get him to Bath. Sophy must write, and beg him to come to Bath. Here are pretty girls enough, I am sure. It would be of no use to go to Uppercross again, for that other Miss Musgrove, I find, is bespoke by her cousin, the young parson. Do not you think, Miss Elliot, we had better try to get him to Bath?"

Anne must have agreed, for the Admiral patted her hand affectionately and launched directly into a different topic, most likely about his beloved Sophy or how something else should *involve* his beloved Sophy. Anne had trouble paying attention. The idea of Frederick—Captain Wentworth—coming to Bath had snared all capability for complex thought.

It had been difficult enough being near to him when he was actively seeking another's hand. Whatever would she do if he came to Bath as a free man? She *prayed* he came to Bath as a free man.

She made her excuses to the Admiral, and he gallantly dropped her off at home. Anne went directly to her room, not pausing to say hello to her father, sister, or Mrs. Clay—the pressing need for solitude overriding even the most basic manners.

When she arrived at her room, she shut the door and leaned against it, her breath whooshing out of her in a sigh as every bone in her body sagged with weariness. She was so *tired*. Tired of being alone, tired of having her needs go unmet, tired of having her love life be the focus of everyone's speculation—just tired.

Unbidden her eyes landed on her bed, and her mind pictured the box of Frederick's letters that she knew were hidden underneath. Longing stole through her, and she resisted as long as she could before she trudged over to the bed, kneeled down on the floor, and pulled the box toward her.

With a steeling breath, Anne opened the box while still kneeling on the unforgiving floor, and Frederick's faint scent wafted toward her from the collection of sentiment inside. With shaking fingers, she sifted through the yellowing letters to the very bottom where she knew she would find his last missive along with the present that had accompanied it.

Her fingers encountered the cool brass first, and she pulled forth the small telescope. She warily eyed the little folded square of paper that was attached to the metal with a sturdy knot while setting the box down on the floor without looking.

She knew what the letter said without having to read it, but she undid the knot with one pull in the right place and unfolded the letter anyway.

Do not stop looking for me, for my heart is never far from yours.
Love,
Frederick

He had sent it after she had broken their engagement, on the day that he left for the sea. Anne had taken to her bed and held the telescope to her chest as she cried without end for days upon days.

And, truth be told, she had obeyed his plea. Never once had she stopped looking for him: around every corner, at every party, during every holiday.

"I have never stopped loving you," she whispered. The lines of Frederick's script blurred, and Anne blinked back tears as she tried to stay the tide of longing for him—for his touch, his kiss, his love—that threatened to sweep her away. "Please." She closed her eyes and held the telescope against her cheek. "Come back to me."

Chapter 19

While Admiral Croft was taking this walk with Anne, and express-
ing his wish of getting Captain Wentworth to Bath, Captain
Wentworth was already on his way thither, and he was very confused as to why he was. He hoped the timing of his journey—
just after finding out he was a free man with Louisa's engagement
announcement—was not as suspicious to others as it was to himself. He was certain—that is to say, not certain at all—that he was
coming to Bath for very good reasons, none of which involved
Anne Elliot or the way their last encounter and its aftermath had
been foremost in his thoughts in her absence. An absence, by
the by, that carried the sharp sting of new heartbreak, a prob-
lem Captain Wentworth had not anticipated. His much-needed
distance, a gift of time, seemed to be a disappearing commod-
ity, and so it was that before Mrs. Croft had written requesting
Captain Wentworth's presence, he was arrived, and the very next
time Anne walked out, she saw him.

Mr. Elliot was attending his two cousins and Mrs. Clay. They
were in Milsom Street. It began to rain, not much, but enough to
make shelter desirable for women, and quite enough to make it very
desirable for Miss Elliot to have the advantage of being conveyed
home in Lady Dalrymple's carriage, which was seen waiting at a
little distance; she, Anne, and Mrs. Clay, therefore, turned into
Molland's, while Mr. Elliot stepped to Lady Dalrymple, to request
her assistance. He soon joined them again, successful, of course;
Lady Dalrymple would be most happy to take them home, and
would call for them in a few minutes.

Her ladyship's carriage was a barouche, and did not hold more than four with any comfort. Miss Carteret was with her mother; consequently it was not reasonable to expect accommodation for all the three Camden Place ladies. There could be no doubt as to Miss Elliot. Whoever suffered inconvenience, she must suffer none, but it occupied a little time to settle the point of civility between the other two. The rain was a mere trifle, and Anne was most sincere in preferring a walk with Mr. Elliot. But the rain was also a mere trifle to Mrs. Clay; she would hardly allow it even to drop at all, and her boots were so thick! much thicker than Miss Anne's; and, in short, her civility rendered her quite as anxious to be left to walk with Mr. Elliot as Anne could be, and it was discussed between them with a generosity so polite and so determined, that the others were obliged to settle it for them; Miss Elliot maintaining that Mrs. Clay had a little cold already, and Mr. Elliot deciding on appeal, that his cousin Anne's boots were rather the thickest.

It was fixed accordingly, that Mrs. Clay should be of the party in the carriage; and they had just reached this point, when Anne, as she sat near the window, descried, most decidedly and distinctly, Captain Wentworth walking down the street. Wherever he had come from, the rain must have already arrived, for his blonde hair was slicked back and drying in waves, and his breeches were just damp enough that they stuck to his thighs and outlined every cord of muscle. Anne's eyes caressed every dip of his legs as they flexed and relaxed with his hurried stride, and her eyes traveled upward until she noticed that his legs were not the only part of his lower body hugged by wet fabric. Even from a distance, Anne could see Frederick's member in vivid detail. She jumped and forced herself to jerk her eyes from their target, though such a move took a good deal of fortitude.

Her start, and the instant arousal that inspired it, was perceptible only to herself; but she instantly felt that she was the greatest simpleton in the world, the most unaccountable and absurd! For a few minutes she saw nothing before her; it was all confusion. She was lost, and when she had scolded back her senses, she found the others still waiting for the carriage, and Mr. Elliot (always obliging) just setting off for Union Street on a commission of Mrs. Clay's.

She now felt a great inclination to go to the outer door; she wanted to see if it rained. Why was she to suspect herself of another motive? Captain Wentworth—*not* Frederick—must be out of sight. She left her seat, she would go; one half of her should not be always so much wiser than the other half, or always suspecting the other of being worse than it was. She would see if it rained. She was sent back, however, in a moment by the entrance of Captain Wentworth himself, among a party of gentlemen and ladies, evidently his acquaintance, and whom he must have joined a little below Milsom Street. He was more obviously struck and confused by the sight of her than she had ever observed before; he looked quite red.

Anne could not resist, she found her gaze drifting south and her lips parting. Just a peek, she promised herself. But when her eyes reached their destination, she was shocked to find the state of things in his breeches to have changed. Even had the cloth of his breeches *not* been wet, anyone could have seen that Captain Wentworth was becoming blatantly aroused at an alarming rate. Most fortunately for Anne, that was not the case, and the wet fabric made his arousal even more pronounced. From the tops of her eyes, she spied Captain Wentworth dip his head, apparently for the purpose of seeing what she was staring at, for he immediately took a stumbling step to the side and leaned against the wall behind a barrel, effectively cutting off the view of his body below the waist from everyone in the room, including Anne. He then crossed his arms over his chest and obviously tried to appear relaxed only to uncross his arms and begin to fidget with the buttons of his coat.

For the first time, since their renewed acquaintance, she felt that she was betraying the least sensibility of the two. She had the advantage of him in the preparation of the last few moments. All the overpowering, blinding, bewildering, first effects of strong surprise were over with her. Still, however, she had enough to feel! It was agitation, pain, pleasure, a something between delight and misery.

For several minutes, they looked at each other without looking at each other, and then she saw him heave a great sigh, push off from the wall, and begin to walk toward her. A quick flick of her eyes southward, and she gained the disappointing knowledge that Frederick had regained control of himself. Her heart beat sped like a racing horse, and she wracked her brain for something—anything—intelligent to say to him as he obviously meant to converse with her. He stopped when he stood before her, and Anne could see none of the rest of the room through the bulk of his height and shoulders. It would not have mattered if the whole of the room was before her eyes anyway, for she could not look away from his face. He watched her warily, as though she may spook at any moment. He spoke to her, though what he said, Anne could not force her mind to interpret, and then turned away, staring at a point over her shoulder, which Anne knew was merely a blank wall. The character of his manner was embarrassment. She could not have called it either cold or friendly, or anything so certainly as embarrassed.

After a short interval, however, his eyes drifted back towards her, and he spoke again. Mutual enquiries on common subjects passed: neither of them, probably, much the wiser for what they heard, and Anne continuing fully sensible of his being less at ease than formerly. They had by dint of being so very much together, got to speak to each other with a considerable portion of apparent indifference and calmness; but he could not do it now. Time had changed him, or Louisa had changed him. There was consciousness of some sort or other. He looked very well, not as if he had been suffering in health or spirits, and he talked of Uppercross, of the Musgroves, nay, even of Louisa, and had even a momentary look of his own arch significance as he named her; but yet it was Captain Wentworth not comfortable, not easy, not able to feign that he was.

It did not surprise, but it grieved Anne to observe that Elizabeth would not know him. She saw that he saw Elizabeth, that Elizabeth saw him, that there was complete internal recognition on each side; she was convinced that he was ready to be acknowledged as an acquaintance, expecting it, and she had the pain of seeing her sister turn away with unalterable coldness. Frederick's only indication that he had seen the snub was a ticking of the muscle along his jaw and an almost imperceptible clenching of his fists. But from that moment, the conversation became even more strained until he and Anne simply stared at one another for several moments without talking.

Lady Dalrymple's carriage, for which Miss Elliot was growing very impatient, now drew up; the servant came in to announce it. Anne sighed in relief, knowing that the awkward encounter with Frederick—curses, *Captain Wentworth*—was coming to a close, and she heard him echo the sigh heartily. Anne nodded toward him briefly, and he stepped aside to allow her to pass him and rejoin her party. As she skirted past him, his scent, enhanced by the rain he had walked through, wafted over her, and her relief that their conversation had ended was replaced by something very akin to disappointment.

It was beginning to rain again, and altogether there was a delay, and a bustle, and a talking, which must make all the little crowd in the shop understand that Lady Dalrymple was calling to convey Miss Elliot. At last Miss Elliot and her friend, unattended but by the servant, (for there was no cousin returned), were walking off; and Captain Wentworth, watching them pair off and leave the shop for the carriage with a dark expression marring his handsome features, suddenly launched forward. His boots fell upon the boarded floor with ominous thuds, and in moments, he was by Anne's side. He paused a moment to gift them all with censorious looks before he turned again to Anne, and by manner, rather than words, was offering his services to her. He extended her his arm and raised both of his brows.

Heat suffused Anne's cheeks, and she did not think she imagined the gasp of outrage that had come from the vicinity of her sister. Yes, she had been snubbed by the rest of her party and had no escort, but she was used to such things. After all, she was only Anne, practically a spinster and nothing to worry about. Anne stared at Frederick's arm for what seemed like an eternity, longing more than anything to slip her hand through the crook of his elbow and allow him to draw her close. The eyes of her party began to heat the back of Anne's neck, and she knew without looking that they were watching the two of them with curious shock and anticipation. "I am much obliged to you," was her answer, "but I am not going with them. The carriage would not accommodate so many. I walk: I prefer walking."

His arm did not waver, but it did flex. "But it rains." His voice was almost a growl.

"Oh! very little. Nothing that I regard."

After a moment's pause, Frederick's arm dropped to his side. Anne could no longer look at him, and he took a deep breath before he said: "Though I came only yesterday, I have equipped myself properly for Bath already, you see," (pointing to a new umbrella that was perched beside the door); "I wish you would make use of it, if you are determined to walk; though I think it would be more prudent to let me get you a chair."

The pressure of the others' eyes was still upon her. She worried that if she accepted *anything* from Frederick—*Captain Wentworth*—her heart would betray her, and their secret history would be revealed. She took a fortifying breath and refused him as kindly as she could. She was very much obliged to him, but declined it all, repeating her conviction, that the rain would come to nothing at present, and adding, "I am only waiting for Mr. Elliot. He will be here in a moment, I am sure."

She had hardly spoken the words when Mr. Elliot walked in. Captain Wentworth recollected him perfectly. There was no difference between him and the man who had stood on the steps at Lyme, admiring Anne as she passed, except in the air and look and manner of the privileged relation and friend, and if Captain Wentworth was not mistaken, a bit more. He came in with eagerness, appeared to see and think only of her, apologised for his stay, was grieved to have kept her waiting, and anxious to get her away without further loss of time and before the rain increased; and in another moment they walked off together, her arm under his, a gentle and embarrassed glance, and a "Good morning to you!" being all that she had time for, as she passed away.

Captain Wentworth clenched and unclenched his hand, the hand belonging to the arm that had *almost* had the privilege of escorting Anne, and did not bother trying not to watch them leave until they were no longer visible. As soon as they were out of sight, the ladies of Captain Wentworth's party began talking of them.

"Mr. Elliot does not dislike his cousin, I fancy?"

Something in the back of Captain Wentworth's neck snapped painfully as he jerked his head around quickly to stare at the woman who had spoken.

"Oh! no, that is clear enough. One can guess what will happen there. He is always with them; half lives in the family, I believe. What a very good-looking man!"

Foreboding settling like a heavy weight in his stomach, Captain Wentworth stared out the door again, though Anne and Mr. Elliot had long disappeared. *Had* Mr. Elliot been good-looking? Captain Wentworth cursed internally. He had not been able to look away from Anne long enough to give the man even a cursory glance.

"Yes, and Miss Atkinson, who dined with him once at the Wallises, says he is the most agreeable man she ever was in company with."

"She is pretty, I think; Anne Elliot; very pretty, when one comes to look at her. It is not the fashion to say so, but I confess I admire her more than her sister."

Pretty? Captain Wentworth had to hastily close his mouth to contain the noise of derision that had tried to escape him. Anne Elliot was *breathtaking*, and these women were simpletons. One did not need to look at her close at all to determine so, either. Her beauty struck him from across crowded rooms. He had wanted her instantly upon sight mere moments ago.

"Oh! so do I."

"And so do I. No comparison. But the men are all wild after Miss Elliot. Anne is too delicate for them."

This time, there was no stopping the noise that came from deep within Captain Wentworth's chest—a sound between a chuckle and a growl. "Anne is no more delicate than I am," he said before he could stop himself.

The eyes of each lady in his party popped wide open, and they all stared at him, aghast. Captain Wentworth groaned as he realized two things: he had just called Anne Elliot by her Christian name in mixed public, and none of them would realize that what he had just said was meant to be a compliment.

Knowing this was one of those situations that was irredeemable, Captain Wentworth bowed curtly to the party, and retreated without another word, hoping the cold drizzle would bring him to his senses.

Anne would have been particularly obliged to her cousin, if he would have walked by her side all the way to Camden Place, without saying a word. She had never found it so difficult to listen to him, though nothing could exceed his solicitude and care, and though his subjects were principally such as were wont to be always interesting: praise, warm, just, and discriminating, of Lady Russell, and insinuations highly rational against Mrs. Clay. But just now she could think only of Captain Wentworth. She could not understand his present feelings, whether he were really suffering much from disappointment or not; and till that point were settled, she could not be quite herself.

She hoped to be wise and reasonable in time; but alas! alas! she must confess to herself that she was not wise yet.

Another circumstance very essential for her to know, was how long he meant to be in Bath; he had not mentioned it, or she could not recollect it. He might be only passing through. But it was more probable that he should be come to stay. In that case, so liable as every body was to meet every body in Bath, Lady Russell would in all likelihood see him somewhere. Would she recollect him? How would it all be?

She had already been obliged to tell Lady Russell that Louisa Musgrove was to marry Captain Benwick. It had cost her something to encounter Lady Russell's surprise; and now, if she were by any chance to be thrown into company with Captain Wentworth, her imperfect knowledge of the matter might add another shade of prejudice against him.

The following morning Anne was out with her friend, and for the first hour, in an incessant and fearful sort of watch for him in vain; but at last, in returning down Pulteney Street, she distinguished him on the right hand pavement at such a distance as to have him in view the greater part of the street. There were many other men about him, many groups walking the same way, but there was no mistaking the body she knew by heart. She looked instinctively at Lady Russell; but not from any mad idea of her recognising him so soon as she did herself. No, it was not to be supposed that Lady Russell would perceive him till they were nearly opposite. She looked at her however, from time to time, anxiously; and when the moment approached which must point him out, though not daring to look again (for her own countenance she knew was unfit to be seen), she was yet perfectly conscious of Lady Russell's eyes being turned exactly in the direction for him—of her being, in short, intently observing him. She could thoroughly comprehend the sort of fascination he must possess over Lady Russell's mind, the difficulty it must be for her to withdraw her eyes, the astonishment she must be feeling that eight or nine years should have passed over him, and in foreign climes and in active service too, without robbing him of one personal grace!

At last, Lady Russell drew back her head. "Now, how would she speak of him?"

"You will wonder," said she, "what has been fixing my eye so long; but I was looking after some window-curtains, which Lady Alicia and Mrs. Frankland were telling me of last night. They described the drawing-room window-curtains of one of the houses on this side of the way, and this part of the street, as being the handsomest and best hung of any in Bath, but could not recollect the exact number, and I have been trying to find out which it could be; but I confess I can see no curtains hereabouts that answer their description."

Anne sighed and blushed and smiled, in pity and disdain, either at her friend or herself. The part which provoked her most, was that in all this waste of foresight and caution, she should have lost the right moment for seeing whether he saw them.

A day or two passed without producing anything. The theatre or the rooms, where he was most likely to be, were not fashionable enough for the Elliots, whose evening amusements were solely in the elegant stupidity of private parties, in which they were getting more and more engaged; and Anne, wearied of such a state of stagnation, sick of knowing nothing, and fancying herself stronger because her strength was not tried, was quite impatient for the concert evening. It was a concert for the benefit of a person patronised by Lady Dalrymple. Of course they must attend. It was really expected to be a good one, and Captain Wentworth was very fond of music. If she could only have a few minutes conversation with him again, she fancied she should be satisfied; and as to the power of addressing him, she felt all over courage if the opportunity occurred. Elizabeth had turned from him, Lady Russell overlooked him; her nerves were strengthened by these circumstances; she felt that she owed him attention. He was a man, for heaven's sake, and a good one. He deserved to be treated as such, and if Anne was the only one from her family to do so, she would simply have to make up for the others' lack in her own actions.

She had once partly promised Mrs. Smith to spend the evening with her; but in a short hurried call she excused herself and put it off, with the more decided promise of a longer visit on the morrow. Mrs. Smith gave a most good-humoured acquiescence.

"By all means," said she; "only tell me all about it, when you do come. Who is your party?"

Anne named them all. Mrs. Smith made no reply; but when she was leaving her said, and with an expression half serious, half arch, "Well, I heartily wish your concert may answer; and do not fail me to-morrow if you can come; for I begin to have a foreboding that I may not have many more visits from you."

Anne was startled and confused; but after standing in a moment's suspense, was obliged, and not sorry to be obliged, to hurry away.

Chapter 20

Sir Walter, his two daughters, and Mrs. Clay, were the earliest of all their party at the rooms in the evening; and as Lady Dalrymple must be waited for, they took their station by one of the fires in the Octagon Room. But hardly were they so settled, when the door opened again, and Captain Wentworth walked in alone. He cut a fine figure in his evening clothes; the dark fabric of his coat only served to set off his light hair and eyes even more than usual. The cut of his breeches accentuated the strength of his body. Anne could not take her eyes off of him, and as she was the nearest to him, and making yet a little advance, she instantly spoke. He was preparing only to bow and pass on, but her gentle "How do you do?" brought him out of the straight line with a visible jolt to his body to stand near her, and make enquiries in return, in spite of the formidable father and sister in the back ground. Their being in the back ground was a support to Anne; she knew nothing of their looks, and felt equal to everything which she believed right to be done.

While they were speaking, a whispering between her father and Elizabeth caught her ear. She could not distinguish, but she must guess the subject; and on Captain Wentworth's making a distant bow, she comprehended that her father had judged so well as to give him that simple acknowledgement of acquaintance, and she was just in time by a side glance to see a slight curtsey from Elizabeth herself. This, though late, and reluctant, and ungracious, was yet better than nothing, and her spirits improved.

After talking, however, of the weather, and Bath, and the concert, their conversation began to flag, and so little was said at last, that she was expecting him to go every moment, but he did not; he seemed in no hurry to leave her; and she was becoming distracted by his close presence. Though in evening clothes, he still carried the ever-present scent of the sea—salt air and sunshine—and he was standing so close, his body giving off great waves of heat, that Anne feared she was flushing bright red. If she were honest, she would confess to herself that it was not the heat of his body that made her red, but the heat that his body inspired in her own. They smiled at each other awkwardly for a few moments before, presently, with renewed spirit, with a little smile, a little glow, he said—

"I have hardly seen you since our day at Lyme. I am afraid you must have suffered from the shock, and the more from its not overpowering you at the time."

She assured him that she had not.

"It was a frightful hour," said he, "a frightful day!" and he passed his hand, with fingers that trembled, across his eyes, as if the remembrance were still too painful, but in a moment, half smiling again, added, "The day has produced some effects however; has had some consequences which must be considered as the very reverse of frightful. When you had the presence of mind to suggest that Benwick would be the properest person to fetch a surgeon, you could have little idea of his being eventually one of those most concerned in her recovery."

"Certainly I could have none. But it appears—I should hope it would be a very happy match. There are on both sides good principles and good temper."

"Yes," said he, looking not exactly forward; "but there, I think, ends the resemblance. With all my soul I wish them happy, and rejoice over every circumstance in favour of it. They have no difficulties to contend with at home, no opposition, no caprice, no delays. The Musgroves are behaving like themselves, most honourably and kindly, only anxious with true parental hearts to promote their daughter's comfort. All this is much, very much in favour of their happiness; more than perhaps—"

He stopped. A sudden recollection seemed to occur, and to give him some taste of that emotion which was reddening Anne's cheeks and fixing her eyes on the ground. After clearing his throat, however, he proceeded thus—

"I confess that I do think there is a disparity, too great a disparity, and in a point no less essential than mind. I regard Louisa Musgrove as a very amiable, sweet-tempered girl, and not deficient in understanding, but Benwick is something more. He is a clever man, a reading man; and I confess, that I do consider his attaching himself to her with some surprise. Had it been the effect of gratitude, had he learnt to love her, because he believed her to be preferring him, it would have been another thing. But I have no reason to suppose it so. It seems, on the contrary, to have been a perfectly spontaneous, untaught feeling on his side, and this surprises me. A man like him, in his situation! with a heart pierced, wounded, almost broken! Fanny Harville was a very superior creature, and his attachment to her was indeed attachment. A man does not recover from such a devotion of the heart to such a woman. He ought not; he does not."

Either from the consciousness, however, that his friend had recovered, or from other consciousness, he went no farther; and Anne who, in spite of the agitated voice in which the latter part had been uttered, and in spite of all the various noises of the room, the almost ceaseless slam of the door, and ceaseless buzz of persons walking through, had distinguished every word, was struck, gratified, confused, and beginning to breathe very quick, and feel an hundred things in a moment. It was impossible for her to enter on such a subject; and yet, after a pause, feeling the necessity of speaking, and having not the smallest wish for a total change, she only deviated so far as to say—

"You were a good while at Lyme, I think?"

"About a fortnight. I could not leave it till Louisa's doing well was quite ascertained. I had been too deeply concerned in the mischief to be soon at peace. It had been my doing, solely mine. She would not have been obstinate if I had not been weak. The country round Lyme is very fine. I walked and rode a great deal; and the more I saw, the more I found to admire."

"I should very much like to see Lyme again," said Anne.

"Indeed! I should not have supposed that you could have found anything in Lyme to inspire such a feeling. The horror and distress you were involved in, the stretch of mind, the wear of spirits! I should have thought your last impressions of Lyme must have been strong disgust."

"The last hours were certainly very painful," replied Anne; "but when pain is over, the remembrance of it often becomes a pleasure. One does not love a place the less for having suffered in it, unless it has been all suffering, nothing but suffering, which was by no means the case at Lyme. We were only in anxiety and distress during the last two hours, and previously there had been a great deal of enjoyment. So much novelty and beauty! I have travelled so little, that every fresh place would be interesting to me; but there is real beauty at Lyme; and in short" (with a faint blush at some recollections, his question about Benwick and the resulting feel of his body pressed against her the most prevalent), "altogether my impressions of the place are very agreeable."

His green and blue eyes roamed her face for several seconds, and Anne felt the sting of her blush increase under his scrutiny. He cleared his throat. "About that—" He paused, and Anne knew from instinct that he had gleaned her thoughts and meant to address his conduct that late, dark night. Anne straightened, prepared to stop him, but he continued. "I fear I have much more than Louisa's accident to apologize for." He stepped closer and lowered his voice. "Can you ever forgive me for accosting you so?"

Anne felt her eyes widen. "C-Captain Wentworth—"

"I was quite overcome by the idea of you and my dear friend as a couple."

The protest Anne had been ready to voice died upon her tongue as her heart twisted at the unexpected declaration. Propriety demanded she accept his apology and move on. Propriety did not win. "Why?" she asked so boldly she surprised them both.

He drew back slightly at her startling volume, and from the corners of her eyes, Anne saw several people within speaking distance pause in their conversations and eye her curiously. Captain Wentworth chuckled self-consciously, offered them all polite smiles, and turned his attention back to Anne. He stepped closer and barely above the sound of a whisper, he said, "I wish I knew."

Anne felt her brows draw together. "That is not good enough."

His brows rose and several awkward beats of silence ensued before his breath left him in a whoosh. "Of course it is not." A smile tilted one side of his lips, and he looked at a spot over her shoulder as he brought one hand up to rub the back of his neck. Anne's gaze was snagged by the way his shoulder and arm flexed with the movement, but his next words were enough to draw her attention from even that. "You never did let me get away with anything." His arm fell back to his side, and his eyes met hers with a sudden intensity. "I could not bear to think of you as Benwick's, because I cannot bear to think of you as anyone else's but mine."

As his cool eyes burned her, Anne felt every part of her body seize and release in rapid succession. She wondered for a moment if her legs would fail her, and she would slump to the floor. His unforgiving gaze demanded she speak, and she forced herself to lick suddenly dry, aching lips. "I f-forgive you."

The sound of her words was so small, she doubted he heard them, but his eyes drifted shut, and she knew he had interpreted the all-encompassing meaning of the simple statement. She forgave him—for everything: for having to watch him court another woman, for the coldness of his manner since they had been reunited, for his unkind words after their first meeting. His honest, heart-felt declaration went a long way toward healing the hurt he had caused in recent months.

When his eyes opened again, they were flooded with conflicting emotions, and Anne knew in that moment that he wished he could say the same back to her. But he could not.

The hurt she had caused him eight years ago was still present in the tumultuous depths of his sea-coloured gaze. She nearly leapt with surprise when she felt his hand grip hers gently. Though they both wore gloves, the heat of his skin burned through the barriers. He held the hand that was hidden from the rest of the crowd by her body, and his thumb slowly caressed the inside of her wrist. "Thank you," he whispered.

Anne knew she was staring at his lips like a wanton woman, but she could focus on nothing else. The feel of his glove-covered hand upon the delicate skin of her wrist was slowly driving her to madness. As she ceased all thought, the entrance door was flung open again, and both of them jumped. Captain Wentworth dropped her hand as a guilty flush crossed his face, and the very party appeared for whom they were waiting. "Lady Dalrymple, Lady Dalrymple," was the rejoicing sound; and with all the eagerness compatible with anxious elegance, Sir Walter and his two ladies stepped forward to meet her. Lady Dalrymple and Miss Carteret, escorted by Mr. Elliot and Colonel Wallis, who had happened to arrive nearly at the same instant, advanced into the room. The others joined them, and it was a group in which Anne found herself also necessarily included. She was divided from Captain Wentworth. Their interesting, almost too interesting conversation must be broken up for a time, but slight was the penance compared with the happiness which brought it on! She had learnt, in the last ten minutes, more of his feelings towards Louisa, more of *all* his feelings than she dared to think of; and she gave herself up to the demands of the party, to the needful civilities of the moment, with exquisite, though agitated sensations. She was in good humour with all. She had received ideas which disposed her to be courteous and kind to all, and to pity every one, as being less happy than herself.

The delightful emotions were a little subdued, when on stepping back from the group, to be joined again by Captain Wentworth, she saw that he was gone. She was just in time to see him turn into the Concert Room. He was gone; he had disappeared, she felt a moment's regret. But "they should meet again. He would look for her, he would find her out before the evening were over, and at present, perhaps, it was as well to be asunder. She was in need of a little interval for recollection."

Upon Lady Russell's appearance soon afterwards, the whole party was collected, and all that remained was to marshal themselves, and proceed into the Concert Room; and be of all the consequence in their power, draw as many eyes, excite as many whispers, and disturb as many people as they could.

Very, very happy were both Elizabeth and Anne Elliot as they walked in. Elizabeth arm in arm with Miss Carteret, and looking on the broad back of the dowager Viscountess Dalrymple before her, had nothing to wish for which did not seem within her reach; and Anne—but it would be an insult to the nature of Anne's felicity, to draw any comparison between it and her sister's; the origin of one all selfish vanity, of the other all generous attachment.

Anne saw nothing, thought nothing of the brilliancy of the room. Her happiness was from within. Her eyes were bright and her cheeks glowed; but she knew nothing about it. She was thinking only of the last half hour, and as they passed to their seats, her mind took a hasty range over it. His choice of subjects, his expressions, and still more his manner and look, had been such as she could see in only one light. His opinion of Louisa Musgrove's inferiority, an opinion which he had seemed solicitous to give, his wonder at Captain Benwick, his feelings as to a first, strong attachment; sentences begun which he could not finish, his half averted eyes and more than half expressive glance, the grip of his hand, the caress of his thumb, all, all declared that he had a heart returning to her at least; that anger, resentment, avoidance, were no more overwhelming him; and that they were succeeded, not merely by friendship and regard, but by the tenderness of the past. Yes, some share of the tenderness of the past. She could not contemplate the change as implying less. He must love her.

These were thoughts, with their attendant visions, which occupied and flurried her too much to leave her any power of observation; and she passed along the room without having a glimpse of him, without even trying to discern him. When their places were determined on, and they were all properly arranged, she looked round to see if he should happen to be in the same part of the room, but he was not; her eye could not reach him; and the concert being just opening, she must consent for a time to be happy in a humbler way.

The party was divided and disposed of on two contiguous benches: Anne was among those on the foremost, and Mr. Elliot had manoeuvred so well, with the assistance of his friend Colonel Wallis, as to have a seat by her. Miss Elliot, surrounded by her cousins, and the principal object of Colonel Wallis's gallantry, was quite contented.

Anne's mind was in a most favourable state for the entertainment of the evening; it was just occupation enough: she had feelings for the tender, spirits for the gay, attention for the scientific, and patience for the wearisome; and had never liked a concert better, at least during the first act. Towards the close of it, in the interval succeeding an Italian song, she explained the words of the song to Mr. Elliot. They had a concert bill between them.

"This," said she, "is nearly the sense, or rather the meaning of the words, for certainly the sense of an Italian love-song must not be talked of, but it is as nearly the meaning as I can give; for I do not pretend to understand the language. I am a very poor Italian scholar."

A broad smile lit his face, and he used the fact that she still held one end of the program and he the other to pull her closer. "Yes, yes, I see you are." He clicked his tongue and shook his head sorrowfully. "I see you know nothing of the matter. You have only knowledge enough of the language to translate at sight these inverted, transposed, curtailed Italian lines, into clear, comprehensible, elegant English. You need not say anything more of your ignorance. Here is complete proof." He held her eyes for several seconds, and soon Anne could not resist returning his smile. At that instant, his own smile morphed from blatantly amenable to something else that was both blatant and embarrassing.

Surely Anne was reading him wrong. She blushed when she realized they were practically nose-to-nose and looked back at the program. "I will not oppose such kind politeness; but I should be sorry to be examined by a real proficient."

"I have not had the pleasure of visiting in Camden Place so long," replied he in a deep voice that felt far too intimate, "without knowing something of Miss Anne Elliot; and I do regard her as one who is too modest for the world in general to be aware of half her accomplishments, and too highly accomplished for modesty to be natural in any other woman."

"For shame! for shame! this is too much flattery. I forget what we are to have next," turning to the bill. His attention was creating quite a reaction within Anne. If she did not know herself better, she would say it was annoying her.

"Perhaps," said Mr. Elliot, moving his lips near to her ear and speaking low, "I have had a longer acquaintance with your character than you are aware of."

Anne jumped back—putting a proper distance between them—with an embarrassed, breathy laugh. "Indeed! How so?

You can have been acquainted with it only since I came to Bath, excepting as you might hear me previously spoken of in my own family."

He stretched his arm across the back of Anne's spot on the bench, and his scent—an entirely different one from Captain Wentworth's, but nonetheless pleasant—wafted over her. He grinned so that a dimple showed in one chiseled cheek. "I knew you by report long before you came to Bath. I had heard you described by those who knew you intimately. I have been acquainted with you by character many years. Your person, your disposition, accomplishments, manner; they were all present to me."

Against her will, Anne felt herself softening to him—to his nearness, his flattery. If the twinkle in his eyes was any indication, Mr. Elliot was not disappointed in the interest he hoped to raise. No one can withstand the charm of such a mystery. To have been described long ago to a recent acquaintance, by nameless people, is irresistible; and Anne found herself leaning toward him, all curiosity. She wondered, and questioned him eagerly; but in vain. He delighted in being asked, but he would not tell.

"No, no, some time or other, perhaps, but not now. He would mention no names now; but such, he could assure her, had been the fact. He had many years ago received such a description of Miss Anne Elliot as had inspired him with the highest idea of her merit, and excited the warmest curiosity to know her."

Anne could think of no one so likely to have spoken with partiality of her many years ago as the Mr. Wentworth of Monkford, Captain Wentworth's brother. He might have been in Mr. Elliot's company, but she had not courage to ask the question.

"The name of Anne Elliot," said he, "has long had an interesting sound to me." At this point, Anne realized how close they were to each other. His mint-scented breath fanned over her heated cheeks, and she could practically taste the spice on his words. He dared to lean even closer so that his next words were barely audible. She felt them more than heard them. "Very long has it possessed a charm over my fancy; and, if I dared, I would breathe my wishes that the name might never change."

Such, she believed, were his words; but scarcely had she received their sound, than her attention was caught by the feather-like stroke of his fingers across her nape. He was using the opportunity of having his arm across the bench to touch her! The physical contact paired with the intimacy of his words jolted Anne fiercely, and she was on the verge of moving away from Mr. Elliot when she detected other sounds immediately behind her, which rendered every thing else trivial. Her father and Lady Dalrymple were speaking.

"A well-looking man," said Sir Walter, "a very well-looking man."

"A very fine young man indeed!" said Lady Dalrymple. "More air than one often sees in Bath. Irish, I dare say."

"No, I just know his name. A bowing acquaintance. Wentworth; Captain Wentworth of the navy. His sister married my tenant in Somersetshire, the Croft, who rents Kellynch."

Before Sir Walter had reached this point, Anne's eyes had caught the right direction, and distinguished Captain Wentworth standing among a cluster of men at a little distance. As her eyes fell on him, his seemed to be withdrawn from her. It had that appearance. It seemed as if she had been one moment too late; and as long as she dared observe, he did not look again. However, the moment she moved to look away, she noticed him shift, and she immediately looked upon his face once more, only to feel the anger of his gaze hit her full force. Any amiability that had been in his countenance when they'd talked before was now absent. His looks were dark and furious, and his fuming gaze flicked down from her face to where Mr. Elliot's fingers still brushed against Anne's skin.

Now Anne jerked away from her cousin, and she longed to relay some sort of silent message to Captain Wentworth with her eyes, to offer some sort of explanation that she dimly realized she did not owe: but the performance was recommencing, and she was forced to seem to restore her attention to the orchestra and look straight forward.

When she could give another glance, he had moved away. He could not have come nearer to her if he would; she was so surrounded and shut in: but she would rather have caught his eye.

Mr. Elliot's speech, too, distressed her. She had no longer any inclination to talk to him. She wished him not so near her.

The first act was over. Now she hoped for some beneficial change; and, after a period of nothing-saying amongst the party, some of them did decide on going in quest of tea. Anne was one of the few who did not choose to move. She remained in her seat, and so did Lady Russell; but she had the pleasure of getting rid of Mr. Elliot; and she did not mean, whatever she might feel on Lady Russell's account, to shrink from conversation with Captain Wentworth, if he gave her the opportunity. She was persuaded by Lady Russell's countenance that she had seen him.

He did not come however. Anne sometimes fancied she discerned him at a distance, but he never came. The anxious interval wore away unproductively. The others returned, the room filled again, benches were reclaimed and repossessed, and another hour of pleasure or of penance was to be sat out, another hour of music was to give delight or the gapes, as real or affected taste for it prevailed. To Anne, it chiefly wore the prospect of an hour of agitation. She could not quit that room in peace without seeing Captain Wentworth once more, without the interchange of one friendly look to assure Anne all was still well.

In re-settling themselves there were now many changes, the result of which was favourable for her. Colonel Wallis declined sitting down again, and Mr. Elliot was invited by Elizabeth and Miss Carteret, in a manner not to be refused, to sit between them; and by some other removals, and a little scheming of her own,

Anne was enabled to place herself much nearer the end of the bench than she had been before, much more within reach of a passer-by. She could not do so, without comparing herself with Miss Larolles, the inimitable Miss Larolles; but still she did it, and not with much happier effect; though by what seemed prosperity in the shape of an early abdication in her next neighbours, she found herself at the very end of the bench before the concert closed.

Such was her situation, with a vacant space at hand, when Captain Wentworth was again in sight. She saw him not far off. He saw her too; yet he looked grave, and seemed irresolute, and only by very slow degrees came at last near enough to speak to her. She felt that something must be the matter. The change was indubitable. The difference between his present air and what it had been in the Octagon Room was strikingly great. Why was it? She thought of her father, of Lady Russell. Could there have been any unpleasant glances? Could the slight touch of Mr. Elliot be upsetting him so greatly? He began by speaking of the concert gravely, more like the Captain Wentworth of Uppercross; owned himself disappointed, had expected singing; and in short, must confess that he should not be sorry when it was over. Anne replied, and spoke in defense of the performance so well, and yet in allowance for his feelings so pleasantly, that his countenance improved, and he replied again with almost a smile. They talked for a few minutes more; the improvement held; he even looked down towards the bench, as if he saw a place on it well worth occupying; when at that moment a touch on her shoulder obliged Anne to turn round. It came from Mr. Elliot. His fingers curved around her collarbone, and he cast an indescribable glance Captain Wentworth's way before leaning down so close that Anne could see every one of his eyelashes. Anne saw Captain Wentworth stiffen as Mr. Elliot spoke to her in a low, intimate voice. He begged her pardon, but she must be applied to, to explain Italian again. Miss

Carteret was very anxious to have a general idea of what was next to be sung. Anne could not refuse; but never had she sacrificed to politeness with a more suffering spirit. She could not even bear to look at Captain Wentworth as she mumbled an apology and turned toward her cousin, who seemed to ignore her pointed glance at his hand where it still touched her.

A few minutes, though as few as possible, were inevitably consumed; and when her own mistress again, when able to turn and look as she had done before, she found herself accosted by Captain Wentworth and his formidable glare, in a reserved yet hurried sort of farewell. "He must wish her good night; he was going; he should get home as fast as he could."

"Is not this song worth staying for?" said Anne, suddenly struck by an idea which made her yet more anxious to be encouraging.

"No!" he replied impressively, "there is nothing worth my staying for;" and he was gone directly.

Jealousy of Mr. Elliot! It was the only intelligible motive. Captain Wentworth jealous of her affection! Could she have believed it a week ago; three hours ago! For a moment the gratification was exquisite. But, alas! there were very different thoughts to succeed. How was such jealousy to be quieted? How was the truth to reach him? How, in all the peculiar disadvantages of their respective situations, would he ever learn of her real sentiments? It was misery to think of Mr. Elliot's attentions. Their evil was incalculable.

Over her shoulder, she heard Mr. Elliot try to regain her attention once more, but this time, Anne flaunted propriety. Captain Wentworth's long stride was quickly taking him out of the room, and she could not bear to let him go without trying to allay some of the tension between them. Without a word of excuse to her cousin, Anne launched to her feet and walked quickly in Captain Wentworth's wake.

She was walking so quickly that those she passed were turning to stare at her, but she paid them no mind. It took all of her fortitude not to call for him before she reached the door, but shouting his name in the midst of a concert hall would only exacerbate matters.

However, this slipped from her control as soon as she reached the Octagon Room once more. She spied him at the opposite side of the completely empty room; he was reaching for the door.

"Captain Wentworth!" She cringed as the desperate twinge to her cry echoed around the empty room long enough for Anne to regret the rashness of her shout.

As though he had expected her to follow him, he immediately changed course, dropping his hand from the doorknob and whipping around on one heel in a moment. He stalked toward her almost faster than she could track, his face an impenetrable mask.

Instinctively, Anne backed away, even though she knew he would never hurt her. But he was an oncoming force to be reckoned with, and Anne was not sure she was ready for whatever was about to come.

He walked forward faster than Anne retreated backward, and soon, they were nose to nose. Captain Wentworth gripped Anne by her upper arms, and she was startled to feel her feet leave the floor. He walked perhaps two more steps before she felt her back meet a wall, surprisingly gently for how he had charged and grabbed her. He crowded into her, and she was pinned between his unforgiving front and the tapestry-covered wall at her back.

Every delicious inch of him was pressed into her. The buttons of his waistcoat pressed into her ribs, and he shoved his lower body between her legs, forcing her to all-but-straddle his thigh.

She sucked in a startled breath and prayed for enough control to keep from moaning. A dim, barely functioning region of her mind recognised that she should not *enjoy* being handled thusly, but enjoy she most certainly did. The pressure of his firm thigh at the apex of her legs was too much, and she could not prevent herself from rocking forward and rubbing herself against him.

He groaned harshly and switched his hold on her in an instant. One hand fell to her hip, gripping roughly and staying a repetition of her movement. The other hand gripped her wrists and forced her arms above her hand. That was the moment Anne realized her hands had wandered to his chest where they had been stroking the planes of muscle most indecently. "Hold *still*," he ordered with a desperation that claimed her attention. "Anne, please." His voice broke, and Anne froze.

"F-Frederick?"

At the sound of his name, his eyes squeezed shut, and she felt a shudder go through him. "It is happening again. Just as it did last time." His words were low and dripping with pain.

She tried to free her wrists from his hold, the desire to somehow touch him, to soothe his hurt, overriding his command to be still.

His hold tightened, but remained gentle. "They are persuading you again," he said in a near moan. "Anne, *think* for yourself! For God's sake!"

Anne's shock forced her head backwards, but instead of thumping her head against the wall painfully, the back of her head met with Frederick's hand. As his fingers, the ones that had been gripping her hip, stroked into her hair, Anne realized he had intentionally shielded her head from harm. However, now he was cradling her head, and their lips were a breath apart.

Anne sighed brokenly. "Freder—"

His lips crashed down upon hers. Her lips parted exultantly, and his tongue swept into her mouth, affording her no choice but to return the favour. He finally—*finally*—released her hands so that he could cradle her face with both of them, and as he tilted her head farther back and deepened the kiss, Anne was able to touch him as she wished.

Her fingers combed through his hair, trailed down the flexing muscles of his jaw, and stroked the column of his neck, wrenching a groan from him that vibrated against her lips.

He broke the kiss for only a moment to whisper, "Never stop touching me," before kissing her once more and allowing his hands to roam as hers were.

She felt both of his large hands land upon her bottom, and he squeezed and pulled her up so that her feet once again left the floor. Anne silently cursed the constricting skirts that kept her from wrapping her legs around his waist, and she whimpered in protest.

As though he knew her thoughts, one of his hands moved from her bottom to behind her knee, and he wrenched her leg up as far as it would go and trapped her knee against his hip. They both moaned harshly as his arousal pressed against the swollen and dripping part of Anne's body that desired him to the point of madness.

"Please," she cried softly against his lips. "Frederick."

He pulled back from their kiss to look at her, and his eyes were glazed. He opened his mouth and his lips formed her name, but the actual sound of her name came from the entrance to the concert hall.

"Anne, are you out here?"

As Anne and Frederick froze, Anne knew that Mr. Elliot's voice had never been more unwelcome. Clarity began to edge back into her thoughts, and Anne realized they were both breathing heavily, their chests rising and falling against one another's. The light was dim, and it was with some relief that Anne saw the tapestry was enshrouding them somewhat, hiding them from the view of any passers-by.

Anne held her breath, hoping her lungs would get the point and stop billowing so. She watched as the light of passion dimmed from Frederick's eyes to be replaced by the hardness that had been in them when he'd watched Mr. Elliot stroke Anne's neck.

"I will not apologize for this," Frederick muttered vehemently while slowly lowering Anne to the ground.

Anne opened her mouth to assure him he had done nothing that she had not most heartily wished for, but he stepped back and perused her coldly. His eyes roamed over her hair, and he reached forward quickly. She felt him adjust one of the pins in her coiffure before he simply turned around without another word and walked back to the door.

The click of the door as it closed behind him shocked through her, but her cousin's repetition of her name forced her to move. She stepped out of semi-hiding and walked toward the sound of Mr. Elliot's voice, hoping she was composed enough to make it through the rest of the evening.

She did not know if matters were better or worse between her and Fre—*Captain Wentworth*—but she knew matters had definitely changed.

Chapter 21

Anne recollected with pleasure the next morning both the feel of Captain Wentworth's bruising kiss and her promise of going to Mrs. Smith, meaning that it should engage her from home at the time when Mr. Elliot would be most likely to call; for to avoid Mr. Elliot was almost a first object.

She felt a great deal of good-will towards him. After all, it was Mr. Elliot's attentions to her that had spurred Captain Wentworth to passion. Captain Wentworth's responses to her last night had been almost too passionate to be excused by a man simply seeking physical gratification. For a moment, she had felt the same tender passion from him that she had felt in their youth when he had touched her. Was it possible that he was developing feelings for her again? In spite of the mischief of Mr. Elliot's attentions, she owed him gratitude and regard, perhaps compassion. She could not help thinking much of the extraordinary circumstances attending their acquaintance, of the right which he seemed to have to interest her, by everything in situation, by his own sentiments, by his early prepossession. It was altogether very extraordinary; flattering, but painful. There was much to regret. How she might have felt had there been no Captain Wentworth in the case, was not worth enquiry; for there was a Captain Wentworth; and be the conclusion of the present suspense good or bad, her affection would be his for ever. Their union, she believed, could not divide her more from other men, than their final separation.

Prettier musings of high-wrought love and eternal constancy, could never have passed along the streets of Bath, than Anne was sporting with from Camden Place to Westgate Buildings. It was almost enough to spread purification and perfume all the way.

She was sure of a pleasant reception; and her friend seemed this morning particularly obliged to her for coming, seemed hardly to have expected her, though it had been an appointment.

An account of the concert was immediately claimed; and Anne's recollections of the concert and what came after were quite happy enough to animate her features and make her rejoice to talk of it. All that she could tell she told most gladly, but the all was little for one who had been there, and unsatisfactory for such an enquirer as Mrs. Smith, who had already heard, through the short cut of a laundress and a waiter, rather more of the general success and produce of the evening than Anne could relate, and who now asked in vain for several particulars of the company. Everybody of any consequence or notoriety in Bath was well known by name to Mrs. Smith.

"The little Durands were there, I conclude," said she, "with their mouths open to catch the music, like unfledged sparrows ready to be fed. They never miss a concert."

"Yes; I did not see them myself, but I heard Mr. Elliot say they were in the room."

"The Ibbotsons, were they there? and the two new beauties, with the tall Irish officer, who is talked of for one of them."

"I do not know. I do not think they were."

"Old Lady Mary Maclean? I need not ask after her. She never misses, I know; and you must have seen her. She must have been in your own circle; for as you went with Lady Dalrymple, you were in the seats of grandeur, round the orchestra, of course."

"No, that was what I dreaded. It would have been very unpleasant to me in every respect. But happily Lady Dalrymple always chooses to be farther off; and we were exceedingly well placed, that is, for hearing; I must not say for seeing, because I appear to have seen very little."

"Oh! you saw enough for your own amusement. I can understand. There is a sort of domestic enjoyment to be known even in a crowd, and this you had. You were a large party in yourselves, and you wanted nothing beyond."

"But I ought to have looked about me more," said Anne, conscious while she spoke that there had in fact been no want of looking about, that the object only had been deficient.

"No, no; you were better employed. You need not tell me that you had a pleasant evening. I see it in your eye. I perfectly see how the hours passed: that you had always something agreeable to listen to. In the intervals of the concert it was conversation."

Anne half smiled and said, "Do you see that in my eye?"

"Yes, I do. Your countenance perfectly informs me that you were in company last night with the person whom you think the most agreeable in the world, the person who interests you at this present time more than all the rest of the world put together."

A blush overspread Anne's cheeks. She could say nothing.

"And such being the case," continued Mrs. Smith, after a short pause, "I hope you believe that I do know how to value your kindness in coming to me this morning. It is really very good of you to come and sit with me, when you must have so many pleasanter demands upon your time."

Anne heard nothing of this. She was still in the astonishment and confusion excited by her friend's penetration, unable to imagine how any report of Captain Wentworth could have reached her. After another short silence—

"Pray," said Mrs. Smith, "is Mr. Elliot aware of your acquaintance with me? Does he know that I am in Bath?"

"Mr. Elliot!" repeated Anne, looking up surprised. A moment's reflection shewed her the mistake she had been under. She caught it instantaneously; and recovering her courage with the feeling of safety, soon added, more composedly, "Are you acquainted with Mr. Elliot?"

"I have been a good deal acquainted with him," replied Mrs. Smith, gravely, "but it seems worn out now. It is a great while since we met."

"I was not at all aware of this. You never mentioned it before. Had I known it, I would have had the pleasure of talking to him about you."

"To confess the truth," said Mrs. Smith, assuming her usual air of cheerfulness, "that is exactly the pleasure I want you to have. I want you to talk about me to Mr. Elliot. I want your interest with him. He can be of essential service to me; and if you would have the goodness, my dear Miss Elliot, to make it an object to yourself, of course it is done."

"I should be extremely happy; I hope you cannot doubt my willingness to be of even the slightest use to you," replied Anne; "but I suspect that you are considering me as having a higher claim on Mr. Elliot, a greater right to influence him, than is really the case. I am sure you have, somehow or other, imbibed such a notion. You must consider me only as Mr. Elliot's relation. If in that light there is anything which you suppose his cousin might fairly ask of him, I beg you would not hesitate to employ me."

Mrs. Smith gave her a penetrating glance, and then, smiling, said—

"I have been a little premature, I perceive; I beg your pardon. I ought to have waited for official information, But now, my dear Miss Elliot, as an old friend, do give me a hint as to when I may speak. Next week? To be sure by next week I may be allowed to think it all settled, and build my own selfish schemes on Mr. Elliot's good fortune."

"No," replied Anne, "nor next week, nor next, nor next. I assure you that nothing of the sort you are thinking of will be settled any week. I am not going to marry Mr. Elliot. I should like to know why you imagine I am?"

Mrs. Smith looked at her again, looked earnestly, smiled, shook her head, and exclaimed—

"Now, how I do wish I understood you! How I do wish I knew what you were at! I have a great idea that you do not design to be cruel, when the right moment occurs. Till it does come, you know, we women never mean to have anybody. It is a thing of course among us, that every man is refused, till he offers. But why should you be cruel? Let me plead for my—present friend I cannot call him, but for my former friend. Where can you look for a more suitable match? Where could you expect a more gentlemanlike, agreeable man? Let me recommend Mr. Elliot. I am sure you hear nothing but good of him from Colonel Wallis; and who can know him better than Colonel Wallis?"

"My dear Mrs. Smith, Mr. Elliot's wife has not been dead much above half a year. He ought not to be supposed to be paying his addresses to any one."

"Oh! if these are your only objections," cried Mrs. Smith, archly, "Mr. Elliot is safe, and I shall give myself no more trouble about him. Do not forget me when you are married, that's all. Let him know me to be a friend of yours, and then he will think little of the trouble required, which it is very natural for him now, with so many affairs and engagements of his own, to avoid and get rid of as he can; very natural, perhaps. Ninety-nine out of a hundred would do the same. Of course, he cannot be aware of the importance to me. Well, my dear Miss Elliot, I hope and trust you will be very happy. Mr. Elliot has sense to understand the value of such a woman. Your peace will not be shipwrecked as mine has been. You are safe in all worldly matters, and safe in his character. He will not be led astray; he will not be misled by others to his ruin."

"No," said Anne, "I can readily believe all that of my cousin. He seems to have a calm decided temper, not at all open to dangerous impressions. I consider him with great respect. I have no reason, from any thing that has fallen within my observation, to do otherwise. But I have not known him long; and he is not a man, I think, to be known intimately soon. Will not this manner of speaking of him, Mrs. Smith, convince you that he is nothing to me? Surely this must be calm enough. And, upon my word, he is nothing to me. Should he ever propose to me (which I have very little reason to imagine he has any thought of doing), I shall not accept him. I assure you I shall not. I assure you, Mr. Elliot had not the share which you have been supposing, in whatever pleasure the concert of last night might afford: not Mr. Elliot; it is not Mr. Elliot that—"

She stopped, regretting with a deep blush that she had implied so much; but less would hardly have been sufficient. Mrs. Smith would hardly have believed so soon in Mr. Elliot's failure, but from the perception of there being a somebody else. As it was, she instantly submitted, and with all the semblance of seeing nothing beyond; and Anne, eager to escape farther notice, was impatient to know why Mrs. Smith should have fancied she was to marry Mr. Elliot; where she could have received the idea, or from whom she could have heard it.

"Do tell me how it first came into your head."

"It first came into my head," replied Mrs. Smith, "upon finding how much you were together, and feeling it to be the most probable thing in the world to be wished for by everybody belonging to either of you; and you may depend upon it that all your acquaintance have disposed of you in the same way. But I never heard it spoken of till two days ago."

"And has it indeed been spoken of?"

"Did you observe the woman who opened the door to you when you called yesterday?"

"No. Was not it Mrs. Speed, as usual, or the maid? I observed no one in particular."

"It was my friend Mrs. Rooke; Nurse Rooke; who, by-the-bye, had a great curiosity to see you, and was delighted to be in the way to let you in. She came away from Marlborough Buildings only on Sunday; and she it was who told me you were to marry Mr. Elliot. She had had it from Mrs. Wallis herself, which did not seem bad authority. She sat an hour with me on Monday evening, and gave me the whole history."

"The whole history," repeated Anne, laughing. "She could not make a very long history, I think, of one such little article of unfounded news."

Mrs. Smith said nothing.

"But," continued Anne, presently, "though there is no truth in my having this claim on Mr. Elliot, I should be extremely happy to be of use to you in any way that I could. Shall I mention to him your being in Bath? Shall I take any message?"

"No, I thank you: no, certainly not. In the warmth of the moment, and under a mistaken impression, I might, perhaps, have endeavoured to interest you in some circumstances; but not now. No, I thank you, I have nothing to trouble you with."

"I think you spoke of having known Mr. Elliot many years?"

"I did."

"Not before he was married, I suppose?"

"Yes; he was not married when I knew him first."

"And—were you much acquainted?"

"Intimately."

"Indeed! Then do tell me what he was at that time of life. I have a great curiosity to know what Mr. Elliot was as a very young man. Was he at all such as he appears now?"

"I have not seen Mr. Elliot these three years," was Mrs. Smith's answer, given so gravely that it was impossible to pursue the subject farther; and Anne felt that she had gained nothing but an increase of curiosity. They were both silent: Mrs. Smith very thoughtful. At last—

"I beg your pardon, my dear Miss Elliot," she cried, in her natural tone of cordiality, "I beg your pardon for the short answers I have been giving you, but I have been uncertain what I ought to do. I have been doubting and considering as to what I ought to tell you. There were many things to be taken into the account. One hates to be officious, to be giving bad impressions, making mischief. Even the smooth surface of family-union seems worth preserving, though there may be nothing durable beneath. However, I have determined; I think I am right; I think you ought to be made acquainted with Mr. Elliot's real character. Though I fully believe that, at present, you have not the smallest intention of accepting him, there is no saying what may happen. You might, some time or other, be differently affected towards him. Hear the truth, therefore, now, while you are unprejudiced. Mr. Elliot is a man without heart or conscience; a designing, wary, cold-blooded being, who thinks only of himself; whom for his own interest or ease, would be guilty of any cruelty, or any treachery, that could be perpetrated without risk of his general character. He has no feeling for others. Those whom he has been the chief cause of leading into ruin, he can neglect and desert without the smallest compunction. He is totally beyond the reach of any sentiment of justice or compassion. Oh! he is black at heart, hollow and black!"

Anne's astonished air, and exclamation of wonder, made her pause, and in a calmer manner, she added,

"My expressions startle you. You must allow for an injured, angry woman. But I will try to command myself. I will not abuse him. I will only tell you what I have found him. Facts shall speak. He was the intimate friend of my dear husband, who trusted and loved him, and thought him as good as himself. The intimacy had been formed before our marriage. I found them most intimate friends; and I, too, became excessively pleased with Mr. Elliot, and entertained the highest opinion of him. At nineteen, you know, one does not think very seriously; but Mr. Elliot appeared to me quite as good as others, and much more agreeable than most others, and we were almost always together. We were principally in town, living in very good style. He was then the inferior in circumstances; he was then the poor one; he had chambers in the Temple, and it was as much as he could do to support the appearance of a gentleman. He had always a home with us whenever he chose it; he was always welcome; he was like a brother. My poor Charles, who had the finest, most generous spirit in the world, would have divided his last farthing with him; and I know that his purse was open to him; I know that he often assisted him."

"This must have been about that very period of Mr. Elliot's life," said Anne, "which has always excited my particular curiosity. It must have been about the same time that he became known to my father and sister. I never knew him myself; I only heard of him; but there was a something in his conduct then, with regard to my father and sister, and afterwards in the circumstances of his marriage, which I never could quite reconcile with present times. It seemed to announce a different sort of man."

"I know it all, I know it all," cried Mrs. Smith. "He had been introduced to Sir Walter and your sister before I was acquainted with him, but I heard him speak of them for ever. I know he was invited and encouraged, and I know he did not choose to go. I can satisfy you, perhaps, on points which you would little expect; and as to his marriage, I knew all about it at the time. I was privy to all the fors and againsts; I was the friend to whom he confided his hopes and plans; and though I did not know his wife previously, her inferior situation in society, indeed, rendered that impossible, yet I knew her all her life afterwards, or at least till within the last two years of her life, and can answer any question you may wish to put."

"Nay," said Anne, "I have no particular enquiry to make about her. I have always understood they were not a happy couple. But I should like to know why, at that time of his life, he should slight my father's acquaintance as he did. My father was certainly disposed to take very kind and proper notice of him. Why did Mr. Elliot draw back?"

"Mr. Elliot," replied Mrs. Smith, "at that period of his life, had one object in view: to make his fortune, and by a rather quicker process than the law. He was determined to make it by marriage. He was determined, at least, not to mar it by an imprudent marriage; and I know it was his belief (whether justly or not, of course I cannot decide), that your father and sister, in their civilities and invitations, were designing a match between the heir and the young lady, and it was impossible that such a match should have answered his ideas of wealth and independence. That was his motive for drawing back, I can assure you. He told me the whole story. He had no concealments with me. It was curious, that having just left you behind me in Bath, my first and principal acquaintance on marrying should be your cousin; and that, through him, I should be continually hearing of your father and sister. He described one Miss Elliot, and I thought very affectionately of the other."

"Perhaps," cried Anne, struck by a sudden idea, "you sometimes spoke of me to Mr. Elliot?"

"To be sure I did; very often. I used to boast of my own Anne Elliot, and vouch for your being a very different creature from—"

She checked herself just in time.

"This accounts for something which Mr. Elliot said last night," cried Anne. "This explains it. I found he had been used to hear of me. I could not comprehend how. What wild imaginations one forms where dear self is concerned! How sure to be mistaken! But I beg your pardon; I have interrupted you. Mr. Elliot married then completely for money? The circumstances, probably, which first opened your eyes to his character."

Mrs. Smith hesitated a little here. "Oh! those things are too common. When one lives in the world, a man or woman's marrying for money is too common to strike one as it ought. I was very young, and associated only with the young, and we were a thoughtless, gay set, without any strict rules of conduct. We lived for enjoyment. I think differently now; time and sickness and sorrow have given me other notions; but at that period I must own I saw nothing reprehensible in what Mr. Elliot was doing. 'To do the best for himself,' passed as a duty."

"But was not she a very low woman?"

"Yes; which I objected to, but he would not regard. Money, money, was all that he wanted. Her father was a grazier, her grandfather had been a butcher, but that was all nothing. She was a fine woman, had had a decent education, was brought forward by some cousins, thrown by chance into Mr. Elliot's company, and fell in love with him; and not a difficulty or a scruple was there on his side, with respect to her birth. All his caution was spent in being secured of the real amount of her fortune, before he committed himself. Depend upon it, whatever esteem Mr. Elliot may have for his own situation in life now, as a young man he had not the smallest value for it. His chance for the Kellynch estate was something, but all the honour of the family he held as cheap as dirt. I have often heard him declare, that if baronetcies were saleable, anybody should have his for fifty pounds, arms and motto, name and livery included; but I will not pretend to repeat half that I used to hear him say on that subject. It would not be fair; and yet you ought to have proof, for what is all this but assertion, and you shall have proof."

"Indeed, my dear Mrs. Smith, I want none," cried Anne. "You have asserted nothing contradictory to what Mr. Elliot appeared to be some years ago. This is all in confirmation, rather, of what we used to hear and believe. I am more curious to know why he should be so different now."

"But for my satisfaction, if you will have the goodness to ring for Mary; stay: I am sure you will have the still greater goodness of going yourself into my bedroom, and bringing me the small inlaid box which you will find on the upper shelf of the closet."

Anne, seeing her friend to be earnestly bent on it, did as she was desired. The box was brought and placed before her, and Mrs. Smith, sighing over it as she unlocked it, said—

"This is full of papers belonging to him, to my husband; a small portion only of what I had to look over when I lost him. The letter I am looking for was one written by Mr. Elliot to him before our marriage, and happened to be saved; why, one can hardly imagine. But he was careless and immethodical, like other men, about those things; and when I came to examine his papers, I found it with others still more trivial, from different people scattered here and there, while many letters and memorandums of real importance had been destroyed. Here it is; I would not burn it, because being even then very little satisfied with Mr. Elliot, I was determined to preserve every document of former intimacy. I have now another motive for being glad that I can produce it."

This was the letter, directed to "Charles Smith, Esq. Tunbridge Wells," and dated from London, as far back as July, 1803:—

"Dear Smith,—I have received yours. Your kindness almost overpowers me. I wish nature had made such hearts as yours more common, but I have lived three-and-twenty years in the world, and have seen none like it. At present, believe me, I have no need of your services, being in cash again. Give me joy: I have got rid of Sir Walter and Miss. They are gone back to Kellynch, and almost made me swear to visit them this summer; but my first visit to Kellynch will be with a surveyor, to tell me how to bring it with best advantage to the hammer. The baronet, nevertheless, is not unlikely to marry again; he is quite fool enough. If he does, however, they will leave me in peace, which may be a decent equivalent for the reversion. He is worse than last year.

"I wish I had any name but Elliot. I am sick of it. The name of Walter I can drop, thank God! and I desire you will never insult me with my second W. again, meaning, for the rest of my life, to be only yours truly,—Wm. Elliot."

Such a letter could not be read without putting Anne in a glow; and Mrs. Smith, observing the high colour in her face, said—

"The language, I know, is highly disrespectful. Though I have forgot the exact terms, I have a perfect impression of the general meaning. But it shows you the man. Mark his professions to my poor husband. Can any thing be stronger?"

Anne could not immediately get over the shock and mortification of finding such words applied to her father. She was obliged to recollect that her seeing the letter was a violation of the laws of honour, that no one ought to be judged or to be known by such testimonies, that no private correspondence could bear the eye of others, before she could recover calmness enough to return the letter which she had been meditating over, and say—

"Thank you. This is full proof undoubtedly; proof of every thing you were saying. But why be acquainted with us now?"

"I can explain this too," cried Mrs. Smith, smiling.

"Can you really?"

"Yes. I have shewn you Mr. Elliot as he was a dozen years ago, and I will shew him as he is now. I cannot produce written proof again, but I can give as authentic oral testimony as you can desire, of what he is now wanting, and what he is now doing. He is no hypocrite now. He truly wants to marry you. His present attentions to your family are very sincere: quite from the heart. I will give you my authority: his friend Colonel Wallis."

"Colonel Wallis! you are acquainted with him?"

"No. It does not come to me in quite so direct a line as that; it takes a bend or two, but nothing of consequence. The stream is as good as at first; the little rubbish it collects in the turnings is easily moved away. Mr. Elliot talks unreservedly to Colonel Wallis of his views on you, which said Colonel Wallis, I imagine to be, in himself, a sensible, careful, discerning sort of character; but Colonel Wallis has a very pretty silly wife, to whom he tells things which he had better not, and he repeats it all to her. She in the overflowing spirits of her recovery, repeats it all to her nurse; and the nurse knowing my acquaintance with you, very naturally brings it all to me. On Monday evening, my good friend Mrs. Rooke let me thus much into the secrets of Marlborough Buildings. When I talked of a whole history, therefore, you see I was not romancing so much as you supposed."

"My dear Mrs. Smith, your authority is deficient. This will not do. Mr. Elliot's having any views on me will not in the least account for the efforts he made towards a reconciliation with my father. That was all prior to my coming to Bath. I found them on the most friendly terms when I arrived."

"I know you did; I know it all perfectly, but—"

"Indeed, Mrs. Smith, we must not expect to get real information in such a line. Facts or opinions which are to pass through the hands of so many, to be misconceived by folly in one, and ignorance in another, can hardly have much truth left."

"Only give me a hearing. You will soon be able to judge of the general credit due, by listening to some particulars which you can yourself immediately contradict or confirm. Nobody supposes that you were his first inducement. He had seen you indeed, before he came to Bath, and admired you, but without knowing it to be you. So says my historian, at least. Is this true? Did he see you last summer or autumn, 'somewhere down in the west,' to use her own words, without knowing it to be you?"

Anne blushed and looked at her hands. "He certainly did. So far it is very true. At Lyme. I happened to be at Lyme."

"Well," continued Mrs. Smith, triumphantly, "grant my friend the credit due to the establishment of the first point asserted. He saw you then at Lyme, and liked you so well as to be exceedingly pleased to meet with you again in Camden Place, as Miss Anne Elliot, and from that moment, I have no doubt, had a double motive in his visits there. But there was another, and an earlier, which I will now explain. If there is anything in my story which you know to be either false or improbable, stop me. My account states, that your sister's friend, the lady now staying with you, whom I have heard you mention, came to Bath with Miss Elliot and Sir Walter as long ago as September (in short when they first came themselves), and has been staying there ever since; that she is a clever, insinuating, handsome woman, poor and plausible, and altogether such in situation and manner, as to give a general idea, among Sir Walter's acquaintance, of her meaning to be Lady Elliot, and as general a surprise that Miss Elliot should be apparently, blind to the danger."

Here Mrs. Smith paused a moment; but Anne had not a word to say, and she continued—

"This was the light in which it appeared to those who knew the family, long before you returned to it; and Colonel Wallis had his eye upon your father enough to be sensible of it, though he did not then visit in Camden Place; but his regard for Mr. Elliot gave him an interest in watching all that was going on there, and when Mr. Elliot came to Bath for a day or two, as he happened to do a little before Christmas, Colonel Wallis made him acquainted with the appearance of things, and the reports beginning to prevail. Now you are to understand, that time had worked a very material change in Mr. Elliot's opinions as to the value of a baronetcy. Upon all points of blood and connexion he is a completely altered man. Having long had as much money as he could spend, nothing to wish for on the side of avarice or indulgence, he has been gradually learning to pin his happiness upon the consequence he is heir to. I thought it coming on before our acquaintance ceased, but it is now a confirmed feeling. He cannot bear the idea of not being Sir William. You may guess, therefore, that the news he heard from his friend could not be very agreeable, and you may guess what it produced; the resolution of coming back to Bath as soon as possible, and of fixing himself here for a time, with the view of renewing his former acquaintance, and recovering such a footing in the family as might give him the means of ascertaining the degree of his danger, and of circumventing the lady if he found it material. This was agreed upon between the two friends as the only thing to be done; and Colonel Wallis was to assist in every way that he could. He was to be introduced, and Mrs. Wallis was to be introduced, and everybody was to be introduced. Mr. Elliot came back accordingly; and on application was forgiven, as you know, and re-admitted into the family; and there it was his constant object, and his only object (till your arrival added another motive), to watch Sir Walter and Mrs. Clay. He omitted no opportunity of being with them, threw himself in their way, called at all hours; but I need not be particular on this subject. You can imagine what an artful man would do; and with this guide, perhaps, may recollect what you have seen him do."

"Yes," said Anne, "you tell me nothing which does not accord with what I have known, or could imagine. There is always something offensive in the details of cunning. The manoeuvres of selfishness and duplicity must ever be revolting, but I have heard nothing which really surprises me. I know those who would be shocked by such a representation of Mr. Elliot, who would have difficulty in believing it; but I have never been satisfied. I have always wanted some other motive for his conduct than appeared. I should like to know his present opinion, as to the probability of the event he has been in dread of; whether he considers the danger to be lessening or not."

"Lessening, I understand," replied Mrs. Smith. "He thinks Mrs. Clay afraid of him, aware that he sees through her, and not daring to proceed as she might do in his absence. But since he must be absent some time or other, I do not perceive how he can ever be secure while she holds her present influence. Mrs. Wallis has an amusing idea, as nurse tells me, that it is to be put into the marriage articles when you and Mr. Elliot marry, that your father is not to marry Mrs. Clay. A scheme, worthy of Mrs.

Wallis's understanding, by all accounts; but my sensible nurse Rooke sees the absurdity of it. 'Why, to be sure, ma'am,' said she, 'it would not prevent his marrying anybody else.' And, indeed, to own the truth, I do not think nurse, in her heart, is a very strenuous opposer of Sir Walter's making a second match. She must be allowed to be a favourer of matrimony, you know; and (since self will intrude) who can say that she may not have some flying visions of attending the next Lady Elliot, through Mrs. Wallis's recommendation?"

"I am very glad to know all this," said Anne, after a little thoughtfulness. "It will be more painful to me in some respects to be in company with him, but I shall know better what to do. My line of conduct will be more direct. Mr. Elliot is evidently a disingenuous, artificial, worldly man, who has never had any better principle to guide him than selfishness."

But Mr. Elliot was not done with. Mrs. Smith had been carried away from her first direction, and Anne had forgotten, in the interest of her own family concerns, how much had been originally implied against him; but her attention was now called to the explanation of those first hints, and she listened to a recital which, if it did not perfectly justify the unqualified bitterness of Mrs. Smith, proved him to have been very unfeeling in his conduct towards her; very deficient both in justice and compassion.

She learned that (the intimacy between them continuing unimpaired by Mr. Elliot's marriage) they had been as before always together, and Mr. Elliot had led his friend into expenses much beyond his fortune. Mrs. Smith did not want to take blame to herself, and was most tender of throwing any on her husband; but Anne could collect that their income had never been equal to their style of living, and that from the first there had been a great deal of general and joint extravagance. From his wife's account of him she could discern Mr. Smith to have been a man of warm feelings, easy temper, careless habits, and not strong understanding, much more amiable than his friend, and very unlike him, led by him, and probably despised by him. Mr. Elliot, raised by his marriage to great affluence, and disposed to every gratification of pleasure and vanity which could be commanded without involving himself, (for with all his self-indulgence he had become a prudent man), and beginning to be rich, just as his friend ought to have found himself to be poor, seemed to have had no concern at all for that friend's probable finances, but, on the contrary, had been prompting and encouraging expenses which could end only in ruin; and the Smiths accordingly had been ruined.

The husband had died just in time to be spared the full knowledge of it. They had previously known embarrassments enough to try the friendship of their friends, and to prove that Mr. Elliot's had better not be tried; but it was not till his death that the wretched state of his affairs was fully known. With a confidence in Mr. Elliot's regard, more creditable to his feelings than his judgement, Mr. Smith had appointed him the executor of his will; but Mr. Elliot would not act, and the difficulties and distress which this refusal had heaped on her, in addition to the inevitable sufferings of her situation, had been such as could not be related without anguish of spirit, or listened to without corresponding indignation.

Anne was shewn some letters of his on the occasion, answers to urgent applications from Mrs. Smith, which all breathed the same stern resolution of not engaging in a fruitless trouble, and, under a cold civility, the same hard-hearted indifference to any of the evils it might bring on her. It was a dreadful picture of ingratitude and inhumanity; and Anne felt, at some moments, that no flagrant open crime could have been worse. She had a great deal to listen to; all the particulars of past sad scenes, all the minutiae of distress upon distress, which in former conversations had been merely hinted at, were dwelt on now with a natural indulgence. Anne could perfectly comprehend the exquisite relief, and was only the more inclined to wonder at the composure of her friend's usual state of mind.

There was one circumstance in the history of her grievances of particular irritation. She had good reason to believe that some property of her husband in the West Indies, which had been for many years under a sort of sequestration for the payment of its own incumbrances, might be recoverable by proper measures; and this property, though not large, would be enough to make her comparatively rich. But there was nobody to stir in it. Mr. Elliot would do nothing, and she could do nothing herself, equally disabled from personal exertion by her state of bodily weakness, and from employing others by her want of money. She had no natural connexions to assist her even with their counsel, and she could not afford to purchase the assistance of the law. This was a cruel aggravation of actually straitened means. To feel that she ought to be in better circumstances, that a little trouble in the right place might do it, and to fear that delay might be even weakening her claims, was hard to bear.

It was on this point that she had hoped to engage Anne's good offices with Mr. Elliot. She had previously, in the anticipation of their marriage, been very apprehensive of losing her friend by it; but on being assured that he could have made no attempt of that nature, since he did not even know her to be in Bath, it immediately occurred, that something might be done in her favour by the influence of the woman he loved, and she had been hastily preparing to interest Anne's feelings, as far as the observances due to Mr. Elliot's character would allow, when Anne's refutation of the supposed engagement changed the face of everything; and while it took from her the new-formed hope of succeeding in the object of her first anxiety, left her at least the comfort of telling the whole story her own way.

After listening to this full description of Mr. Elliot, Anne could not but express some surprise at Mrs. Smith's having spoken of him so favourably in the beginning of their conversation. "She had seemed to recommend and praise him!"

"My dear," was Mrs. Smith's reply, "there was nothing else to be done. I considered your marrying him as certain, though he might not yet have made the offer, and I could no more speak the truth of him, than if he had been your husband. My heart bled for you, as I talked of happiness; and yet he is sensible, he is agreeable, and with such a woman as you, it was not absolutely hopeless. He was very unkind to his first wife. They were wretched together. But she was too ignorant and giddy for respect, and he had never loved her. I was willing to hope that you must fare better."

Anne could just acknowledge within herself such a possibility of having been induced to marry him, as made her shudder at the idea of the misery which must have followed. It was just possible that she might have been persuaded by Lady Russell! And under such a supposition, which would have been most miserable, when time had disclosed all, too late?

It was very desirable that Lady Russell should be no longer deceived; and one of the concluding arrangements of this important conference, which carried them through the greater part of the morning, was, that Anne had full liberty to communicate to her friend everything relative to Mrs. Smith, in which his conduct was involved.

Chapter 22

Anne went home to think over all that she had heard. In one point, her feelings were relieved by this knowledge of Mr. Elliot. There was no longer anything of tenderness due to him. He stood as opposed to Captain Wentworth, in all his own unwelcome obtrusiveness; and the evil of his attentions last night, the irremediable mischief he might have done, was considered with sensations unqualified, unperplexed. Pity for him was all over. But this was the only point of relief. In every other respect, in looking around her, or penetrating forward, she saw more to distrust and to apprehend. She was concerned for the disappointment and pain Lady Russell would be feeling; for the mortifications which must be hanging over her father and sister, and had all the distress of foreseeing many evils, without knowing how to avert any one of them. She was most thankful for her own knowledge of him.

She had never considered herself as entitled to reward for not slighting an old friend like Mrs. Smith, but here was a reward indeed springing from it! Mrs. Smith had been able to tell her what no one else could have done. Could the knowledge have been extended through her family? But this was a vain idea. She must talk to Lady Russell, tell her, consult with her, and having done her best, wait the event with as much composure as possible; and after all, her greatest want of composure would be in that quarter of the mind which could not be opened to Lady Russell; in that flow of anxieties and fears which must be all to herself.

She found, on reaching home, that she had, as she intended, escaped seeing Mr. Elliot; that he had called and paid them a long morning visit; but hardly had she congratulated herself, and felt safe, when she heard that he was coming again in the evening.

"I had not the smallest intention of asking him," said Elizabeth, with affected carelessness, "but he gave so many hints; so Mrs. Clay says, at least."

"Indeed, I do say it. I never saw anybody in my life spell harder for an invitation. Poor man! I was really in pain for him; for your hard-hearted sister, Miss Anne, seems bent on cruelty."

"Oh!" cried Elizabeth, "I have been rather too much used to the game to be soon overcome by a gentleman's hints. However, when I found how excessively he was regretting that he should miss my father this morning, I gave way immediately, for I would never really omit an opportunity of bringing him and Sir Walter together. They appear to so much advantage in company with each other. Each behaving so pleasantly. Mr. Elliot looking up with so much respect."

"Quite delightful!" cried Mrs. Clay, not daring, however, to turn her eyes towards Anne. "Exactly like father and son! Dear Miss Elliot, may I not say father and son?"

"Oh! I lay no embargo on any body's words. If you will have such ideas! But, upon my word, I am scarcely sensible of his attentions being beyond those of other men."

"My dear Miss Elliot!" exclaimed Mrs. Clay, lifting her hands and eyes, and sinking all the rest of her astonishment in a convenient silence.

"Well, my dear Penelope, you need not be so alarmed about him. I did invite him, you know. I sent him away with smiles. When I found he was really going to his friends at Thornberry Park for the whole day to-morrow, I had compassion on him."

Anne admired the good acting of the friend, in being able to shew such pleasure as she did, in the expectation and in the actual arrival of the very person whose presence must really be interfering with her prime object. It was impossible but that Mrs. Clay must hate the sight of Mr. Elliot; and yet she could assume a most obliging, placid look, and appear quite satisfied with the curtailed license of devoting herself only half as much to Sir Walter as she would have done otherwise.

To Anne herself it was most distressing to see Mr. Elliot enter the room; and quite painful to have him approach and speak to her. She had been used before to feel that he could not be always quite sincere, but now she saw insincerity in everything. His attentive deference to her father, contrasted with his former language, was odious; and when she thought of his cruel conduct towards Mrs. Smith, she could hardly bear the sight of his present smiles and mildness, or the sound of his artificial good sentiments.

She meant to avoid any such alteration of manners as might provoke a remonstrance on his side. It was a great object to her to escape all enquiry or *éclat*; but it was her intention to be as decidedly cool to him as might be compatible with their relationship; and to retrace, as quietly as she could, the few steps of unnecessary intimacy she had been gradually led along. When he leaned close, she leaned back; when he tried to grasp her hand, she reached for her tea. She was accordingly more guarded, and more cool, than she had been the night before.

He wanted to animate her curiosity again as to how and where he could have heard her formerly praised; wanted very much to be gratified by more solicitation; but the charm was broken: he found that the heat and animation of a public room was necessary to kindle his modest cousin's vanity; he found, at least, that it was not to be done now, by any of those attempts which he could hazard among the too-commanding claims of the others. He little surmised that it was a subject acting now exactly against his interest, bringing immediately to her thoughts all those parts of his conduct which were least excusable.

She had some satisfaction in finding that he was really going out of Bath the next morning, going early, and that he would be gone the greater part of two days. He was invited again to Camden Place the very evening of his return; but from Thursday to Saturday evening his absence was certain. It was bad enough that a Mrs. Clay should be always before her; but that a deeper hypocrite should be added to their party, seemed the destruction of everything like peace and comfort. It was so humiliating to reflect on the constant deception practised on her father and Elizabeth; to consider the various sources of mortification preparing for them! Mrs. Clay's selfishness was not so complicate nor so revolting as his; and Anne would have compounded for the marriage at once, with all its evils, to be clear of Mr. Elliot's subtleties in endeavouring to prevent it.

On Friday morning she meant to go very early to Lady Russell, and accomplish the necessary communication; and she would have gone directly after breakfast, but that Mrs. Clay was also going out on some obliging purpose of saving her sister trouble, which determined her to wait till she might be safe from such a companion. She saw Mrs. Clay fairly off, therefore, before she began to talk of spending the morning in Rivers Street.

"Very well," said Elizabeth, "I have nothing to send but my love. Oh! you may as well take back that tiresome book she would lend me, and pretend I have read it through. I really cannot be plaguing myself for ever with all the new poems and states of the nation that come out. Lady Russell quite bores one with her new publications. You need not tell her so, but I thought her dress hideous the other night. I used to think she had some taste in dress, but I was ashamed of her at the concert. Something so formal and *arrangé* in her air! and she sits so upright! My best love, of course."

"And mine," added Sir Walter. "Kindest regards. And you may say, that I mean to call upon her soon. Make a civil message; but I shall only leave my card. Morning visits are never fair by women at her time of life, who make themselves up so little. If she would only wear rouge she would not be afraid of being seen; but last time I called, I observed the blinds were let down immediately."

While her father spoke, there was a knock at the door. Who could it be? Anne, remembering the preconcerted visits, at all hours, of Mr. Elliot, would have expected him, but for his known engagement seven miles off. After the usual period of suspense, the usual sounds of approach were heard, and "Mr. and Mrs. Charles Musgrove" were ushered into the room.

Surprise was the strongest emotion raised by their appearance; but Anne was really glad to see them; and the others were not so sorry but that they could put on a decent air of welcome; and as soon as it became clear that these, their nearest relations, were not arrived with any views of accommodation in that house, Sir Walter and Elizabeth were able to rise in cordiality, and do the honours of it very well. They were come to Bath for a few days with Mrs. Musgrove, and were at the White Hart. So much was pretty soon understood; but till Sir Walter and Elizabeth were walking Mary into the other drawing-room, and regaling themselves with her admiration, Anne could not draw upon Charles's brain for a regular history of their coming, or an explanation of some smiling hints of particular business, which had been ostentatiously dropped by Mary, as well as of some apparent confusion as to whom their party consisted of.

She then found that it consisted of Mrs. Musgrove, Henrietta, and Captain Harville, beside their two selves. He gave her a very plain, intelligible account of the whole; a narration in which she saw a great deal of most characteristic proceeding. The scheme had received its first impulse by Captain Harville's wanting to come to Bath on business. He had begun to talk of it a week ago; and by way of doing something, as shooting was over, Charles had proposed coming with him, and Mrs. Harville had seemed to like the idea of it very much, as an advantage to her husband; but Mary could not bear to be left, and had made herself so unhappy about it, that for a day or two everything seemed to be in suspense, or at an end. But then, it had been taken up by his father and mother. His mother had some old friends in Bath whom she wanted to see; it was thought a good opportunity for Henrietta to come and buy wedding-clothes for herself and her sister; and, in short, it ended in being his mother's party, that everything might be comfortable and easy to Captain Harville; and he and Mary were included in it by way of general convenience. They had arrived late the night before. Mrs. Harville, her children, and Captain Benwick, remained with Mr. Musgrove and Louisa at Uppercross.

Anne's only surprise was, that affairs should be in forwardness enough for Henrietta's wedding-clothes to be talked of. She had imagined such difficulties of fortune to exist there as must prevent the marriage from being near at hand; but she learned from Charles that, very recently, (since Mary's last letter to herself), Charles Hayter had been applied to by a friend to hold a living for a youth who could not possibly claim it under many years; and that on the strength of his present income, with almost a certainty of something more permanent long before the term in question, the two families had consented to the young people's wishes, and that their marriage was likely to take place in a few months, quite as soon as Louisa's. "And a very good living it was," Charles added: "only five-and-twenty miles from Uppercross, and in a very fine country: fine part of Dorsetshire. In the centre of some of the best preserves in the kingdom, surrounded by three great proprietors, each more careful and jealous than the other; and to two of the three at least, Charles Hayter might get a special recommendation. Not that he will value it as he ought," he observed, "Charles is too cool about sporting. That's the worst of him."

"I am extremely glad, indeed," cried Anne, "particularly glad that this should happen; and that of two sisters, who both deserve equally well, and who have always been such good friends, the pleasant prospect of one should not be dimming those of the other—that they should be so equal in their prosperity and comfort. I hope your father and mother are quite happy with regard to both."

"Oh! yes. My father would be well pleased if the gentlemen were richer, but he has no other fault to find. Money, you know, coming down with money—two daughters at once—it cannot be a very agreeable operation, and it streightens him as to many things. However, I do not mean to say they have not a right to it. It is very fit they should have daughters' shares; and I am sure he has always been a very kind, liberal father to me. Mary does not above half like Henrietta's match. She never did, you know. But she does not do him justice, nor think enough about Winthrop. I cannot make her attend to the value of the property. It is a very fair match, as times go; and I have liked Charles Hayter all my life, and I shall not leave off now."

"Such excellent parents as Mr. and Mrs. Musgrove," exclaimed Anne, "should be happy in their children's marriages. They do everything to confer happiness, I am sure. What a blessing to young people to be in such hands! Your father and mother seem so totally free from all those ambitious feelings which have led to so much misconduct and misery, both in young and old. I hope you think Louisa perfectly recovered now?"

He answered rather hesitatingly, "Yes, I believe I do; very much recovered; but she is altered; there is no running or jumping about, no laughing or dancing; it is quite different. If one happens only to shut the door a little hard, she starts and wriggles like a young dab-chick in the water; and Benwick sits at her elbow, reading verses, or whispering to her, all day long."

Anne could not help laughing. "That cannot be much to your taste, I know," said she; "but I do believe him to be an excellent young man."

"To be sure he is. Nobody doubts it; and I hope you do not think I am so illiberal as to want every man to have the same objects and pleasures as myself. I have a great value for Benwick; and when one can but get him to talk, he has plenty to say. His reading has done him no harm, for he has fought as well as read. He is a brave fellow. I got more acquainted with him last Monday than ever I did before. We had a famous set-to at rat-hunting all the morning in my father's great barns; and he played his part so well that I have liked him the better ever since."

Here they were interrupted by the absolute necessity of Charles's following the others to admire mirrors and china; but Anne had heard enough to understand the present state of Uppercross, and rejoice in its happiness; and though she sighed as she rejoiced, her sigh had none of the ill-will of envy in it. She would certainly have risen to their blessings if she could, but she did not want to lessen theirs.

The visit passed off altogether in high good humour. Mary was in excellent spirits, enjoying the gaiety and the change, and so well satisfied with the journey in her mother-in-law's carriage with four horses, and with her own complete independence of Camden Place, that she was exactly in a temper to admire everything as she ought, and enter most readily into all the superiorities of the house, as they were detailed to her. She had no demands on her father or sister, and her consequence was just enough increased by their handsome drawing-rooms.

Elizabeth was, for a short time, suffering a good deal. She felt that Mrs. Musgrove and all her party ought to be asked to dine with them; but she could not bear to have the difference of style, the reduction of servants, which a dinner must betray, witnessed by those who had been always so inferior to the Elliots of Kellynch. It was a struggle between propriety and vanity; but vanity got the better, and then Elizabeth was happy again. These were her internal persuasions: "Old fashioned notions; country hospitality; we do not profess to give dinners; few people in Bath do; Lady Alicia never does; did not even ask her own sister's family, though they were here a month: and I dare say it would be very inconvenient to Mrs. Musgrove; put her quite out of her way. I am sure she would rather not come; she cannot feel easy with us. I will ask them all for an evening; that will be much better; that will be a novelty and a treat. They have not seen two such drawing rooms before. They will be delighted to come to-morrow evening. It shall be a regular party, small, but most elegant." And this satisfied Elizabeth: and when the invitation was given to the two present, and promised for the absent, Mary was as completely satisfied. She was particularly asked to meet Mr. Elliot, and be introduced to Lady Dalrymple and Miss Carteret, who were fortunately already engaged to come; and she could not have received a more gratifying attention. Miss Elliot was to have the honour of calling on Mrs. Musgrove in the course of the morning; and Anne walked off with Charles and Mary, to go and see her and Henrietta directly.

Her plan of sitting with Lady Russell must give way for the present. They all three called in Rivers Street for a couple of minutes; but Anne convinced herself that a day's delay of the intended communication could be of no consequence, and hastened forward to the White Hart, to see again the friends and companions of the last autumn, with an eagerness of good-will which many associations contributed to form.

They found Mrs. Musgrove and her daughter within, and by themselves, and Anne had the kindest welcome from each. Henrietta was exactly in that state of recently-improved views, of fresh-formed happiness, which made her full of regard and interest for everybody she had ever liked before at all; and Mrs. Musgrove's real affection had been won by her usefulness when they were in distress. It was a heartiness, and a warmth, and a sincerity which Anne delighted in the more, from the sad want of such blessings at home. She was entreated to give them as much of her time as possible, invited for every day and all day long, or rather claimed as part of the family; and, in return, she naturally fell into all her wonted ways of attention and assistance, and on Charles's leaving them together, was listening to Mrs. Musgrove's history of Louisa, and to Henrietta's of herself, giving opinions on business, and recommendations to shops; with intervals of every help which Mary required, from altering her ribbon to settling her accounts; from finding her keys, and assorting her trinkets, to trying to convince her that she was not ill-used by anybody; which Mary, well amused as she generally was, in her station at a window overlooking the entrance to the Pump Room, could not but have her moments of imagining.

A morning of thorough confusion was to be expected. A large party in an hotel ensured a quick-changing, unsettled scene. One five minutes brought a note, the next a parcel; and Anne had not been there half an hour, when their dining-room, spacious as it was, seemed more than half filled: a party of steady old friends were seated around Mrs. Musgrove, and Charles came back with Captains Harville and Wentworth. The appearance of the latter could not be more than the surprise of the moment. It was impossible for her to have forgotten to feel that this arrival of their common friends must be soon bringing them together again. Their last meeting had been most important in opening his feelings; she had derived from it and from their kiss a delightful conviction; but she feared from his looks, that the same unfortunate persuasion that he had perceived her to be under, which had hastened him away from the Concert Room, still governed. He did not seem to want to be near enough for conversation.

She tried to be calm, and leave things to take their course, and tried to dwell much on this argument of rational dependence:—"Surely, if there be constant attachment on each side, our hearts must understand each other ere long. We are not boy and girl, to be captiously irritable, misled by every moment's inadvertence, and wantonly playing with our own happiness." And yet, a few minutes afterwards, she felt as if their being in company with each other, under their present circumstances, could only be exposing them to inadvertencies and misconstructions of the most mischievous kind. *Not* talking to one another only seemed to be cementing Captain Wentworth's notion of Anne's imminent persuasion to marry another man.

"Anne," cried Mary, still at her window, "there is Mrs. Clay, I am sure, standing under the colonnade, and a gentleman with her. I saw them turn the corner from Bath Street just now. They seemed deep in talk. Who is it? Come, and tell me. Good heavens! I recollect. It is Mr. Elliot himself."

"No," cried Anne, quickly, through an intense pang of dread "it cannot be Mr. Elliot, I assure you. He was to leave Bath at nine this morning, and does not come back till to-morrow."

As she spoke, she felt that Captain Wentworth was looking at her, the consciousness of which vexed and embarrassed her, and made her regret that she had said so much, simple as it was. She realized belatedly that knowing Mr. Elliot's comings and goings betrayed an intimacy that simply did not exist.

Mary, resenting that she should be supposed not to know her own cousin, began talking very warmly about the family features, and protesting still more positively that it was Mr. Elliot, calling again upon Anne to come and look for herself, but Anne did not mean to stir, and tried to be cool and unconcerned. Her distress returned, however, on perceiving smiles and intelligent glances pass between two or three of the lady visitors, as if they believed themselves quite in the secret. It was evident that the report concerning her had spread, and a short pause succeeded, which seemed to ensure that it would now spread farther. She could feel tension radiating from Captain Wentworth's seat, and Anne wished severely that this conversation would pass.

"Do come, Anne," cried Mary, "come and look yourself. You will be too late if you do not make haste. They are parting; they are shaking hands. He is turning away. Not know Mr. Elliot, indeed! You seem to have forgot all about Lyme."

To pacify Mary, and perhaps screen her own embarrassment, Anne did move quietly to the window. She was just in time to ascertain that it really was Mr. Elliot, which she had never believed. He was leaning toward a woman, whose back was to them, and his face was impassioned. When the woman turned her face to the side, Anne saw that it was indeed Mrs. Clay. Anne had the passing thought that maybe he had been lecturing Mrs. Clay about Sir Walter, before he disappeared on one side, as Mrs. Clay walked quickly off on the other; and checking the surprise which she could not but feel at such an appearance of friendly conference between two persons of totally opposite interest, she calmly said, "Yes, it is Mr. Elliot, certainly. He has changed his hour of going, I suppose, that is all, or I may be mistaken, I might not attend;" and walked back to her chair, recomposed, and with the comfortable hope of having acquitted herself well.

The visitors took their leave; and Charles, having civilly seen them off, and then made a face at them, and abused them for coming, began with—

"Well, mother, I have done something for you that you will like. I have been to the theatre, and secured a box for to-morrow night. A'n't I a good boy? I know you love a play; and there is room for us all. It holds nine. I have engaged Captain Wentworth. Anne will not be sorry to join us, I am sure. We all like a play. Have not I done well, mother?"

Mrs. Musgrove was good humouredly beginning to express her perfect readiness for the play, if Henrietta and all the others liked it, when Mary eagerly interrupted her by exclaiming—

"Good heavens, Charles! how can you think of such a thing? Take a box for to-morrow night! Have you forgot that we are engaged to Camden Place to-morrow night? and that we were most particularly asked to meet Lady Dalrymple and her daughter, and

Mr. Elliot, and all the principal family connexions, on purpose to be introduced to them? How can you be so forgetful?"

"Phoo! phoo!" replied Charles, "what's an evening party? Never worth remembering. Your father might have asked us to dinner, I think, if he had wanted to see us. You may do as you like, but I shall go to the play."

"Oh! Charles, I declare it will be too abominable if you do, when you promised to go."

"No, I did not promise. I only smirked and bowed, and said the word 'happy.' There was no promise."

"But you must go, Charles. It would be unpardonable to fail. We were asked on purpose to be introduced. There was always such a great connexion between the Dalrymples and ourselves. Nothing ever happened on either side that was not announced immediately. We are quite near relations, you know; and Mr. Elliot too, whom you ought so particularly to be acquainted with! Every attention is due to Mr. Elliot. Consider, my father's heir: the future representative of the family."

"Don't talk to me about heirs and representatives," cried Charles. "I am not one of those who neglect the reigning power to bow to the rising sun. If I would not go for the sake of your father, I should think it scandalous to go for the sake of his heir. What is Mr. Elliot to me?" The careless expression was life to Anne, who saw that Captain Wentworth was all attention, looking and listening with his whole soul; and that the last words brought his enquiring eyes from Charles to herself. His eyes had an obvious question in their depths, which she tried to answer with her own, and she was relieved beyond words when a small smile tilted his lips before he looked away from her.

Charles and Mary still talked on in the same style; he, half serious and half jesting, maintaining the scheme for the play, and she, invariably serious, most warmly opposing it, and not omitting to make it known that, however determined to go to Camden

Place herself, she should not think herself very well used, if they went to the play without her. Mrs. Musgrove interposed.

"We had better put it off. Charles, you had much better go back and change the box for Tuesday. It would be a pity to be divided, and we should be losing Miss Anne, too, if there is a party at her father's; and I am sure neither Henrietta nor I should care at all for the play, if Miss Anne could not be with us."

Anne felt truly obliged to her for such kindness; and quite as much so for the opportunity it gave her of decidedly saying—

"If it depended only on my inclination, ma'am, the party at home (excepting on Mary's account) would not be the smallest impediment. I have no pleasure in the sort of meeting, and should be too happy to change it for a play, and with you. But, it had better not be attempted, perhaps." She had spoken it; but she trembled when it was done, conscious that her words were listened to, and daring not even to try to observe their effect.

It was soon generally agreed that Tuesday should be the day; Charles only reserving the advantage of still teasing his wife, by persisting that he would go to the play to-morrow if nobody else would.

Captain Wentworth left his seat, and walked to the fire-place; probably for the sake of walking away from it soon afterwards, and taking a station, with less bare-faced design, by Anne.

As soon as he sat down beside her, a knot of tension within Anne's belly relaxed. It was all she could do not to lean toward him and draw in a deep breath. The smell of sunshine and ocean overwhelmed anyway, and Anne curled her hands in her lap to keep from reaching for him.

"You have not been long enough in Bath," said he in a low voice for her alone, "to enjoy the evening parties of the place."

"Oh! no," Anne said, her eyes occupied with drawing in every plane and angle of his handsome face. "The usual character of them has nothing for me. I am no card-player."

His smile was gentle and intimate. "You were not formerly, I know. You did not use to like cards; but time makes many changes."

"I am not yet so much changed," cried Anne, and stopped, fearing she hardly knew what misconstruction. After waiting a few moments he said, and as if it were the result of immediate feeling, "It is a period, indeed! Eight years and a half is a period."

Whether he would have proceeded farther was left to Anne's imagination to ponder over in a calmer hour; for while still hearing the sounds he had uttered, she was startled to other subjects by Henrietta, who flounced down upon the sofa at Anne's other side, eager to make use of the present leisure for getting out, and calling on her companions to lose no time, lest somebody else should come in.

They were obliged to move. Anne talked of being perfectly ready, and tried to look it; but she felt that could Henrietta have known the regret and reluctance of her heart in quitting that chair, in preparing to quit the room, she would have found, in all her own sensations for her cousin, in the very security of his affection, wherewith to pity her.

Their preparations, however, were stopped short. Alarming sounds were heard; other visitors approached, and the door was thrown open for Sir Walter and Miss Elliot, whose entrance seemed to give a general chill. Anne felt an instant oppression, and wherever she looked saw symptoms of the same. The comfort, the freedom, the gaiety of the room was over, hushed into cold composure, determined silence, or insipid talk, to meet the heartless elegance of her father and sister. How mortifying to feel that it was so!

Her jealous eye was satisfied in one particular. Captain Wentworth was acknowledged again by each, by Elizabeth more graciously than before. She even addressed him once, and looked at him more than once. Elizabeth was, in fact, revolving a great measure. The sequel explained it. After the waste of a few minutes in saying the proper nothings, she began to give the invitation which was to comprise all the remaining dues of the Musgroves. "To-morrow evening, to meet a few friends: no formal party." It was all said very gracefully, and the cards with which she had provided herself, the "Miss Elliot at home," were laid on the table, with a courteous, comprehensive smile to all, and one smile and one card more decidedly for Captain Wentworth. The truth was, that Elizabeth had been long enough in Bath to understand the importance of a man of such an air and appearance as his. The past was nothing. The present was that Captain Wentworth would move about well in her drawing-room. The card was pointedly given, and Sir Walter and Elizabeth arose and disappeared.

The interruption had been short, though severe, and ease and animation returned to most of those they left as the door shut them out, but not to Anne. She could think only of the invitation she had with such astonishment witnessed, and of the manner in which it had been received; a manner of doubtful meaning, of surprise rather than gratification, of polite acknowledgement rather than acceptance. He glanced at Anne over the edge of the card with a look that contained much. She knew him; she saw disdain in his eye, and could not venture to believe that he had determined to accept such an offering, as an atonement for all the insolence of the past. Her spirits sank. He held the card in his hand after they were gone, as if deeply considering it. Anne watched him stroke the embossed words of false and too-late acceptance with his thumb.

"Only think of Elizabeth's including everybody!" whispered Mary very audibly. "I do not wonder Captain Wentworth is delighted! You see he cannot put the card out of his hand."

Anne caught his eye once more, saw his cheeks glow, and his mouth form itself into a momentary expression of contempt, and turned away, that she might neither see nor hear more to vex her.

He crushed the invitation within his fist and dropped it carelessly to the floor where it rolled beneath one of the chairs.

The party separated without Captain Wentworth ever looking at Anne again. The gentlemen had their own pursuits, the ladies proceeded on their own business, and they met no more while Anne belonged to them. She was earnestly begged to return and dine, and give them all the rest of the day, but her spirits had been so long exerted that at present she felt unequal to more, and fit only for home, where she might be sure of being as silent as she chose.

Promising to be with them the whole of the following morning, therefore, she closed the fatigues of the present by a toilsome walk to Camden Place, there to spend the evening chiefly in listening to the busy arrangements of Elizabeth and Mrs. Clay for the morrow's party, the frequent enumeration of the persons invited, and the continually improving detail of all the embellishments which were to make it the most completely elegant of its kind in Bath, while harassing herself with the never-ending question, of whether Captain Wentworth would come or not? They were reckoning him as certain, but with her it was a gnawing solicitude never appeased for five minutes together. Even though she had seen him crumple the invitation, she generally thought he would come, because she generally thought he ought; but it was a case which she could not so shape into any positive act of duty or discretion, as inevitably to defy the suggestions of very opposite feelings.

She only roused herself from the broodings of this restless agitation, to let Mrs. Clay know that she had been seen with Mr. Elliot three hours after his being supposed to be out of Bath, for having watched in vain for some intimation of the interview from the lady herself, she determined to mention it, and it seemed to her there was guilt in Mrs. Clay's face as she listened. It was transient: cleared away in an instant; but Anne could imagine she read there the consciousness of having, by some complication of mutual trick, or some overbearing authority of his, been obliged to attend (perhaps for half an hour) to his lectures and restrictions on her designs on Sir Walter. She exclaimed, however, with a very tolerable imitation of nature:—

"Oh! dear! very true. Only think, Miss Elliot, to my great surprise I met with Mr. Elliot in Bath Street. I was never more astonished. He turned back and walked with me to the Pump Yard. He had been prevented setting off for Thornberry, but I really forget by what; for I was in a hurry, and could not much attend, and I can only answer for his being determined not to be delayed in his return. He wanted to know how early he might be admitted to-morrow. He was full of 'to-morrow,' and it is very evident that I have been full of it too, ever since I entered the house, and learnt the extension of your plan and all that had happened, or my seeing him could never have gone so entirely out of my head."

Chapter 23

One day only had passed since Anne's conversation with Mrs. Smith; but a keener interest had succeeded, and she was now so little touched by Mr. Elliot's conduct, except by its effects in one quarter, that it became a matter of course the next morning, still to defer her explanatory visit in Rivers Street. She had promised to be with the Musgroves from breakfast to dinner. Her faith was plighted, and Mr. Elliot's character, like the Sultaness Scheherazade's head, must live another day.

She could not keep her appointment punctually, however; the weather was unfavourable, and she had grieved over the rain on her friends' account, and felt it very much on her own, before she was able to attempt the walk. When she reached the White Hart, and made her way to the proper apartment, she found herself neither arriving quite in time, nor the first to arrive. The party before her were, Mrs. Musgrove, talking to Mrs. Croft, and Captain Harville to Captain Wentworth. The others paused in their conversations to say hello, but Captain Wentworth refused to even look at her. Anne immediately heard that Mary and Henrietta, too impatient to wait, had gone out the moment it had cleared, but would be back again soon, and that the strictest injunctions had been left with Mrs. Musgrove to keep her there till they returned. She had only to submit, sit down, be outwardly composed, and feel herself plunged at once in all the agitations which she had merely laid her account of tasting a little before the morning closed. There was no delay, no waste of time. She was deep in the happiness of such misery, or the misery of such happiness, instantly. Two minutes after her entering the room, Captain Wentworth said—

"We will write the letter we were talking of, Harville, now, if you will give me materials."

Materials were at hand, on a separate table; he went to it, and nearly turning his broad back to them all, though Anne felt the rebuff was meant solely for her, was engrossed by writing.

Mrs. Musgrove was giving Mrs. Croft the history of her eldest daughter's engagement, and just in that inconvenient tone of voice which was perfectly audible while it pretended to be a whisper. Anne felt that she did not belong to the conversation, and yet, as Captain Harville seemed thoughtful and not disposed to talk, she could not avoid hearing many undesirable particulars; such as, "how Mr. Musgrove and my brother Hayter had met again and again to talk it over; what my brother Hayter had said one day, and what Mr. Musgrove had proposed the next, and what had occurred to my sister Hayter, and what the young people had wished, and what I said at first I never could consent to, but was afterwards persuaded to think might do very well," and a great deal in the same style of open-hearted communication: minutiae which, even with every advantage of taste and delicacy, which good Mrs. Musgrove could not give, could be properly interesting only to the principals. Mrs. Croft was attending with great good-humour, and whenever she spoke at all, it was very sensibly. Anne hoped the gentlemen might each be too much self-occupied to hear.

"And so, ma'am, all these thing considered," said Mrs. Musgrove, in her powerful whisper, "though we could have wished it different, yet, altogether, we did not think it fair to stand out any longer, for Charles Hayter was quite wild about it, and Henrietta was pretty near as bad; and so we thought they had better marry at once, and make the best of it, as many others have done before them. At any rate, said I, it will be better than a long engagement. They can barely contain themselves and keep their hands off one another now. Yes, best to be married right away when things descend to such a state."

Anne blushed furiously and kept her eyes turned upon the floor. It was certain that everyone in the room had heard Mrs. Musgrove's audacious words, and Anne could not bear to see how Captain Wentworth reacted to them. They had been in "such a state" once.

Mrs. Croft chuckled. "That is precisely what I was going to observe," cried Mrs. Croft. "I would rather have young people settle on a small income at once, and have to struggle with a few difficulties together, than be involved in a long engagement. I always think that no mutual—"

"Oh! dear Mrs. Croft," cried Mrs. Musgrove, unable to let her finish her speech, "there is nothing I so abominate for young people as a long engagement. It is what I always protested against for my children. It is all very well, I used to say, for young people to be engaged, if there is a certainty of their being able to marry in six months, or even in twelve; but a long engagement—"

"Yes, dear ma'am," said Mrs. Croft, "or an uncertain engagement, an engagement which may be long. To begin without knowing that at such a time there will be the means of marrying, I hold to be very unsafe and unwise, and what I think all parents should prevent as far as they can. Ruination is nothing to trifle with."

Anne found an unexpected interest here. She felt its application to herself, felt it in a nervous thrill all over her; her control slipped and at the same moment that her eyes instinctively glanced towards the distant table, Captain Wentworth's pen ceased to move, his head was raised, pausing, listening, and he turned round the next instant to give a look, one quick, conscious look at her. His eyes quickly skidded away, but not before Anne had seen the heat of remembered dalliances in their depths. Lady Russell's dire admonition that she was more like her father than her mother did not bear the same sting now that it had in her youth. Had Lady

Russell attempted that warning now, Anne was not sure that it would have convinced her to break with Frederick. Anne could not help but think that, in her case, ruination had been very much worth it.

The two ladies continued to talk, to re-urge the same admitted truths, and enforce them with such examples of the ill effect of a contrary practice as had fallen within their observation, but Anne heard nothing distinctly; it was only a buzz of words in her ear, her mind was in confusion, replaying every touch and every kiss as she stared blankly at Frederick's wide, beautiful back.

Captain Harville, who had in truth been hearing none of it, now left his seat, and moved to a window, and Anne seeming to watch him, though it was from thorough absence of mind, became gradually sensible that he was inviting her to join him where he stood. He looked at her with a smile, and a little motion of the head, which expressed, "Come to me, I have something to say;" and the unaffected, easy kindness of manner which denoted the feelings of an older acquaintance than he really was, strongly enforced the invitation. She roused herself and went to him. The window at which he stood was at the other end of the room from where the two ladies were sitting, and though nearer to Captain Wentworth's table, not very near. As she joined him, Captain Harville's countenance re-assumed the serious, thoughtful expression which seemed its natural character.

"Look here," said he, unfolding a parcel in his hand, and displaying a small miniature painting, "do you know who that is?"

"Certainly: Captain Benwick."

"Yes, and you may guess who it is for. But," (in a deep tone,) "it was not done for her. Miss Elliot, do you remember our walking together at Lyme, and grieving for him? I little thought then—but no matter. This was drawn at the Cape. He met with a clever young German artist at the Cape, and in compliance with a promise to my poor sister, sat to him, and was bringing it home for her; and I have now the charge of getting it properly set for another! It was a commission to me! But who else was there to employ? I hope I can allow for him. I am not sorry, indeed, to make it over to another. He undertakes it;" (looking towards Captain Wentworth,) "he is writing about it now." And with a quivering lip he wound up the whole by adding, "Poor Fanny! she would not have forgotten him so soon!"

"No," replied Anne, in a low, feeling voice. "That I can easily believe."

"It was not in her nature. She doted on him."

"It would not be the nature of any woman who truly loved."

Captain Harville smiled, as much as to say, "Do you claim that for your sex?" and she answered the question, smiling also, "Yes. We certainly do not forget you as soon as you forget us. It is, perhaps, our fate rather than our merit. We cannot help ourselves. We live at home, quiet, confined, and our feelings prey upon us. You are forced on exertion. You have always a profession, pursuits, business of some sort or other, to take you back into the world immediately, and continual occupation and change soon weaken impressions."

"Granting your assertion that the world does all this so soon for men (which, however, I do not think I shall grant), it does not apply to Benwick. He has not been forced upon any exertion. The peace turned him on shore at the very moment, and he has been living with us, in our little family circle, ever since."

"True," said Anne, "very true; I did not recollect; but what shall we say now, Captain Harville? If the change be not from outward circumstances, it must be from within; it must be nature, man's nature, which has done the business for Captain Benwick."

"No, no, it is not man's nature. I will not allow it to be more man's nature than woman's to be inconstant and forget those they do love, or have loved. I believe the reverse. I believe in a true analogy between our bodily frames and our mental; and that as our bodies are the strongest, so are our feelings; capable of bearing most rough usage, and riding out the heaviest weather."

"Your feelings may be the strongest," replied Anne, "but the same spirit of analogy will authorise me to assert that ours are the most tender. Man is more robust than woman, but he is not longer lived; which exactly explains my view of the nature of their attachments. Nay, it would be too hard upon you, if it were otherwise. You have difficulties, and privations, and dangers enough to struggle with. You are always labouring and toiling, exposed to every risk and hardship. Your home, country, friends, all quitted. Neither time, nor health, nor life, to be called your own. It would be hard, indeed" (with a faltering voice), "if woman's feelings were to be added to all this."

"We shall never agree upon this question," Captain Harville was beginning to say, when a slight noise called their attention to Captain Wentworth's hitherto perfectly quiet division of the room. It was nothing more than that his pen had fallen down; but Anne was startled at finding him nearer than she had supposed, and half inclined to suspect that the pen had only fallen because he had been occupied by them, striving to catch sounds, which yet she did not think he could have caught.

"Have you finished your letter?" said Captain Harville.

"Not quite, a few lines more. I shall have done in five minutes." His voice was hoarse, and Anne did not think she imagined that his back was stiffer than it had been moments ago. The content of his letter must be troubling him. "There is no hurry on my side. I am only ready whenever you are. I am in very good anchorage here," (smiling at Anne,) "well supplied, and want for nothing. No hurry for a signal at all. Well, Miss Elliot," (lowering his voice,) "as I was saying we shall never agree, I suppose, upon this point. No man and woman, would, probably. But let me observe that all histories are against you—all stories, prose and verse. If I had such a memory as Benwick, I could bring you fifty quotations in a moment on my side the argument, and I do not think I ever opened a book in my life which had not something to say upon woman's inconstancy. Songs and proverbs, all talk of woman's fickleness. But perhaps you will say, these were all written by men."

"Perhaps I shall. Yes, yes, if you please, no reference to examples in books. Men have had every advantage of us in telling their own story. Education has been theirs in so much higher a degree; the pen has been in their hands. I will not allow books to prove anything."

"But how shall we prove anything?"

"We never shall. We never can expect to prove any thing upon such a point. It is a difference of opinion which does not admit of proof. We each begin, probably, with a little bias towards our own sex; and upon that bias build every circumstance in favour of it which has occurred within our own circle; many of which circumstances (perhaps those very cases which strike us the most) may be precisely such as cannot be brought forward without betraying a confidence, or in some respect saying what should not be said."

"Ah!" cried Captain Harville, in a tone of strong feeling, "if I could but make you comprehend what a man suffers when he takes a last look at his wife and children, and watches the boat that he has sent them off in, as long as it is in sight, and then turns away and says, 'God knows whether we ever meet again!' And then, if I could convey to you the glow of his soul when he does see them again; when, coming back after a twelvemonth's absence, perhaps, and obliged to put into another port, he calculates how soon it be possible to get them there, pretending to deceive himself, and saying, 'They cannot be here till such a day,' but all the while hoping for them twelve hours sooner, and seeing them arrive at last, as if Heaven had given them wings, by many hours sooner still! If I could explain to you all this, and all that a man can bear and do, and glories to do, for the sake of these treasures of his existence! I speak, you know, only of such men as have hearts!" pressing his own with emotion.

"Oh!" cried Anne eagerly, "I hope I do justice to all that is felt by you, and by those who resemble you. God forbid that I should undervalue the warm and faithful feelings of any of my fellow-creatures! I should deserve utter contempt if I dared to suppose that true attachment and constancy were known only by woman. No, I believe you capable of everything great and good in your married lives. I believe you equal to every important exertion, and to every domestic forbearance, so long as—if I may be allowed the expression—so long as you have an object. I mean while the woman you love lives, and lives for you. All the privilege I claim for my own sex (it is not a very enviable one; you need not covet it), is that of loving longest, when existence or when hope is gone."

She could not immediately have uttered another sentence; her heart was too full, her breath too much oppressed.

"You are a good soul," cried Captain Harville, putting his hand on her arm, quite affectionately. "There is no quarrelling with you. And when I think of Benwick, my tongue is tied."

Their attention was called towards the others. Mrs. Croft was taking leave.

"Here, Frederick, you and I part company, I believe," said she. "I am going home, and you have an engagement with your friend. To-night we may have the pleasure of all meeting again at your party," (turning to Anne.) "We had your sister's card yesterday, and I understood Frederick had a card too, though I did not see it; and you are disengaged, Frederick, are you not, as well as ourselves?"

Captain Wentworth was folding up a letter in great haste, muscles bunching beneath his coat, and either could not or would not answer fully. Anne noticed with some shock that his hair was ruffled as though he had put his hands through it.

"Yes," said he, "very true; here we separate, but Harville and I shall soon be after you; that is, Harville, if you are ready, I am in half a minute. I know you will not be sorry to be off. I shall be at your service in half a minute."

Mrs. Croft left them, and Captain Wentworth, having sealed his letter with great rapidity, was indeed ready, and had even a hurried, agitated air, which shewed impatience to be gone. Anne knew not how to understand it. She had the kindest "Good morning, God bless you!" from Captain Harville, but from him not a word, nor a look! He had passed out of the room without a look!

She had only time, however, to move closer to the table where he had been writing, when footsteps were heard returning; the door opened, it was himself. He begged their pardon, but he had forgotten his gloves, and instantly crossing the room to the writing table, he drew out a letter from under the scattered paper, placed it before Anne with eyes of glowing entreaty fixed on her for a time. His eyes dipped from hers to her lips, and then, hastily collecting his gloves, he was again out of the room, almost before Mrs. Musgrove was aware of his being in it: the work of an instant!

The revolution which one instant had made in Anne, was almost beyond expression. The letter, with a direction hardly legible, to "Miss A. E.—," was evidently the one which he had been folding so hastily. While supposed to be writing only to Captain Benwick, he had been also addressing her! On the contents of that letter depended all which this world could do for her. Anything was possible, anything might be defied rather than suspense. Mrs. Musgrove had little arrangements of her own at her own table; to their protection she must trust, and sinking into the chair which he had occupied and which was still warmed from his body, succeeding to the very spot where he had leaned and written, her eyes devoured the following words:

"I can listen no longer in silence. I must speak to you by such means as are within my reach. You pierce my soul. I am half agony, half hope. Tell me not that I am too late, that such precious feelings are gone for ever. I offer myself to you again with a heart even more your own than when you almost broke it, eight years and a half ago. Dare not say that man forgets sooner than woman, that his love has an earlier death. I have loved none but you. Unjust I may have been, weak and resentful I have been, but never inconstant. You alone have brought me to Bath. For you alone, I think and plan. Have you not seen this? Can you fail to have understood my wishes? I had not waited even these ten days, could I have read your feelings, as I think you must have penetrated mine. I can hardly write. I am every instant hearing something which overpowers me. You sink your voice, but I can distinguish the tones of that voice when they would be lost on others. Too good, too excellent creature! You do us justice, indeed. You do believe that there is true attachment and constancy among men. Believe it to be most fervent, most undeviating, in F. W.

"I must go, uncertain of my fate; but I shall return hither, or follow your party, as soon as possible. A word, a look, will be enough to decide whether I enter your father's house this evening or never."

Such a letter was not to be soon recovered from. Half an hour's solitude and reflection might have tranquillized her; but the ten minutes only which now passed before she was interrupted, with all the restraints of her situation, could do nothing towards tranquillity. Every moment rather brought fresh agitation. It was overpowering happiness. And before she was beyond the first stage of full sensation, Charles, Mary, and Henrietta all came in. Anne quickly tucked Frederick's letter between her breasts and out of sight.

The absolute necessity of seeming like herself produced then an immediate struggle; but after a while she could do no more. She began not to understand a word they said, and was obliged to plead indisposition and excuse herself. They could then see that she looked very ill, were shocked and concerned, and would not stir without her for the world. This was dreadful. Would they only have gone away, and left her in the quiet possession of that room it would have been her cure; but to have them all standing or waiting around her was distracting, and in desperation, she said she would go home.

"By all means, my dear," cried Mrs. Musgrove, "go home directly, and take care of yourself, that you may be fit for the evening. I wish Sarah was here to doctor you, but I am no doctor myself. Charles, ring and order a chair. She must not walk."

But the chair would never do. Worse than all! To lose the possibility of speaking two words to Captain Wentworth in the course of her quiet, solitary progress up the town (and she felt almost certain of meeting him) could not be borne. The chair was earnestly protested against, and Mrs. Musgrove, who thought only of one sort of illness, having assured herself with some anxiety, that there had been no fall in the case; that Anne had not at any time lately slipped down, and got a blow on her head; that she was perfectly convinced of having had no fall; could part with her cheerfully, and depend on finding her better at night.

Anxious to omit no possible precaution, Anne struggled, and said—

"I am afraid, ma'am, that it is not perfectly understood. Pray be so good as to mention to the other gentlemen that we hope to see your whole party this evening. I am afraid there had been some mistake; and I wish you particularly to assure Captain Harville and Captain Wentworth, that we hope to see them both."

"Oh! my dear, it is quite understood, I give you my word. Captain Harville has no thought but of going."

"Do you think so? But I am afraid; and I should be so very sorry. Will you promise me to mention it, when you see them again? You will see them both this morning, I dare say. Do promise me."

"To be sure I will, if you wish it. Charles, if you see Captain Harville anywhere, remember to give Miss Anne's message. But indeed, my dear, you need not be uneasy. Captain Harville holds himself quite engaged, I'll answer for it; and Captain Wentworth the same, I dare say."

Anne could do no more; but her heart prophesied some mischance to damp the perfection of her felicity. It could not be very lasting, however. Even if he did not come to Camden Place himself, it would be in her power to send an intelligible sentence by Captain Harville. Another momentary vexation occurred. Charles, in his real concern and good nature, would go home with her; there was no preventing him. This was almost cruel. But she could not be long ungrateful; he was sacrificing an engagement at a gunsmith's, to be of use to her; and she set off with him, with no feeling but gratitude apparent.

They were on Union Street, when a quicker step behind, a something of familiar sound, gave her two moments' preparation for the sight of Captain Wentworth. He joined them; but, as if irresolute whether to join or to pass on, said nothing, only looked. Anne could command herself enough to receive that look, and not repulsively. The cheeks which had been pale now glowed, and the movements which had hesitated were decided. He walked by her side. Anne was nearly driven mad by the heat of his body as he walked so closely that the back of his hand brushed against the back of hers with each step. Presently, struck by a sudden thought, Charles said—

"Captain Wentworth, which way are you going? Only to Gay Street, or farther up the town?"

"I hardly know," replied Captain Wentworth, his eyes finding Anne's and posing the same question.

"Are you going as high as Belmont? Are you going near Camden Place? Because, if you are, I shall have no scruple in asking you to take my place, and give Anne your arm to her father's door. She is rather done for this morning, and must not go so far without help, and I ought to be at that fellow's in the Market Place. He promised me the sight of a capital gun he is just going to send off;

said he would keep it unpacked to the last possible moment, that I might see it; and if I do not turn back now, I have no chance. By his description, a good deal like the second size double-barrel of mine, which you shot with one day round Winthrop."

There could not be an objection. There could be only the most proper alacrity, a most obliging compliance for public view; and smiles reined in and spirits dancing in private rapture. In half a minute Charles was at the bottom of Union Street again, and the other two proceeding together: and soon words enough had passed between them to decide their direction towards the comparatively quiet and retired gravel walk, where the power of conversation would make the present hour a blessing indeed, and prepare it for all the immortality which the happiest recollections of their own future lives could bestow. There they exchanged again those feelings and those promises which had once before seemed to secure everything, but which had been followed by so many, many years of division and estrangement. There they returned again into the past, more exquisitely happy, perhaps, in their re-union, than when it had been first projected; more tender, more tried, more fixed in a knowledge of each other's character, truth, and attachment; more equal to act, more justified in acting. And there, as they slowly paced the gradual ascent, heedless of every group around them, seeing neither sauntering politicians, bustling housekeepers, flirting girls, nor nursery-maids and children, they could indulge in those retrospections and acknowledgements, and especially in those explanations of what had directly preceded the present moment, which were so poignant and so ceaseless in interest. All the little variations of the last week were gone through; and of yesterday and to-day there could scarcely be an end.

She had not mistaken him. Jealousy of Mr. Elliot had been the retarding weight, the doubt, the torment. That had begun to operate in the very hour of first meeting her in Bath; that had returned, after a short suspension, to ruin the concert; and that had influenced him in everything he had said and done, or omitted to say and do, in the last four-and-twenty hours. It had been gradually yielding to the better hopes which her looks, or words, or actions occasionally encouraged; it had been vanquished at last by those sentiments and those tones which had reached him while she talked with Captain Harville; and under the irresistible governance of which he had seized a sheet of paper, and poured out his feelings.

Of what he had then written, nothing was to be retracted or qualified. He persisted in having loved none but her. She had never been supplanted. He never even believed himself to see her equal. Thus much indeed he was obliged to acknowledge: that he had been constant unconsciously, nay unintentionally; that he had meant to forget her, and believed it to be done. He had imagined himself indifferent, when he had only been angry; and he had been unjust to her merits, because he had been a sufferer from them. Her character was now fixed on his mind as perfection itself, maintaining the loveliest medium of fortitude and gentleness; but he was obliged to acknowledge that only at Uppercross had he learnt to do her justice, and only at Lyme had he begun to understand himself. At Lyme, he had received lessons of more than one sort. The passing admiration of Mr. Elliot had at least roused him, and the scenes on the Cobb and at Captain Harville's had fixed her superiority.

In his preceding attempts to attach himself to Louisa Musgrove (the attempts of angry pride), he protested that he had for ever felt it to be impossible; that he had not cared, could not care, for Louisa; though till that day, till the leisure for reflection which followed it, he had not understood the perfect excellence of the mind with which Louisa's could so ill bear a comparison, or the perfect unrivalled hold it possessed over his own. There, he had learnt to distinguish between the steadiness of principle and the obstinacy of self-will, between the darings of heedlessness and the resolution of a collected mind. There he had seen everything to exalt in his estimation the woman he had lost; and there begun to deplore the pride, the folly, the madness of resentment, which had kept him from trying to regain her when thrown in his way.

From that period his penance had become severe. He had no sooner been free from the horror and remorse attending the first few days of Louisa's accident, no sooner begun to feel himself alive again, than he had begun to feel himself, though alive, not at liberty.

"I found," said he, "that I was considered by Harville an engaged man! That neither Harville nor his wife entertained a doubt of our mutual attachment. I was startled and shocked. To a degree, I could contradict this instantly; but, when I began to reflect that others might have felt the same—her own family, nay, perhaps herself—I was no longer at my own disposal. I was hers in honour if she wished it. I had been unguarded. I had not thought seriously on this subject before. I had not considered that my excessive intimacy must have its danger of ill consequence in many ways; and that I had no right to be trying whether I could attach myself to either of the girls, at the risk of raising even an unpleasant report, were there no other ill effects. I had been grossly wrong, and must abide the consequences."

He found too late, in short, that he had entangled himself; and that precisely as he became fully satisfied of his not caring for Louisa at all, he must regard himself as bound to her, if her sentiments for him were what the Harvilles supposed. It determined him to leave Lyme, and await her complete recovery elsewhere. He would gladly weaken, by any fair means, whatever feelings or speculations concerning him might exist; and he went, therefore, to his brother's, meaning after a while to return to Kellynch, and act as circumstances might require.

"I was six weeks with Edward," said he, "and saw him happy— so very happy in his marriage. They nearly drove me to the brink,

Anne. They were constantly touching each other and stealing kisses, and all I could think of was you and how I may have for ever ruined my chances to regain your love. I could have no other pleasure. I deserved none. He enquired after you very particularly; asked even if you were personally altered, little suspecting that to my eye you could never alter."

Anne smiled, and let it pass. It was too pleasing a blunder for a reproach. It is something for a woman to be assured, in her eight-and-twentieth year, that she has not lost one charm of earlier youth; but the value of such homage was inexpressibly increased to Anne, by comparing it with former words, and feeling it to be the result, not the cause of a revival of his warm attachment.

He had remained in Shropshire, lamenting the blindness of his own pride, and the blunders of his own calculations, till at once released from Louisa by the astonishing and felicitous intelligence of her engagement with Benwick.

"Here," said he, "ended the worst of my state; for now I could at least put myself in the way of happiness; I could exert myself; I could do something. But to be waiting so long in inaction, and waiting only for evil, had been dreadful. Within the first five minutes I said, 'I will be at Bath on Wednesday,' and I was. Was it unpardonable to think it worth my while to come? And to arrive with some degree of hope? You were single. It was possible that you might retain the feelings of the past, as I did; and one encouragement happened to be mine. I could never doubt that you would be loved and sought by others, but I knew to a certainty that you had refused one man, at least, of better pretensions than myself; and I could not help often saying, 'Was this for me?'"

Their first meeting in Milsom Street afforded much to be said, but the concert still more. That evening seemed to be made up of exquisite moments. The moment of her stepping forward in the Octagon Room to speak to him: the moment of Mr. Elliot's appearing and tearing her away, and one or two subsequent moments, marked by returning hope or increasing despondency, and then their meeting in the Octagon Room were dwelt on with energy.

"To see you," cried he, "in the midst of those who could not be my well-wishers; to see your cousin close by you, conversing and smiling, and feel all the horrible eligibilities and proprieties of the match! To consider it as the certain wish of every being who could hope to influence you! Even if your own feelings were reluctant or indifferent, to consider what powerful supports would be his! Was it not enough to make the fool of me which I acted? How could I look on without agony? Was not the very sight of the friend who sat behind you, was not the recollection of what had been, the knowledge of her influence, the indelible, immoveable impression of what persuasion had once done—was it not all against me?"

"You should have distinguished," replied Anne. "You should not have suspected me now; the case is so different, and my age is so different. If I was wrong in yielding to persuasion once, remember that it was to persuasion exerted on the side of safety, not of risk. When I yielded, I thought it was to duty, but no duty could be called in aid here. In marrying a man indifferent to me, all risk would have been incurred, and all duty violated."

"Perhaps I ought to have reasoned thus," he replied, "but I could not. I could not derive benefit from the late knowledge I had acquired of your character. I could not bring it into play; it was overwhelmed, buried, lost in those earlier feelings which I had been smarting under year after year. I could think of you only as one who had yielded, who had given me up, who had been influenced by any one rather than by me. I saw you with the very person who had guided you in that year of misery. I had no reason to believe her of less authority now. The force of habit was to be added."

"I should have thought," said Anne, "that my manner to yourself might have spared you much or all of this. I do not—" Anne blushed "—do those *things* with just anyone."

"No, no! your reaction might be only the cause which your engagement to another man would give. Your eyes as you looked upon me when we were interrupted by Mr. Elliot—they cut right through me. I assumed you were bereft because I had stolen something from you that belonged to *him*! I left you in this belief; and yet, I was determined to see you again. My spirits rallied with the morning, and I felt that I had still a motive for remaining here."

Anne stopped him with a hand to his upper arm. "Frederick," she whispered, "I was *bereft* because you stopped kissing and touching me. No other reason."

She was standing so close to him, and with her hand upon his arm, that she felt when her words caused every muscle in his body to clench.

"Will I ever do the right thing with you?" he asked in dismay, his eyes cast down to where his fingers traced a shape on the back of her hand.

The simple movement of his finger across her skin was setting fire to her body. "That depends on what you plan to do right now."

The nearly audible snap of his head jerking up so he could stare at her betrayed that her words had shocked him nearly as much as they had shocked herself. The blatant invitation in her tone had not been missed.

Frederick stared at her for several moments before his face split in a slow smile. "Indeed," he said, his voice a rumble.

In the next heartbeat, he was obviously scouring their location. Her eyes joined his in the search, and they both spotted the stable at the same time.

He did not have to stop to ask her if she would join him there, for she began walking in that direction immediately. His chuckle sounded in her ear, raising goose bumps across her chest, as he quickly followed in her wake.

A door on the side of the building stood open, and he reached it first, opening it wider for her and allowing her to slip into the cool, hay-scented air ahead of him.

A quick perusal showed the stable to be empty of all but a lone, sleeping donkey in one of the far stalls.

"Thank heaven," Frederick breathed on a laugh. "I have no idea what I would have said to some one if they had been in here."

Anne used the opportunity of his attention being focused elsewhere to look upon him. He was so much handsomer than he had been over eight years ago, and even then, she had never seen anyone who matched him. He was so big and broad that his presence dwarfed the roomy stable. Her eyes devoured every inch of him, and when her silence caught his attention and he turned toward her, he caught her in the act of ogling him.

Immediate and intense heat flared in his eyes. "Anne," he breathed, turning toward her fully and stroking the back of his finger down her cheek. His breath hitched in his chest. "I cannot believe I am permitted to touch you once more." He tilted his head to the side and closed his eyes as his simple stroke of her cheek morphed until his fingers wove through her hair.

He pulled her forward, and she went willingly, stepping into his tall, warm body and wrapping her arms about his waist. She turned her head and rested her ear against his chest. The solid thumping of his heart sounded through every fibre of her being, and his arms enclosed her and squeezed her tightly.

She squeezed him in return, though his body gave a lot less than she suspected hers did. His middle was firm, and her hands splayed across cords of muscle in his back. She felt that muscle shift, and she raised her head to find he was lowering his.

Her heart grew nearly too big for her chest as she tilted her face up and accepted his kiss. The sigh of relief that left her when their lips touched she heard echoed from him as he gently swept his lips back and forth across hers.

His touch was light, his hold upon her loose—it spoke of the confidence he now felt that she was truly his, that he did not have to hold her tightly or lose her.

"Anne," he spoke between kisses. "I am so sorry." His hold did grow slightly tighter as he continued to breathe a litany of apologies and what sounded like *such a fool* while tasting her lips and allowing his hands to wander her back.

She shushed him as well as she could with her lips occupied.

He began to walk her backwards, and next she knew, he was lowering her to the ground. She went without question and found herself lying upon a mound of hay. He immediately followed her down and stretched out atop her. The weight of his body pressed her deliciously into the softness at her back, and she sighed once more as she clutched his jacket with both hands and pulled him even closer. She widened her thighs and silently thrilled when his body fell into the area she had meant it to.

His hard, unforgiving arousal pressed against her centre, and they both broke the kiss to suck in a startled breath. His eyes searched her face, and it was a few moments before she realized that he was asking permission.

"Oh, Frederick," she whispered. "Love me. Please."

He paused only long enough to gift her with a beauteous smile, and then he lowered his head once more. This time, his kiss was determined. Gone were the soft sweeps of his lips. He licked his way into her mouth and stroked her tongue languidly. His hand gripped the sides of her thighs, and she felt him tugging her dress up.

She moaned into their kiss and reached down to help him. Together, they bunched her skirts around her waist, and his hand slipped into her drawers. Two fingers stroked down her centre, and she gasped as they passed over the throbbing bundle of nerves at the top of her sex, but he did not stop there. His two thick fingers slid into her sheath, stretching and filling her so swiftly, she nearly peaked on the spot.

"Frederick!" Her gasp echoed around the empty stable, and it quickly turned into a moan as he shifted his body to the side so he could stroke the top of her sex with his thumb.

Things were moving so quickly. Her body was carrying her away. She was going to reach her pleasure any second, and it would be without him inside of her body. That she could not abide.

"Slow down," she pleaded breathlessly, clutching his jacket and tugging fretfully. "Frederick, not yet."

He immediately stopped, and a look of horror flashed across his features. His body immediately moved away from hers, and the slow drag of his fingers against the sensitive skin of her core was almost her undoing. Thankfully, enough of her mind remained in command to recognise that he had misinterpreted her passion-addled words. Her grip upon his arms tightened, and she yanked him back down upon her with more strength than she thought she possessed.

"No," she whispered. "Inside me. Please."

He stilled, and through the haze of passion, Anne saw the conflict and confusion in his eyes.

"I do not want to finish without you inside me."

His body relaxed, and she knew all was well when a breathless laugh escaped his lips and his fingers returned to their deep-seated position. His thumb stroked a sure circle around her bud, and he leaned down to kiss the shell of her ear. "If I enter you now," he breathed into her ear, "I will never last."

His thumb continued to circle, and Anne moaned fretfully, knowing she should be focusing on his words instead of the sensations he was wringing from her body, but being unable to do anything but revel in the slow, steady rhythm of his hand.

His breath teazed the hair at her temple as he spoke once more. "It's been eight and a half years since I have loved a woman, Anne." His thumb picked up the pace, and Anne's back bowed involuntarily. "The moment I enter your body, I am done."

As soon as his words registered, Anne's body threw itself into paradise. Her lips parted as she moaned long and low. Her thighs tightened, and her fingers flexed in his jacket. She heard herself breathe his name, and he thrust his fingers even deeper inside of her, crooking them slightly and rubbing them against a spot that wrenched a haggard gasp from her lungs. The pleasure grew in intensity until it was so great spots flashed behind Anne's eyes. "Now!" she half-sobbed. "Please, now."

She heard his bitten off curse and the sound of his breeches rustling, and in the next instant, he pulled his fingers from her body. The scalding hot skin of his arousal branded her entrance, and he never paused. He grasped behind her knee, pulled her leg over his hip, and thrust forward. Her drenched body gladly accepted him, and he slid in to the hilt.

"God," he choked out, throwing his head back and setting the cords of his neck into stark relief. "So tight," he groaned as every muscle in his body flexed and then began to tremble.

Anne's hands wandered over his chest and up his neck, and she pulled him down so that he was lying heavily upon her once more. She raised her head and bit his lower lip. "Move," she begged while grinding her hips against his in a circle.

"*Anne*, it is too good." He shook his head, but his body contrarily took over as he pulled back his hips and thrust into her once more. Another pained noise rumbled in his chest, and he buried his face in her neck. She heard him pray for control as his hips again moved, and then continued to move, quickly picking up the pace until the sound of his hips slapping against her echoed in the air.

The loose, gentle hold he had used when they'd first entered the stable had certainly vanished. He touched her everywhere, and he touched her hard. His beard rasped against her neck. One hand squeezed her breast while the other's fingers dug into her flank. She felt the edge of his teeth as he nibbled a path down her neck to her collarbone where he bit and then sucked. Her fingers clutched his hair and held him close, and he gifted her with another bite.

Impossibly, Anne felt the peak she had already met once looming before her, and his dire warning of not being able to last suddenly mattered a great deal. "Do not stop," she moaned as she wrapt her legs around his hips and crossed her ankles over his bottom. "*Please.*"

"Oh, God, Anne." His fingers flexed into her flesh, and she heard him swear violently. His thrusts grew deeper, and it was this new depth that had him grinding against the top of her sex.

Anne sucked in all of her breath as her body reached completion, and Frederick crushed his lips against hers, bruising them and capturing her scream at the same time. He thrust his tongue deeply into her mouth, and his groan rumbled through her as his thrusts grew erratic and his muscles shook. She felt him jet hotly into her womb, and her eyes stung from an overwhelming rush of emotion.

Their bodies stilled, but their breaths billowed out of their chest in almost perfect synchronicity. He kissed her slowly and softly one last time before pulling back to look into her eyes. As she met his gaze, she knew the happiness she saw glowing from his every feature was mirrored in her own face.

They heard voices outside, and they both tensed as they realized they had just made love—rather *loud* love—in the middle of the day and in the middle of Bath.

Anne laughed softly, and the trace of worry that had edged into Frederick's expression vanished. He rolled to the side with a groan, pulled down Anne's skirt, and pressed a kiss to her temple before setting his breeches to rights.

"I cannot believe we did that," he said in a soft, amused voice.

"I can," Anne said with a smile. "I have been wanting to do so since you first arrived in this city."

He chuckled and turned to wink at her, one lock of his blonde hair falling rakishly across his brow. She reached up to brush it with her fingers, and he captured her hand and pressed a kiss to her fingertips.

"We must go, love," he said with a reticent smile. "Charles will beat you home and use his new rifle on me." He rose effortlessly to his feet and turned to help her to hers.

Anne brushed her skirt, and Frederick plucked several pieces of hay from her hair. He clucked his tongue and passed a finger over a sensitive spot on her collarbone. Her eyes followed his touch to find a mark upon her skin.

"I bit you?" he asked incredulously.

Anne smiled. "Oh, yes." At his horrified look, she laughed once more and drew her shawl over the spot. "I rather liked it. Remember that for the future."

His instantaneous smile dazzled her. "The future," he repeated dazedly. "Indeed."

At last Anne was at home again, and happier than any one in that house could have conceived. All the surprise and suspense, and every other painful part of the morning dissipated by this conversation and by their love, she re-entered the house so happy as to be obliged to find an alloy in some momentary apprehensions of its being impossible to last. An interval of meditation, serious and grateful, was the best corrective of everything dangerous in such high-wrought felicity; and she went to her room, and grew steadfast and fearless in the thankfulness of her enjoyment.

The evening came, the drawing-rooms were lighted up, the company assembled. It was but a card party, it was but a mixture of those who had never met before, and those who met too often; a commonplace business, too numerous for intimacy, too small for variety; but Anne had never found an evening shorter. Glowing and lovely in sensibility and happiness, and more generally admired than she thought about or cared for, she had cheerful or forbearing feelings for every creature around her. A pleasant ache burned at the apex of her thighs and overshadowed any ill feeling. Mr. Elliot was there; she avoided, but she could pity him. The Wallises, she had amusement in understanding them. Lady Dalrymple and Miss Carteret—they would soon be innoxious cousins to her. She cared not for Mrs. Clay, and had nothing to blush for in the public manners of her father and sister. With the Musgroves, there was the happy chat of perfect ease; with Captain Harville, the kind-hearted intercourse of brother and sister; with Lady Russell, attempts at conversation, which a delicious consciousness cut short; with Admiral and Mrs. Croft, everything of peculiar cordiality and fervent interest, which the same consciousness sought to conceal; and with Captain Wentworth, some moments of communications continually occurring, several stolen caresses, and always the hope of more, and always the knowledge of his being there.

It was in one of these short meetings, each apparently occupied in admiring a fine display of greenhouse plants though he used the opportunity to stroke his finger down her arm, that she said—

"I have been thinking over the past, and trying impartially to judge of the right and wrong, I mean with regard to myself; and I must believe that I was right, much as I suffered from it, that I was perfectly right in being guided by the friend whom you will love better than you do now. To me, she was in the place of a parent." His finger stilled upon her skin, and she felt him tense. "Do not mistake me, however," she hurried to say. "I am not saying that she did not err in her advice. It was, perhaps, one of those cases in which advice is good or bad only as the event decides; and for myself, I certainly never should, in any circumstance of tolerable similarity, give such advice. But I mean, that I was right in submitting to her, and that if I had done otherwise, I should have suffered more in continuing the engagement than I did even in giving it up, because I should have suffered in my conscience. I have now, as far as such a sentiment is allowable in human nature, nothing to reproach myself with; and if I mistake not, a strong sense of duty is no bad part of a woman's portion."

He looked at her, looked at Lady Russell, and looking again at her, replied, as if in cool deliberation—

"Not yet. But there are hopes of her being forgiven in time. I trust to being in charity with her soon. But I too have been thinking over the past, and a question has suggested itself, whether there may not have been one person more my enemy even than that lady? My own self. Tell me if, when I returned to England in the year eight, with a few thousand pounds, and was posted into the *Laconia*, if I had then written to you, would you have answered my letter? Would you, in short, have renewed the engagement then?"

"Would I!" was all her answer; but the accent was decisive enough.

"Good God!" he cried, "you would! It is not that I did not think of it, or desire it, as what could alone crown all my other success; but I was proud, too proud to ask again. I did not understand you. I shut my eyes, and would not understand you, or do you justice. This is a recollection which ought to make me forgive every one sooner than myself. Six years of separation and suffering might have been spared. It is a sort of pain, too, which is new to me. I have been used to the gratification of believing myself to earn every blessing that I enjoyed. I have valued myself on honourable toils and just rewards. Like other great men under reverses," he added, with a smile. "I must endeavour to subdue my mind to my fortune. I must learn to brook being happier than I deserve."

Chapter 24

Who can be in doubt of what followed? When any two young people take it into their heads to marry, they are pretty sure by perseverance to carry their point, be they ever so poor, or ever so imprudent, or ever so little likely to be necessary to each other's ultimate comfort. This may be bad morality to conclude with, but I believe it to be truth; and if such parties succeed, how should a Captain Wentworth and an Anne Elliot, with the advantage of maturity of mind, consciousness of right, and one independent fortune between them, fail of bearing down every opposition? They might in fact, have borne down a great deal more than they met with, for there was little to distress them beyond the want of graciousness and warmth. Sir Walter made no objection, and Elizabeth did nothing worse than look cold and unconcerned. Captain Wentworth, with five-and-twenty thousand pounds, and as high in his profession as merit and activity could place him, was no longer nobody. He was now esteemed quite worthy to address the daughter of a foolish, spendthrift baronet, who had not had principle or sense enough to maintain himself in the situation in which Providence had placed him, and who could give his daughter at present but a small part of the share of ten thousand pounds which must be hers hereafter.

Sir Walter, indeed, though he had no affection for Anne, and no vanity flattered, to make him really happy on the occasion, was very far from thinking it a bad match for her. On the contrary, when he saw more of Captain Wentworth, saw him repeatedly by daylight, and eyed him well, he was very much struck by his personal claims, and felt that his superiority of appearance might be not unfairly balanced against her superiority of rank; and all this, assisted by his well-sounding name, enabled Sir Walter at last to prepare his pen, with a very good grace, for the insertion of the marriage in the volume of honour.

The only one among them, whose opposition of feeling could excite any serious anxiety was Lady Russell. Anne knew that Lady Russell must be suffering some pain in understanding and relinquishing Mr. Elliot, and be making some struggles to become truly acquainted with, and do justice to Captain Wentworth. This however was what Lady Russell had now to do. She must learn to feel that she had been mistaken with regard to both; that she had been unfairly influenced by appearances in each; that because Captain Wentworth's manners had not suited her own ideas, she had been too quick in suspecting them to indicate a character of dangerous impetuosity; and that because Mr. Elliot's manners had precisely pleased her in their propriety and correctness, their general politeness and suavity, she had been too quick in receiving them as the certain result of the most correct opinions and well-regulated mind. There was nothing less for Lady Russell to do, than to admit that she had been pretty completely wrong, and to take up a new set of opinions and of hopes.

There is a quickness of perception in some, a nicety in the discernment of character, a natural penetration, in short, which no experience in others can equal, and Lady Russell had been less gifted in this part of understanding than her young friend. But she was a very good woman, and if her second object was to be sensible and well-judging, her first was to see Anne happy. She loved Anne better than she loved her own abilities; and when the awkwardness of the beginning was over, found little hardship in attaching herself as a mother to the man who was securing the happiness of her other child.

Of all the family, Mary was probably the one most immediately gratified by the circumstance. It was creditable to have a sister married, and she might flatter herself with having been greatly instrumental to the connexion, by keeping Anne with her in the autumn; and as her own sister must be better than her husband's sisters, it was very agreeable that Captain Wentworth should be a richer man than either Captain Benwick or Charles Hayter. She had something to suffer, perhaps, when they came into contact again, in seeing Anne restored to the rights of seniority, and the mistress of a very pretty landaulette; but she had a future to look forward to, of powerful consolation. Anne had no Uppercross Hall before her, no landed estate, no headship of a family; and if they could but keep Captain Wentworth from being made a baronet, she would not change situations with Anne.

It would be well for the eldest sister if she were equally satisfied with her situation, for a change is not very probable there. She had soon the mortification of seeing Mr. Elliot withdraw, and no one of proper condition has since presented himself to raise even the unfounded hopes which sunk with him.

The news of his cousin Anne's engagement burst on Mr. Elliot most unexpectedly. It deranged his best plan of domestic happiness, his best hope of keeping Sir Walter single by the watchfulness which a son-in-law's rights would have given. But, though discomfited and disappointed, he could still do something for his own interest and his own enjoyment. He soon quitted Bath; and on Mrs. Clay's quitting it soon afterwards, and being next heard of as established under his protection in London, it was evident how double a game he had been playing, and how determined he was to save himself from being cut out by one artful woman, at least.

Mrs. Clay's affections had overpowered her interest, and she had sacrificed, for the young man's sake, the possibility of scheming longer for Sir Walter. She has abilities, however, as well as affections; and it is now a doubtful point whether his cunning, or hers, may finally carry the day; whether, after preventing her from being the wife of Sir Walter, he may not be wheedled and caressed at last into making her the wife of Sir William.

It cannot be doubted that Sir Walter and Elizabeth were shocked and mortified by the loss of their companion, and the discovery of their deception in her. They had their great cousins, to be sure, to resort to for comfort; but they must long feel that to flatter and follow others, without being flattered and followed in turn, is but a state of half enjoyment.

Anne, satisfied at a very early period of Lady Russell's meaning to love Captain Wentworth as she ought, had no other alloy to the happiness of her prospects than what arose from the consciousness of having no relations to bestow on him which a man of sense could value. There she felt her own inferiority very keenly. The disproportion in their fortune was nothing; it did not give her a moment's regret; but to have no family to receive and estimate him properly, nothing of respectability, of harmony, of good will to offer in return for all the worth and all the prompt welcome which met her in his brothers and sisters, was a source of as lively pain as her mind could well be sensible of under circumstances of otherwise strong felicity. She had but two friends in the world to add to his list, Lady Russell and Mrs. Smith. To those, however, he was very well disposed to attach himself. Lady Russell, in spite of all her former transgressions, he could now value from his heart. While he was not obliged to say that he believed her to have been right in originally dividing them, he was ready to say almost everything else in her favour, and as for Mrs. Smith, she had claims of various kinds to recommend her quickly and permanently.

Her recent good offices by Anne had been enough in themselves, and their marriage, instead of depriving her of one friend, secured her two. She was their earliest visitor in their settled life; and Captain Wentworth, by putting her in the way of recovering her husband's property in the West Indies, by writing for her, acting for her, and seeing her through all the petty difficulties of the case with the activity and exertion of a fearless man and a determined friend, fully requited the services which she had rendered, or ever meant to render, to his wife.

Mrs. Smith's enjoyments were not spoiled by this improvement of income, with some improvement of health, and the acquisition of such friends to be often with, for her cheerfulness and mental alacrity did not fail her; and while these prime supplies of good remained, she might have bid defiance even to greater accessions of worldly prosperity. She might have been absolutely rich and perfectly healthy, and yet be happy. Her spring of felicity was in the glow of her spirits, as her friend Anne's was in the warmth of her heart. Anne was tenderness itself, and she had the full worth of it in Captain Wentworth's affection. She went with him wherever he went, on land and on sea. His profession was all that could ever make her friends wish that tenderness less, the dread of a future war all that could dim her sunshine, but she loved the water, and she loved travelling it with Frederick. As he came up behind her while she watched the setting sun from the deck of the ship, he wrapt his arms around her and splayed his hands across the swell of her belly that housed their growing child. He pressed a kiss to her neck, and Anne turned her face from the warmth of the sun to bask in the warmth of his love. She gloried in being a sailor's wife, but she must pay the tax of quick alarm for belonging to that profession which is, if possible, more distinguished in its domestic virtues than in its national importance.

More from This Author

(From *Of Consuming Fire*)

Dr. Grace Tucker pulled herself deeper into the corner and tucked her arms tighter around her unshapely belly. As her hands and arms touched her large middle, it repulsed her nearly as much as it seemed to repulse the opposite sex. No, there was no disappearing a plus-sized woman, but her sloppy appearance got most people to look away quickly, which was as close as Grace was ever going to get to being blessedly invisible.

And, not for the first time, she desperately wished to be invisible.

Grace huddled in the main room of the top-secret government facility where the Trees stood. As always, she ignored them. She was never awed by the ancient trees. She'd taken one cursory glance at their branches that most described as majestic. Their fruit—covered in glittering diamonds for the Tree of Eternal Life, swirling black and white for the Tree of the Knowledge of Good and Evil—was interesting only in that it loosely related to her work. She didn't stand there and stare at them for hours as she was told was the expected behavior for new employees.

And yet right now, Grace wasn't the only one ignoring the Trees. The somber mood in the facility was nearly suffocating. Not one of the dozens of employees had spoken in hours. They moped from room to room, desk to desk, casting great, wide-eyed glances upon everyone they crossed. But that wasn't the reason Grace retreated to the corner.

They were *touching* one another.

Any person they came into reaching distance with. A hand on the shoulder. A hug. A squeeze of the arm or lingering pat on the back.

It was only a matter of time before one of them tried to touch *her*. And that simply was not going to work. End of story.

And, so, she was in the closest thing to a corner the domed room provided.

A young soldier in army fatigues walked by, and Grace went rigid, holding her breath until he passed.

He didn't once glance in her direction. Grace's breath flew from her frozen lungs even as her heart seized at the casual snub. She hugged herself tighter as she cursed her weak emotions. Without fail, every time her carefully cultivated armor of acerbic wit and slovenly appearance actually worked as she'd meant it to by keeping others away, her irrational side would come up bruised, as though it didn't know perfectly well the reasons human contact was not in Grace's cards.

She sighed almost silently, and forced herself to look cheerfully upon the fact that standing in the corner was working. She would make it through this. She *would*. It wouldn't be like all of the other times. There would be no scene. No gut-wrenching screams shooting from her body without her control. No hysterical sobs. No sedation. No awkward return to work. No inevitable summons to the boss. No starting over with the knowledge that this was her life—on repeat.

She closed her eyes. The sad truth was, this *was* her life. And right now, she was huddled in the corner, praying to be invisible, worrying with all of her strength that someone would touch her.

But her friend's impending death? Not even a blip on her emotional radar. Jericho Edwards was dying, and Grace was worried about herself.

Jericho was everyone's favorite, but for a reason Grace couldn't explain, he was *her* favorite as well. It had been thirteen long years since Grace considered a man as anything other than something to be avoided at all costs. Thirteen years since Grace had carefully erected a wall around her heart. And yet, somehow, Jericho found his way around that wall the tiniest bit.

It might have been the very obvious fact that Jericho would never, ever pose a threat to her. She'd known two seconds after being introduced to him that he was head over heels in love with someone: his Impulse mate, Dahlia. Jericho was nice to *everyone*, men and women alike. In fact, Grace had never met anyone so good.

And he'd taken one look at her—her frumpy clothes, excess body weight, bird's nest of red hair, black-rimmed glasses, and man-hating glare—and deemed her a friend, working tirelessly at cultivating a relationship with her when everyone else just avoided her.

And now, he was dying. Worse, his survival depended upon *Grace* and Grace's work.

Three months and a week or so ago, Jericho cut his finger on the sword—the artifact that Grace was commissioned to work on. It was a flesh wound that should have healed in seconds given that Jericho, Dahlia, Eli, and Abilene were all immortal after eating the fruit from the Tree of Eternal Life. But the simple wound hadn't healed. And things came to a head a few days ago when Jericho returned to the facility with his brand new wife, Dahlia. In the process of moving, Jericho managed to rip the tiny, unhealed wound wide open from the tip of his finger into his palm. It had been bleeding profusely ever since, and his body couldn't keep up.

And suddenly, Dr. Grace Tucker was very much in demand. She couldn't count the number of times she had to remind them "I'm not that kind of doctor." Their situation was so unique that her PhD in dead languages made her much more qualified to help

Jericho than an MD would on its best day, but her work took more time than medication or surgery ever would.

She'd made her breakthrough this morning.

The ancient, dead language on the sword said *What the Tree gives, the Sword takes. What the Sword takes, the Tree gives.*

At least, she was ninety-nine percent sure that's what it said.

Grace gritted her teeth, closed her eyes, and reassured herself that she was never wrong when it came to her work. Never. She was wrong when it came to everything else, but her work was infallible.

That's why she was here. She was the single most prestigious language expert in the world. And it was going to change her life. That was the plan. She'd worked hard to make sure no one noticed her. The weight she'd gained, the fashion-backward wardrobe, the overt hostility—when she couldn't disappear into her surroundings, she kept people away with every weapon her extensive intelligence and vast vocabulary could come up with.

But Grace's secret dream *was* recognition. She just wanted it on her terms. She was going to make *the* discovery of all time with this sword. It was the work she'd been waiting for her entire career. And now it was here. And, as long as her translation was right, it was about to save one of only four immortal human beings on the planet.

Career. Made.

Everyone would know her name; everyone would know she was something. And the best part? She'd be absolutely untouchable in a way she could not dream of cultivating on her own. No one walked up to the winner of the Nobel Prize and gave them a hug. They got the recognition without all the messy social baggage associated with being members of the human race. They were members of a class considered above such things. And Grace couldn't wait to be admitted into their ranks.

Grace's eyes snapped open when she heard the sharp clack of men's shoes on the hard floor of the facility. Sergeant Collins was approaching.

Grace shrank back further into her corner, her shoulders bending in on themselves, but it was too late: he was looking right at her, and double damn, he'd noticed she was trying to turn into wallpaper if the arch of one of his salt and pepper eyebrows was any indication.

He stopped before her, and Grace couldn't prevent the hitch in her breathing. Reaching distance. The man was within reaching distance. She bit her bottom lip to avoid a whimper.

"Dr. Tucker?" Sergeant Collins asked in his smooth, Southern whisky drawl. He then looked her over once more. His eyes softened. He took a step back and crossed his arms behind him, effecting "at ease" posture.

Relief flooded through her so strongly it momentarily overshadowed the embarrassment she felt at having someone else recognize her reticence at human contact. But only momentarily. Damn it, why couldn't she be normal?

She straightened to her full height—a whole five feet five inches—and worked her hardest to look as un-crazy as possible. "What can I do for you, sir?" A lock of her frizzy, red hair fell over her glasses, blocking Sergeant Collins from sight. She shoved it out of the way, tucking it behind one of the pencils stuffed into her "style" of the day.

"Nothing more than you've done, ma'am," he said with polite distance. "I've come to report that your findings seem to be accurate."

Grace wanted to sag in relief, but was so wary of causing Sergeant Collins to think any less of her that she clenched her jaw and forced iron into her spine. No one would know how worried she'd been about her translation. She'd emit cool confidence all day long. Her "findings" included the recommendation that whatever damage the sword caused could be un-done by administering the fruit of the Tree of Eternal Life topically. They'd been forcing the fruit down Jericho's throat for days to no effect. It was a nuance of the language that had given Grace the idea to apply the fruit to the site of Jericho's wound.

"So, Jericho's recovering?" Grace forced herself to ask, alarmed a little at the obvious worry in her voice. She didn't care about him that much, did she?

A new voice sounded as it approached. "His skin is knitting together before our eyes." Dahlia Edward's brown eyes peeked around Collins's shoulder, warm for the first time ever that Grace witnessed.

Grace actually liked Dahlia a lot, and not just because Jericho did. Grace hadn't met many people who seemed to hate all others as much as Dahlia did. She was even more socially hostile than Grace. It was . . . refreshing.

"They think he'll wake up any moment now, and I want to be there when he does, but I had to come thank you first," Dahlia continued.

Grace felt her eyes widen. "Thanks" often involved touch of some kind. "That's not necessary," Grace muttered, crowding the corner again.

Dahlia rolled her eyes. "Relax, Red," she said with a laugh. "God, it's not like we're going to attack you with hugs or anything."

Grace didn't laugh. She didn't even notice when the two before her exchanged a worried look as her eyes glazed, and her mind turned over one of Dahlia's words.

Attack. Attack. Attack.

A loud snap erupted in front of her face.

Grace refocused to see Dahlia's fingers before her eyes as the woman snapped again, this time accompanied by a sharp, "Grace!"

Grace sucked in a breath.

"Is she . . ." Sergeant Collins trailed off as both women's heads snapped around to glare at him.

Grace opened her mouth to speak, but was cut off with Dahlia's curt, "She's fine, Collins, God." She then stood directly in front of Grace, blocking her from Collins's sight, giving her a chance to compose herself. "Nothing some lunch and a good night's sleep won't fix. We've run her ragged. Give her some *grace*." Dahlia snorted.

Collins threw Dahlia a wobbly smile. "I'll just . . . um . . . call Miss Esperanza then. Tell her Jericho's fine." His mouth moved like a caress over the name of Dahlia's former mother-in-law, his accent adding at least two syllables, and his eyes twinkling like a kid.

Dahlia looked at Grace and winked. "You do that, Collins."

He cast one more concerned look toward Grace's corner, not quite meeting her eyes, and backed off, hurrying away to his office.

As Dahlia watched him go, her hand fell to the small bump beneath her shirt. Grace was pretty sure she was the only person in the facility who had guessed that Jericho and Dahlia were expecting. There had been no announcement; there hadn't been time before Jericho fell gravely ill. But Dahlia made that little movement often when she thought no one was looking.

She turned to Grace now and arched a perfect eyebrow.

"I really am fine," Grace offered weakly.

Dahlia scoffed and muttered something in Spanish that Grace perfectly understood—dead languages weren't her only specialty. Grace bristled. "Look, I'll just get back to work." The news of Jericho's recovery was already spreading if the increased chatter in the room was any indication. She could re-join life now. She needed to get started on writing this up, though she knew publishing any of her top-secret findings was going to be an uphill battle. Possibly an impossible one.

Dahlia nodded once and began to turn away.

"Hey," Grace blurted. Dahlia turned back to her. "Um . . . when he wakes up. Tell Jericho . . . I'm glad he's okay." Grace was shocked to find out she meant it.

Dahlia's eyes roved Grace's face for a moment, but then she smiled. "You've got it, Red." She took two steps toward the medical wing, then stopped.

Grace watched the black waves cascading down Dahlia's back rustle as the stunning Latina tilted her head to the side.

"Do you hear that?" Dahlia asked.

Grace frowned. "Hear what?"

Just then, the lights flickered. A distant rumbling seemed to seep in through the walls of the facility.

All of the hopeful chatter in the room faded and then fizzled out as people began to look around curiously.

A huge clap of thunder rent through the building with such force that loose items throughout the main room clattered where they sat.

The lights went out completely.

Emergency lights along the walls illuminated, casting Dahlia's caramel skin in an unearthly glow as Grace stared at her in barely subdued panic. The others in the room began to mumble to each other, their voices rising in pitch. She felt her nails digging into the skin of her arms and realized she was hugging herself again.

A man in a lab coat raced into the main room, skidding around the door and barreling toward Dahlia as soon as he spotted her. "He's waking!" he yelled at Jericho's wife. "Come quickly."

Dahlia took a quick step toward him, but then stumbled. She threw out an arm to catch herself against the wall. "*Shit*," Grace heard her mutter.

Dahlia spun around and pinned Grace with a wide-eyed look. "Earthquake," she told Grace in an odd, disbelieving tone. "Big one."

Dahlia lunged forward and grabbed Grace by the arm, hauling her quickly to a nearby desk and shoving herself and Grace in the small area beneath it.

Shooting pains emanated from the skin Dahlia's fingers touched. Grace hissed and tried to wrench her arm from Dahlia's grip as she spluttered, "What—how do you—"

"I can hear it coming," she said impatiently. "Take cover!" she bellowed to all the gawkers.

No sooner had the words left her mouth than the first wave hit the building. A sound, louder than the eardrum-cracking clap of thunder, ricocheted through the room like a freight train, and Grace watched with wide eyes as the floor began to ripple at the edge of the room and move toward them like oncoming ocean waves.

And, even though paralyzed with fear, all Grace could think of was the scorching pain of Dahlia's fingers where they still clutched her arm.

Screams began to echo as the men and women who worked at the facility realized what was happening. Feet thundered as everyone sought shelter.

But Grace scrambled away from Dahlia and out into the open as soon as the woman's grip on Grace's arm slackened.

Dahlia's arm snaked out and captured the back of Grace's jacket. "What the *hell*?"

"Don't *touch me*!" Grace shrieked so loudly that Dahlia drew back in shock.

A huge chunk of plaster fell from the ceiling to land right beside Grace. A cloud of white exploded from its impact and dusted both of them. Desks began to skitter across the floor.

"Do you want to die?" Dahlia yelled, blinking the white powder from her lashes.

Die or be touched? No contest. Grace didn't move.

The earthquake gained in intensity. The glass that made up the ceiling of the dome tinkled and Grace looked up as a crack spider-webbed from one end of the dome to the other.

"Okay," Dahlia said fast and low. "I won't touch you. Just get your ass under here right now!"

Grace dragged her eyes from the ceiling to look into the dim space beneath the desk. Dahlia pressed herself against the side, leaving more than enough room for Grace to fit without having to be against the other woman. And still she hesitated.

Across the dome, bookshelves began to fall like dominoes, each one hitting the ground with a resounding boom. The tinkling of the glass ceiling increased and one or two shards escaped and plummeted toward the ground.

With a deep breath for courage, Grace dove into the area beside Dahlia just as the ceiling gave way.

The glass chimed like clock-tower bells as it fell. It tinkled off of every surface and bounced from the floor in glittering arcs. Grace watched in horror as a huge shard caught one of the soldiers as he tried to dive under a desk a few feet away. His scream cut off as the glass sliced through his chest and pinned him to the floor right where Grace had been kneeling seconds before.

Grace huddled into the corner and buried her face against the wood of the desk so hard she thought her nose might break.

The waves of the ground moved as though alive beneath Grace, hitting her in the shins and knees again and again as she knelt and causing her stomach to lurch as though seasick. Beside her, she heard Dahlia begin to recite the rosary in Spanish in a low, breathless voice. As a backdrop, the glass on the floor clacked and pinged as the entire building shimmied with the rage of the earth.

And in the next heartbeat, everything stopped.

Grace's frantic breaths in the sudden absence of sound were excruciatingly loud, but the silence didn't last for long. Moans from the wounded began to fill the air.

She heard her boss, Eli Johnson, bellowing his past-due pregnant wife's name as he barreled through the dome from his office and toward the medical wing.

"Jericho," Dahlia breathed next to her. Then she scrambled from her hiding spot, sliding in the blood that slicked across the floor from the impaled man before gaining purchase and sprinting in Eli's wake.

Grace stared dumbfounded at the glassy eyes of the dead man in front of her before forcing herself to emerge from the desk.

Utter destruction waited for her. Her eyes skimmed over the demolished main room of the facility. Everything was . . . gone. Desks were smashed. Books were flung to every wall of the room. The glass on the floor glittered like diamonds among the pools of blood. It looked like after-pictures of a tornado.

But the trees stood resolute in the center of the room. Not one fruit had fallen from their branches. And on the desk beneath them, where Grace did her work, the sword glowed. The sword, usually covered with flickering green and gold flames, was now . . . *angry*. It was the only word she could use to describe what she was seeing. The green and gold flames had morphed into red and black. The metal, engraved with the words she had translated to say *what the tree gives, the sword takes; what the sword takes, the tree gives* was now pulsing with emotion. And coming off of the sword in waves was an otherworldly *heat*. The sword had always emitted a cool indifference. Now it was raging.

"Oh, God," Grace gasped. Her breathing sped up even more, and black began to edge in on her vision.

Something had angered this inanimate object. Fear, so familiar and yet, in this case, so different, choked Grace's throat. She had a gut feeling that in completing her job she betrayed a secret. The sword's secret.

Someone was coming. Coming for them. Coming for her.

She had one thought before losing consciousness: *What have I done?*

Micah Persell is also the author of Emma: The Wild and Wanton Edition, Of the Knowledge of Good and Evil, and Of Eternal Life

In the mood for more Crimson Romance?
Check out *Daisy Miller: The Wild and Wanton Edition*
by Gabrielle Vigot and Henry James
at *CrimsonRomance.com*.

Printed in the United States
By Bookmasters